MORTAL REVENGE

First Edition January 2026
by Indies United Publishing House, LLC

Cover design by Vila Design

This is a work of fiction. Names, characters, places, and incidents are either the product of the author's imagination or are use fictionally, and any resemblance to actual persons, living or dead, business establishments, events or locales is entirely coincidental.

ISBN: 978-1-64456-875-0 [Paperback]
ISBN: 978-1-64456-876-7 [Kindle]
ISBN: 978-1-64456-877-4 [ePub]
ISBN: 978-1-64456-878-1 [Audiobook]

Library of Congress Control Number: 2026901837

INDIES UNITED PUBLISHING HOUSE, LLC
P.O. BOX 3071
QUINCY, IL 62305-3071
indiesunited.net

The JadeAnne Stone Mexico Adventures

Set Up (2018)

The Hydra Effect (2019)

Nothing Comes After Z (2022)

Coyote (2022)

Backlash (2023)

The Dafne Olabarrieta Mexico Mysteries

Kickback (2024)

Other books

Saints and Skeletons
A Memoir of Living in Mexico (2023)

Praise for the Dafne Olabarrieta Mexico Mysteries

Kickback

Literary Titan Gold Award for Fiction 2024
Longlisted for the CIBA Clue Award for Suspense/Thriller 2025

Literary Titan
Kickback is a crime thriller that is a testament to the complexities of human relationships and the strength required to confront life's darkest moments. With its engaging narrative and deep emotional undertones, this is a book that will leave readers eager for the next chapter in Dafne Olabarrieta's journey.

Readers Choice 5-Star Review
Manwaring skillfully blends intense action with emotional stakes, ensuring readers are as invested in Dafne's internal struggles as they are in the plot. I loved the high-stakes story, the intensity of the action, and the character development that accompanied the plot. There was never a dull moment. I finished this book in one sitting and enjoyed it immensely. I highly recommend it.

Praise for the JadeAnne Stone Mexico Adventures

Backlash

Literary Titan Gold Award for Fiction 2023
Shortlisted for the CIBA Clue Award for Suspense/Thriller 2023

Midwest Book Review, Diane Donovan
Ana Manwaring does an outstanding job of crafting a story … steeped in Mexican culture and mayhem, with the lingering effects of Vietnam relationships. The result is a vivid portrait of traitors and a dangerous man whose wrath and cleverness threaten everyone Quint has believed in and loved.

Coyote

Literary Titan Silver Award for Fiction 202

Literary Titan Review
The author has sent her characters on a heart-pounding mission in the fourth installment in her series. The ensemble cast and suspenseful story remind me of the consistently entertaining *Fast and Furious* series... [*Coyote*] successfully brings together action and adventure in this explosive thriller set against the unique backdrop of Mexico.

*US Review Kat Kennedy*This novel, with its backdrop of human trafficking, is a riveting read that puts one into the center of Mexican culture with its descriptive narrative of landmarks and cuisine.

Nothing Comes After Z

Literary Titan Silver Award for Fiction 2022

Literary Titan Review
Nothing Comes After Z is a riveting crime thriller with a strong female protagonist. I appreciated the grounded nature of the crime and how it relates to some headlines we see in the news today. Before she can safely leave Mexico and return to her life, she has to uncover some hard truths and catch the perpetrators. I enjoyed how well the emotion is weaved into this action novel because it ensure we're invested in the protagonist and we're biting our nails when the action intensifies. Author Ana Manwaring knows how to create a storyline that easily sets up the hard-hitting action.

Michelle Chouinard, USA Today bestseller of A Serial Killer Guide to San Francisco Mystery Series
A well-written, engaging story with a bad-ass protagonist I loved spending time with. Bring on more JadeAnne!

The Hydra Effect

Lisa Towles, multi-award-winning author of The A&E Investigations Series
The Hydra Effect sizzles with action, tension, and peril. Great writing combined with regional flare and international intrigue make this sequel a delightful ride!

Jan M Flynn, award winning author
JadeAnne heads to Mexico City for a break from her partner and now ex-boyfriend. But her sharp intelligence, curiosity and inability to stay in her own lane land her in a snarl of trouble. In short order she's evading cartel thugs, uncovering a human trafficking network and confronting high-level Mexican politicos with questionable connections, all in a lushly realized setting one can just about smell. And taste—JadeAnne might be in the middle of a gunfight, but she's never immune to the temptation of a good plate of tacos al pastor. She and her loyal dog Pepper are a team you can't but cheer for.

Set Up

Heather Haven, multi-award-winning author of the Alvarez Family Murder Mysteries
This is a blowout of a story. It starts on the backroads of Mexico in the middle of the night—just a woman, a dog, and Mexican Banditos—and escalates from there. If you are looking for a fast-paced, action-filled thriller about the adventures of a young PI and her lethal but well-trained dog, this will be your cup of tea. Or should I say Margarita? Jack Reacher step aside. You have met your match in JadeAnne Stone.

Kirkus Reviews
With a likeable duo and a vivid, appealing setting, this adventure series is off to a promising start.

Praise for Ana Manwaring's Memoir of Living in Mexico

Saints and Skeletons

Recipient of the Literary Titan Gold Book Award 2023

Literary Titan Review
Saints and Skeletons is a captivating and introspective work that encourages readers to embrace life's complexities. Ana Manwaring's unflinching honesty and willingness to bare her soul are both brave and inspiring. This memoir stands as a testament to the transformative power of storytelling and the remarkable human capacity for growth and resilience.

In Memory of Victor "Toto" León Torrens, Diego León

Torrens, and Blanca Torrens Anguiano lost to corruption.

May they rest in peace knowing their stories have been told.

Acknowledgements

I am deeply grateful to my writing partner, Fernando León Torrens, for searching cyberspace to find me after thirty years of silence. Thank you Fer for bringing me your story and allowing me to turn it into fiction. I didn't know when we started how difficult it would be to work in a second language, but I owe you big time for your patience and good-humored Spanish lessons. I hope you love our book!

I also owe my First Readers a huge debt of gratitude. Mortal Revenge is more deeply steeped in Mexican culture than my previous books. More than read the story, my readers had to decipher an unfamiliar culture and come up with suggestions to smooth over the bumps. Thanks to my "BritCrit" women: Aletheia Morden, Kerry Granshaw, and Susan Savage; "my siblings" in Sisters in Crime: Bruce William Johnson, Mac Daly, and T.E. MacArthur; and my "publisher-in-training" Jeanette Tomson. Your analyses and comments helped shape this story immensely.

Thank you, Cindy Davis, The Book Doctor. You really had your work cut out for you on this novel! I appreciate your excellent "doctoring" of all my books and look forward to working with you for books to come.

Don't let me forget my amazing cover designer, Tatiana Vila of Vila Design who put up with probably too many changes. The cover rocks! That half-blind Justice is brilliant! And to my publisher, Lisa Orban of Indies United Publishing House. You've been waiting for this one, and finally—here it is! I know you'll work your magic, and the book will be totally fabulous.

As always, big hugs to David, Alfie, and Beto. How would I keep this up without your love, encouragement, and purrs?

To all my Spanish teachers, especially Susana Ackerman who corrected my "Mexicano" to proper Spanish. Without these many kind mentors, I'd never have been able to write this book.

MORTAL REVENGE

Ana Manwaring
Fernando León Torrens

INDIES UNITED
PUBLISHING HOUSE, LLC

Prologue

December 2019

Surprise! Alex's mother invited him to come for the Christmas holidays. Most years, he was ignored. This year he wanted some comfort and cheer, yet he couldn't shake the dread. Confront his family again? What did Irene want? *But she's my mother. I have to go.*

Since his girlfriend had betrayed him, he needed his family. What should he do? Like his conniving ex, his mother wanted something. *What?*

"It's stomach cancer," Lucas, his brother, claimed when he arrived.

Then why leave Irene to die alone in pain in her house with a caregiver instead of a hospital? Or better yet, at Lucas's house with family? Worse, Alex was forbidden to stay at Irene's house for the weeks of his visit, forced to take a costly short-term rental next door to his brother and drive back and forth to care for his mother.

What the hell was Aimee, the hired caretaker, doing? Not much he could see, beyond flirting with Lucas when he came, which was often. The two sat up in the spare bedroom drinking and doing who knows what while Irene suffered in the next room. Alex could hear the middle-aged servant giggling like a teenager.

By the third day, he had a clear idea of Irene's condition. His mother was being starved, left in her own filth, and over-sedated. To top it off, if she truly had stomach cancer, her medications were wrong. He should know—top pharmaceutical salesman nine years running.

He took on his mother's personal care—bathing and dressing her, cooking her meals, feeding her, and cleaning the house while Aimee watched t.v.

One morning over coffee on the patio in a patch of warm sun, Alex quizzed the caretaker.

"I'm from Veracruz, a jarocha pure through," she said, giggling, as though this was the greatest joke. "I live in the next block. Irene and I have known each other for years."

"You married? Kids?"

"My husband took off after I caught him with my sister. Good riddance. I've had to work to support our daughter. He doesn't send anything." The woman minced a coy smile over her cup.

Alex wasn't interested. He felt manipulated—*pitching for a raise?* Aimee should be fired, not rewarded for her poor caretaking. Did Irene really have cancer? She wasn't taking her medicine per instructions. He counted the number of pills in the containers and the dates the medications had been purchased. He'd call the prescribing doctor, a Dr. Lionel Fierro, on the 27th when he returned to work after Navidad. That is, *if I still have a job.*

"Aimee, I'm concerned for my mother's care. Have you any background in administering medications?"

She stiffened, pulled away from the table, frowning, eyes defiant. "I do exactly what Lucas instructs me to do."

Nervous. Covering her tracks. Was Lucas involved? That she referred to him as Lucas, not Señor, troubled him too. That and the drinking in the spare room.

"I'd like to see that, Aimee, and I'd like to watch you do things to learn how to take care of my mother on Navidad when you'll be with your daughter. I don't want you to worry I would make a mistake." He smiled as sincerely as he could muster.

Aimee's voice belied her words. "Of course, Señor." She checked her watch and continued like she'd won the upper hand. "Irene is due for her next injection soon and I always give her the cancer medicine before she naps."

She was lying. Oh, not about the order in which she administered the medicines, but her willingness to "teach" him was fake. Did the woman think placating him with a moment of compliance would make it okay she was not doing her job? *Why does Lucas keep her on?*

When the cups were empty, Aimee cleared the coffee service to the kitchen and proceeded to make a soft-boiled egg and toast for Irene. When she was finished, she called Alex in from hanging out the laundry to dry on the line. They mounted the narrow stairs and entered Irene's room.

The shuttered room still smelled of unwashed bedding and body, old food, incontinence, and illness. The low wood-frame bed took up most of the floor with a chair placed by it facing a TV mounted on the wall, playing a telenovela at low volume. On the other side of the bed, a cabinet with several drawers held an array of medicine bottles, small paper cups, and syringes on a plastic tray, but the room was too dark to actually read the labels on the drugs. Alex pulled open the heavy curtains. Irene groaned, jerking her thin arm across her face.

"Mother, does the light hurt your eyes?"

She whispered something. Aimee slammed the breakfast tray on the bureau and snapped, "Your eyes will adjust. I've brought your eggs and toast." She bent to haul the old woman to a semi-sitting position.

Irene cried out in pain. Alex nudged Aimee aside. Gently he propped his mother upright with the bed pillows. "Are you comfortable now?"

Her lips barely curved upwards as she uttered, "Thank you, Alex."

"Aimee, why don't you prepare the medicines while I help Mother eat?"

The woman edged around the bed to the bureau to count the pills into the paper cup.

Alex took up the bowl of eggy toast and encouraged Irene to taste it. She swallowed several bites and waved her hands, croaking, "No more."

Not eating was a sure sign a patient was ready to go. He'd seen too many patients dying. But watching Aimee prepare Irene's medication, he wondered if it might be drug poisoning, not cancer, killing her.

Aimee set aside the cup to prepare the sedative. When she finished filling the syringe Alex was certain the woman was about to administer triple the dose a frail old lady required to rest comfortably.

"Thanks, Aimee. You can leave the rest to me. I'll help Mother take her pills, clean her up, and settle her back into bed before the sedative. You'd like that, wouldn't you, Mother?" Irene nodded. "Find those instructions for me," he added.

Aimee's face took on a narrow-eyed, tight-lipped expression, but she shrugged and left the room.

Once Irene was clean and settled into the pillows, he emptied the syringe into the toilet and dropped the needle into the medical waste container. Then he read the labels on the drugs, verified through the internet what each was for, and adjusted the paper cup for only those she should take with her meal. Four pills, not nine.

Aimee, of course, had not appeared with Lucas's list. It was just as well. He helped Irene find a comfortable position and bent to kiss her cheek. She smiled.

When Lucas showed up, Alex asked for the list of medications and doses. His brother stonewalled him, disappearing upstairs to drink with Aimee. He heard her shrill voice arguing with Lucas. And crept up the stairs to listen to the row.

"Get him out of here, Lucas. He's in my way. I can't take care of your mother. He's questioning everything I do. I can't stand him."

Lucas shouted, "Shut up Aimee. You'll wake up Mother. My brother will be go—" His voice lowered.

Alex retreated to the bottom of the stairs.

What was going on? Lucas was well aware of Alex's training and jobs with pharmaceutical companies. Why should it bother him that Alex wanted to understand his mother's diagnosis and treatment? The creeping feeling Irene had been mis-diagnosed and was receiving improper care overtook his thoughts to the point of obsession. It wasn't so far-fetched that she had stomach cancer. His youngest brother had died of it a couple of years earlier. His father had died of it too. Both had worked at the nuclear plant; cancers were common in the area.

But Alex and Lucas lived in Mexico City for much of their lives; Lucas moving to Veracruz as an adult where he worked at the nuclear plant as well. But not for much time. Was his family victim to radiation? Would Lucas eventually be diagnosed with stomach cancer?

The powers that be claimed the plant was secure, radiation free—clean. But this was Mexico—Veracruz, with a notoriously corrupt government. He didn't believe the claims. The only family member who never worked there, Alex, was the control group. The future would tell.

When Alex arrived one morning, there was no doubt about what was going on. The moaning he heard was not his mother's. He kicked open the guestroom door and caught them—*fucking like street dogs*—liquor bottles strewn across the floor.

Lucas reared up and roared obscenities as he hustled into his clothes and fled; Aimee screamed. Alex bent, scooped her clothing from the heap on the floor. "Get dressed and get out of here. You're fired!" He tossed the clothes into her bare chest. "Cover yourself!"

The woman wailed, "You're not my jefe. I don't need to do anything you say. Lucas says—"

"I don't care what Lucas says. *I* say, get out of this house and don't come back."

Aimee, bawling, asked, "How will I take care of my girl?" while pulling on her clothes. Her hands shook.

"I don't care. Be glad I'm not going to the police."

The caretaker shoved past Alex. At the bottom of the stairs she shouted, "You'll never get away with this, you stupid man. Lucas won't let you. I'll have what's promised!"

What was promised? Money? *It was always about money, wasn't it?* He prepared Irene's breakfast and carried it up to her room. She was sitting up in bed; some color had returned to her sallow cheeks.

"Good morning, Mother. Hungry?"

"What was all that shouting, Alex?"

"I'm so sorry, did they wake you up?"

"Who?"

"Lucas and Aimee."

"Lucas! Lucas is here?" Her cheeks pinked.

"No Mother, Lucas and I argued over the care Aimee gives you. I don't think she is doing a good job. I fired her. Lucas left."

Irene's voice dropped to barely a whisper. Alex had to lean down, his ear near her mouth, to hear. "Lucas promised to give Aimee my house."

Could it be true? He had taken her off most of the drugs and all the sedative. Her mind was clearer. He pondered the evidence as he cleaned the house, starting in the spare room, clearing away twenty-three brandy bottles and a bag of sex toys he found under the bed. He changed the sheets. He was probably going to spend the night.

It was getting dark when he heard a commotion at the gate. Lucas and Aimee came in. She threw herself onto the couch, and Lucas marched to the table where Alex studied receipts for Irene's medical visits and prescriptions for cancer medicines.

"You have no authority to fire my employee,

brother. You may leave now. We won't need you tonight. Adios."

Alex grabbed his keys, slammed out of the house, clanging the gate behind him. His only solace was he'd disposed of all the unnecessary drugs and the sedative.

On Christmas Day, Irene was feeling better and appeared happy to see him. She wanted to go downstairs. His mother was not dying, she was stronger, happier and alert as she settled into her chair. Heartened, he opened a streaming station of Christmas music for her.

For lunch, she devoured a Christmas atole to go with the tamales and buñellos he picked up en route from his rental.

"Alex, can you ever forgive me?"

Alex's stomach danced with butterflies at her words. She never spoke intimately with him. "For what, Mother?"

"Get me a stool, would you?" she asked.

He pulled up the footstool and lifted her legs onto it. He could feel the stiffness and began to rub each leg.

Irene sighed in pleasure. "Thank you, my son. That feels lovely."

"I forgive you, but what for?" he asked again.

Irene's mouth pursed into a tight line. Eventually she said, "I need one hundred fifty thousand pesos. Your brother needs it." She looked around the modest, poorly constructed government-built home Lucas had given her, waiting.

Alex knew the house came through some double-dealing Lucas was involved in. He had been lucky with his deals, and he earned a good salary. "Why?" he asked. But he knew. It was always about the money with Lucas and his spendthrift wife Ana.

"He needs money to pay his credit cards. You owe it to your family to help, Alex."

Before Alex answered, Lucas and Ana breezed through the gate with arms full of wrapped gifts. He ignored them, asking, "Mother, I'm confused. Why should I forgive you?" He sure as hell wasn't confused about the plea for money.

As always, Irene lit up when Lucas entered the house. Lucas glowered at Alex. Ana shoved a box his way while Lucas announced, "With Mother doing so well now, Ana and I have decided we don't need you here anymore. Go on back to Mexico, Alex. Merry Christmas."

Chapter 1

The Award

Friday, March 27, 2020

Alex Deltoro chained up his motorcycle, pulled off his helmet, and shrugged his toned frame out of his leather jacket. He smoothed his unruly silver-streaked auburn curls into place, adjusted his blue striped tie, then trotted up the steps to push through the heavy doors into the foyer of La Mansion. A hostess greeted him, checked his helmet and jacket, brushing his arm as she directed him to the private room Laboratorios Salud Integrales booked for the annual product roll-out and awards dinner. He smiled. He may be fifty-three, but somebody thought he still had it.

This year was special. The COVID pandemic raged across the world and their new antivirus was working miracles with patients in the trials. Alex grinned with pride. In part, it was his project making the extensive trials possible. He was certain he was going to be acknowledged—and not fired for his indiscretion with the traitorous Avelina.

He paused in the doorway, embarrassed by the

unusual rush of self-pride and accomplishment. How could he feel on top of the world when the last he heard from his mother was a whispered, "She's trying to kill me."

Guilt for leaving on Christmas day washed over him—again—and worry cast its shadow. It had been days; he couldn't reach anyone in the family.

Director Ivan Castellanos Palacios waved him to an empty stool, shouting "Alex, over here."

Alex squeezed through the gathering crowd of lab techs at the end of the bar, greeted several by name, and eased onto the stool Ivan held for him.

"Glad you could make it. Have a drink?" Ivan said.

Mustering some enthusiasm, Alex said, "I wouldn't have missed this for anything, jefe. We've done it. What are you all drinking?" he asked, eyeing the row of seated executives chatting among themselves. The head of the virology department looked up and nodded toward Alex. He tipped up his chin and smiled. The bar was littered with shot glasses and a dark bottle inscribed in blue: Casa Dragones Añejo. A fine sipping tequila.

Ivan grabbed the bottle and called for another round. The bartender scurried over, swept aside the dirty shot glasses, and set a fresh one in front of each man, then brimmed them with the golden liquid.

The director turned, raised his glass, and shouted over the din, "To Laboratorios Salud Integrales and our new antiviral! We're gonna beat that COVID dragon!"

"To LSI and Viru-out!" chorused the crowd. Ivan and some shot back their drinks. Others raised their glasses in the air, cheering.

The tequila went down around him like water, but

Alex ordered a whisky neat with a mineral water chaser. Shots weren't his thing. He could see some of the employees already showing signs of inebriation. He planned to stay sober to give the obligatory dreaded speech. He swiveled on his stool then leaned back against the bar to watch the excited crowd. The bar was packed with LSI employees, most in their party best, especially the women. Ivan had given the entire company the afternoon off to get ready.

Alex felt blessed to have been hired by LSI. Even after a decade, he was excited to go to work every day. Castellanos was an excellent director—caring, humane, inspiring. He maintained an encouraging atmosphere of innovation, excellence, and family within his company. People who wanted to work hard and rise up the ranks were offered every opportunity to do so, and each contributor received deserved praise. Better yet, the pay was excellent and the raises regular.

Alex was no novice. He'd worked his way up through several pharmaceutical manufacturers, starting as a junior salesman to reach his current position as Director of Sales and Promotion. Public heath was his passion; he cared about people—like his mother alone in the Port of Veracruz. Why hadn't she called him back? Why hadn't he brought her here to Mexico in December? His stomach tanked along with his good spirits. The entire family had shut him out. He took a gulp of the whisky and let the burn relax his tense muscles. *Not tonight güey,* he told himself. *It's my night.*

"Well hello, Alex. So nice to see you again," a voice crooned into his ear.

He spun to the right, recognition sending his nerves through the ceiling. Avelina Fogle. He frowned. What the hell was that bitch doing at LSI's annual product roll-out and awards dinner? She'd been fired for stealing company secrets.

"Avelina. I'm surprised you'd show your face here."

She fluttered her fake eyelashes over her smirk. "So nice to see you too, Alex." She turned to a burly man wearing a bespoke navy suit with a school tie. "I believe you know my *novio*, Jesus Bonillo?"

Bonillo held out his hand to shake.

Chingao. The evening had barely started, and it was already going to shit. "Yeah, we are acquainted. Chucho, 'sup?" He did not offer his hand and the man dropped his, turning away.

Avelina crowded in closer, laughing. In his ear, she said, "You can't stand I dumped your wimpy ass for a real man, can you?"

"Excuse me, Avelina, they're calling us to the dining room. Take care," he intoned in a patronizing voice as he pushed past her into the crowd. *Jesus Cristo.* How had he ever been attracted to that woman? A self-serving painted doll with a heart of stone and criminal greed. Bonillo would find out what Avelina Fogel was about when she made off with his clients and company secrets. He had to hand it to Ivan—Alex should have been fired for his lapse in judgement. He was the king of picking the wrong women; Avelina was kicked out of LSI—and his house—before the holidays. He changed his passwords then notified his contacts she was no longer representing the company or him. She should have been prosecuted, but Ivan was right, the press would have been disastrous for the company.

The Director's personal assistant greeted Alex at the door to the private dining room and pointed out his seat at the head table between the Director of Development and the head of Marketing. He sat down, ordered another whisky as the waiter passed by with a tray of tempting mini huitlacoche quesadillas, and watched the LSI staff stream into the room. The table was positioned in front of a narrow riser with a lectern and two microphones. A small table loaded with plaques and envelopes sat next to it. Behind the lectern on the wall, hung a banner touting LSI and the new antiviral drug, Viru-Out. A clutch of capsule-shaped helium filled balloons floated overhead in a rainbow of colors. Alex's drink arrived and he settled in to endure the evening.

"Good to see you, Alex. I'd hoped to talk to you," Abramov from Marketing greeted him. "I hear you're having a huge success with your trials, and sales are skyrocketing through your network. I want to create a campaign featuring you and your foundation's work. Interested?"

"I'm flattered, Levi. We do our best. Because of Margarita," he elbowed the Development director, "Viru-Out is helping hundreds of low-income COVID patients beat this damned virus. And provide the necessary trials. We should include her—"

"Good evening gentlemen. Include me in what?" Margarita interrupted.

"Hola, Directora, I was just suggesting to Alex we run a campaign on the foundation and your efforts to get LSI products into the hands of the needy. It would make an excellent marketing tool. Especially now that

Viru-Out is proving safe and effective."

Alex asked, "What's your idea? A video? I'd be happy to talk to you. Margarita?" He turned to her, eyebrows raised—and choked on the skewered shrimp he was nibbling. There she was again, taking a chair at the next table. Avelina, staring at him with an air of triumph. She winked, then threw a mincing smile his way.

Alex coughed. Turned away. "Sorry, shrimp down the wrong pipe."

Margarita patted his back. "Okay?"

"Okay," he lied.

Surreptitiously he watched Avelina and Chucho Bonilla chatting up the guests as the table filled. What the hell were they doing at the LSI product launch?

"Camarones al diablo. Shall I schedule a couple of meetings to interview you?" the marketing director asked, an expectant smile below his trim mustache.

We should go do it right now. Anything to get away from that bitch. He turned Margarita and said, "Shall we do it?"

"Of course. Say, isn't that your ex with the owner of Aplicaciones Farmaceuticos? Bonillo? Wasn't she fired four months ago? What are they doing here?"

Abramov cut in. "I don't remember her. But he's competition and ruthless. I don't much like his methods. How do you know him Margarita?"

"Long story, long ago. Let's say my opinion is similar to yours. You know him, Alex?"

"No, not really. Avelina introduced us at a party once. He pestered me for info on our products and access to Ivan and the board. Looks like he got what he wanted."

"You're better off without her, Alex. She had a sneaky side and acted as though she were entitled to more than anyone else when she worked under me. I would have fired if you hadn't gotten her," Margarita said.

"I don't miss her, but I'm missing some videos that walked out around the time she did. It wasn't enough to call the authorities, but—"

The waiter interrupted the conversation. "Excuse me, folks. The buffet is ready when you are." He recited the menu, then asked, "May I bring you anything to drink?"

After jotting down the drink orders, the waiter moved on to re-count the menu to the newcomers. The room had filled to capacity. It looked to Alex as if the entire company had turned out, even the janitorial team.

"Let's get some food while it's hot off the grill," Margarita said.

Eventually, a pretty waitress came around with trays of delicious looking dessert assortments. Alex resisted the urge to try both the flan de coco and cajeta crepas.

Alex and Levi were in an intense conversation on the merits of social media marketing versus traditional print advertising when Ivan strode to the lectern and shouted, "Bienvenido to our tenth annual awards dinner!"

The crowd, except Avelina and Bonilla, cheered, hooted and shouted encouragement. Ivan patted down the air with his hands. Someone yelled, "Let him talk!" Someone else tapped a water glass with a fork.

Finally, Ivan commanded, "Quiet down! Quiet down, we have a special guest, and we don't want to give him the impression we are a herd of hyenas." The group laughed and settled.

"Before I introduce this year's award winners, let me pat our collective back on the incredible job Laboratorios Salud Integrales has done with our new antivirus, Viru-Out." He quoted some statistics collected through the trials on efficacy combatting COVID and the steady rise in sales as the pandemic swelled. "If our analysts' projections are anywhere near their expectations for sales, every employee of LSI will receive a fat holiday bonus come December. And we can thank the teams that made this happen."

Ivan gave a short history of the development lab's discovery of compounds that in tests killed viruses, and Margarita's expert leadership in bringing the new drug to human trials. "Alex, escort Margarita up here," he shouted.

Alex jumped to his feet and offered his arm. Ivan welcomed her with a hug and a hearty gracias. He thanked her staff then handed over one of the plaques and a fat envelope "for Margarita and the team".

Alex stood back waiting to hand her down from the stage.

"Of course we couldn't have done it without the development team, but even a miracle drug can't sell itself. I thought this guy was a nut case when he approached me to start a foundation to serve the needs of our nation. I wasn't buying his Boy Scout attitude. LSI didn't need a do-gooder, we needed trials and positive proof Viru-Out would work. A lot of money poured into developing it. For the patent, we needed proof it worked—and didn't kill anyone in the process." The audience laughed. "Listen, I said, you do your magic with sales and keep us afloat. We're not giving anything away, not until we're the Pfizer of Mexico. But this dumb-ass kept hammering away at me. Then Margarita came at me. And before you know it, the crazy scheme was making sense. I want you all to honor our very own crazy man, Alex Deltoro. A bull in the ring. For the tenth year, Alex's team receives the award for the year's top sales. But that's not all. I finally listened to his cockamamy idea, and folks, Mr. Alex Deltoro's do-good heart has created a system to get medicine free of charge to the most in-need in exchange for participating in our trials, and he has boosted sales of our drugs to the very doctors who care for these people in the government run IMSS and ISSST hospitals, not to mention the free clinics across our city and beyond. With COVID, we have thousands of patients in trials and we're winning the battle against the virus, *and* our competition! Come over here, Alex," he said.

Margarita hugged him. Alex stepped to the lectern. Ivan took his wrist and raised his arm in a gesture of winning. "You deserve this man. Thank you from LSI." He handed Alex one of the plaques and two envelopes. "One for Sales Team of the Year and the rest for Highest Contributor to the Company. Alex, a plaque doesn't say it clearly enough. We are impressed with your dedication, drive, loyalty, innovation and know-how. I, and the Board, want you to step into the Director of Operations position when Zugasti retires in May. Congratulations, Deltoro!"

The employees went wild. Avelina glared daggers at

him. *What was that about?*

Ivan handed him the mic; Alex pulled Margarita next to him to acknowledge her participation in the foundation's, and the antiviral's, success. "I'm grateful to LSI, a company that values innovation and hard work. Ten years ago, I came in as part of the sales team hoping to do well enough to help my family. I never thought I'd receive such an honor. Thank you!"

"So, you'll take the job?" Ivan asked, winking.

"You're the boss, I can't say no," Alex quipped back to chuckles across the room.

The men shook hands; the audience applauded as Alex returned to his seat.

Ivan called up the other department heads and introduced each to the room. The heads reported on their 2020 projects and 2019 outcomes, awarding envelopes to each department team member of the year.

As the last award recipient returned to her table, Ivan called Jesus Bonillo to the podium. Alex's chilis en nogadas turned to cement in his stomach. *What the hell?* He shot a side-glance at Avelina. The gloating look on his ex-protege cum lover's face burned him up. Suddenly, he understood how people could be pushed to murder.

He turned back to the stage as Ivan introduced Bonillo, ". . . Director of Aplicaciones Farmaceuticos, formerly our biggest competitor in the antivirus market, now our co-collaborator. LSI has just signed a contract with AF to co-develop a version of Viru-Out for children. We'll market the two together and beat this deadly virus!"

Bonillo grinned and the men shook hands. Alex

couldn't listen to his speech. He knew where the formulations came from. Stolen from LSI by Avelina. He ordered a third whisky.

Champagne corks popped, waiters circulated with brimming flutes, attendees milled and chatted. The music changed to some popular dance tunes and the party kicked into gear. Alex gazed at the exit longing for his soft bed and the cuddly kitten who had adopted him, both waiting at home. And someone to answer his call to Veracruz.

Chapter 2

The Call

Saturday, March 28, 2020

Between too much whisky and the shock and shame of Avelina and Bonillo attending the dinner, the motorcycle ride home was a blur—a miracle he'd made it at all. Driving in Mexico City was crazy enough without adding alcohol and anger. But that was water under the bridge.

Shouldn't he be walking on clouds after his success? He may have been roasted first, but a $50,000 peso award, another rung higher on the corporate ladder—a directorship with a 35% raise were nothing to scoff at. He was going to run the department and there wouldn't be any leaks. He would control that.

So why was he so upset? Because still no communications from either his mother or the family. Was she still alive? Surely Lucas would let him know if she'd died. Or maybe she'd gone into remission? Why wouldn't anyone communicate with him? He'd called Lucas, his sister-in-law, and his niece, Morticia. All ignored him. *Hadn't it always been like this?* He was the outsider. He'd always be the outsider with the Deltoros, and his pattern had been to run the other way. Yet this was his mother; he had to keep trying. He dialed again. The line rang and rang and rang.

By now, his tongue stuck to the roof of his mouth, and someone was trying to jackhammer his skull. He got up to swallow four aspirins, refilling his glass from the five-gallon bottle on the kitchen counter to swill them down. He should go to bed; he could still catch the eleven o'clock news. Maybe he'd see himself being recognized. A news crew had been in the room at the beginning of the ceremony. He flicked on the TV and dialed into the local station, planting himself in the leather easy chair with the control in his hand.

In several minutes a business newscaster announced Laboratorios Salud Integral's big roll out and showed a short clip of the director's speech. The newscast barely mentioned Alex's promotion. The announcer cut to another story, announcing Aplicaciónes Farmaceuticos new antiviral and rolled a short interview with that pendejo Jesus Bonilla. Alex turned it up. Bonilla claimed his new miracle drug would save the lives of thousands of Mexican children with COVID, and he owed it all to his head of development, Avelina Fogle. The final shot showed the two of them smirking at Alex right through the airwaves.

Not even a mention of the joint project with LSI. He thought back several years when Bonilla had come to LSI to apply for a job. Alex had disliked him upon meeting. Something untrustworthy about him convinced Ivan to pass over Bonilla for Levi. How did Bonilla get the capital to take over Aplicaciónes

Farmaceuticos, anyway?

The alarm shrilled. Seven a.m. Alex's head still pounded. Champagne had never agreed with him—and mixed with whisky. Was he stupid? He was too old to party late and work all day anymore—about thirty years too old. He whacked the snooze button and rolled over to catch another half hour of sleep before he had to get up. A muffled yowl followed by sharp pricks to his side sent him flying out of bed. After cleaning the scratches with hydrogen peroxide and choking down three more aspirins, he padded to the bodega to scoop a quarter cup of kitten food into Daisi's bowl.

Damn, the kitten wasn't even his. Daisi showed up on the doorstep one day and made herself at home. He didn't want a pet. He didn't have enough time to take care of a cat, but the little creature was too skinny and needed care—yeah, his middle name: Caregiver.

He put on the kettle and ground his Frijoles Mayos coffee beans. While he waited for the water to boil, he checked his messages. Nothing. He'd try again after his Foundation gig at the IMSS—always a depressing stop on his rounds. Noisy, dirty, and many of the staff uncooperative. At least the chief of Virology worked well with him.

The new anti-viral was combating COVID, but tired and hung-over, he questioned his efforts as he poured the steaming water over the grounds and plunged them to the bottom of the French carafe. His success with landing a government contract for Viru-Out—for any drug—was wasted effort. The AMLO government wasn't interested in saving lives. Worrying about sales was futile.

Just like worrying about his mother.

Why doesn't she return my call?

Now Lucas, he was another story. Alex's brother had been doted on; he could do no wrong. His mother thought the sun rose and set on his older brother. The pinche drunk. Alex poured a dollop of milk into his hot coffee. He knew his thought train was headed for a crash, or at least a side spur. Thinking of his family would not improve his day. But he couldn't stop.

The sun shone on the patio. Small white bells bloomed amid dark green sword-like leaves in a large Talavera pot. The neighborhood was quiet this early on a Saturday morning and he'd placed a small iron table in the sunniest corner. A moment of warm peace and vitamin D would help banish his dark thoughts. He carried his coffee out and sat down. Daisi followed him, jumping onto the other chair to groom. They sat companionably until he finished his cup and went back to the kitchen for a refill.

The gloom of the house cast its shadow over his tenuous mood improvement. He caught a look at himself in the mirror near the entrance to the kitchen. Haggard, tired, old. The circles under his eyes turned his usual sea blue irises into the color of storm clouds over slate. A bit like Lucas's after one of his all-too-often benders. Alex pictured how much Lucas looked like their mother. He looked like his father, so much so there could be no question of whose child he was. But the question nagged: was Irene his mother? Last December Irene had almost admitted she wasn't. He'd brought her a series of a new cancer medicine, and she responded well; for once she obviously felt kindly toward him. She wanted to talk. Yet, as soon as Irene showed an interest in Alex, Lucas and Ana sent him home.

They were up to something and wanted to keep Alex from finding out. Maybe it had to do with the inheritance.

He pondered this as he stirred a spoonful of sugar into his third coffee. He didn't even know if there *was* anything to inherit. But what point was there to thinking about all of these things? He'd try Irene again after his shower.

The phone rang as he dried off. He grabbed it from the edge of the sink and answered. A low, scratchy-sounding voice cut in and out with the poor signal in the bathroom. He stepped into the hall near the router.

"Hello? I can't hear you. Who is it?"

"Help me, Alex. She's trying to kill me." The line went dead.

Who? What? It sounded sort of like his mother. What was going on? He checked the number. Blocked. Hit redial. Rang once and ended. He dialed Ana. Dread descended upon him. *What if?* No, they wouldn't...it was too terrible to consider.

The phone rang and rang. Lucas didn't answer either. Frustrated, Alex filled Daisi's water bowl, checked that the upstairs window was cracked open enough that she could get out, and grabbed his helmet. The rush of wind on the motorcycle always made him feel better. He'd forget about his family. Move on. Get ready to step up into top management of his company.

The nagging message dogged him.

What if it were true?

What if he didn't respond?

What if they really were trying to kill Irene?

If only he knew how to reach a neighbor.

Oh God, I'll never be able to live with myself if I don't go to Veracruz.

Chapter 3

The Mission

Traffic was light between Naucalpan and Tlalnepantla. The wind banished the dregs of whisky from his brain, but not his worry. Alex rechecked his mental task-list for the day at the IMSS Hospital General de Zona #51. He knew it well and looked forward to his talk with the jefa de pabellon, unit manager, Doctor Milagros Bondad.

Dr. Milagros, a great supporter of Alex's work, was a virus specialist trained in the U.S., and in charge of the COVID unit. She not only arranged for a high percentage of the patients for the Viru-Out trials; she kept meticulous notes, complying with all the regulations. Best, her private practice actively purchased LSI's medicines and entered patients into trials. He owed her a lot as one of the first doctors to sign on to his foundation's mission.

The Satellite towers blurred by. Traffic picked up as Alex approached the exits for the big shopping centers. He slowed down anticipating his Santa Monica exit. *Five minutes.*

He had time to stop and pick up two drinks to go.

Dr. Milagros loved her chai lattes. He needed more jet fuel.

The first order of the day was to deliver the coffee and go over the results of the past month. The second was to spread the news about the Viru-Out launch and his promotion. He planned to drop by all the doctors tending COVID patients and invite them to assemble in the patio for lunch—six feet apart—to spread the word of the drug's success. Milagros would come. She wasn't one of those skinny women who ate half a lettuce leaf and shoved the plate away. She loved to eat and talk about medicine. Her lovely apple-cheeked face always lit up when Alex suggested a lunch meeting. Today would be no different, he wagered, although the pandemic was creating an untenable schedule for medical staff. The hospitals were full to overflowing and the staffs overworked.

Next Alex planned to make the rounds of the patients and assess who might qualify to receive Viru-Out. He would lend a hand to anyone needing extra help while he was there. It satisfied him to help out, knowing he was making people's lives better. Some had suggested he attend medical school, but that ship had sailed.

Several horns blasted; Alex swerved around a snarl and pulled into a small space between two Suburbans outside the Multiplaza Arboledos.

He yanked off his helmet, secured it to his sample case and chained the case and bike to a streetlamp with a special chain designed to need a giant metal cutter to break—he'd lost one motorcycle to thieves, and had learned his lesson.

Business was brisk inside the coffee shop although

the line was short. Most of the tables were occupied with people wearing masks, working on laptops, tablets, and phones. People at few tables actually talked; the constant staring at devices irritated Alex. He loved to talk, share ideas, and get to know people. A rousing debate on most any topic energized him. His penchant for talk was the secret to his success as a salesperson.

He eyed the pastry case.

"Buenos dias, may I take your order?" asked a pretty morena when he reached the counter.

"Please. I'd like an Americano with cream and a chai latte, both grande to go." He glanced at a delicious looking cake in the case and asked, "What's the cake?"

"Walnut with cream filling and mocha frosting. Want a slice?"

"Absolutely! Make it two packaged separately. Thanks. And can the barista write Viru-Out on the chai?"

"Maybe," the girl answered then called, "Luci, can you write something special on a chai latte?"

"Depends on what he wants. Can you write it down for me, Señor?"

Alex jotted the drug name onto a paper napkin and pushed his debit card under the reader.

"Thanks, have a great day," he said as he dropped a twenty-peso note into the tip jar. The girl grinned.

The chai latte looked perfect with Viru-Out in cream on top. The barista had even managed a heart around the words after Alex explained what it was. He packed the bag of coffees and cake into his saddlebag, freed the bike, and roared out of the movie plaza, arriving at the hospital parking lot with exactly enough time to get to his meeting.

He felt energized. Visiting Dr. Milagros tended to have that effect on him. Her ample curves and her brightly flamboyant style of dressing turned him on, but it was her brilliant mind that was the real attraction. Too bad she was married. That seemed to be his luck—the good ones didn't need him—unlike his ex-wife and a string of losers and takers like Avelina Fogel.

Alex strode through the wide entry to the hospital astounded by the miserable conditions that greeted him. The lobby had been turned into a COVID ward, or so it appeared. Beds were everywhere with patients coughing or gasping for air. People and staff milled about, many unmasked. He added a second mask over his N95 respirator and took the broad stairs to the second floor. But it was worse; crammed with beds, gurneys, and cots filled by men, women, and children struggling to breathe. Struggling to live. Some as waxy pale as cadavers. Surely the hospital was removing the deceased. He skirted his way through the mishmash of patients to Milagros's office and knocked. Ten o'clock. Right on time. As if it mattered in this hell hole.

The doctor let him in and quickly shut the door against the din of coughs, moaning, beeping machines, crying, calls for help, and harried nursing staff trying to do their job. The misery weighed on Alex. His case containing twenty-four free courses of Viru-Out— laughable.

"Hijole, Milagros, I had no idea. . ." He handed over her bag of coffee and cake. "You look like you need this."

"Thanks." She peeked into the bag, removing her

drink and prying off the top, then slipping off her mask. The writing had begun to melt into the hot liquid, but she smiled. "Viru-Out. If only we had enough for everyone. And what's this? Cake?" Her dark eyes lit up for a short moment.

"Walnut cake with creme and mocha. I couldn't resist. I can't believe the change since last month. It's like purgatory." He moved a pile of clean masks from the visitor chair to the corner of the file-laden desk and sat down to open his Honey Coffee bag.

"It's rough, Alex. No one believed in February how virulent COVID 19 is. People refused to wear masks and stay home. The government is trying to educate the populace, but it's a disaster. People are losing their jobs, people with cash can't find necessities because the stores are sold out, others are starting to go hungry. There's no vaccination and no immunity. The kids go to school, and in a week the entire family is sick. The very young and very old are dying at alarming rates. I don't know what to do. My team pleaded with the governing board to invest in the best chance we have of saving lives and shortening the duration of the virus, your Viru-Out, but IMSS just won't do it. We're running out of medicines. We're out of beds. I'm so angry I could spit." She sipped her chai latte and drooped into her chair.

"Alex, I'm tired. My staff is tired. All of the staff is tired. And the Director and his top staff don't even come to help. Already we're losing nurses and doctors to the virus, or they're quitting before they catch it." She took a bite of the cake. "Mmmm, delicious."

"I'm free all day, Milagros. Put me to work. I have twenty-four fourteen-day courses of Viru-Out. We've just rolled it out onto the market. We've made some improvements in efficacy since the last batch. Of course, we still need to assess, but the big trials have proven the drug works. It's not a cure, but it's attacking the virus directly. As you know from the last trial, it's shortening the length and severity of the illness for otherwise healthy adults. We are starting development of a version for children, but so far, we haven't made inroads," he said between bites. "This final formulation addresses some of the contraindications from the last batch."

"Come on, it's time for my rounds. Walk with me. I've selected forty-eight potential recipients from my patient load." She rose, slipped her arms into her lab coat, secured her mask, and hung her stethoscope around her neck. Grabbing her medical bag, she ushered Alex through the door locking it while he put on his mask.

"You need to lock your door?"

"If I didn't, I'd return to find five new patients on my desk." Her chuckle sounded more like a groan.

They walked to the nurses' station to collect patient charts for the people the doctor had chosen to see first. Alex detailed the current contraindications as they entered the ward.

"Yours and other trials show negative reactions to Viru-Out in patients with hypertension, hepatitis, especially C, diabetes, and kidney disease. Also, alcoholic patients and all the patients with advanced COVID, have shown more severe symptoms. I'm not sure why the alcoholics have adverse reactions. Maybe you understand that. We don't really have much data on it, in part because the alcoholics won't always own up to being alcoholic. The last group is the group most in need of Viru-Out—those over seventy."

Milagros paused at the bed of a woman breathing through a ventilator then flipped open the top chart. "Mariella Espinosa, twenty-three, student, and my usual waitress at Honey Coffee. She does not drink, is in perfect health, other than COVID, and qualifies financially for the trial."

"She's on a ventilator."

"Does it matter?"

"No, not really. She could have a long life if we can beat this plague. I'll add her to the list."

The next ten qualifying patients ranged in aged between thirty-two and sixty-seven. Five on ventilators, and the rest laboring for breath. All with high temperatures. But none with other medical complications. Alex added them to the list.

As they proceeded through the overcrowded ward, he stopped to help patients drink water. He covered others in the cool room, and he spoke gently to many.

Finally, Dr, Milagros said, "That's half. It's my shift lunchtime. Shall we round up the others and invite everyone to the cafeteria? They'll want to hear about your success with Viru-Out. Several of them have people fitting your criteria, too. Our private practices are overwhelmed. We could all use it, if not for the good of our patients, then for lightening our loads." She giggled. "Did I say that out loud?"

Alex laughed. "I hear you, Milagros. I'm appalled at how rapidly this is spreading. I'm in and out of hospitals every week, but this is by far the worst I've seen. I'll beg more courses off Ivan Castellanos. Hundreds more. We'll buy it. The foundation has donors. We'll do something."

It was true. He understood her feelings. Seeing first-hand the awful situation in IMSS #51 and multiplying it by how many IMSS hospitals in the country? Not to mention all the other hospitals, clinics, and health centers, made him realize that this wasn't just a serious outbreak. In one month, the outbreak had exploded into the pandemic newscasters described in other countries.

For all the misery, lunch was a reasonably jovial affair. Besides Milagros, five doctors with patients in his trials, and one new doctora, Purita Ayala her nametag said, attended.

Alex picked up the tab for the meals he carried from the cafeteria and made his pitch. Doctor Purita asked a lot of questions. Alex and the doctors enjoyed a rousing discussion of the pros and cons of Viru-Out and several of the drugs the hospital administered. Laboratorios Salud Integral won the competition, but it didn't make any difference, IMSS was a government hospital with a low budget and lower interest in actually healing its patients, especially under the MORENA government. IMSS wouldn't buy Viru-Out, no matter how effective it was. Doctor Purita said she'd be willing to give it a try.

"Thank you, Doctora. I'll come to your office when Dr. Milagros and I finish rounds. You'll still be here in about three hours?"

"Of course, Señor Deltoro. I think I live here now. I didn't know when I received my license to practice before the holidays I'd be working fifteen hours a day."

"Fifteen? When do you sleep?" one of the other

doctors asked.

"On my feet, I think," she replied. The group laughed. "I drink a lot of coffee," she said, tipping her cup toward the group. Everyone agreed.

Back on rounds, Alex and Milagros discovered three of her patients had died while they were at lunch. The lighter atmosphere generated at the luncheon table darkened. Alex felt a heavy weight descending onto his shoulders.

"It's been like this every day since I last saw you, Alex. You're doing so much, but none of us can do enough. Millions will die from COVID. Mark my words."

They had identified five more candidates and initiated treatment. These might live, but what about the hundreds more dying in front of his eyes?

"Go help Purita. She's just starting out. Get in with her and you'll have her as a customer for the rest of your career. She's an excellent doctor. Stanford in California, top of her class, interned at the UC Med Center in San Francisco, and took her residency at the famous Mayo Clinic in infectious diseases."

"With that background, why on earth is she working at an IMSS?"

"She's like you, a caregiver. She really cares and money isn't her objective. I interviewed her for hire. She's dedicated. But she's green. Go give her a hand."

They shook hands. Alex thanked the doctora, saying he'd be in touch soon, that he would move mountains to get more antivirus to her patients, then made his way to the next floor to doctor Purita's ward.

He found the young woman slumped over her desk in a cat nap. She woke when he knocked.

It was a repeat of his meeting in Milagros' office, but with more questions and note taking on the part of Purita. She had already assessed her patients for good fits and had their charts stacked neatly on the desk. They read through each and agreed on the five who would have the greatest success.

On the ward over the next three hours, Alex and Purita offered comfort and attention to the thirty-five people under her direct charge. Purita's unit had many children. It broke Alex's heart to see these little people suffering so much. Purita gave detailed histories of each child's illness and background.

With tears glistening in her eyes, she said, "This is Yuliana. She is nine and has been caring for her five younger siblings because both her parents contracted COVID. Her father died in this hospital several weeks ago. The mother came down with it a week later, and the young family has not had food or care until Yuliana got here. I'm taking care of them now, but even I'm a poor caregiver, being here so much of the time. And this is only one of the stories we hear."

"Aren't there any services for kids like this?"

"Churches maybe, but these little ones don't know how to find help. They'll just starve to death or come down with this dreaded virus and die because there's no one to take care of them."

"Purita, I have some resources. I can put you in touch." Alex gulped a breath. The weight he felt before had become a building-sized cement block pressing down on him. "I promise you I'll do everything in my power to get Viru-Out into your hands."

She checked her watch and thanked Alex for his work. It was seven, she had a meeting with the supervisors.

Alex collected his now-empty case and made his way back to his motorcycle. Eight people had died while he was in the hospital. The heavy block now felt like a hot volcano burning him with fear. He wore his double masks except at lunch and washed his hands raw. COVID was the last thing he wanted. As he roared into his garage, he prayed he hadn't been exposed. Didn't he already have enough problems?

It all rushed back. His mother, the family ghosting him. He entered the house and dialed his mother. Nothing. He dialed Lucas and left a message. He dialed his niece Morticia. More of the same.

Chapter 4

The Decision

Sunday, March 29, 2020

Daisi pounced on Alex's chest and meowed loudly. He stirred, pulled his pillow over his head to block the ray of morning sun slicing through a gap in the curtains. The kitty was probably hungry, but a night of tossing and turning with worry left him exhausted. From the angle of the sun, he knew it was early. No point in trying to call the family at six a.m. No one would answer that early on a Sunday morning.

He covered his head with the pillow. "Daisi, you'll just have to wait." Alex drifted into a fugue state where all his failures paraded in costume around him in an empty arena. There was Irene with her duster shooing little Alex to his room as she cuddled Lucas and their baby brother. His father strode past, a look of disgust on his face, pointing to the door. The girl he married pirouetted into a leap, landing in front of Alex, a gun pointed at his head. Next a chorus of cheerleaders, chanting, "loser, user" to a crowd materialized into the stands. Avelina minced behind, a siren, her taunting laughter filling the air.

He shook himself awake, depression that cement block weighing him down. A glance at his cell phone said it was eight thirty. Alex roused himself, sitting up on the edge of the bed. Daisi was gone, but the hangover of his dream lingered. Why did he feel so low? He'd just been honored, promoted, and awarded a fat cash bonus. Not to mention the coming raise. He had friends and close colleagues. He made the world a little better. Alex had it all. Didn't he?

In the kitchen he made two carafes of coffee and heated up the conchas he'd bought on the way home from the hospital. His mind churned. Maybe he cared too much. If he didn't care, it wouldn't make much difference that the women he dated generally were after his youthful fair skinned, blue-eyed European looks and his good salary—not *him*. Only one woman had truly loved him and demanded nothing from him but that he love her. He'd blown that.

He slathered butter on his sweet roll and took a bite. The sugar rushed into his bloodstream, perking him up. Between the coffee and the pastry, the tatty cobwebs of failure tore off and drifted away.

But still there was the uncertainty of his mother. Was Irene alive? Were the family keeping him away from her? Why? He buttered the second concha and considered the possibilities. None sounded good. She didn't want to talk to him—nothing new there. Or, his brother, the chosen son, was after her estate, or her love, or just wanted to hurt Alex. Or the family had neglected Irene, and she lay dying in her crummy government-built house, alone, and they didn't want to own up to it.

Or she was dead and Alex's final tie to his family severed.

He picked up his phone and dialed Morticia. She answered on the fifth ring.

"Morticia, I'm so glad to reach you. How are you? What's going on?"

"Hello Tío, I'm fine. Nothing's new. Gabriel and I are taking care of the kids and spending time with my grandmother. Why?"

"I've called and called, Morticia. My mother never returns my calls anymore. Lucas doesn't answer my calls, your mother never has, and I've left at least four messages for you. How is my mother?"

"You were here at Christmas Tío. She got a little better, you remember. She's doing pretty well, but she doesn't like talking on the phone. She's old and forgets to call. I didn't realize you'd phoned her."

"Okay, busy then? Work?" asked Alex.

"The kids keep me going night and day. I help Papi out some of the time too. What about you? How's work?"

Alex summarized his success and asked, "And Lucas? What's so pressing he can't call his brother?"

"Tío, the truth is, you live in Mexico City and are not here taking care of your mother. Papi has to do everything. Grandma isn't going to live forever and he's having to take care of it all. Maybe you should help support her. Papi would probably talk to you more if you showed more interest in the family." Morticia paused. Alex remained silent. She added, "I'm just saying, Tío."

"I'm calling now. I want to know exactly what's going on with Mother. You're not answering me,

Morticia. All this about how I don't care or help? You know what I've done. The farm, the house, the business? Do you really believe yourself? Tell me the status of my mother," he demanded.

"Tío Alex, tu mamá is doing as well as a very old lady can. We're taking good care of her. I'll ask her to call you."

Was Alex just being paranoid, or did his niece's voice carry a tinge of insincerity? He said, "Please, Morticia. I need to know she's all right. Will you also ask your dad to call me?"

"Sure Tío. Te amo. Bye."

The line went dead. There was no doubt in Alex's mind. Morticia was lying through her teeth. Irene was not all right. That phone call Friday night. After this conversation, Alex was certain it had come from Irene, and his mother was dying. But who was the "she" trying to kill her? The caretaker? And why wouldn't Lucas call him? Especially if he was complaining to the family Alex didn't do enough for his mother? He needed to go to Veracruz.

What luck LSI granted him two weeks off before taking his new position, Alex thought as he finished his third coffee. He had planned on fulfilling his obligations to his department, closing out his current files and handing off the work to the new manager during his time off. Not to mention the work with the foundation. It skyrocketed with COVID and Viru-Out was needed more than ever. But that all would have to wait.

He pulled his motorcycle backpack out of the closet, tossed it on the bed, and began stuffing it with tee-shirts, shorts, underwear. He wouldn't need much. Veracruz was warm.

When the pack was almost full, he added his grooming kit and set about assembling needed files, laptop, and a portable printer. He would do the administrative work at Irene's house while he sorted out whatever was going on.

When everything was ready, he carried the pile down to the gated side yard to load the motorcycle, returning to the house to bathe and dress. He'd laid out his leather pants and jacket with the helmet. It was a seven-hour ride over the highest mountain in Mexico. No telling what the mountain weather would be like. It was still early spring. He might encounter snow. He added gloves and a scarf to the mix.

Finally dressed and groomed, he set out Daisi's bed and the auto dispensing food and water bowls onto the balcony where she liked to hang out. He hoped she'd be okay for a few days—no more than a week, anyway. He'd call his neighbor to check in on her.

The computer equipment wobbled on the back of the bike. Not secure, and not dust or waterproof. He wasn't thinking straight. Alex went back to the garage and scrounged for the heavy-duty cardboard box he knew was there somewhere. He admonished himself to pay attention, stop anguishing over things he couldn't control.

He picked through containers of old clothes, books, things Avelina left behind after he threw her out in December, for a reinforced box lined with Styrofoam. Something from LSI, which had contained some sort of delicate lab equipment. He had forgotten why he had it, but the laptop, portable printer, cables, and chargers fit perfectly. He unwound several bungee cords from his rarely used bicycle, carrying everything to the motorcycle and securing his files and equipment first with the cords then with the locking metal cable. Finally, he called his assistant at the foundation and left a message to have someone deliver the Viru-Out he'd promised.

All he had to do now was lock the garage, check the doors and windows to make sure they were secured, shrug into the backpack, and be off. Seven hours at 100 km. If he was lucky, he'd arrive in time for dinner. His watch said twelve-thirty. Alex's anxiety grew as he closed up the house. The trip was not just long, but perilous through some of the remote regions. Besides poorly maintained roads, he would have to pass through territories known for roadblocks and robbing travelers. Generally, when Alex traveled, he used the bus, which stuck to the toll roads. But he didn't have time to wait for the next one to Veracruz.

As he secured the last lock and pulled the curtain closed, he heard Daisi crying in the stairwell. He met her at the landing where she wove between his ankles meowing and purring loudly, visibly agitated. Alex scooped her up and crooned, "It's okay, Daisi. I'll be back before you know it. Come on," he said and carried her back to the balcony, showing her the bed, food, and water. "You'll be okay. Señora Vasquez will come check on you." She scrambled onto his shoulder and yowled, trying to burrow into his jacket. It was obvious Daisi was unhappy. Alex couldn't leave her. He opened his collar, and she crawled in, curling onto his chest. He cleared the food and bed into the house and dialed the neighbor.

But how would he carry her across four states in his jacket? He hoped the little carrier from a long-lost puppy was still stored. It would have to do. He grabbed the fleece off the kitty bed and again searched.

It was after one when Alex finally had Daisi in the carrier, the motorcycle packed, secured, and the gate locked behind him. He'd been forced to move the files to the paneers and ditch the printer. The laptop now resided in the backpack. He could manage.

Alex and Daisi cruised the couple of hours out of the city toward Puebla. City traffic eventually thinned under a weak sun. The thermal inversion blanketed out any cheer the sun might have added to the day, and his thoughts were as bleak as the landscape.

Automotive businesses, warehouses, and strip malls bordering the highway thinned into a countryside of grazing goats and sheep. Dusty, gray, matching his mood. The highway skirted the western range denuded, on the eastern slope, of vegetation while slowly rising. Far in the distance, the high peaks showed the dull green of pines and the highest peak, Orizaba, gleamed white. Alex took the turn toward Texcoco and Tlascala aiming for the town of Perote about three and a half hours into the trip. Halfway. *Probably a good place to stop for lunch and let Daisi out.*

The autopisto, federal highway, terminated at sprawling Perote. Alex exited onto the business loop to search out food and gas. At the second gas plaza, he found Restaurante Doña Maria, a small, but gleaming truck stop, with excellent hot coffee and the best torta de jamón y queso he'd eaten in ages, served with American style fries and slaw, all for a pittance. He understood why the plaza was crammed with big rigs. Good food, cheap prices, unlimited coffee refills, and clean bathrooms. He felt the altitude he'd gained after walking Daisi for a few minutes and running out of breath. 7800 feet—and it was cold. The coffee was a godsend.

Alex secured the kitten back into her carrier and readjusted the tarp covering it. He didn't want her to freeze.

The autopisto narrowed here to a typical two-lane mountain road, twisting uphill for an hour until he reached Xalapa and began the descent into Cardel and tropical Veracruz. This leg of the journey was where he might to run into rain, fog, and possibly snow, but the scenery was lovely with pines, Holsteins, and cold. It always reminded him of Switzerland. As he entered the highway, he checked his watch. In two hours, he'd be in humid Xalapa. Twenty minutes later, hot, humid Actopan, arriving at Irene's soon after.

The ride was all he expected. Beautiful vistas, fog, cold. He pulled over at a roadside joint for coffee to warm up and check the kitten outside Xalapa, then hopped onto the federal highway into Veracruz.

The closer he got to his mother's the more his mood sank.

Chapter 5

The Declaration

The air, heavy with moisture, pressed into the sugarcane fields with the gloaming as Alex and Daisi cruised past Cardel. Only twenty more minutes, he thought as he crossed Rio de Antigua. Highway 180 curved toward the coast and the port city of Veracruz. Within minutes, the countryside turned from rural to the urban outskirts of a working port. He passed plaza after plaza of shipping container storage, tractors and their trailers. Lines of cargo loaded trucks crawled onto the highway at several entrances, bound for the port. From a rise, he saw the hazy acres of city bordering the deepening gray of the Gulf. If he were on vacation, Alex would be excited. Veracruz had a certain charm, some excellent seafood restaurants, and plazas full of musical groups competing for tourist pesos. The Naval base and working port added interest beyond shops full of artesania for tourists, mostly produced in China, he'd noticed on his last visit.

Traffic slowed as the highway morphed outside the Walmart Plaza into a wide divided boulevard of long blocks and stop lights. Big rigs, taxis, peseras, cars, and a surfeit of motorcycles vied for space and position. Alex cringed when a stream of policía and military pickups loaded with armed men passed on patrol. Some of the trucks mixed military and police in the same pickup bed. *More than usual?* He swung around a big rig pulling two container-laden trailers and caught the light at his turn. Making the right, he immediately cut left into the Pemex station for a fill-up. The station was in front of the Chedraui, a giant supermarket. After filling the tank, he putted into the parking lot.

His mother might need food, but it would be better to check out the house first. He grabbed a Coke from a cold case near the cash registers, found a bag of kitty crunchies and another of litter and strode toward the grocery section where he selected a bunch of wilting yellow roses for Irene. Hopefully they would perk up once he trimmed the stems and arranged them in a vase with baking soda.

He hoped the roses would soften the blow of his unexpected arrival and help open the door to her confiding what was going on. She could be so difficult —had always been difficult when it came to him. He was determined to get her to answer the question always dogging him. Always, since he was a tiny child being handed off to that kind woman on the weekends or sent to his room when Irene was passing out hugs to Lucas or being criticized for nothing more than existing.

It embarrassed him to realize he'd spent over fifty years trying to make Irene love him. His father had, and Alex had idolized him, but ultimately Irene essentially managed to push him out of the family when she and Lucas had taken over Alex's share of the inheritance. Why was he here?

Because family comes first.

Back on the bike, he drove directly to his mother's Las Brisas home, parking in front of the entry gate. He undid the cords, then lifted the cage off the bike, speaking softly to the kitten. Poor Daisi needed to get out of the tiny cage and meowed her displeasure at being cooped up so long.

"We're here, Daisi. I'll let you out in just minute," Alex crooned to the little cat. She meowed louder.

The gate, as usual, was chained and locked. He sifted through his keyring and found the key, swung it open, and wheeled the motorcycle into the small courtyard. Daisi watched through the air grates of her cage and cried again.

"Hang on, little girl. Almost in the house."

The front door was locked. Odd when his mother, if she was his mother, was home. Maybe she was out? Again, he fished out the correct keys to unlock the security gate, then the door. Inside, he set the carrier on the floor and opened the grate. Daisi took a tentative step forward, assessing the new territory with trepidation. He left her to figure out for herself where she was.

After putting on a mask, he shouted, "Hello? Hello! It's me, Alex. Anybody here? Madre? Aimee?"

The house felt stuffy as though it had been closed up for some time. It smelled of dirty linens. And it was tomb silent. No answer. No creaks, no ticking clock, no drone of T.V. Was Irene upstairs in bed? Well, Alex would deal with Irene as soon as he'd fed, watered and provided the kitty box for Daisi. Then he searched out a vase and arranged the roses, which now looked droopier than they had wrapped in their paper. He carried his sad offering upstairs to the landing and knocked on his mother's door. No answer.

He peeked into the guest room. The bed had been stripped and the windows locked. He stepped up the last stair to Irene's door and pushed it open. He stepped back, overpowered by the disgusting stench.

The room was stripped of ornamentation, the bed unmade and filthy. Her wardrobe was mostly empty. He looked for her medications. Gone. The whole place a filthy, neglected sickroom. Had Irene died and no one bothered to contact him? No, they wouldn't be that mean. If she were alive, where was she?

He opened the window, stripped the bed, and searched for clean bedding. Alex already knew how useless the caretaker was, but the condition of the house was beyond neglected. How could Lucas allow his mother to live like that? No wonder she was ill. As usual, there was no answer at Lucas's.

Alex rolled up his sleeves and set to work. Two hours later he had made up his bed, his mother's bed and cleaned the two bathrooms, dusted the furniture, and washed the kitchen floor. He sank onto the couch, exhausted. He needed some sleep. It was full-on night, long past the hour Irene would have returned. He searched for his cell phone, finding it in the kitchen next to the open can of cat food. "Daisi. Daisi! Where are you?" he called.

With typical cat behavior, Daisi was hiding. Alex wandered the house checking under all the furniture, in every cranny, closet, cupboard and behind every curtain. He finally found her cowering in the service patio. She looked relieved to see him. He was certainly happy to see her. Now that he was beginning to relax, he realized the place was giving him the creeps. Had his mother died here and left her ghost behind?

He pulled the phone from his pocket and dialed Lucas. No answer. Again. He tried the house phone. Nada. He finally called Morticia. The boyfriend answered but hung up when Alex identified himself. What was going on? He slammed his fist into the couch cushion. This was no time for the family to ignore him. Irene had called him. Morticia had lied.

"To hell with the hour, Daisi," Alex said, spitting the words. "I'll see you later. I'm checking out what's going on."

Ana, Alex's sister-in-law, opened the door with a look of shock and disdain on her heavy, square face. It was late, but Alex didn't care. He barreled in demanding, "Where's my mother?"

Ana pressed herself against the wall but screeched a challenge. "How dare you come to my house, Alex!"

He spun back to her. "Dare? You've forced me to come." His words came out low and clipped. She took a step towards him. "No you don't, Ana." He held his hand up to stop her. His voice rising, he said, "Keep your distance. I demand to see my mother. You people have ignored me long enough." He was shouting now.

Lucas shuffled into the entry hall from the living room, shocking Alex. His brother had aged ten years since Christmas. Lucas's skin looked yellow and drawn. Was he ill? The broken blood vessels across his nose stood out more than Alex remembered. Dark circles lined his flaccid cheeks and sagging chin. His movement was labored, jelly-like, his slow, fat body jiggling with each tired step.

"What are you doing here, Alex?" he said as he placed himself in front of the stairs.

"You know what I want, brother. Where is my mother? Get out of my way."

Ana rushed to Lucas and snarled, "No! You get out of my house, or I'll call the police." She started toward Alex, her manicured claws out.

"Do whatever you have to, Ana. I'm going to see my mother." He elbowed his way past her, butting away Lucas's feeble attempt at restraining him, and ran up the stairs. At the first floor, he beelined to the guest room and burst in. Irene lay in bed sleeping. Her breath came in labored gasps. A soft light illuminated her wizened face, once full and lovely, now pale and dull. He stopped in the doorway. Tears formed in his eyes. He swiped the moisture away with the edge of his mask and proceeded to her bed.

"Hello, Mother. I'm here."

He reached out and stroked her cold skin. Irene didn't move. For a moment, Alex couldn't discern any breathing. He squatted, his head dropping to the edge of the bed. Had his mother just died?

A hand cupped his cheek. He looked up into her eyes.

"Alex, you've come. Take me home." Her voice was weak, but he recognized the pleading.

"I'm here to get you, Madre," he replied.

In the hallway, the voices of Ana and Lucas rose into a heated argument. Alex tuned them out while he cradled his mother, promising to take her home. In a few moments some of their words registered.

Lucas shouted, "She's my mother, Ana!"

"And we've been taking care of her. We've paid her upkeep. We gave her a house. What has Alex done for her?"

"So, what do you want, Ana? You don't take care of her, Morticia does."

Ana lowered her voice. Alex missed her reply, but he had heard enough. He resolved to stay with his mother, care for her, for as long as he was needed.

Lucas charged into the room, Ana on his heels, steaming in anger. "Alex, take her home. Use my car. Mother is your problem now.

Chapter 6

The Neighbor

Monday, March 30, 2020

Finally, Irene lay in her freshly made bed, sleeping. Alex drooped with exhaustion. Moving his mother was difficult enough without the barrage of recriminations from Lucas and Ana. Ana went beyond hateful. She put up a fight to prevent Alex from taking Irene home. In turn this agitated Irene.

His brother was in no condition to control his wife. Alex was forced to help Lucas shove her into her room. Ana flew across the room and landed on the bed, not hurt, but screaming to bloody hell. She needed a time-out. Alex slammed the door, scooped the frail old lady from the bed, and hustled down the stairs. Lucas met him at the door with the keys.

"Hermano, what's the matter with your wife? She doesn't want to care for our mother. You'd think she'd be happy I'm willing to take over."

"She's not my wife anymore. I have an obligation to take care of my family, or I'd leave."

Alex let the revelation sink in for a beat while he

maneuvered the stairs. Once at the car, he asked, "Because you had that affair with Aimee?"

Lucas's laugh lacked mirth. "No. She betrayed me with another man."

Heat rushed up Alex's neck into his face. He didn't know what to say. Ana had an affair? *Who would want that cow?* He adjusted his mother in his arms, hoping she didn't hear what they were saying.

Lucas unlocked the door and helped Alex settle Irene into the backseat, then handed him the keys. "Bring the car back first thing. I have to leave before nine."

Alex nodded and slid behind the wheel.

After checking on his mother who slept peacefully, Alex dropped off the car and returned on his motorcycle before seven. Someone—Lucas?— had put Irene's medications in his saddlebag with the instructions withheld in December. Over coffee, Alex studied the list, reading about each on the manufacturers' websites. Most were drugs for pain. He planned on cutting back on these. He would use the morphine when her pain warranted, but the opioids he planned on phasing out. Two other drugs turned out to be small-molecule cancer targeted therapies, tablets easily swallowed. The bottle of Capecitabine was almost empty. The sedative they were injecting was not among the drugs left on the bike.

When Irene awoke, Alex gave her the prescribed cancer medicine and made breakfast. She ate two bites and pushed it away. He helped her wash and get into clean bedclothes. While she napped, he left a message for Dr. Fierro. He had many questions for the doctor, especially—when was he seeing Irene again, and where?

By mid-afternoon Alex slumped to the sofa. Daisi had taken to Irene. They slept curled together upstairs. Alex closed his eyes. The day was warm, and the door stood open. He heard a whistle at the gate. Through the windows he made out a figure standing in the lane. His face was obscured by the motorcycle helmet he wore. Alex called, "I'm coming," and went outside to find out what the man wanted.

As he approached, the man laughed and said, "You been gone so long you've forgotten your friends?" He took off the helmet.

Alex recognized Pancho López. Behind him stood Irene's best friend Rosa from next door. He hadn't seen her in several years. Now her pure white hair contrasted with her dark complexion. For an old lady, she was stunning.

Alex grinned at the man, a long-time friend of the Deltoros. "Hello, you two. Did you come together? Come on in." He unlocked the pedestrian gate and ushered them into the house, handing them masks from the stack on the table, then indicating they should take a seat. "Coffee? I can make a new pot."

"Que amable, Alex, but water is fine for me," Rosa said.

"Actually, güey," Pancho said, "I saw you come in last night and came to invite you for a cold one. You look like you need it."

"Let me get Señora Rosa her water, I think I saw some beers in the fridge." He went into the tiny kitchen, returning with water. "Sorry Pancho, all out."

"Let's go out then."

"I can't leave my mother, mano—"

"Sure you can, dear," Rosa said. "I'll sit with Irene. I have my knitting—" She pulled a fluffy pink ball of yarn from her bag— "and two hours free. I planned to visit with Irene if she feels up to it, anyway."

Pancho said, "Then it's decided. Get your helmet. Let's go."

Alex shrugged. He was tired. Pancho was really Lucas's friend, but he said, "Are you sure it's okay with you, Señora?"

Rosa nodded her white head and smiled. "I'll go up now." Alex gave her a hand, helping her off the low sofa, but didn't think she'd make it up the stairs. He watched her as she trudged up.

"Get your helmet and let's go," Pancho demanded impatiently.

Alex complied, wondering what the rush was, as he climbed onto the back of Pancho's bike. Had Lucas put him up to it?

"Where we going Pancho?" he asked.

"You know that cantina about ten blocks north?"

"Not really. I may have been there once. Probably with you and Lucas."

The motor roared to life backfiring as Pancho put the bike into gear. He turned left, idling between the stanchions closing the cobbled alley to through-traffic, and hitting the gas when they reached tarmac.

The cantina was a run-down hole-in-the-wall in a seedy neighborhood. Corrido music blared out from under the rain tarp drooping over some dingy plastic tables set on a cemented patio in front. Inside the bar, the music distorted under the high volume. Alex slipped on his mask and led them to a metallic table painted with Corona beer logos in the farthest corner from the over-driven speakers so they could talk. In a few moments, a chunky waitress wearing a very short, skin-tight shiny black dress and no mask showed up and asked what they wanted.

"Two very cold caguamas, por favor," Pancho ordered.

Alex shoved another mask across the table. "Put this on, Poncho. This place is a petri dish for God knows what."

"No mames, pendejo. It's flu."

The waitress returned in a few minutes with two huge beers. The dark room was cool, cave-like in the heat of the day, and the cold beer went down quickly while they caught up. Pancho ordered another round. The conversation turned to Alex's family and Lucas in particular.

"Your brother is a great man, Alex." He recounted several anecdotes as he swilled down the liquid. "Lucas is splendid. He and I like visiting the bars; he is so generous—he always picks up the tab. He has a chingo of partying friends." Pancho paused to signal the waitress for a third round.

Alex already felt a little woozy. He wasn't much of a drinker, and he was way too tired. Not to mention the conversation didn't make him happy, but he grinned as if he liked what was being said, remaining silent to keep Pancho talking. If Lucas had put him up to this, it'd backfired. He was learning a lot about his brother.

Pancho now slurred his words. He pushed out from the table, saying, "I've gotta piss." He wove behind the jukebox and giant speakers hanging on a support post and beam blasting ranchero music.

Alex watched him stagger into a black curtained tunnel labeled "restroom" between a storage area and where the suspicious bowl of fatty meat and unrecognizable, limp vegetables in oily broth came from—a kitchen, he supposed. Another woman, stuffed into a size-too-small black dress like a salchicha, scuttled in behind Pancho. Alex was starting to get the picture.

"Another round?" the waitress asked, circling her finger over the table.

"Thanks, I'm good, but one for my friend, please."

Pancho returned five minutes later grinning. He launched right into a story about the time Lucas took him to Las Vegas. The man didn't acknowledge he had a fresh beer, just guzzled it down.

"The casino sent him two courtesy plane tickets to go stay and play and we went to this chigno hotel, a very nice atmosphere. . ."

Alex lost track of the story. Most likely Lucas was sent tickets so he could drink the free drinks and lose at the tables. To Alex, gambling was an unadulterated waste of resources. He felt his blood begin to boil. How dare Lucas waste money on gambling, partying, and drinking. Lucas's capital was not the product of his work but was the family patrimony—*his* money. Pancho jabbered on about the cute waitresses and the sexy call girls. *Unlike the overweight hags in this joint.*

He plastered the phony grin to his lips again, hoping it would reach his eyes, and thought about how Lucas had never distributed the inheritance from his father. The greedy bastard. Pancho was making it clear just how dishonest his brother really was. He held up his empty glass and raised his eyebrows. Pancho grinned and signaled for yet another round then continued his story.

Lucas's escapades depressed Alex. He drifted into a different story. The story of visiting his father's ranch in Campeche and finding out Lucas had forged his father's signature to sell it. Of course, Alex never saw any of that money. He doubted their younger brother did either. Lucas had it planned. In that moment, Alex realized that he made a big mistake by not telling the police. It was a serious crime. If prosecuted, his brother would have gone to jail without the possibility of parole. But it would have killed his mother out of sadness. Irene's life was Lucas.

Despite his advancing drunkenness, Pancho recognized the shift in Alex's mood and changed the conversation. "I admire your brother very much. He went for your mother in Mexico to bring her here, gave her the house, and took responsibility for her. You know he is the one who takes her to the doctor and sees to her upkeep. He complains a lot that you never come to see her, but I see that's just Lucas being a pendejo.

"When I went to see Irene recently; she was in a bad way. I went over to see Lucas, and he finally picked Irene up and took her to his place. The three times I visited; Lucas wasn't home. His wife was inhospitable. She didn't want me to see your mother, but one time your niece took me up and I could see Ana was giving her what I thought was too much sedative. Then I understood. Ana didn't want me to know what she was doing. If I were you, I'd watch out for Lucas, too. He spends money he doesn't have."

"What do you mean?"

"I dunno, güey. But his house is gonna crumble down on him one of these days. He lives too big."

Alex was left alone at the table again when Pancho staggered up. This time the bartender scurried in after him but came right out. Pancho couldn't get it up, probably. As if Alex cared. He felt sad a woman had to sell herself to awful men like Pancho. Anyway, he had enough depressing things to think about.

Memories of other abuses his brother instigated swirled through his brain. The house in Mexico City he was forced to sell so Lucas could give the money to Irene. Two days after signing the agreement, Alex had arrived home from work to find the gate chained, the doors locked, and a mattress on the sidewalk. Not even a goodbye. Lucas and his precious mother were gone.

Sipping at his brew, he wallowed in a mental tour of the huge mistakes he made trusting Irene and Lucas. Lucas had forged his dead father's signature to sell Alex's property in Tamarindo, a pig farm with a house and orchard, which his father had given to Alex after Lucas sold the pigs and used the money to buy a hot car. It irked him still that Lucas made Irene sell the hamburger stand with a soda fountain located in front of a school, which Alex bought for her. Worst, Irene always complained that Alex was a bad son and never looked after her.

Poncho finally returned to the table. He'd staggered from the bathroom to the bar to chat up the bartender. Exacerbated by the alcohol, Alex slumped sad and disappointed under the weight of his thoughts. It was time to go. He said, "Oye, Pancho, I'm tired, I need to go. Thanks." He rose, went to the bar, paid the tab, and grabbed a cab disgorging a couple of cops he recognized, coming to the putero for a little action. Everything was so sad. Lucas's behavior was worse than he thought.

What have I gotten myself into?

Chapter 7

The Funeral

Into Wednesday, April 1, 2020

Ana showed up at Alex's door shortly after the taxi left him at the gate. Just what he didn't need. But out of politeness, he invited her in. She joined Rosa in the living room, accepting the offered coffee. "How is your mother, Alex?" Ana asked, stirring in a spoonful of sugar into the cup.

Rosa answered. "I sat with her while Alex took a break. She's resting now, but we had lovely chat. She says she's feeling much better now that she's home. She asked after Lucas."

Ana stiffened at the mention of Lucas. Or was it the fact that Irene was alert and chatting with her friend? He didn't have time to play footsie with his sister-in-law. Her arrival boded no good. "Not to be rude, but why are you here, Ana?"

She frowned, drawing her mouth into that tight line. But she didn't appear to be shocked. More annoyed than anything else. "Why do you ask, Alex? Irene is my family, and I want to know she's being taken care of."

The look of feigned innocence was laughable.

Rosa smiled. "Of course you do dear. Alex, I'm surprised at you."

Her tone sounded mild, but he knew he was being criticized. Ana smirked.

He said, "Rosa, you missed the show last night. Ana made it clear she was not taking care of my mother." He looked at Ana. "And by her condition, I'd judge that to be the only truth you've told since I arrived. What's the matter with you? Are you here to apologize?"

"Me? Apologize, Alex? For what? You're the one who barged into my house uninvited and dragged a sick old woman away from her family."

"I am her family, Ana."

"Pues, I beg to differ." Ana was shouting now.

"Lower your voice, Ana. You'll wake Irene," the neighbor said, placing her hand on Ana's arm.

Ana looked at the boney work-worn paw like it was a snake about to strike and jerked away. "I'll go up and check on her." She set her cup on the glass coffee table and rose.

Alex sprang from the chair. "No. My mother is resting. I do not want you to agitate her."

Ana gritted her jaw and with a low, controlled voice said, "I don't care what you want, Alex." She moved toward the stairs.

He sprang after her blocking the way, as a weak voice filtered down from the second floor. "Alex? Alex, are you there?"

Irene! He spun to mount the steps, but Ana beat him to it. As she ran up, he saw she pulled a syringe from her little purse.

"No!" he yelled. Taking two steps at a time, he raced into the room as Ana was reaching for his mother's arm. He batted her hand away. The syringe flew against the wall and shattered to the tiles. Ana shoved Alex aside and ran. In moments, the gate clanged behind her.

Irene had gone white with fear. She whimpered, shaking. He gathered his mother into his arms and rocked her, whispering soothing sounds until she calmed.

"Thank you, Alex. She was going to kill me," she said so quietly Alex wasn't sure she'd actually spoken.

"Why would Ana want to do that, Mother?"

"She wants the money."

Alex had considered that. It certainly looked suspicious that every time Alex and his mother started to have a conversation, Ana swooped in and filled her full of drugs, rendering Irene incapable of talking. It wasn't to care for her or keep her comfortable, the syringe was to dope her into unconsciousness.

Over the next two days, Alex and Irene entertained a stream of visitors. Rosa arrived daily to give him a rest. Lucas came in and out. Morticia arrived on Wednesday evening while her father sat in the living room with Alex. She handed her father a file marked "Mother". The talk turned to the boyhood times the brothers spent with their father. They reminisced over Irene's photo albums, laughing, choking up, and quibbling over their memories. Alex felt peaceful and accepted for a change.

During a lull in the conversation, a wavering voice filtered down the stairs. "Alex. Alex."

He rushed up from the armchair, scattering the photos. He didn't stop to pick them up but ran to Irene's room. He found her turning blue, desperately trying to take in a breath of air. He lifted her, squeezing and releasing her chest in hopes to make her lungs respond. But in vain. Irene stared into his eyes in anguish and terror. His mother was dying. Alex held her close as her soul slipped from her body. In a panic, Alex tried to revive her with a heart massage.

But Irene ceased to exist.

Alex stilled. He hugged his mother, crying silently through that moment where silence is heard. His life with his mother in childhood looped through his mind, a great sadness filling his heart. Had she really been his mother? He would never know, and what was most hurtful, he no longer had the chance to repair their contentious relationship. Alex felt the loss deeply. He'd loved this woman who raised him, even as she rejected him. He felt shipwrecked, cast away to some distant shore with no route home.

Gently he placed her back in her bed, arranging the sheet to give her a peaceful appearance. Kissing her cheek, he set about the tasks her death required.

He tucked the drugs into a baggie he found in the bureau drawer. He would double-check his assessment of her prescriptions later. He already knew she was being given far more painkillers than she should have taken. Ana had administered four times more than the doctor prescribed, he reckoned. The idea crossed Alex's mind again that Ana did it so that Irene would be unconscious and could not talk to him, or anyone else. But to what end? Irene thought Ana wanted to kill her for money. Did Irene have anything more than this crummy house?

He dragged himself down the stairs to deliver the news. Lucas's florid face twisted from smiling to pain, but he was not surprised. Morticia stifled a sob. She excused herself to sit with her grandmother.

Alex squeezed his brother's shoulder and asked, "You okay?"

Lucas didn't answer. Instead, he slid the file Morticia delivered into Alex's his hands. He opened it, discovering both the funeral arrangements and Irene's medical file. Lucas had anticipated this day. Did he suspect the death was premature? Why else would he give Alex the medical records? He skimmed the pages. Lucas went upstairs.

Before Alex could study the medical file, he needed to call the funeral home and arrange for Irene's remains to be collected. The family and the mortuary had only twenty-four hours to organize everything before the funeral. He tapped his finger nervously on the table as the line rang.

A man answered, his voice calm, reassuring. Alex gave the contract number and his name. "I'm Irene's son. Lucas Deltoro's brother."

"Yes, I see, Señor Deltoro. You will be with your mother until the hearse arrives? Our driver will collect her from her home in Las Brisas?" He rattled off the address.

Alex confirmed.

"All our paperwork is in order. Please include the outfit you wish her to be dressed in. The car will arrive in approximately forty-five minutes. Please rest easy knowing we will take care of everything, including notifying the authorities and obtaining the death certificate."

He confirmed Lucas's requests as Alex read along from the contract. Lucas had spared no expense, but Alex didn't find the invoice. Why would his brother leave it out of the file?

Finally, the funeral director said, "We are truly sorry for your loss, Señor Deltoro." The ring of sincerity in his voice sounded genuine.

Alex choked on his next words. "Thank you."

In forty-five minutes, the hearse arrived with two attendants wearing tuxedoes. Alex opened the gate for the vehicle and ushered the staff inside.

"We are so sorry for your loss," the driver said. "Where will we find the deceased?"

"Upstairs but permit me to go up to prepare my brother and niece first."

He climbed the narrow stairs and tapped lightly on Irene's door. "They're here."

Lucas opened the door. He had transformed into an old man, hunched with blotchy drooping skin. He stepped back to the bed, kissed his mother's forehead, and gathered Morticia into his arms. She openly sobbed. They each murmured, "Goodbye," and disappeared into the guest room. Morticia's cry of grief stabbed his heart. Alex descended to tell the attendants where to find his mother.

The next evening, the mortuary called to say they were ready to receive the family and guests. It was the same smooth-voiced man Alex had spoken to the night before.

He wore dark slacks and shoes he'd bought during

the day. The ride to Lucas's house was short; he arrived in time to meet his black-clad family to pay his respects. Ana was subdued and polite. Alex was the only one who wore a mask.

Señor Flores, the man who Alex had talked to, met the Deltoros at the entry. He wore a black suit with a white flower pinned to his lapel, and a mask. He asked that before Irene was moved to the viewing, someone needed approve her makeup and dress. Alex thought whatever Irene looked like, the sight would be horrible. Morticia accompanied Alex to the workroom, which stank of formaldehyde. Morticia complained the makeup was wrong although she had applied it earlier in the day.

An hour and a half later, Irene in her open casket was moved to what they called the wake room. Alex noted it's grand size, set with rows of chairs and filled with urns and vases of flowers forming a backdrop to his mother's placement. Flowered horseshoes, crosses, stars, and hearts on tripods announced their good wishes above the coffin. The room took on that sticky odor of hothouse flowers. More floral arrangements kept arriving. Alex didn't know Irene had so many friends.

The wake room was actually a suite. With two bedrooms and two full baths. It would be their home for the next twenty-four hours. Like a five-star hotel, it was appointed with attractive furniture and art in soothing colors. When Alex entered the room on the left to use the bathroom, he found Ana sprawled on the bed.

"Get out of my room, Alex," she snarled.

Always gracious, he thought before he quipped, "My

condolences, Ana. I know you're hurting. We all are. But I'll leave when I'm ready." He closed the bathroom door behind him and exhaled. He wanted to hide.

In the main room, Lucas had ordered a sound system to play Irene's favorite music. She enjoyed standards, especially those sung by her niece, singer Lucero, and many of her songs played softly as friends came to say goodbye. People Alex recognized, and many he didn't, milled around chatting or lounging in the ample leather chairs, comfortable enough for sleeping. Few wore masks.

A steady stream of people flowed in and out of the cafeteria on the mezzanine for unlimited snacks, drinks and coffee. Alex idly wondered who was paying for this. Probably the cost of her funeral was why his mother had asked Alex for the one hundred fifty thousand pesos in December.

At midnight, the assembled guests quieted down when three robed women arrived to say the rosary. The service lasted an hour. Ana did not come out of the room. Morticia sobbed and Lucas stared into space.

In the morning, Lucas appeared from the room Ana had not claimed, bathed and groomed, but wearing comfortable pants and huaraches rather than his formal wear.

Alex had slept fitfully in one of the chairs, waking with a start when his brother entered the room. Lucas looked sad, but Alex saw something else. His face had taken on a sickly pale-yellow cast and his feet had swollen to almost twice their normal size, bulging out of the strappy sandals.

Alex sat up. "Buenos días, brother. You look

terrible. Are you sick?"

Lucas grimaced. "I haven't been feeling well lately."

"I can see. Where's your mask? I'm worried about your feet. Show me your legs."

Lucas frowned but yanked up the hems of his pants to expose extreme inflammation. Alex stifled a gasp. Lucas's legs bore a yellowish color; from his movement, Alex knew they were stiff. He feared if he didn't do something, his brother might lose both legs, but he didn't say anything. He let Lucas drop the hems and move next to the casket. He discreetly left the room to sit in the corridor and allow Lucas his grief. After what he saw, Alex had a new job—to watch over Lucas.

Soon people began to arrive again for the next Rosary. After prayers, a twelve-member mariachi band trooped in to set up and play two hours of favorites. Alex especially loved the old mariachi songs. He'd always referred to it as music for barrachos, drunks, but held his tongue. Instead, he greeted mourners and tried to make people comfortable. Neither Lucas nor Morticia had the capacity to host the event. Morticia's boyfriend appeared with the two kids for the music then took them to the cafeteria. Ana did not appear.

When Ana, red-eyed and haggard, finally entered the room, Lucas stared blankly at his mother through the glass window in the casket. Alex greeted his sister-in-law, offering his sincere condolences—at some point, Ana had loved his mother.

Ana snipped, "I don't feel bad. I feel good. Everything is as it should be."

Lucas collapsed.

Ana turned away. Her brother, Doctor Victor Mata, rushed forward, calling to his wife to bring his bag from the truck. Alex offered to help.

"Thank you, Alex. My condolences for the loss of your mother. She was quite remarkable, living as long as she did with that terrible stomach cancer."

Alex remembered the medical file Lucas had given him claimed Mata as the attending physician, not Irene's doctor of record, Dr. Fierro. And Mata had written there was no treatment for the cancer. Then why so many drugs?

"Thank you, Victor. That's kind of you."

"Help me move him to the private room."

As soon as they had deposited Lucas on the bed, Mata examined the patient. He took Lucas's temperature, blood pressure, and listened to his heart, then commented, "It's nothing serious."

Alex remained silent, but wanted to shout, "Look at his color. Look at his feet and legs!"

Dr. Mata removed his prescription pad from his case and wrote up prescription for Firac injectable, then suggested Alex pick up a package of Firac 250 mg. while he was at the farmacia. He instructed him to immediately find the nearest pharmacy and buy it. Alex took Lucas's car.

When he returned, the doctor applied an intramuscular injection. The remaining vials he put in his briefcase, setting off alarm bells in Alex's head. Mata opened the box of the Firac 250 mg. and gave Lucas one tablet with the comment that he takes one every twelve hours if he had pain.

"Don't worry about it, Lucas," he said. "you'll be fine in no time. I'd say you suffer from exhaustion and grief."

An hour later, Lucas was fully restored. He left the

room to listen to the closing mass. Alex wondered what Victor Mata had given him, and why he absconded with five vials Alex had paid for. But he couldn't bring himself to ask, to make waves. *Not today.*

At the end of the service, the funeral staff whisked Irene's coffin to the crematorium. People started to leave, and by the time the staff returned with the ashes in a beautiful silver urn engraved with Irene's name, dates of birth and death two hours later, only the family remained.

Señor Flores delivered the ashes into Alex's hands along with the bill. He bowed slightly as he said, "Thank you, Señor. Deltoro. It has been a pleasure to offer you comfort in your time of loss. We hope everything was to your satisfaction. Shall I charge this to your credit card? Please take the flowers. They're yours."

Chapter 8

The Showdown

Thursday, April 2, 2020

With the help of the mortuary staff, Alex and Morticia loaded as many of the arrangements as possible into the back of Lucas's SUV. The flowers overflowed the interior of the vehicle leaving little room for the passengers. Of course, Ana and her daughter shared the front seat, so Alex had to squish in with the flowers. He propped up vases to keep them from spilling.

"Take it easy, Lucas. You'll be driving an aquarium if you don't. I only have two hands."

Lucas slowed. No one spoke. The atmosphere inside the SUV resembled the air of the wake room. Not surprising with all the flowers and stinky now-dirty flower water. Alex's stomach churned. He hoped he wouldn't puke before they reached the house. That was just what the atmosphere needed. All he wanted was to jump on his motorcycle, return to Irene's, and take a long shower.

The ride took forty-five minutes. Lucas swung into

the privada, stopping in front of the house. Ana leaped out and scurried to the gate, unlocking it and pushing it open. Alex watched her disappear into the house. He thought she was hurrying to prepare dinner; at least he hoped she was going to. He hadn't gone to the cafeteria. The fresh air coming through the door made him feel better. He was starving.

Lucas got out, opened the garage, then backed around to unload. He released the door to let Alex out and grabbed several arrangements. "You two start unloading the flowers into the garage. We'll have to figure out what to do with them. I'm going up to change. I'll be right back."

Alex and Morticia complied, lining up the vases in rows until the garage looked like a florist shop. The mood remained somber, each in their own thoughts.

Several minutes later, Lucas appeared wearing shorts. He set to work organizing the congestion of arrangements to fit in the rest. As Alex set a tall vase of calla lilies by his brother's feet, he noted the extent of his brother's edema. He gasped. Lucas's legs were not only swollen with a yellow cast to the skin, but looked rough, stippled. Why wasn't Lucas, or his doctor, taking care of this?

"Hey, bro, what's up with your legs? Have you been standing too much? Sitting too long? I don't know, but they don't look good. How about if I give them a massage after we finish this? Get the blood moving. Maybe bring down the swelling?"

"Thanks, Alex. I don't know what's going on. They've been getting worse."

Alex handed him two small vases slopping water onto the pavement. "Have you asked your doctor to take a look?"

"I haven't been able to get in. Morticia got me some anti-inflammatory medicine, but it doesn't seem to work."

"Why didn't you ask Mata while he attended you?"

Lucas shrugged.

Alex handed over another vase filled with white roses. *Is there no color in heaven?* Heaven. That's where he hoped his mother was.

"What's left, Morticia?"

"That's it, Tío. Papi, you'll need to get the SUV cleaned. It's pretty wet and there are petals everywhere," she said.

"Thanks, Morticia. I'll leave the windows open. I'll meet you in my room, Alex."

It turned out Lucas no longer shared the master bedroom with his wife. He slept in a small space off the living room.

"What's up with the room, Lucas? You can't manage the stairs?" He was confused. Lucas handled Irene's stairs okay.

"I haven't been well for some time. Mostly I sleep in the recliner. It started when Ana complained I woke her up all night getting in and out of bed when I can't sleep." He looked around, lowered his voice. "It started when she was screwing that pendejo over in Boca de Rio. Frankly, I'm just as happy to be away from her."

Morticia came into the room and sprawled onto the couch. "I need a nap. I slept like crap in the room with Mami last night. I'm glad it's all over."

"Don't get too comfortable," Alex said. "I'm going to rub your dad's legs to see if we can improve the circulation. Can you go find me some oil or greasy

75

lotion?"

"Sure." She swung her lean frame from the cushion. "I've been worried about him. Papi's legs look bad." She glared at her father. "Tío, he refuses to see Doctor Fierro."

After twenty minutes of manipulation, the change in Lucas's legs was miraculous. Alex rubbed out the swelling; the skin returned to its normal color.

"Lucas, why aren't you taking care of yourself? *You* could have done this."

"No te preocupes, hermanito. Don't worry little brother, I'm fine. Fierro doesn't have time with this flu going around. I'll pay more attention if you think I should."

"You should, Papi. And you need to cut back on your drinking. I'm worried about you," Morticia admonished him as she set a tray of snacks and soft drinks on the coffee table.

Alex recognized the look of annoyance mixed with shame on Lucas's face. It was obvious he didn't want to talk about his health, or his drinking.

"Quit ganging up on me, you two, I'm taking my medicines," Lucas volunteered.

"Speaking of which, what do you take?"

"Tío, the meds are all here—" She walked into the dining room across the entry hall and opened a drawer of the credenza. She smiled over her shoulder at Alex who had followed her, then turned to the drawer and gasped. "It's empty! Where are the medications Papi?"

Alex saw how much Morticia cared about her father. He was glad his brother had someone on his side. Lucas was no saint, but he had always taken his responsibility to his family seriously. They wanted for nothing. Probably because Alex's inheritance paid for it.

"Papi, did you move them?"

"No, why would I? Maybe your mother did."

"I'll go up and ask." Morticia darted to the stairs taking two at a time. Alex remembered the days. . .

But why would she have moved them? Alex wondered. Wouldn't it have been easier to add the new prescription with the others? Alex had a bad feeling about Ana. What was she up to? He heard the women's voices echoing down the stairwell but couldn't discern the words. He started up the stairs. At the landing, he heard Ana forbid Morticia from telling him anything, especially from showing Alex the medicines.

Morticia responded to her mother angrily, "Why not? My uncle asked me for them and wants to know what treatment Dad has. He knows all about drugs."

Ana's voice rose, her words angry and clipped. "Alex. Does. Not. Need. To. Know. Your father's treatment is private. Your uncle is not a doctor. Morticia, I forbid you to share intimate family matters with Alex."

"Mother, you forget he *is* family. He has a right to know what's going on. I will not be disloyal."

The bedroom door slammed. Alex smiled to himself. At least he had one true ally in this fucked up family. He turned around, descended to the living room, and sat down. Morticia would tell him just what was going on. One thing for certain, Ana had not rushed into the house to cook dinner. She rushed in to hide her husband's medications. Because she was perfectly aware of what Alex did for a living. *But why would she want hide Lucas's medical treatment?* His brow wrinkled as he pondered the problem. He heard Lucas in the dining room. The sound of crystal clinking onto the table told him his brother was already drinking. The only answer to his question: Ana was hiding something the medications would reveal. He'd questioned Ana's treatment of Irene and now he suspected something bigger was going on. *She's trying to kill me.* He would have to confront his sister-in-law.

Of course, Ana's door was shut and locked. He pounded on it shouting, "Open this door Ana and explain yourself. I know you have hidden my brother's medicine, and I want to know why."

When she didn't respond, he pounded harder. "Open the pinche door or I'll kick it in," he bellowed giving a kick for emphasis.

The lock clicked. Ana sneered up at him through the open doorway. "This doesn't concern you, Alex."

"Oh, yes it does. My brother needs help and I'm here to give it. What the fuck are you up to?"

"Your brother? You mean your half-brother. And he doesn't want anything from you, you bastard."

Alex's jaw dropped. Ana knew what he suspected? "What are you talking about? Are you crazy?" She didn't respond, just shot him a malevolent smile as she tried to close the door. He slid his foot in front of it, shouting, "Show. Me. The. Medications." His fists balled. Ana backed up, but the sneer remained on her lips. How he wanted to wipe it away with one of those fists. He rushed in, demanding, "The medications, now!"

Ana's voice softened. She patted Alex's arm. "Think Alex, this is a private matter of my family. Would you accept it if I barged in on your privacy?"

"Ana, Lucas is my brother. He's not well and I demand to know his condition and treatment."

Her voce rose again. "No way! Get out of my room. Get out of my house!"

"I won't go until I know everything. Show me the meds, Ana." He shouted.

They heard Lucas trudging up the stairs. Morticia stopped him in the hall. He shouldered past her and stormed into Ana's room. His room.

"Ana. Give my brother the pinche meds!"

She stomped to her bathroom where Alex heard her rummaging in a drawer. When she returned, she carried a freezer sized plastic bag filled with bottles and packets, which she flung at Alex's face. He dodged a direct hit, but the bag opened, and the contents flew across the floor. The cap came off one of the prescriptions. Little blue pills fanned across the tiles. Alex, Lucas, and Morticia stared, dumbfounded by Ana's behavior; the room plunged into silence.

Ana retreated to her bathroom and slammed the door. The others picked up the medications. One glass bottle shattered, its contents forming a brown puddle on the floor. Alex gathered the shards and tossed them in a waste basket, saving only the label in the baggie.

Over the few minutes they cleaned up, the high tension settled. Alex asked, "What's the matter with your wife?"

"Let's go back downstairs and cool off," Lucas said.

"Yeah, go downstairs, Alex, it's okay. But I'm not taking care of your brother anymore," she shouted from the bedroom. "Do it yourself if you're foolish enough to want it."

Chapter 9

The GP

Downstairs, Morticia related a story about taking her father for a medical exam in January and the treatment he'd received.

"Papi was having trouble breathing, so I took him to the emergency room. Tío Mateo was there and hustled him off to a room while I waited outside. When I went in, Papi was restrained to the bed and Tío said he couldn't breathe. He was going to intubate Papi." She shook her head. "You know Papi said never to do that—it's in his medical chart. Pues, Papi heard and started fighting to get loose, damaging the equipment bar above the bed, and freeing himself. He was naked! Not even a hospital gown, but Papi ran. I grabbed his clothes and ran after him to the car. It's a miracle we got away and made it home."

Alex sat at the table in shock. The incident was beyond believable, and right in range of alarming. Could she have made it up? "I, uh—are you serious Morticia?"

She shoved her phone into his hands. "It's all there. . ." Alex hit PLAY. Now Ana's attempt to suppress evidence made sense. Lucas never said a word, but by the time Alex said goodnight, the bottle of brandy was empty. He helped Lucas stagger to bed and tucked him in.

Morticia walked him out. She hugged him at the gate. "Thank you for listening to me, Tío. My parents won't speak to each other, Papi is out of the house as much as possible, and when he's home, she leaves. I do what I can for them, but the truth is, I'm nothing more than a weapon they can point at each other. I don't know what Papi has done, but he's smoking and drinking himself to death. My mother encourages him. It's like she wants him to die. The entire Mata family has turned against him."

"What do you mean?" Alex asked.

"A gut feeling. Uncle Victor is here a lot, sequestered with Mami in her room. I know they talk about my father. I heard him say she should divorce him."

Alex grunted something like a laugh. "You listening through the door?"

Morticia nodded. "Yep. I have a right to know what's going on. At times all of them treat me like a child. I'm a psychologist, for the grace of God. I can't work because my own dysfunctional family needs care so badly." She sighed. "My parents are harder to raise than my children. Gabriel is little help. He's great with the kids, but if Papi didn't support us, we'd go begging. I've wondered if that's why Mami doesn't leave him— or throw him out. He has other houses, Irene's for instance. Say, when will we read the will?"

Morticia's interest in the will disturbed him. "I don't know. Have you seen it? I'd put my money on

Lucas inheriting everything."

"Is that why my mother stays? To inherit?"

The idea had crossed Alex's mind more than once. "You'll have to ask her. Morticia—why don't you talk to her? Ask Ana what she wants—and why she doesn't do it. No offense, but she is acting ugly. If it's the drinking, I'd be happy to mount an intervention with you and your mother to send him to a program to get sober. I'm alarmed at his physical health. I don't think he's as rational as he could be, either. But I'm keeping you—go on home. I'll stay here until you're in the door."

She leaned toward him and kissed his cheek. "Good night, Uncle."

Daisi greeted Alex at the door, meowing vociferously. She trotted to the kitchen and back, talking all the time. He tossed the bag of medicines on the table. "You hungry, girl?" Daisi replied something he took to be, "I'm starving, you fool. Where have you been?"

He let her lead him to the kitchen where she planted herself next to her empty bowls. Once she was eating and he had patted her, he went to the bathroom to wash his hands and face. It had been several very long, fraught days and he wanted to sleep for the next week—at home in his own bed in Naucalpan. But he had work to do.

At the table in the dining alcove, the only reliable spot for the internet signal, he booted his laptop. He arranged the vials, bottles, and packs of drugs in a line with their labels showing. With the notes he had taken at Lucas's house to his right, Alex looked up each drug for manufacturers' information, jotting the uses and the contraindications of each on the list. An hour and a half later, with Daisi purring in his lap, he had confirmed his suspicions. Used together per manufacturer's instructions, the drugs would negate each other—or kill his brother.

According to Morticia, the drugs were not dispensed per manufacturers' instructions. *Just like with Irene.* Those labeled one every twelve hours was given every eight hours according to Morticia. Then Lucas was given several medications such as hydralazine, used for hypertension; that combined with sildenafil, could be fatal. Alex didn't rule out his brother had not been prescribed VIAGRA. But there it was on the list he gave Morticia. After all, he had to keep Aimee, or whomever he was screwing happy, didn't he? All that booze was sure to interfere with his sex life. The medication was also indicated for pulmonary hypertension, but he had no proof his brother suffered from that. He would ask the doctor.

In another half hour of note taking, he went up to sleep. Alternating brooding and sleep, he whipped the bedclothes into a tangled mess.

Friday dawned for Alex at 5:30 a.m. A morning person, he usually climbed out of bed alert and chipper with the rising sun. This day he felt like he need toothpicks to prop his eyes open. Even the tepid shower didn't help. His only motivation was the cup of delicious Café 88, the Veracruzano mountain grown coffee, he would drink with his eggs.

After breakfast, he got ready to go to Lucas' house.

It was 6:10; the sun was climbing over the rooftops from the Gulf. The morning was still, quiet, and pretty with a buildup of cumulous clouds reflecting the early rays.

Alex now had a copy of the door keys. He let himself in and found Lucas awake. All the ground floor lights were on, yet they did not dispel the gloom. Alex wanted to go back out, climb onto his motorcycle, and ride to the shore, walk in the sand and feel the sun. This was the best time of day, before the heat and humidity settled down, turning everyone grumpy and tired. But he had to grin and bear it—the unpleasantness of the house, of Ana, and the self-inflicted misery of his hung-over brother.

"Good morning, Lucas. How do you feel?"

Lucas's face looked dull, deeply lined, haggard, and despairing. But he answered, "Well, enough. My stomach hurts. I must have eaten something that disagreed with me."

Alex smiled cheerfully, but he felt as sad as Lucas looked. He opened the drawer in the dining room containing instruments to monitor Lucas's vitals, removed the glucometer, Baumanometer, oximeter, and thermometer, placing them on the table. "Sit down, Lucas. I'll check you out. Do you want something for your stomach?"

"No, leave it. Always the same pinche Gato," he grumbled, but did as told, holding out his finger.

Alex pricked the finger, collected a drop of blood onto a strip of sterile paper, and placed it in the glucometer to monitor his blood sugar. Amazing, after drinking a bottle of brandy the night before, his reading remained in the normal range. He applied the

Baumanometer cuff to his arm and checked Lucas's blood pressure. Alex directed the oximeter over Lucas's finger before activating it to measure his brother's oxygenation. Finally, he put the thermometer in Lucas's armpit to check his body temperature. He jotted down the results into a notebook and compared it to the recent notebook entries. All the readings remained within the normal parameters, if perhaps a little low in oxygen. Nothing to be alarmed about. Alex put away the equipment and dispensed the first series of Lucas's daily medications, at least, those he knew were safe to take together. According to what he learned, there were three different medication schedules each day.

Once this routine was finished, Alex went to the kitchen to serve Lucas a snack of fruits, juice, and coffee. While he ate, Alex sat down to entertain him a little. His idea was that his brother would loosen up and start talking about what was going on. Didn't he feel the evil lurking in the corners? Alex certainly did. He wanted to get out of this house.

At eleven Morticia arrived with Gabriel and her two children. "Good morning, Papi," she greeted him. "I got an appointment with the doctor for you at 3:30. Ready for breakfast?"

He nodded and the older boy shouted, "I'm ready, Mami!"

Lucas smiled. "He's just like you were at that age, Morticia. Always hungry."

The smaller boy shouted, "I'm hungry too!"

"Then come on and help me make it." Morticia disappeared into the kitchen with her tribe following. Alex heard them laughing and talking amid the clank of pans and thumps of cabinet doors.

A bit later, Morticia sent Gabriel into the dining room with plates, forks, and glasses following with platters of carne asada, some delicious smelling Manchego cheese quesadillas accompanied by refried beans, chocolate milk, and pan dulces. She arranged everything on the table and went upstairs to let her mother know that breakfast was ready, but Ana did not appear.

"Mother said she's not hungry," Morticia announced as she took her place at the table with the family. Alex expected the truth was closer to not wanting to be anywhere near Alex or Lucas. Or perhaps Gabriel, who gave off uncomfortable vibes and kept his mouth shut except to shovel in helping after helping of carne asada. The children chattered. Lucas seemed to have relaxed, other than several piercing glares he sent Gabriel's way. Gabriel didn't notice, just kept shoveling in Lucas's food. Alex wondered what the story was. Morticia had admitted Lucas was supporting them. Why didn't Gabriel work? He'd ask Lucas when the kids left.

Once breakfast was over and Morticia had cleared the table, he reminded his father they had an appointment with his doctor in the afternoon. Gabriel took the boys home while Morticia washed up after the meal, returning to go over the drug inventory with Lucas to prepare for Dr. Fierro.

Although Alex had his annotated inventory, they made an inventory of the existing medications without any medical criteria. Apparently this was a pattern. They asked for what they wanted or whatever came to mind without taking into consideration if Lucas actually felt better, or if there were changes in his health. Alex intervened in the conversation to ask about the Viagra.

"Lucas, did you ask for this, or are you taking it under medical supervision?"

"He prescribed it."

"If you haven't seen your doctor in several years, how exactly did he prescribe it? I studied your medicines last night. The Viagra cannot be taken with the hydralazine without serious reactions. I don't believe your doctor is aware of what you take, or he doesn't know the contraindications."

Lucas and Morticia continued their inventory, ignoring Alex's comments. He would have to leave it under the responsibility of the doctor. Their list was longer than what he'd inventoried. He didn't care so much about the over-the-counter drugs, but when they got to the controlled substances, Alex wondered if perhaps Lucas used them to get high. He bit his tongue—better to listen politely like a fly on the wall. He'd learn more. How they carried out this task month after month, he could not fathom. *So irresponsible!*

His brother was an expert in electrical engineering, a very important executive with a lot of responsibility for the safety of the only nuclear electricity production plant in Mexico located nearby in Laguna Verde. Alex couldn't imagine someone so educated with such total ignorance of his health care.

At three, Lucas, Morticia and Alex climbed into the SUV for the visit with Lucas's GP. Alex insisted they wear masks, then drove to the IMSS facility, Adolfo Ruiz Cortines Specialty Hospital No. 14, located on

Cuauhtémoc Avenue. They had an appointment at 3:30 but, after picking their way through makeshift wards of COVID patients in the halls, had to sit in the waiting area for thirty minutes with the hordes of mostly unmasked patients.

Finally, Lucas's name was called, and they were ushered into Dr. Fierro's office. Alex's first look at the masked doctor told him Fierro was about fifty, small in stature, very thin, with a dark-complected hairless face. Alex pegged him as a naco, an ignorant, closed-minded type.

Dr. Fierro stood and greeted Lucas in a friendly manner, but speaking in the rapid, overly familiar, clipped accent of the coastal jarochos. Alex was taken aback when the man gave Alex the once-over and bluntly said, "Tu? Quien eres, Papi?"

He's calling me Daddy?

Morticia greeted the doctor warmly then introduced Alex.

The doctor stepped forward and brayed, "Good to meet ya, Alex," and shook hands with him. His palm felt sweaty.

"Morticia, what have you got for me?" Fierro asked.

She handed over the medication list and sat down.

Open-mouthed, standing behind Morticia's chair, Alex observed the doctor, if that was what he could be called. No, 'How are you feeling?' or 'What can I do for you?' In fact, Fierro never acknowledged Lucas, who had retreated to the door.

Fierro took Lucas' file from a filing cabinet, opened it on the desk. From another drawer he plucked out his prescription book. Exactly as the order for medicines was written on Lucas and Morticia's sheet, he transferred the drug names to the prescription pad and signed it to be filled. A case of malpractice if Alex had ever seen one. How could a doctor, who had vowed to 'do no harm' be so irresponsible? *Unless he was being bought off—by Ana?* This was Mexico, so why not? He sat down in the other chair.

Morticia and the doctor chatted and joked while Alex scrutinized the man's actions. Everything was jovial laughter and witty banter. He frowned and drummed his fingers on the desk. He couldn't hide it; he was upset. This was no medical consultation. He had not come for a coffee klatch between Morticia and the doctor. Lucas's state of health? Hell, Lucas, was forgotten, ignored. Not even his name was mentioned. *Was Morticia really this naïve—or was she in on it?* Alex interrupted the jocular talk. "Doctor. I need to know the correct dosages of these medications, the contraindications, and the efficacy of combining some of these."

Fierro's countenance and attitude radically changed. His face flushed and he angrily replied, "Your brother continues to drink."

Alex said, "Yes he does. That is one of my concerns. He should not be prescribed—"

Fierro interrupted. "I did not prescribe that list. I gave it to Dr. Mata, the wife's brother. I didn't have the time to see Lucas. This COVID pandemic, you know. Anyway, who are you to question my treatment of my patient!" Fierro snarled. "I do not know if the medications are being used properly. I gave Mata's instructions to his wife. If the patient does not follow the instructions, it is not my fault."

Evading the answer. Alex repeated, "Doctor, can

you answer my question? How are these medications to be used? Is it correct for Lucas to take so many drugs for the same condition as in the case of peripheral circulation?" He glared back at the medical man. "I need you to explain it to me so I can administer his treatment correctly, now that I am the one who attends to the patient."

Alex continued talking, informing Fierro of the leg massage that relieved the symptoms of Lucas's peripheral circulation failures, emphasizing the problem disappeared entirely.

Again, Fierro took the floor, angrily shouting, "I DON'T HAVE TIME TO WASTE ON PEOPLE WHO ARE NOT WORTH IT. IF HE CONTINUES TO DRINK IT'S NOT MY PROBLEM. What's more," he continued, but now sneering. "Your brother has cancer and he's going to die. You'll see. Regardless of whether he regulates his blood pressure or diet, he's going to die." His sneer morphed into a triumphant grin.

Alex flew out of his chair but grasped the back of Morticia's to steady himself. They both stared in shock.

Outside the office no one would have heard what was going on. Masked voices didn't carry well, but Lucas had gasped, backed out of the doorway, and disappeared.

Morticia panicked, rising from her chair, her breath coming in short bursts. She choked out, "My dad is going to die, he lost the strength of his legs. He's going to die." She collapsed back down, crying.

Alex came around the chair to console his niece with a hug. He turned to see Dr. Fierro frowning at them through bone-withering eyes. He let go of Morticia to grab his brother's file from the desk. He skimmed it, flipping through the pages.

The tension in the atmosphere built-up until Dr. Fierro reacted, "Put that file down. These documents are private. You have no right to read them."

The look Alex levied at Fierro could have frozen Hell. He replied tersely, "Where are your medical ethics? You haven't given me an explanation of Lucas's health or treatment. All I've seen here is a party with Morticia, and a complete disregard for your patient. It looks like malpractice to me. You tell me my brother has cancer, and I ask, why do I find no tests or prescribed cancer treatment in the file, nor cancer medications among the medications you prescribed. I asked you to please tell me how to administer the medications that you have prescribed, and you verbally insult my family. This is outrageous. I will report it to the medical licensing board."

Dr. Fierro had turned purple with rage. Shouting louder he replied, "MY WORK IS NEEDED BY OTHER PEOPLE WHO ARE TRULY WORTHWHILE. I CAN'T WASTE MY TIME ON A DRUNK!" He backed toward the exit then bolted through the door, abandoning Alex and Morticia. She sobbed.

He deserves to lose his license. Taking Morticia's arm, he said, "Let's go, we can't stay here any longer, or we'll catch COVID."

They collected Lucas, slumped in a chair in the waiting area, and exited the hospital, Fierro's words ringing in Alex's ears.

91

Chapter 10

The Pain

Friday, April 3, 2020

Alex felt like he was in a prison transport on his way to a life sentence, not returning to the house. Was this how everything would go with Lucas's care? He understood Ana's decision to stop caring for him, if today was an example of how things operated. No wonder his brother drank himself into a stupor every day. Yet, what was he going to do about the doctor? The way these government hospitals worked Lucas couldn't get treatment without Fierro's signature. And Alex had blown up *that* bridge. Lucas needed a new doctor, but Alex had no personal experience with the IMSS system to know how to get one.

Nearing the house, Morticia's sobs subsided. She was more capable than Alex had realized. He hoped she'd cried out her shock and anger enough to help him.

"We're here," Alex announced. The children were kicking a ball in the callejon in front of the house with a couple of boys Alex assumed were from the neighborhood. "Someone get the gate?"

Lucas hunched over. Holding his middle, he lumbered out, fished keys from his pocket, and unlocked the gate, pushing it open for the SUV. Alex pulled in, set the brake, and turned off the engine.

"Morticia, we need to find your dad a new doctor. Can you help me?"

"I thought Dr. Fierro was a friend. I've known him for ages. Let me talk to him and see if I can straighten things out."

Good luck with that, Alex wanted to say.

They got out of the vehicle. He closed the gate, squeezing the padlock shut with a click. Morticia stood gazing through the fence at her boys happily playing their version of futból. "Life is easy for them, Uncle. Look how happy they are to kick a ball. Sometimes I wish I could play with friends and not worry." She swung around to face him. "Do you think it's true?"

"No, I don't." Alex knew what she meant—cancer. He tossed the medical file on the dining room table as they entered. "He was lying."

"How do you know? And why?"

He opened the file folder to reveal a second file inside. "See for yourself. Nothing in your father's medical file indicates cancer. Why don't you read this over while I make us some coffee. Lucas," he yelled, "can I make you cup of coffee?"

From the living room came groaning.

"What's the matter? My coffee that bad?"

Morticia smiled. Her father groaned again. "It's my stomach. It hurts worse."

Alex had to agree with Fierro that his brother's alcoholism was at the root of his problems. Then again, why the hell didn't Lucas speak up? *But it's a disease.* The doctor was sworn to help sick people, yet he refused to treat Lucas. That bastard. "Relax, Lucas. I'll bring you something for it."

Alex started the water heating then popped two slices of bread into the toaster and peeled a banana. Toast was the best stomachache remedy going. He delivered the food to the coffee table in front of Lucas.

"Lucas, dry toast and banana should calm your stomach. Eat them. Use the butter if you must."

"I'm not pregnant, brother," Lucas said through a wan smile.

At least he's making an attempt at humor. "Are you sure?" Alex winked.

"May I have a slice of toast too?" asked Morticia, as Alex passed en-route to the kitchen.

"Sure. Changed your mind about that coffee?"

"No, thanks. Look here." She pointed to a page of notes by Fierro.

"Read it to me."

"First, he's noted that my tío asked Dr. Fierro his opinion of the possibility of my father developing cancer. Then Fierro notes my father might have liver failure for his drinking." She slumped to the table. "Tío, is my papi going to die?"

"Not if we can get him to stop drinking."

She sighed. Then straightened up. "Aver! Listen to this. My doctor says he's not to refer Papi to the specialists, but it doesn't say who told him or why."

"You're kidding me! Let me see."

Morticia pushed the file toward Alex, her purple fingernail tapping the passage. "I don't understand why Dr. Fierro wouldn't send Papi to the doctors he needs."

Alex took his iPhone from his pocket and snapped a photo of the page, then a close up of the entry. He grinned, *we got the pendejo.*

Lucas ate his toast and banana. He claimed his stomach felt better, but he was going to lie down and disappeared into his small room. It had been a library. Shelves contained a wide array of books, from Lucas's books on engineering to classic novels to biographies to pulp fiction and comic books. The shelves of mysteries were empty. Ana had loved those, especially a series set in Mexico. He thought for a moment. The Dafne Olabarrieta Mexico Mysteries—he'd liked that first one —but other than the comics, Alex wasn't sure anybody else ever read anything. TV was more popular in Lucas's house. He wasn't much of a TV man, except for American football. It was a toss-up who he preferred: the San Francisco 49ers or the Miami Dolphins, Unfortunately the 49ers had just been tromped by the Kansas City Chiefs at the Super Bowl.

He delivered a glass of water to his brother. "Shout if you need me. I'm going to work at my computer."

Morticia left to round up her kids and get dinner on the table. She said she would make enough for everyone and be back later.

After his coffee and seeing the note in Fierro's handwriting, Alex felt more positive. Now they had two pieces of evidence if it came to a malpractice suit. He looked at his watch: six. He had a couple of hours to look into the possibility of opening the area to his foundation. Alex couldn't see himself sitting around making toast for Lucas all day—he needed to do something. And Ivan couldn't prevent it.

He had fought to open Medicina Para Todos A.C. and make it functional. The foundation had made strong advances and resounding successes in greater Mexico City. It satisfied Alex to help people get access to decent healthcare and medicines.

The government regularly stole the economic resources out of the health sector; the papers were full of reports—especially since AMLO became president. Now it had ceased supplying medicines to government hospitals, leaving poor people to die when they could have lived. The real data was alarming; in the month of January alone millions of prescriptions were not filled in the country after the new AMLO government cut funding from health services such as the Seguro Popular that had served millions of families who did not have any other options. The death toll rose.

In Alex's mind, it was up to the private sector to protect the less advantaged. His short sojourn to the IMSS today had reinforced his convictions. The place was jammed with people dying from COVID 19. His company's Viru-Out could save most of them. He searched, experimenting with keywords to get current statistics on the pandemic and the situations and outcomes in the various local hospitals. There were plenty of statistics—mostly depressing.

Morticia returned with a platter of chicken enchiladas, squash cooked in tomato and chili, rice and black beans, and a green salad. She set the dinner on the table and went to wake her father. Alex set the table. Ana did not join them.

Lucas looked worse for wear. He was aging rapidly

from the drink and poor sleep. During dinner he pushed his food around his plate, eating barely a quarter of his serving. Alex watched him look anxiously toward the credenza several times. *He wants a drink.*

"Brother, how is your stomach?"

"Not so good, but I managed to sleep a bit."

"Papi, I brought some medicine to settle it. You should feel better soon. But you can't drink with it." Morticia put it on the credenza with a note on how to take it.

"Leave it. I'll take it if I need it. My stomach isn't that bad."

Alex and Morticia exchanged a look. They both knew what he meant.

"Don't look at each other like that," Lucas complained. "I'm going to bed. It's been a tiring day."

Alex said, "Okay. Do you want a shower first? It might help you relax and sleep."

"Yes. I'm going up to the penthouse. Morticia, can you find me a pair of clean pajamas?"

She put her fork on her plate and stood up. "There's a stack of clean clothes in the laundry." She excused herself and disappeared through the kitchen door.

"Do you need any help?" Alex asked.

"No. Thanks, Alex. I'm good. You can go back to Mother's house. I'll be fine."

"I guess I'll help Morticia clean up then," he said and started collecting the dirty dishes. "Before you go up, Lucas, I need to monitor you and give you the last round of meds."

"We never picked them up."

"And we aren't going to until you've seen a doctor

for a real examination. I'll give you the drugs I know you need. There's a supply for a week or so."

"Yeah, you're the drug expert."

Did Lucas's voice sound sarcastic? Or disappointed? Maybe he did like getting high. Alex pulled everything out of the drawer and repeated the morning routine. His results looked normal, but the problem of the stomach was disturbing. What if he did have cancer? Their mother had just died of stomach cancer. Others in the family, too. Could the fact nothing had been prescribed to Lucas be that the hospital simply didn't have the drugs? But Lucas bought his medicines privately through one of the cartel owned pharmacies —or it was reputed to be a cartel-controlled outlet. Alex had no proof.

Morticia returned during the monitoring and, after dropping clean night clothes on the table, counted out the drugs. She'd found his slippers, too. "Shall I get him some water?"

"Please. Sorry, I cleared the table without thinking."

"No worries, Uncle. It's no biggie." She stole into the kitchen, returning in moments with a full glass.

"Okay, bro, here you go." Alex handed over a saucer with the pills and the glass of water, waiting until Lucas had swallowed everything, including all the water. Alex estimated dehydration was part of the problem in his legs.

Lucas collected his night clothes and said goodnight. Morticia put the leftovers into containers, Alex washed the dishes, and they both left for home. On the way out the door Alex asked, "Morticia, should I stay and see your dad to bed?"

"If you mean, stay to make sure he doesn't drink, I don't think you can stop him. I went up to the penthouse today and cleared out all the bottles I could find. He'll be pissed off, but I'm sure he had one or two stashed somewhere I didn't find."

"I'll say it again, I'm happy to arrange an intervention with an alcohol treatment center. Say the word. We'll need your mother to sign off on it too. Please talk to her."

"Mami denies it's a disease. She's not going to do anything. I think she's waiting for my father to drink himself to death."

Yeah, with a little help from some drugs that, mixed with alcohol, will kill him. "Good night then. Sleep well. I'll see you in the morning. Let's hope a good meal and a night's sleep takes care of the stomachache."

"Yes, let's hope, Tío. Ojalá. Good night."

Alex was too tired to do anything more than rough out a new proposal to his boss on his legal pad. He had good data, which needed tabulation into a spreadsheet. It would have to wait. He cleaned the cat box instead, showered, and hit the hay, Daisi purring next to him.

In the morning, he repeated his routine of coffee, breakfast, feeding Daisi, and putting together everything he wanted to take to Lucas's. He arrived at six thirty. Lucas was sleeping in the recliner, an almost empty brandy bottle on the coffee table. He cleared it away, dumping the last bit and putting the bottle in the trash already overflowing with Lucas's empties. Considering how much he drank, Lucas must have the constitution of a bulldozer to produce the blood sugar and blood pressure readings he got.

Alex decided to let him sleep. His round of pills could wait. He couldn't risk his stomach being full of booze when he swallowed them. He made himself a pot of coffee and carried the cup as he mounted the stairs to the penthouse.

Lucas's glass and an empty bottle were on the counter. Several cabinets stood open, as if someone had been looking for something. He began opening and closing cupboards and closets to see if there were more. Sure enough, he found three more bottles. One in the pantry behind an empty bread box; another hiding inside a rubber boot in the coat closet; the third in the bathroom under the sink beside toilet cleaner and rubber gloves. Classic alcoholism. Maybe he should search the whole house.

When he had hunted everywhere but Ana's suite and returned to the first floor, he heard groaning. Lucas. Alex put the bottles in the garbage container, filled a coffee for his brother, and went in to see what was going on. Lucas was on the floor doubled over holding his stomach. No surprise after how much he had drunk. He would arrange an intervention. He prayed he could get it taken care of before the week was out when he had to return to work.

But how would he get Ana to participate?

Chapter 11

The Choice

Saturday, April 4, 2020

Ana's declaration, and the visit to Fierro, had made it clear: Lucas needed more help than Alex had originally expected. His heart sank. He knew it in his bones— accepting his familial responsibility meant staying in Veracruz to take care of Lucas. It would jeopardize all he'd worked for: his Directorship—the reward for almost thirty years of hard work. His head sank into his hands. What should he do? If Lucas did not have care, or even the lousy care he was getting, he was going to lose his legs at best, or his life at worst.

In a way, Alex understood. Lucas had always been difficult. He suffered from advanced alcoholism and only God knew what medical conditions caused by it. He cheated on his wife. He stole his brothers' inheritance from under them. The list expanded as Alex remembered all the shitty things Lucas had done throughout their lives.

How about all the times Lucas spent their support money on alcohol, drugs, and parties when their father had left them in the Mexico house to finish school, while their parents and younger brother moved to Veracruz? The teens had lived on junk food and beer until their father showed up, pulled them out of school, and stuck them on a pig farm outside the port—to learn responsibility and a trade. What did Lucas do? Drink and party with new friends and Ana. She'd entered the picture by then. The image of his father's face when he and Alex returned from the nuclear plant's cafeteria with a pickup load of leftover food for the pigs and discovered a brand-new muscle car in the yard and the pigs sold, haunted him. Then somehow, Lucas sold the farm, which had been deeded to Alex. He hadn't seen a dime of that money.

His stomach turned over, cramping. What should he do? Now Ana vowed to abandon her husband, *the bitch*. Who would take care of Lucas?

Alex had never made such a difficult decision. Lucas had cost him so much already. Should he let his older brother take the last shred of his dignity and success? Staying in Veracruz to care for him would cost his savings. Possibly his health. And certainly, his promotion. But it had been a long, emotion packed week starting with his mother's death, the funeral, the ashes, the flowers, this terrible situation with Lucas, then Ana's declaration. Alex needed to sleep. The family problems would wait until morning.

Alex awoke at his usual pre-dawn hour with his answer and an idea, an idea that would handle his potential economic losses. If he could open new hospitals to the work of his foundation, perhaps he could at least continue to sell in Veracruz. LSI's drug sales in the state weren't as strong as they could be, and with COVID, thousands of potential trial candidates existed. He opened his laptop to write a letter:

Ivan Castellanos Palacios, Director General
Laboratorios Salud Integral S.A. de C.V
Nicolas San Juan 1046, Col. Del Valle
México D.F, México
4 Abril, 2020

Estimado Ivan,

You may not know I have traveled to the Port of Veracruz to attend my mother who has now died. Her funeral ended yesterday, but during this family time, I have discovered my brother is quite ill. Due to the seriousness of his symptoms, I am obligated to remain in Veracruz for an undetermined time to arrange adequate medical attention for him.

As this may take time, I propose I be granted a leave of absence to open the market for the foundation to run trials and simultaneously to inform new doctors of Viru-Out and our other drugs, therefore increasing sales in the State of Veracruz, a state which does not now meet sales quotas. My research shows all hospitals here exceed capacity of care due to the COVID 19 pandemic, especially the government-run hospitals.

I have seen first-hand the abysmal conditions in one such hospital lacking sufficient personnel to care for the overflow and maintain hygienic conditions, increasing contagion. Doctors are worried and helpless here, and I suspect, nationwide. It could be a goldmine for LSI.

I hope you find this arrangement satisfactory. I realize you will have to find a temporary Director for the department, and I offer my sincerest apology for this. Please forgive and understand I must fulfill my duty to my family.

He read it over several times, making small corrections, finally typing his name, title, and a notation this was backup to his email. He printed two copies, added his signature to one and filed the other in his work folder. He opened his email, cut and pasted the letter into the body, titled it Request for Medical Leave, and hit send.

Feeling more positive and relaxed, he fixed eggs with salsa and tortillas for breakfast. Ivan would jump at the idea of making more money for LSI; it was his job after all. Alex potentially could make more money here in this untapped, over-stressed market than in Mexico City. A win-win. And the idea of foiling Ana's dastardly plans tickled him. Ana had never been his favorite. A big-boned woman with rather bushy, mousy colored hair, she'd aged into an unattractively corpulent harridan. She'd always been a bit dim.

Probably why his brother had liked her. Ana in the early days was pretty wild. She liked to drink, get high, and she apparently loved sex. A perfect match for Lucas.

But after Morticia was born, Ana was forced to be more responsible and the trouble started in their marriage. Not that Lucas had discussed it with him, Alex was too much of an outsider for that. During the times he spent with his family, he observed their interactions and concluded Ana and Lucas hated each other, pitting Morticia's loyalty against one or the other depending on who was manipulating her at the time. Morticia had grown up in a dysfunctional home and eventually became a therapist. Probably because she was a bit nuts. *Aren't all therapists loco?*

The director's response was quick—Ivan was up early too— detailing the coverage LSI already had in Veracruz, claiming it was competent, and anyway, the salespeople were under contract. There was nothing he could do at the moment, but Alex was right to take a leave to care for this brother. Of course, it would be unpaid leave, for which Ivan apologized, and as soon as it was resolved Alex could return to work in his newly granted position.

One short paragraph dashed Alex's hope to pieces. Again, he considered his decision to stay in Veracruz. Was it the right one? He passed the next hour thinking while he separated Irene's clothing and personal items to boxes for donation and garbage. It crossed his mind to fuck it, leave instructions for Morticia on how to do things, and return to Mexico to work. It was the response everyone expected of him.

As his mind seesawed up and down, he remembered his childhood with his big brother, and the fun they'd had together. The time they'd truly been brothers. He missed that. How could he fail Lucas now? But the Lucas now was a different person. He'd become a careless drunk. A philanderer. A greedy, lying cheater. Why the hell should Alex give up his life for a man like Lucas Deltoro? Because Alex knew inside the layers of lust, greed, and infidelity, Lucas was his brother. Family.

Alex could not let him die alone.

Chapter 12

The Ultrasound

Sunday, April 5, 2020

Lucas was on the floor, clutching his gut. He stank of old cocktails, halitosis, and sweat. Alex's heart raced. "Lucas. Lucas! Can you get up?"

Lucas opened one eye and groaned again. "My stomach is killing me," he slurred.

"You're drunk, bro. Let me help you up and I'll make you more toast." Alex steadied him as he crawled to his feet.

"Not drunk. Took some of that medicine Morticia brought and started to feel knives stabbing me."

"When?"

"When I woke up. Didn't know you were here."

"I was quiet. Letting you sleep."

Lucas doubled over again. Alex latched onto his arms to keep him from falling and pushed him onto the couch. "I'm calling Morticia. You need a full examination. She'll have to beg Fierro."

"Not him. You heard what he said."

"He's your assigned doctor. You can't see anyone

else without his signature. Hold on. I'll get toast."

Alex ran out of the living room into the kitchen, dropped slices of bread into the toaster and called Morticia. She answered on the fifth ring.

"Tío?" She yawned. "What's going on? Is Papi okay?"

"No. His stomach is worse. I need you to call and get him in for a real exam. Can you do that?"

"I'll try. I have to get the boys up, fed, and to school. I'll come over just after nine. Give him some of that medicine I left yesterday."

"Can't Gabriel do that?" Morticia ignored his question. "I think that's part of the problem. He drank last night and took the medicine while the alcohol was still in his system."

"Oh, this is bad."

"Milk and toast. Where did he get the drink?"

"I went up yesterday and found three more bottles. We have to search the whole house, again."

"Sounds like a plan." She hung up. Alex returned with the toast and milk.

He helped Lucas sit up and watched him as he finished off the food. He was almost crying with the pain. Alex decided it was time to administer some uncontrolled painkillers specific for the type of discomfort his brother presented. In twenty minutes, Lucas felt better, and he was able to sit up.

"Lucas, you need to shower and dress. Morticia is working on getting you in to see someone. She'll be here pretty soon, then we'll go."

He shook his head. "She'll never get me in."

"They have to take you. We'll go to emergency if need be. Come on. Where can I find clean clothes for you?"

"They leave my things in the laundry. Ana doesn't want me in her room. You can look in the guest room, but I probably don't need a suit."

"Can you shower down here?"

"No, the guest bath."

"Okay, come on. You shower, I'll find clothes."

Morticia arrived about the time Lucas finished dressing. Alex pulled her into the kitchen. "Did you get an appointment?"

"Not exactly. The receptionist said Dr. Fierro was not there. He's been commissioned in a COVID brigade. You know, the 'people who are worth it'," she added in snarky tone. "I'll call back later. She said she would leave a message for him and ask what time he'll return."

"Well, if that's the best we can do. Lucas is feeling better right now."

The hospital was filled beyond capacity with COVID patients and masked attendants; the energy in the waiting area rumbled with fear.

After forty-five long minutes of waiting outside the consultation room, Alex was wound tight—a bundle of nerves over his brother's condition. It felt like an eternity. Alex had watched Lucas's discomfort turn into severe pain as the analgesic wore off and his symptoms worsened. He tried to comfort Lucas, but without any painkillers or toast, he had nothing to combat what Lucas called "knives stabbing his gut". The misery surrounding them exacerbated things.

Finally, the doctor in charge called out through her open office door, "Deltoro, Lucas."

Alex jumped from his chair and hastened to the office, leaving Lucas where he was. The doctor's round face looked weary, but Alex could see she was a woman of experience and wisdom. She needed a few pounds, but her straight black hair, tied up into a loose bun gleamed over her brown apple-round cheeks. She wore large glasses with thick lenses, which made her almost grey eyes look small. Her shapeless out-of-fashion dress, embroidered in bright flowers, stood out cheerfully from her white lab coat in stark contrast to the illness and pain surrounding her.

She smiled, waving him in. Alex stepped into her tiny office drowning under patient files.

"Good afternoon." She looked at the file and said, "Lucas Deltoro? I'm Doctora Aurora Rodríguez. Please sit down."

Only one chair was empty. Alex sat. "Good afternoon, doctor. I'm Alex Deltoro, the patient's brother."

Her expression changed to confusion. "Not the patient. Then how can I help you?"

Alex explained why they had come, leaving out that he'd threatened to go to the medical board on Dr. Fierro. "My brother is having severe stomach pains. His regular doctor is unavailable, but suggested Lucas has cancer. Both our mother and our younger brother died of stomach cancer. Dr. Fierro said to make an appointment to have him tested, but he's on a COVID rotation and we can't get Lucas in."

"I see. What exactly are his symptoms? Where is he now?"

"In the waiting area," he said and pointed. "The man holding his stomach."

She craned her neck to see around the door then nodded kindly. "Yes. He's in a great deal of pain." She took out an intake sheet from the desk drawer and picked a pen from the cup. "Please, slowly detail his history, symptoms, and medications."

Alex began with Lucas's alcoholism. "Doctor, I'm sure this is the root of the problem, but he has problems with his circulation and now he describes feeling knives stabbing him in the stomach. He fainted recently, too. His vitals are normal, but he doesn't sleep. Here's the list of medicines he has been taking." He handed over the list he generated with his notations.

She scanned it her pleasant expression fading to alarm, then asked Alex to again detail the symptoms.

He thought for a moment to remember everything and answered describing the rough yellow skin, the elephant legs, the loss of appetite, the amount he was drinking, and his experience in the hospital in January. "Now he has acute pain in his gut."

Alex saw the shadow of fear cross her face. "Los gangleos!" She exclaimed aloud. "What have you done for him?"

"Milk and dry toast relieved him some, but I was afraid to give him any drugs that might react with his alcohol or other drugs."

She pulled her prescription pad from the drawer and scribbled something on it. "Señor Deltoro, I want you take Lucas immediately for an ultrasound." She handed over the paper. "When you have the results, bring them to me. This test is very important."

"Thank you so much, Doctor." Alex left the office and asked the receptionist stationed in the hall,

111

"Excuse me, can you direct me to the ultrasound?

She answered without looking up from her paperwork, "On the ground floor, Señor." She pointed to the stairs.

He thanked her, helped Lucas from his chair, and hustled him to the elevator.

They wandered through a maze of passages until someone pointed out the ultrasound consultation room. Alex handed over the request to the doctor in charge.

He kindly said, "We will gladly attend Señor Deltoro, but I need the floor supervisor's authorization. Let's make the appointment and you can bring me the signed slip as soon as you get it. What day is good for you?"

Alex said, "The doctor was alarmed. She said it should be immediately."

"I'm sorry, we are overbooked already." He handed the appointment calendar to Alex. "Pick a slot. It's the best I can do."

Alex saw the next day three appointments were open. "We'll take 7:00 a.m., but if you get a cancellation, can you call me?"

The doctor sighed. "The waiting list already has five names on it, but I'll do my best. Go get that authorization from the floor supervisor."

"Where do I find this person?"

"You were just there. You'll find her office down the hall from Doctora Rodríguez."

He dragged Lucas back up to the waiting area and deposited him in a chair. "Stay here until I come for you. I'll get it sorted out."

Alex found the doctor in charge of the floor and presented himself along with Doctora Rodríguez's order. He explained the urgency of the order.

"It can't be done," the stern-faced administrator said.

"I'm sorry. Why not?"

"The hospital is not conducting ultrasounds at this time." She smiled up at him exposing a set of sharp teeth gleaming under her long, pointed nose. Alex thought all she needed was a broom.

"I'm surprised. Maybe some wires got crossed. I just came from that department and my brother has an appointment for seven tomorrow morning."

The administrator's voice rose. Several heads turned toward the open door. "I said there are no appointments for ultrasounds at this time. You may not have my signature. Close the door on your way out."

Alex tensed, his hands balling. Angrily he growled something and forced himself out the door before he decked the witch. He skittered between beds and personnel back to Doctora Rodríguez's office. She looked up sharply then smiled.

"What happened?"

Alex explained the chain of events.

"No, she's wrong. We are using ultrasound as usual. Go tell her I said it is urgent."

Alex again went to the office of the floor manager and explained the urgency of the procedure.

Again, she flatly refused.

Alex wasn't letting this go. Lucas was ill and this bitch was standing in the way of his treatment. He raised his voice, demanding the authorization.

The floor manager requested her secretary bring Doctora Rodríguez to the office. When the doctor arrived, she introduced herself and the women began to argue. Doctora Rodríguez was annoyed and heatedly demanded the administrator comply with her medical order. She didn't plead, but she spoke in a loud voice. Everyone nearby could hear her, humiliating the powerless floor manager.

The administrator signed.

Equally loudly, she ordered Dra. Rodriguez and Alex out of her office. The doctora ran out the back door—probably embarrassed to have had to argue for her patient. The floor manager gave her secretary the signed document to be given to Alex, although he was standing there.

"Thank you for your help," he managed to utter with a straight face.

Without wasting anymore time, he ran down the stairs and found ultrasound again to hand over the authorization.

The next morning, Alex deposited Lucas for the ultrasound at 6:45 a.m. They weren't going to be late for this. Lucas was in extreme pain, and to have secured this appointment—regardless of how stressful securing it was—in less than a day was miraculous. He blessed Doctora Rodríguez.

Lucas was scanned and Alex took him home. The results would not be available for twenty-four hours. Alex planned to swing by the hospital in the morning on his way to Lucas's house. The day progressed much as was becoming the routine.

Morticia came to make them breakfast. Ana, as usual, did not join them. She lived like a ghost, sneaking out of her room to eat or to disappear out of the house for hours at a time. When he did see her, Ana either ran back to her room or was nasty to him. She was like living with a crazy, rabid dog. He was about over his sister-in-law. She should be taking care of Lucas, not him.

Lucas rested in the afternoon. Alex used the time to work on his project to bring his foundation to Veracruz. It felt like it was taking a long time, but the reality was, he still had a couple of days left on his vacation. His leave hadn't started. Depending on the outcome of Lucas's ultrasound, he and Daisi might be able to head home by the end of the week. He prayed to whatever power was listening to be able to walk into his new position next Monday morning.

Morticia, Gabriel, and the kids came with tacos for dinner. She was thrilled to hear Lucas had finally started getting the tests he needed. Everyone was in a happy mood, expecting good results and a fast recovery now that they would know what the trouble was. Lucas got up and ate a few tacos. It was clear how much he loved his daughter and grandkids. They seemed to give him energy.

Alex asked, "How're you feeling, bro?"

Lucas smiled at him. "Alex, thank you so much for being here and helping me. I love you, brother."

Alex's heart swelled with the hot pinpricks of tears behind his eyes. Maybe this was for something after all. Maybe redemption.

Chapter 13

The Catch-22

Tuesday, April 7, 2020

At dawn, Alex stood in front of the ultrasound department waiting to pick up the results of Lucas's test. An attendant assured him they would be ready in fifteen minutes. He sat down.

Thirty minutes later he received a sealed envelope. The attending doctor had arrived. Alex asked, "How'd my brother do?" His heart pounded and his gut roiled.

The Doctor replied, "It's all good. There are no lesions, but it is important that another study is carried out, a CT scan. Your brother could not hold the positions to be able to be fully examined."

Alex was satisfied with the doctor's answer although he still sensed a twinge of trepidation. He thanked him and went upstairs to the appointment area to schedule the scan with Doctora Rodríguez, the treating physician. Without any argument, it was scheduled for that same afternoon. Fortune had smiled on Alex. After a bad patch, he was coming out on top again. He was winning! He raced to Lucas's house with the good news.

He parked outside the gate and ran in waving the envelope. Lucas was not in the recliner nor the dining room. He found his brother in the shower. Alex should wait to read the results, but curiosity overtook him. He ripped into the envelope and read through the eight-page results from beginning to end, shouting over the running water.

Later in the afternoon, Alex returned to the IMSS hospital to deliver the ultrasound results to Doctora Rodríguez, and hopefully make the appointment for Lucas's next examination. Maybe she would have some time to consult with him on the test results. As he picked his way between the overflow of COVID patients suffering in beds, on cots, on mattresses on the floor in the hallway, he passed the doctor's office and found himself face-to-face with Dr. Fierro.

"Alex Deltoro, isn't it? How are you doing?" Dr. Fierro said. "What are you doing here? Is Lucas worse?" His smile didn't reach his eyes; it matched his hypocritical attitude. "Come on in, my patient has just left. The next isn't due for twenty minutes." He gallantly gestured toward the office door.

"Thank you, Dr. Fierro. I'm actually here to see Doctora Rodríguez with the results of Lucas's ultrasound." Alex trailed the doctor into his office. It was in more disarray than before. He moved a pile of folders to the floor and sat down. He bet the doctor hadn't noticed Lucas's file was gone. How could he tell amid this mess?

Fierro pinched his lips but refrained from saying anything. He rounded the desk and sat. *Score one for me*, Alex thought.

"Doctora Rodríguez? I'm not so sure why you would be seeing her. I did not authorize your brother to see a specialist or waste resources on unnecessary tests."

"We had an emergency. Lucas needed attention and you were on your COVID rotation." Alex explained the situation.

"I see. Pass me those results and I'll evaluate our next move."

"Doctora Rodríguez already is familiar with the case, and she is expecting me. I better not hold her up." Alex stood.

"Sit, sit. She's tied up. We're all tied up with this pandemic. I'll read and give my opinion to her." He held out his hand, wiggling his fingers impatiently.

Although Alex was loathe to let Fierro take any part in his brother's health care, he handed over the envelope. Fierro pretended to read for five minutes, then pushed back from the desk, the wheels on his chair ground backward over the spilled files on the floor. "I told you it's cancer."

Alex heard the challenge in the man's voice. He stood up, stepped to the desk, and snatched the studies. Fierro opened his flappy lips, but Alex began to read before the doctor could get his words out. He read the pages from beginning to end, including the letterhead, signatures and the named technician who carried out the exam. It took eight minutes. A suffocating silence ensued.

He tossed the pile back onto Fierro's desk. "Nowhere in this document does it say cancer has been detected in my brother."

Fierro colored. In a quiet voice he almost

whispered, "But it's cancer, man."

Alex was pissed. *What a fool.* He replied, "Dr. Fierro. What is needed is a CT scan, which the competent doctors we saw Monday have advised my brother to take. You will authorize it."

"Yes, I can authorize the scan." His grin reminded Alex of the expressions he'd seen on European gargoyles. "However, it's not as easy as all that. These devices are in high demand right now, and if your family is very lucky, in about six months maybe you'll get an appointment." The sound he made could easily have come from some creature from Hell. He scribbled something on his pad and handed it to Alex. "Go to the floor administrator to see if she authorizes it. Good luck."

Well, that explained the horrid treatment Alex had received the last time he'd dealt with the administrator. She and Fierro were in cahoots. Displeased, he went to the administrator's receptionist and asked to see the supervisor.

"Go right in. She's waiting for you."

Her office was the exact opposite of Fierro's. Neat as a pin. One file lay on the desk. "Good afternoon, I'm here for your signature for a CT scan for Lucas—"

"I know what you want. Give me Dr. Fierro's request."

Alex passed the request to the boney witch.

She scrutinized it, then wrote up the order. "You'll need the signature of Lucas Deltoro's general practitioner before you can take this to the department for your appointment."

Exasperated, Alex marched back to Dr. Fierro's office. The doctor was already busy giving another consultation, but he had the door open, Alex stood in front of the door waving the order.

Dr. Fierro shouted at Alex, "What do you want now?"

Alex replied, "The administrator said you have to sign it."

Dr. Fierro didn't try to hide his anger. He stormed from his chair, his patient, a young woman cowering at his unprofessional behavior, and snarled, "Madre de Dios, let's see." He snatched the document from Alex's hands, the patient jerked in surprise and got up.

Alex expected this behavior and shrugged, shaking his head. The woman collected her purse, stepping toward the door as Fierro stormed out in the direction of the floor administrator's office. Alex followed him. They met the administrator in the hallway, and Fierro shouted, "It's that pendejo, Deltoro."

The witch reacted without saying anything. She pushed Fierro back the way he'd come and shook her head, but Dr. Fierro continued, "I am busy, and I have many patients. Fix this."

Alex intervened. "Doctor, you must sign the order according to your floor administrator."

The doctor was drawing attention now. "I already told you, there is no available tomography service. Many patients need it, and apart from that, the device is broken."

Fierro handed the document to the administrator. She took it, saying, "I'm sorry, Mr. Deltoro, I did not know that the equipment was broken. I have to cancel this order."

Everyone present in the corridor watched as the witch tore up the document. Standing between the two shouting, Alex tried to look shocked and frightened. This was rolling out in the presence of receptionists and patients waiting to be served. Alex wanted witnesses to the bad behavior of these two.

He yelled, "Stop! Dr. Fierro, what a disappointment. You are not a doctor. You have betrayed your oath to do no harm. Alcoholism is a disease, and you have to treat it as such, you cannot discriminate against a person and deny him service because you don't approve of his lifestyle." He gulped a breath. All eyes were on Alex. "You cannot let a person die because of prejudice. No one, I say NO ONE has the right to kill another person in this country. You cannot discriminate in such a violent way against a person who worked all his life and paid for the service that you arbitrarily denied."

The onlookers clapped. Fierro crept back to his office, face red, shoulders hunched. But nothing changed. The CT scan was canceled at Dr. Fierro's own discretion with the support of the floor administrator.

Without another word Alex left the hospital. How could the hospital administration allow such poor treatment of its patients? Not to mention the substandard level of care. Did everyone have such negative experiences here?

It wasn't cancer, but Lucas was going to die if he didn't get the care he needed. Alex had to act. The intention of the doctor was clear.

This was war.

Chapter 14

The Confession

Friday, April 10, 2020

Alex brooded. The knives in Lucas's stomach turned into axes. He and Morticia rattled through the daily routine of toast, milk, and painkillers without much effect. The few times Alex ran into Ana, the Mona Lisa smile she wore baffled and horrified him. He tried to talk to her, stressing the urgency of the CT scan. Would she intervene through her brother Victor? Her response, "Not my husband, not my problem."

The behavior of Dr. Fierro and the witchy floor administrator deeply disturbed him. He couldn't mistake their alliance. They were allies. For what? Or maybe he should consider they aligned *against* something. Lucas? Why? He found it next to impossible to believe the hospital regulations allowed personnel to fight in the hallways. The government hospitals had been founded on good intentions, but like most bureaucracies, they'd become small fiefdoms for the top brass. Was money being diverted from healthcare to the pockets of the directors and top doctors? It wouldn't surprise him if Fierro was somehow profiting from the abuse of patients. But the floor administrator? No way. Her payoff came from perceived power. Still, why Lucas?

Damn, damn, damn. *What is the connection?* he wanted to shout.

A quiet trill from his laptop, the laptop he had not touched in three days, told him it was time to make dinner. A week of personal care, housework, food shopping, cooking, and more personal care ground Alex down. Paralyzed by tedium and worry, he had deserted the war before it officially was declared.

Forget dinner. Lucas wouldn't eat it anyway. Alex found his cell phone on the dining table and dialed Lucas' brother-in-law, Doctor Victor Mata, Director of the IMSS General Hospital No. 71. Not Fierro's hospital, his best shot to get the necessary tests.

"Dr. Mata. How may I help you?"

"Victor, it's Alex Deltoro. I need some help." After summarizing Fierro's strange behavior, he asked, "Do you have time to talk to me?"

"Listen, Alex. It's after 17:30 and I've a meeting before dinner. I'll be over to visit Ana tonight. We'll speak then."

The drumroll of battle sounded. A zap of electricity charged through him. Maybe now he'd make some headway and be back in Mexico to start his new directorship on Monday.

Victor rumbled up in his Urban truck just after 21:00 hours. Alex paced outside, taking in the cool night air. He wished he smoked. A cigarette would taste good and get his blood pumping. He missed his daily workouts, but Lucas didn't have any equipment.

The doctor clambered out and set the alarm. Alex greeted him. "Let me get the gate for you, Victor."

"Thanks. How are you? Holding up okay? You must be at the end of your leave."

"That I am, but I've extended until I can resolve Lucas's situation. Why don't we stay out here. The family is already stressed enough. Lucas is worse."

"I assumed that would be the case." Mata pulled two aromatic Cubanos from his jacket, tilting one in Alex's direction, eyebrows raised.

"Thanks, not for me, but knock yourself out."

"I'm not allowed to smoke in the house. I made a habit if dropping by and smoking one with Lucas now and then. Ana never minded."

"I'm sure she would now. From what I can see, if he enjoyed it, she'd forbid it. I don't know what's between them. She should leave him or show him out. They have other houses. But that's not what I wanted to talk about."

Mata blew a couple of smoke rings into the night air. The smoke drifted upwards a thin line making the ring look like an inverted noose in the still night. Alex's palms sweated. *Here goes.*

He narrated the facts to the doctor. Mata swayed foot to foot in an uneasy dance as Alex talked. A glint of moonshine showed beads of sweat on his forehead. *Nervous.* Mata wiped his brow and cast his eyes toward the ground. "Alex, leave it at that. I'll arrange the tests at my hospital."

"I'd appreciate that, Victor. It's urgent. How soon can you get him in?"

"Call me tomorrow at noon and I'll let you know."

"Thank you so much. You coming in?" He held out

his hand, inviting the doctor in. "If we can get these scans taken care of, I can get home."

"Just to say hello. A quick bite, if I know my sister."

The men entered the house discussing the early success of the new LSI antiviral.

"Alex, you should come see me once everything is settled and give me your pitch. If Viru-Out is as efficacious as you say, we might save some lives. This damn pandemic is a cabron."

"Hola, Tío," Morticia exclaimed, bouncing off the couch to give her Uncle Victor a hug.

"Morticia, Lucas, good evening."

Lucas lurched up, turned a weak smile on his brother-in-law, and drooped back into his chair.

The rattle of Ana's door opening echoed down the stairs. She shouted, her voice cheerful for a change, "Good evening little brother, how are you?"

She pranced down the stairs nicely dressed with her square face fully made-up, and hair freshly styled. *Is she going somewhere?* Alex watched her hug Victor. She said, "You hungry? I can make you some dinner."

"Something light, Ana. I'm in a hurry."

She skipped to the kitchen, returning in record time with platters of carne asada accompanied by red enchiladas and soda. Brother and sister took up residence in the dining room, talking and laughing between sounds of eating, while Alex's stomach growled and he, Lucas, and Morticia watched a soccer game on TV. The weird vibes in the Deltoro house made him shiver.

Victor finished eating then poked his head into the living room to say goodbye. Ana accompanied him to the door. "Good night, Victor," she said, closing the door and turning the lock. Alex listened to her climb the stairs and slam her bedroom door. He glanced at Morticia. She wore a sad expression. "I'll go clean up. Then I'm due back home," she said.

At noon the next day, Alex dialed Dr. Mata. A receptionist answered and when he gave his name she said, "Hold, please."

Mata answered immediately. "You just caught me. I have good news. We have the appointment for the tomography tomorrow morning at eight a.m. Can you get Lucas here? I've got my tech coming in before the lab opens."

"Yes, of course, Victor. Thank you so much. How quickly will you have answers?"

"Same day. See you in the morning." He hung up.

Alex brayed a woohoo and pumped his fist into the air. He was winning the first skirmish. *Take that, Fierro.*

Lucas bucked against the early departure from his recliner.

"Get over it, brother. We're going."

Alex maneuvered Lucas to the SUV and put up with his brother's complaints and groans for the fifteen minutes it took to reach IMSS No.71 on Salvador Diaz Mirón.

Once inside, Alex asked the way to Victor's office. They took the elevator. Lucas looked grey and spotty. He'd lost a few kilos since Alex arrived; his skin hung loose and wrinkled.

At the door, Alex knocked.

"Come in," Victor said. "Listen, before we go down, I

have to check with the lab tech. Make yourselves comfortable and I'll be right back."

"Victor is in good spirits today," Alex said.

"Why not? I bought him a nice meal last night."

"Really, Lucas? Try a little gratitude for a change. You're sick and he is providing you with care. We'll know today if you have cancer."

It took Victor fifteen minutes to return. He stuck his head through the doorway. "Follow me."

Like in the other hospital, they wound through a labyrinth in the basement. The technician who would perform the study already waited. The man ordered Lucas to undress and put on a gown, then get on the device. Lucas lay down and kept still for twenty minutes as he was scanned. Alex waited in the hall until he was called to help Lucas dress.

Exhausted and irritated by the scan, Lucas staggered to the changing room and slumped down onto the bench.

Alex handed him his clothes. "Can you manage?"

Lucas grabbed his t-shirt from his brother and yanked it over his head, missing the armhole. "Anything to get out of this dungeon." He struggled for a moment then popped his arm through. "What the fuck was that all about? Took too long. It was the same as yesterday. Why do I need all this?" He banged out of the changing room and hissed, "I'm fed up, Gato. Let's go."

A wave of sadness engulfed Alex. Seeing his brother like this, an old sick man, hurt more than he imagined. "I'll call and thank Victor later."

They left without saying goodbye. Mata did not call with the results.

The doorbell rang the next evening while Alex was clearing up from dinner. One look at Mata's face and he knew the news was bad. "Doctor, hello, come in," he said, forcing his voice to sound light.

Alex ushered him into the living room where Lucas sat. He glared at Mata.

The doctor sat down across from him. For moments he gazed at his sister's husband. "Lucas, you know I love you like a brother. I've always been able to count on you for anything—"

Alex slumped onto the couch and interrupted the doctor. "What's wrong, Victor? Lay it out. What did the scan find?"

"Yes, I have news," he said, and continued to address Lucas. "We've spent many happy moments—"

"Is there cancer?" Alex blurted.

"Yes."

Lucas sank into his wrinkled shell, diminishing before Alex's eyes. "Has it metastasized?"

Mata's "Yes" could not be misconstrued. Alex turned away; Lucas couldn't see him cry. He excused himself and walked into the hallway, his pain and anger like a thing dogging his steps. He couldn't go back into the living room and let Lucas see him like this. His brother needed every ounce of vitality he could muster, not a pissed off, scared little brother sapping him of more energy. Deep breaths. That's what he needed. Or a stiff drink.

Dr. Mata met Alex at the dining table as he poured a measure of Lucas's brandy. "Bring Lucas to the hospital tomorrow. I'll put you in touch with some specialists. We'll get more tests and start treatment immediately. Goodnight, Alex, Take courage. Go in and take care of your brother."

Take courage, Alex. How could he say that so calmly? Alex hated the man. Go in to keep his brother company? His anger and grief boiled over. He pounded the table, tears streaming.

He sucked in the deep breath then ordered himself to calm down. Silence engulfed him like an evil omen. It was time to do his duty like the doctor ordered: take care of his brother.

The living room air felt dead. Neither Alex nor Lucas spoke. Alex's head exploded with all the things he should say but couldn't. Finally, he croaked, "We should get Ana."

"No, Gato, I don't want her here with her mean little smile. Let me sit with this awhile."

"Shall I go?"

"No, stay here. I'll tell her tomorrow." He gave a short laugh. "She probably already knows. She and Victor are mad at me."

Monday morning Alex found Dr. Mata ensconced in his office, the chairs outside the door filled with people waiting for an audience. Masked secretaries and receptionists scuttled about, answered phones and consulted with workers at various desks placed around the anteroom to the Director's and manager's offices. He gave his name at the first desk.

"The Director is expecting you, Señor Deltoro. Please take a seat in the waiting area and I'll come for you in a few minutes.

"Thank you, Señorita," he said.

The receptionist blushed, eyes twinkling. "I haven't

been called señorita in forty years."

"No? You had me fooled," he said with a wink.

Alex's new friend tottered from behind her desk and nodded to Alex from the door five minutes later. He rose, smiling and mouthed *thank you* as he passed into Doctor Mata's office. The eye-daggers aimed at him as he skirted the row of chairs did not go unnoticed.

"Buenos tardes, Victor. Thanks again for this," Alex said, leaning over the desk to shake the doctor's hand.

"Don't mention it, Alex," he replied and tossed him a bottle of hand sanitizer. "Be sure you clean your hands regularly when you're here. It's clear now COVID is passed both through the air and from infected surfaces." He gazed out the partially shrouded window overlooking the front office and beyond into the hospital. "This pandemic is getting worse. Our staff is catching the virus from the patients. A quarter of the nursing staff is down with it. Many occupy beds in our halls. We don't have anywhere else to put people. But that's my problem. Let's solve yours."

"Victor, I could perhaps be of help. You know about Viru-Out. Come by the house when you can, and I'll explain my foundation and its program."

The doctor nodded. "I will."

"So, what can we do to get treatment for my brother?"

"He needs a consultation with our gastroenterologist. However, that specialty is not available here in No. 71. You need to talk to Dr. Juan Carlos Figueroa." He handed over a card with the doctor's contact information. "He's the director of the Tarimoya IMSS and he is expecting you." Mata outlined the procedure. His pass would be waiting when he arrived. The specialist would personally perform the endoscopy. "And please stress to your brother, this is being performed as a courtesy to me. We both know how he gets around doctors." He laughed.

Alex laughed too. Victor was right. Lucas was a terrible patient. "What does he drink? I'll bring him a bottle."

"That's not necessary. But if you're determined, he's a mezcal drinker." Mata stood, offering his hand.

Alex shook it. "And you, Victor? What do you prefer?"

"Tequila!"

"I'll find the best bottle in Veracruz."

Alex raced back to where he'd parked his motorcycle. He wasn't going to let any time pass to make the appointment with Dr. Juan Carlos Figueroa. The Tarimoya hospital was about twenty minutes away if traffic wasn't too bad. He laid on the gas.

It took Alex seventeen minutes to arrive, park, and jog to the front door. Because of the pandemic, this hospital allowed entry through appointments only. He announced his name and the doctor's. An attendant wearing scrubs and the obligatory facemask, directed him to the reception desk where Alex received his pass and the consultation appointment for the following day —with a dose of kindness.

Alex and Lucas showed up punctually at 8:15 the next morning. Pass in-hand, they were welcomed inside and directed to the third floor to the doctor's office.

Doctor Juan Carlos Figueroa greeted them with a

rebuke, "Señor Deltoro, you have not taken care of yourself. You know you've brought this on—" he rapped his is index finger on the open medical file in front of him. "Your brother-in-law says you drink too much—"

He glared at Lucas with, to Alex, the appearance of a rotund butcher—one who had just cut up a pig.

The gastroenterologist continued. "You have to stop drinking or you'll die."

Lucas had gone pale, but Alex had googled him and read a few reviews. This doctor's reputation preceded him. The man was notorious for his shitty bedside manner, *and* for being one of the best gastroenterologists in the city. Why he worked through IMSS when a private practice would make him wealthy was the question. Probably because he was so mean. And the prognosis *was* discouraging.

Alex intervened. "He's trying to stop, doctor."

The doctor swirled his chair to face Alex. "Shut up and listen! Don't get your hopes up too high. There is no possibility of success."

"What do you mean?" Lucas, now blanching to the look and texture of a boiled potato.

"I mean, I'll follow protocol. That's it. Lie down on the table." He cocked his head to the examination table. "Nurse, I don't need you."

The nurse stepped out, but did not close the door. Alex could see her listening. Lucas lay down.

To Lucas, the doctor said, "We'll scope out your gut now—it's through your mouth, in case you don't know —and then we'll sort out a treatment plan. I don't want to say more until we have a clear picture of what's going on in your stomach. Ready? Yes? Let's go. Unzip your pants."

Lucas complied. The doctor ran his hands over Lucas's stomach, tapping here and there and squeezing certain spots. "Tell me where it hurts."

Lucas said, "No. No. No." To the various points the hands touched until the doctor hit a tender spot. "Ow! That spot hurts."

"Here?" He pressed, letting his full bodyweight fall on Lucas's stomach.

Lucas screamed. He curled up and turned onto his side to protect himself, working to get off the examining table. Alex flew from his chair to land between Lucas and the doctor with his fists ready. His better judgement shouted, *calmate güey*, and he inhaled sharply. He couldn't afford the serious trouble he'd be in if he decked a doctor.

From the corner of his eye, he saw movement outside the back door. The nurse who had been dismissed. Their eyes met. Her's said she was scared by what she had seen.

The doctor yelled, "Didn't I tell you to get out?" Was he yelling at the nurse or at him?

Lucas stood by the table, buttoning up his jeans. Alex stepped to his side and helped him out of the office and down to the parking lot. No one said a word.

The endoscopy was never carried out.

Alex, breaking for a red light, broke the silence. "Lucas, I don't get it. The inconsistencies and weird events are bothering me. This can't all be random. I feel like the Veracruz medical community has a vendetta against you. You don't even know the half." He described his experiences. "What have you done, Lucas?"

Lucas dropped his head into his hands. Only the SUV's seatbelt held him up. Alex glanced over, alarmed.

Lucas's face turned crimson, and he slowly wagged his head side to side. "Nothing."

Angrily Alex lashed, "I don't believe you, brother. It is not possible for all the doctors in this city to treat you this way. What did you do?"

"I'm sorry, Alex. It-it's just retaliation for the skirt issue."

Alex rolled his head toward his brother. "What the fuck? You aren't making any sense Lucas. Skirt issue?"

Lucas launched into a confession.

"And you trusted your health to Mata and his cronies? After betraying your brother-in-law?" Alex shouted. "Are you an idiot?" He couldn't keep his incredulous tone neutral—or pleasant.

Lucas sat up, confusion spreading thick across his's face. "That's another thing, Gato. One thing at work and another personally. We're good friends."

By the time they arrived at the house, Alex understood just what a betraying, traitorous pendejo his brother was. And for this he was losing the biggest honor and advancement of his life? He wanted to pummel Lucas, squash him like a bug. But he didn't need to lift a finger, Victor Mata and his colleagues were doing the job—systematically destroying Lucas Deltoro.

Chapter 15

The Wife

Lucas pulled a cigarette out of the glove compartment and punched in the lighter.

"Chingao! Are you crazy, Lucas?" Alex snapped, pulling the cancer-stick from his brother's fingers. "You're sick! You want to smoke?"

"Leave me alone, Gato. I need to relax."

"Well, I can't stand the smoke. I'll be inside." Alex turned off the SUV then slammed the door behind him. He didn't want to see his brother kill himself. What was the matter with him? His hands shook as he turned the front door's knob and rushed in, almost bowling over Ana, carrying a tray of food.

"Watch where you're going, Alex." She steadied the tray, turned her back, and thudded up the stairs to avoid him.

He gritted his teeth. Ana. Exactly what he needed —he was ready to spit. *Might as well add one more reason to throttle someone.* "Stop, Ana. I need to talk to you." His voice sounded threatening, even to his ears. He was so tired of her attitude. Why did she stick around? Her husband had betrayed her. Ana had every right to leave, *but this?*

She mounted the staircase as quickly as her ponderous body allowed.

"Trying to escape?" Alex sprinted after her, catching her on the landing before she could disappear into her bedroom. He snatched the tray, sliding it onto a hall table. Closing his fist around her arm, he forced her down to the living room, shoving her into the recliner. She shrank back, baring her teeth.

He towered over her, the force of his intention pinning her to the chair. "Not this time, Ana." Alex blocked her way. "Not going to escape. You're going to sit there and tell me what you're hiding." As he said it, he realized, that's exactly what was going on. And he knew what her secret was.

Ana clamped her jaw. Alex watched her close the blinds, go dark. It was like she turned out a light and was no longer there, infuriating him more. He took a deep breath.

When Alex spoke, it was loud and clear. "Ana," he said, giving her shoulder a shake, "why are you refusing to care for your husband? He needs you. I believe he is dying, and *you* are making it worse." He glared, waiting for Ana's lies.

"Alex, I'm no longer your brother's wife." She hung her head. "I failed as a partner." The last came in a whisper. Tears dripped from her downturned face.

Alex stepped back, surprised. His voice softened. "Why do you say that?"

Her head flew up. She looked him in the eye, "Your brother is a wretch, he cheated on me with your mother's maid, and I don't know how many more."

So Ana knew.

"I caught him. Not once. Not with just Aimee." She was shouting. She twisted in the chair, the tears flooding her face. ". . .so angry. So angry. He made me do it." Her reddened eyes bored into Alex's. "He made me disrespect my family. I'm as bad as Lucas. Worse." She gazed at the wall, lost in thought.

"Your family? What do you mean?" Alex sat down. He felt her desperation; took her icy hand. Maybe Ana was a victim of his brother too. Maybe he, Alex, was wrong about her. He heard the click of the front door, then the scrape of the glass cabinet closing, the clink of glass on wood.

Sobbing, she choked, "There were more. My husband fornicated with my niece Leticia, the daughter of my older sister. . ." The rest was lost to her cries.

Alex's guard crumbled. Floored, he did not expect news like this. No wonder she hated Lucas, but what was Lucas's problem? *Skirts* he called it. Who else had Lucas screwed? How deep did the betrayals go? Victor Mata's image flashed through his mind. His sequestered visits upstairs with his sister. The treatment of the doctors. It was all becoming clear— retribution. Vengeance. Revenge. Ana was the nexus.

Ana continued complaining.

"Ana I don't want to know anything more about your family, or Lucas, or anyone who has to do with you. What I want to know is, why don't you divorce hm? It would be for the best. If what you tell me is true, you owe it to your marriage, your daughter, and yourself to cut ties. You don't think this illness is, in part, caused by the stress of your dysfunctional relationship? Ask Morticia. She's a psychologist. Ana, end it before Lucas dies. You'll carry that guilt for the rest of your life."

"My daughter can never know. Promise me you won't tell her. I can't leave him, Alex. I can't divorce Lucas. It would kill her. I have to guarantee her economic stability."

"You don't think your secrets and lies aren't hurting your daughter?"

"Too much of our wealth is tied up together. It's the only thing stopping me."

The living room tilted, the brightly colored artwork swirled, a vortex spinning, spinning. Alex grabbed his head, a scream forming deep in his gut. The room blacked out—no longer a theory, her motivation was clear. Ana wanted the inheritance. His stomach knotted. Now he felt the knives Lucas had complained about. Fillet knives cutting out his heart. Ana was willing to let her husband die to get the money—and part of that money belonged to Alex.

Or is she conspiring to kill him?

Chapter 16

The Beach

Alex didn't bother to comment. He got up, turned his back on his sister-in-law, growled, "Go back to your cave, you greedy bitch." He had to get away from these awful people. He turned at the door to see Ana sobbing in the living room. Lucas drinking in the dining room.

He ran.

The motorcycle waited, pawing the pavement, snorting. Anxious to ride away. Traffic slowed him. Finally, Alex was on the open road and cranked on the gas. He had no destination in mind, no goal beyond distancing himself from his terrible, sad family. He crossed the river, spun through the cane fields toward the shore. Another bridge, another small town full of topes.

The *rico* smell of street tacos brought his awareness back to his whereabouts. He pulled over and walked back to the taco stand, stomach growling, ordered a beer and half a dozen tacos, which he doused in the hottest salsa the vender offered. At a small table placed at the edge of the road, he sat. Ate. Focused on the flavors, the burning on his tongue and down his throat. Salsa so hot it stripped away the cruel words he wanted to shout at his brother and sister-in-law; at the doctors; at his mother—she was part of this, too. Wasn't it Irene who had created the Lucas monster?

When the beer was gone, he ordered more. He needed it.

The entrance to the beach lay at the end of the short block. Alex returned the plastic plate to the vendor, placed his bottles in recycling, dirty napkins in the trash, then ambled toward the Gulf of Mexico stretching before him—murky, steel grey, flat. He kicked off his running shoes at the sand and walked away from the crowds of people taking a day at the shore.

Soon he left behind the laughter, shrieks of children, calls of vendors, cook-fire smoke, growling motorcycles, and squawks of sea gulls. The beach rolled out before him as he walked, the quiet of lapping waves, soft breeze, and crunch of sand calmed his mind. Now it was time to sit and ponder the situation. He should have accepted it was about the money. Wasn't it always?

Before his mother died, Alex had come upon Lucas going through her financial files. "What's up, Lucas? Can I help?"

Lucas had slammed the files closed and retorted, "You going to start, Gato? All you care about is the money. We don't see you for months and here you are when my mother is dying."

Alex hadn't taken up the argument, but he'd noted it was Lucas hiding what he was doing. That was when he knew for certain he couldn't trust his brother. He'd cheated Alex, their younger brother, and probably Irene out of his father's inheritance. When Lucas left, Alex had pulled out the files and taken a look.

On the top was a life insurance policy on his little brother. He'd left everything he had to Irene. He carried the file into his mother, "Madre, did you receive the inheritance from Hugo's life insurance?"

"Yes, Alex. Lucas deposited the three thousand pesos to my account for me. I don't want you asking questions or meddling."

Alex said, "No Mother, it was three hundred thousand pesos." He showed his mother the numbers on the document. "Where's the deposit receipt? Or your statements. Maybe there was an error."

"In my drawer. But Lucas doesn't make mistakes."

No, Alex thought, as he read over his mother's bank statements, it was no mistake.

He'd let it go, apologizing to his mother. He got no advantage from upsetting a sick old woman. But there was more. Once Alex knew Lucas was stealing his mother's money, he studied the files. It was clear Lucas didn't only come to drink and screw the servant, he also came to screw over his mother—and him.

He discovered Lucas was transferring ownership of Irene's properties to Morticia and her boys. He found certificates with notary public seals, but they did not have Irene's signature. They had Lucas's. It was clear, Lucas was illegally transferring the family inheritance, but not according to Irene's will, which Alex remembered he had witnessed when she made it after his father died. There was no question, Lucas was paying off the notaries.

Alex didn't care so much about the money, but he

did not want his family's assets to eventually wind up with Ana and the Mata family. Apparently, Lucas didn't want that either. Nothing had been transferred to his wife.

More clouds built over the Gulf as the sun shifted west. The wind picked up and the pleasant temperature dropped. Alex dug his toes into the sand and watched the dark line of a loaded cargo ship slowly disappear below the horizon. He made a recount of the facts and thought that the same thing was happening with the remaining assets of his recently deceased mother. And Ana wanted her share.

A conversation they'd had at Christmas came back to him. They'd been talking about Hugo, the fickleness of life, and the importance of making wills.

He'd asked, "Ana, are you telling me that the only important thing is my family's money?" He hadn't expected her nasty reply. He'd bulls-eyed one of her buttons.

"There is nothing from your family! Your father only left debts, and I envy your brother who didn't need to live to find out how bad Enrique Deltoro Bandenboosh was. My husband is an alcoholic because of your father."

Alex had been furious. Ana defamed his late father! For Alex, his father was the most valuable man on the planet. He had responded to Ana, saying, *"Why would you say these things, Ana?"*

Morticia had come in, said hello and disappeared into the kitchen. Luckily, she didn't realize her mother and uncle were arguing.

A seagull swooped down on the remains of a dead sea creature. Three more circled, landed, and began a noisy fight over the precious inheritance. The birds reminded him of the feelings Ana brought up in him. Alex had been a sensitive kid, easy to hurt, and volatile. Ana was determined to restore that Alex back to life. At the time, he could not contain himself insisting on an answer to his question. Ana had gleefully obliged him.

"Yes, the only thing your father came to my house for was to get drunk with Lucas."

Alex had shouted to silence her. *The hateful woman.* And perhaps to let Morticia hear the terrible things her mother said about her grandfather. He had reminded her who drank with teen-aged Lucas.

"My brother became an alcoholic when he was your boyfriend. Every day he came home with a bottle of brandy in the car and ashtrays from different motels. Once I asked Lucas who he spent his time with, and he replied with you. When I met you, indeed, you drank and smoked together. Have you already forgotten? I want you to clarify this to your daughter, because I do not like the image your lies have created of her grandfather. Morticia's opinion of my father is important to me and she's listening to us now."

He laughed to himself. The first gull grabbed the carcass and flew off, leaving the rest of the family squabbling at the tideline. Ana had been speechless not knowing what to answer. She had tried to divert the subject by saying, *"The only thing your dad left us were debts."* This infuriated Alex more. He'd lashed out, *"That is not true! My father was a hardworking, successful man. I know he left us a sound inheritance."*

Ana had tried to defend herself, but Alex shouted

over her. *"Lucas was appointed to be executor before a notary public and you cannot deny it, you were present. You signed as a witness. We discussed the will, the Campeche ranch with more than 400 hectares and a thousand head of cattle, the Palma Sola Veracruz ranch, the bank accounts, the jewelry, the collection of cars. What happened to it all? I never got my share, nor did Hugo. Ana, tell me what you and Lucas did with our inheritance?"*

She had struggled to justify her lies, saying she didn't remember. He had angrily reminded her. *"Well,"* she'd said, *"I have no knowledge of it, I don't handle the money, the one who has access to the bank accounts is Lucas."*

Alex totted up what Ana had conveniently forgotten. With their shares, he and Hugo had paid for the remodel of Lucas's and Ana's house, a modest two-story home expanded to a four-story mansion filled with fine art and furniture; millions of pesos paid to Casa de Hierro, and VISA and MasterCard for nice clothes, appliances, dinners, parties, trips; for luxury cars; parcels of land deeded to Ana—and who knows what.

The anger rushed back. Alex felt his face transform into that of the bull tormented in the ring.

Then the worst, but why hadn't he expected it? Hearing the long-ago argument, Morticia had barreled out of the kitchen and shouted at Alex. *"Stop talking like that to my mom!"*

Lucas had appeared to investigate the commotion. Ana took Alex's momentary inattention to slip away, running up to her room, and slamming her door, Morticia on her heels. Was she part of this too?

That had taken place on December 23rd, the night before Lucas and Ana had dismissed him, sent him home to Mexico City. And now, here he was, sitting on an empty beach as the sun went down, trying to make sense of the terrible mess Lucas had made of his life, and the lives of everyone around him. The Mata family was out for vengeance—Ana and her brother Victor planned to profit on Lucas's bad behavior.

A divorce settlement wasn't enough.

Chapter 17

The Operation

Tuesday, April 14, 2020

The tension permeating Lucas's house after Alex's talk with Ana felt palpable. Lucas had heard most of Ana's revelations. His health nose-dived, adding an additional burden on Alex's days. Morticia stopped eating; every time she tried, she vomited. In a matter of three days, she lost weight from her already slender frame. Alex encouraged her to phone her doctor. She called her uncle Victor.

To Alex's dismay, Mata showed up in the afternoon, but when the doctor saw his niece, he summoned her to the hospital the next day for a series of tests. He warned her she might require an operation.

Morticia told her father.

Lucas asked, "What does Victor think you might have?"

"Uncle Victor says it's nothing serious, but he has to correct the problem as quickly as possible. He won't know what the complications are until after the tests."

Alex could not believe his family had so many

health problems at the same time. It had to be from Lucas's work at the nuclear power plant. He told his niece he would drive her to the hospital. Hopefully this would distract Lucas from continuing to ask about a diagnosis, because Alex knew that the answer would not be easy to hide. He feared the diagnosis would be spelled *cancer.*

On the way to the hospital the next day, Alex tried to cheer up Morticia. "Take it easy, kid, everything is going to be fine."

She didn't respond until they arrived a few minutes early for the appointment. Making no move to get out of the SUV, "Tío," she said, looking straight into his eyes, "What happened to Grandfather Bandenboosh's inheritance? I think my dad is making moves to change the property ownerships, but I don't really know which ones. You know something about it. I heard you tell my mom that Dad is my grandfather's executor. Mami told me Abuelo left a lot of debts."

Alex really didn't want to discuss her father's lies and betrayals when the woman already felt unwell, twitching with raw nerves. The conversation would just make her upset, and with an operation looming, now was not the time. He said, "Morticia your grandfather didn't leave any debt. On the contrary, he left some assets that, to date, have not been distributed. But this is not important today. For now, we have to put positive energy into your successful operation, and your dad's recovery." He pulled past the hospital, making a right at the corner of the campus and looking for a parking space.

"My dad is preparing to die. He's putting his affairs in order. I know, I've taken him to his notary. If my grandfather left you something, Papi is arranging your share too. Tío, the documents are in the liquor cabinet. Papi and the lawyer are working on them."

A lump formed in Alex's throat. Morticia was too trusting. He knew she was being taken care of, but she was wrong about Lucas. Her father was a greedy thief, illegally protecting his family with money and assets belonging to Alex and deceased Hugo. Why would his older brother change his ways? He'd been an entitled money-grubbing teen. It was a pattern he'd followed throughout his life. Alex cleared his throat but didn't say anything. Again, he asked himself, *why am I taking care of him*? But he had no right to put this on Morticia.

Finally, he replied, "I'm sure you're right. But for now, focus on staying calm. You'll come out of your surgery well. The most important thing in life is health."

A car pulled out of a spot not too far from the corner, Alex maneuvered into the tight space, got out of the SUV, walked around to the passenger door, and helped Morticia out. He gathered her things from the backseat: her carry-on bag, a small case with personal hygiene items, and some books.

"I'll take those, Uncle, don't bother." She took all but the personal bag. They went around to the front door and slipped on their masks.

Things had gotten so bad with the pandemic, only Morticia was allowed entry. They said goodbye with a hug and tears.

Alex felt a weight descend upon him. He tried to smile. "Morticia, cariño, good luck. I'll come back for you when you're ready to be discharged."

He analyzed the conversation with his niece as he drove back to Lucas's colonia. He worried. Morticia knew about the asset transfers. Lucas had actually lied to his own daughter. He was so tired of the deceit and the cheating. Disgusted, disheartened, and yes, angry, he almost wanted to say, *Take it. Take it all, Lucas.*

His pattern was to run, hide his head in his work. But he knew he had to broach the subject—and quickly. The behavior of his sister-in-law, the hypocrisy of his brother, and the comments of his niece had turned on the red lights.

He let himself into the house, attended to Lucas's morning routines, gave him his meds, and prepared breakfast. He barely ate; he barely could sit upright at the table, wanting nothing more than to shrink, curl up—disappear. *Let the greedy coyotes take it all.* But Alex knew if he couldn't find a decent doctor soon, Lucas would die. Could he live with that weight on his shoulders?

He also knew, no doctor in Veracruz would competently care for Lucas. Victor Mata had seen to that. Probably Alex's share of his father's inheritance was greasing their palms via Ana. *Yes, Ana is deep into this.*

He should let it go, drop the rebukes, the allegations, the threats. Lucas would never admit he'd taken Alex's inheritance. To Lucas, Alex wasn't a true member of the family. Ana had made that clear. And where would she have gotten the idea? But once the huevos a la mexicana and tortillas were on the table, Alex could not contain himself. "What are you doing at the notary, brother?

He watched Lucas's nervous smile appear. He shoved a forkful of eggs into his mouth. *Stalling for time to think up an answer?*

Lucas chewed, sipped his juice, then said, "Nothing, Gato. Why?"

"You think I don't know who you are working with, brother? I've read the papers in Mother's files."

Lucas's fork shook as he tried to navigate his mouth with another bite. He spoke again, quietly with an imperious tone of voice. "You're paranoid, Alex. I don't know what you're on about."

Oh, yes you do, liar. Alex understood the attitude. As always, Lucas worked to abuse the occasion, as if it wasn't already his brother's habit to deflect and lie.

"It's all coming out, Lucas. You have ripped-off your brothers and everyone else you could. You're a drunk, a liar, a cheater, and a mujeriego—womanizer. For once, be straight with me. You may not have much time left, despite everything I've tried to do for you. You've pissed off too many people and they are stronger. Your own wife! Admit what you've done, brother."

Lucas rose and tottered from the kitchen.

Alex finished his eggs. He cleared the table and washed the dirty dishes in the kitchen. Through a mirror he watched Lucas silently go to the cabinet and remove a medium-sized black leather briefcase, surely containing the documents Morticia talked about. Alex hurried into the dining room, surprising Lucas. He asked his voice friendly, "What are you carrying there, bro?"

Lucas had the decency to blush, but his answer was his standard, "Nothing, Gato. Personal papers." He turned and slowly mounted the stairs to Ana's room.

It was another of Lucas's bad moves. He'd had a chance to come clean. Alex wasn't letting it be this time.

Chapter 18

The Virus

Friday, April 17, 2020

On Friday, when Alex returned from grocery shopping, Morticia was in the living room armchair. Surprised, he almost dropped the bags of food.

"Morticia what are you doing here?" A zing of fear shot through
him.

"I was discharged, Uncle. I'm fine, thanks."

Alex put the bags on the table and returned to the living room. "I'm relieved you're okay, but I'm concerned you've come contaminated with COVID 19 and will infect us all. This is risky for your dad, Morticia. At least put on a mask."

She made a face. "I'm fine. I wanted to talk to him. He needed to know I'm okay. Mami, too."

Alex groaned inwardly. His words were harsh. "Morticia, you've been in the hospital, and for sure you've been exposed to COVID. Your father can't risk exposure. If you pass it to him, he'll die."

Her face pinked slightly. Not quite contrite. "No,

Tío. I wasn't near those sick people. Really. I'm fine."

"I hope so, for Lucas's sake. Who brought you home?"

"Uncle Victor told the ambulance driver to bring me here. I was anxious to get home. See the kids. My parents."

Victor was well aware of the risk. Alex could not believe the blatant disregard of medical procedure committed by Dr. Victor Mata. He sent a little prayer to any deity listening to protect his family.

"Morticia, the hospital is the breeding ground. Please go home. You'll, infect your father. He's not strong enough to combat this plague. I insist you mask up when you see him."

"Oh, Uncle, it's just a virus."

Alex gave up. Morticia and Mata were signing a death warrant. The irony didn't escape him. Alex had been doing everything he could to keep his brother alive and safe from his enemies. He feared his family would be who killed him. Unfortunately, in his gut he knew Victor had won this round.

Morticia asked for help getting home. Although her house was a mere 300 meters away, Alex took his mother's wheelchair from under the stairs, helped Morticia to settle into it, and took her home.

In three days Morticia tested positive for COVID. Alex bought masks for the family and prayed again his brother had not been exposed.

Lucas fought against him every time Alex handed him a mask, but Alex won those skirmishes. Lucas wasn't stupid—just ornery.

Morticia was worse. She'd ripped off the mask as

soon as she exited the ambulance, refusing to put a fresh one on at Lucas's house—or her own.

Alex's days lengthened. Without Morticia's help, he was burdened with all of the household chores, as well as caring for Lucas. Ana refused to help, and even put in her personal orders for food. *Who is she kidding?*

On the twenty-fifth, what Alex feared could happen, happened. Not only Lucas came down with COVID, but Ana, Gabriel, and the children. Morticia was still in bed. Only Alex remained healthy. He kept himself double masked, gloved, and washed. Alex's fear was great. He understood perfectly well, with his brother's health conditions, the risk of death multiplied. Over the next several days, his brother got worse.

Lucas slept and lost weight. When Ana showed signs of contagion they went for tests at a local laboratory, receiving positive results. Only Alex was spared, confirming his theory of having built up immunity in Mexico City when he'd presented all the COVID symptoms early in the pandemic. Viru-Out had saved him, he was sure. Why hadn't he brought any to Veracruz?

With the entire family down with the virus, the household work became exhausting. Two houses of sick people to care for, feed, and clean up after. Ana was the worst. She required a special diet for her hypertension and diabetes. She was grossly overweight and at very high risk of complications. She fought him tooth and nail. He had scratches to prove it. It wasn't just feeding, it was bedpan, bathing, bed changing. In three days, Alex thought he'd keel over from the exertion.

When Mata found out about his sister and niece's infections, he sent specialists in infectious diseases to the houses. Not one checked Lucas. It was incredible. This convinced Alex his paranoia about Mata wanting to kill Lucas was correct.

In one of his brother's lucid moments, Alex described what was going on. He said, "You only exist when they want you to pay their bills. They talk to me demanding I pick up the medications. They've given me a list to pick up today. Can you believe it? Like I'm their pinche assistant. The bastard demanded I go today—and pay for Ana's medicine. I can't do this anymore, Lucas. I'm two weeks late for my new job. Castellanos isn't going to hold it forever. I can't afford to stay. Lucas, you've got to get better. I need to go back to work."

Lucas had fallen asleep again. Alex called over to Morticia's and asked her to cover things for an hour. She was almost well and could manage her boyfriend and her own children now, although she'd been lying in bed expecting him to wait on her.

"Get up. Take care of your parents. I'm going to the pharmacy for your mother's meds."

Alex resented caring for Ana. She hated him and let him know every time she saw him—especially since her confession. Now he'd spent another thousand pesos on medicine for her. A thousand pesos he couldn't afford. He may be on leave, but it was without pay.

He stashed the pills in his saddlebag and started back. Two blocks from the house, while stopped at a red light, an older model white Tsuru sped across the intersection and knocked him over. Traffic blocked the white car from running. The stopped cars honked. The driver got out of the Tsuru, helped Alex and the bike up.

He said, "Sorry man, foot slipped. You okay?" He fished into his pocket and drew out a wad of bills.

Alex inspected his bike. He didn't see any damage. His head was protected in his helmet, and he had on his leather jacket. He wasn't particularly hurt. "I should make a report. Insurance, you know."

Traffic honked again, impatient to go. The man, older, close-cropped brown hair shot through with grey, a ropy scar across his eyebrow, fanned the bills. "Why don't we settle right here."

Alex took the cash, and traffic started moving again. Later he counted his pay-off. His body ached where he'd hit the pavement on one side and where the heavy motorcycle had landed on the other. If he didn't need to go to the hospital—definitely not an IMSS—or a repair shop, he's just made couple grand. More than enough to return to Mexico and his life. The family would get well, and he'd be off.

The days passed and everyone was finally back to normal. Then Lucas began having more acute pain.

Chapter 19

The Injection

Wednesday, April 29, 2020

First he complained. Then he swore. Finally, he doubled over clutching his middle.

Lucas moaned. "Gato, you've got to do something. I can't take it anymore. Find me a doctor," he gasped out, sweat running down his face.

"Can you make it to Mexico City? I can take you to my doctor. We can trust her."

"Ay, pinche idiota." Lucas paused taking, short, shallow breaths. "I'll die before we arrive. Call Victor," he whispered.

Alex had considered that—but he was positive the man was trying to kill his brother. "How can we trust him?"

Lucas's skin had turned ashen. He struggled for breath. Maybe he could make a deal with Fierro? He'd been acting under Mata's directions as had the others. He gave Lucas's shoulder a gentle shake.

Lucas opened his eyes. "I'm dying, Alex."

Alex's hopes plummeted—the sensation of falling

with no net. His heart raced. "No! I won't let you. Hang on, Lucas. The doctor will be here soon." Lucas settled back into the recliner, closing his eyes again. His breathing slowed and a bit of normal color crept into his skin.

He considered Mata again. Alex could not erase the thought of the economic benefit Lucas's death would generate for Ana, and apparently for Mata as well. He'd overheard the two of them whispering—planning something to do with the transfers of assets Lucas had been making. He didn't know what, but he'd distinctly heard Ana say, "Alex should not find out." He'd heard by accident, as he passed by her room on the way to shower during the COVID crisis. The door had slammed and shortly after, Mata ran down the stairs and out of the house.

What was worse? Calling Mata, demanding he take care of his brother-in-law? Probably handing Lucas over to his assassin? Or letting him die here in his recliner in pain? They'd tried before—Morticia's story, complete with video, of the intubation—a direct attempt to kill him orchestrated by Ana's and Victor's cousin, Dr. Mateo Zambada. And the over-prescribing conflicting drugs? Drugs that would ultimately kill him? Alex's sense they wanted to murder his brother expanded. But why? Because Lucas betrayed his wedding vows? That was on Ana, not her family. For the money and assets? She was getting them anyway, and the longer Lucas earned, the more she'd get. *She* didn't add anything to the family coffers.

Alex watched Lucas fitfully sleep, his breath labored, but at least he wasn't suffering so much pain for the moment. Alex watched and thought, cell phone in-hand. Pressured by the obvious state of his brother's health, he forced himself to make a decision—to act. After meditating, analyzing, and praying for guidance, it was the cries of pain from Lucas that stabbed his heart.

He dialed.

"Victor Mata, how can I help you?"

"Victor, it's Alex. We need you to come. Now. Lucas is failing."

"I'm sorry, Alex," the doctor said, a note of glee belying his sympathy. "What symptoms does he present?"

After describing the details of each symptom he said, "Victor, I know you want to punish my brother. I don't know why. But haven't you done enough? Please, please—save him. You can stop the pain you are inflicting on Ana and Morticia. And me," he added. "Please, I'm begging you. We're all still reeling from Irene's death. It will kill Morticia. She idolizes her father."

Mata's voice was gruff, angry. "I don't know what bullshit you are talking about. He's my family too. I can't get to the house right now, but if you come here, I'll have pain medicine ready for you at the information desk. Is Ana aware of what's happening?"

"I don't know what she thinks. You know full well she avoids me." Alex lifted the SUV keys from the hook in the kitchen. "I'm leaving now."

When he reached the main avenue, he realized the traffic was intense. Schools had just let out. The sidewalk was filled with uniformed children running around, mothers pushing strollers gathering the older kids, trains of families holding hands, weaving through the people and cars stopped to collect them.

It would be worse in front of the high school, where a taco stand on the curb would have a huge crowd of teens surrounding it, spilling into the street. The teens paid no attention to traffic, crossing anywhere. Those with cars sped around, showing off. It would take thirty minutes to crawl through this traffic. He made a U-turn racing home for his motorcycle. In twenty minutes, he arrived at the IMSS No. 51, drove onto the crowded sidewalk, chained the bike, and ran into the building, dialing Mata.

Mata met him at the main reception desk and handed over a small bag. Alex slid out the hypodermic needle and a box containing an ampule with a rubber stopper, the prescription affixed to the box.

"Thank you, Victor. I'm able to administer this." He turned and ran back to his motorcycle. He'd been gone for forty-five minutes, all the while praying Lucas hung on. Accelerating, he passed cars at excessive speeds, driving between the lanes—no risk too great.

The gods watched over him. In no more than fifteen minutes, he ran into the house. Lucas was not in the recliner. Frantically he called out, but no one answered. Taking three steps at a time, he checked the guest room. Not in the bathroom. Up the next flight, shouting, "Lucas, Lucas?" No answer. He wasn't on the third floor. Desperate, thinking the worst, he sprinted to the fourth floor and found Morticia. His heart pounded in his chest and his legs wobbled. Panting from the exertion he took a deep breath and approached his niece.

"Hurry, Uncle. Papi can't take the pain anymore.

Hurry!"

Lucas lay on the couch grasping his heart. His breathing was shallow, labored, and the feral sounds he made alarmed Alex. Was Lucas having a heart attack?

He removed the small bag of pain killer from his leather jacket. Pulled the contents out onto the table and read the label. "Oh no! This is NUBAIN. Lucas can't take it." He shrugged off the jacket, letting it drop to the floor and pulled his phone from his jeans pocket. A quick Google search confirmed his suspicions: NUBAIN was contraindicated to generate respiratory arrest in alcoholics within twenty minutes.

"Morticia," he barked. "Call Victor. He needs something else; this will kill him." He went to his brother and tried to calm him.

Morticia shot a hate-filled glance at Alex, then turned to her father. He writhed, his breathing rapid and shallow, the pain obviously unbearable. She dialed her uncle, punched on the speaker, and cried out, "Uncle you must come. Papi will die if he takes the painkiller you sent. Tío Alex read me the contraindications. Papi can't take it. He's in so much pain. What can we do? Hurry!"

Alex's stomach dropped and murderous energy surged through him as he listened to Mata's reply.

"Tell Alex to apply half. I'm on my way." He hung up.

"No!" he shouted. "Morticia. I can't administer this. It'll kill him. It's better we find another doctor for a second opinion."

Hysterical, Morticia screamed, "Alex, you are not a doctor. If my Uncle Victor says it's okay, then it's okay."

She glowered at him. *"Poncela!"* she shouted, demanding he administer the drug.

Alex shouted right back. "I refuse to do it. If you want to kill my brother, your own father, do it yourself!" He threw the medicine onto the couch and turned away from Morticia, clenching his fists.

She drew a syringe from the bag and began to extract the drug. She refused to look at Alex who watched, horrified. With the syringe ready, she commanded her father to pull down his pants.

Lucas felt relief almost immediately, his face transformed from pain to relief to relaxation. Alex saw he was under the influence of the opioid. Lucas actually was smiling. He asked for more. Morticia started to refill the syringe, but Alex slapped her hand away, stopping her. She yelped and opened her mouth to argue. He held up his phone, the timer running, and shook his head.

In exactly twenty minutes, Lucas began to gasp and clutch at his chest. "Morticia, give me more. I feel really bad. It's not working. I'm dying."

Alarmed, this time Alex called Mata.

"Victor Mata—"

"Lucas can't breathe. He's having a terrible reaction to the NUBAIN. What do we do? How soon can you get here?"

"I'm at the door, Alex. Let me in."

Alex ran down jumping the steps three by three, opened the door and hustled Mata to the penthouse. As they passed her door, Ana, called out, "Victor? What's going on?"

Mata didn't answer.

Lucas was suffocating. Morticia, terrified crouching at the edge of the sofa, wailed, "What's wrong with you, Papi? Don't die, please don't die."

"We have to get him to the hospital immediately," Mata ordered.

Alex watched as Lucas, making a superhuman effort, stood up and said, "I'll be okay, my daughter."

To Alex he whispered, "Gato, take care of my wallet. I left it in my mother's bureau in the bedroom. And my phone. Get my phone. It's in the socks."

Morticia clung to his arm, sobbing. Alex grabbed his own phone and hurried to steady Lucas down the three flights of stairs. As they reached the second floor. Ana opened the door of her room. Alex recognized the farewell in her eyes when she saw Lucas' face. She knew. She'd been waiting for this. Her husband was dead in life to her, but it would be the last time she would see him alive. She hugged him and started to cry.

Lucas stiffened. The pained expression crossing his face was for everything had lost, not for his physical body. He turned away from her without hugging her back as Alex drew him toward the last flight of stairs. He wanted so badly to say, *Ana, you got what you wanted. Your brother and your daughter have killed your husband.*

In the driveway, Alex helped him board the SUV, then ran to the driver's side. Victor and Morticia got into Victor's truck. Alex led the caravan to the IMSS Cuauhtémoc five minutes away, Morticia called his cell.

"Tío, they won't admit him. We have to go to the other hospital."

"No. My brother's condition is critical; every minute counts."

Mata took Morticia's cell phone. "Then don't waste time arguing. Follow me."

Alex had no choice. The drive felt eternal. Lucas coughed and gasped and moaned on the backseat. They must have hit every red light, traffic snarl, and police slowdown. Finally, Alex pulled up the ramp to the emergency entrance. Victor, Morticia, the administrator holding Lucas's red admittance card, and several nurses, waited in front of the door. They quickly transferred Lucas from the SUV to a gurney and in a blur of activity, disappeared into the hospital.

Alex was left to park the SUV. It didn't take him more than three minutes to mask up and return to the emergency room, but by the time he found Lucas, the doctors had already intubated him.

On the verge of exploding in rage, he shouted, "How could you allow that? You know perfectly well your father gave instructions that he wasn't to be intubated."

Morticia cringed, hanging her head. An attending doctor intervened and said, "You didn't see your brother collapse. The Director didn't say anything, and they went ahead with procedure."

Lucas' condition was critical. Victor shoved a series of documents in front of Morticia to sign. He also thrust papers at Alex; he rapidly gave instructions, pointing to signature lines, without allowing either of them time to read them over. "Hurry, there's no time to lose. Lucas is critical. We have to get him to intensive care."

Alex's nerves burned him up. He felt hopeless, beyond desperate. He signed the one document, which negated everything Lucas had requested. His brother was denied his final requests. As he flipped through the copy he'd been handed, he saw that Victor Mata and Morticia had authorized it all. He paced the waiting area as Morticia disappeared with her uncle.

With all that talk of "no time to lose", Lucas wasn't transferred out of the Emergency Unit for two hours. Alex trailed him up to the second floor but was blocked from entering his room.

Hours later, he was allowed to visit his brother. The array of medical devices installed on Lucas to keep him alive for a few more moments overwhelmed him. Lucas was alive only for the devices. This, he thought as he sat down in the single chair, is exactly what Lucas did not want. He leaned toward the bed, took his brother's icy hand, and started to talk.

Alex remembered the happy moments they lived as children. He affectionately patted Lucas' naked arm, the skin responded with goosebumps, and tears seeped from both brother's eyes.

A doctor Alex didn't recognize approached him. "Are you a relative?"

Alex was unable to form words around the lump blocking his throat. He nodded.

She asked, "What happened? He was my patient in the E.R. and he was not like this when he came in."

Alex shrugged, silently shaking his head. His dismay and sense of culpability overtaking his ability to communicate. The doctor understood, and without a word, squeezed his shoulder. He felt her kind sentiment more than heard her words. "I'll leave you to your loss. Feel better."

He watched her walk away, her shoulders slumped.

The kind E.R. doctor's comments got him thinking again. "Everything is wrong, Lucas. Too many coincidences. This smacks of planning. Treachery. They murdered you."

Lucas's eyelids fluttered. He seemed to squeeze Alex's hand. Alex squeezed back. It was his only touchstone. Lucas's hand the single safety line preventing Alex's mind from spinning out of control. He lay his cheek on the edge of the bed trying to grasp the swirling thoughts. Nothing made sense. He'd called Mata, gotten a drug Mata knew would kill his brother. Mata standing on the doorstep exactly when Lucas started to die. The wrong hospital, the waiting attendants, the authorizations signed by Mata, not him. The life support. Why did Mata want Lucas dead? What did Ana's brother have to do with anything?

Lucas's voice swirled, a matter of the. . .of the? It was a matter of *skirts*. Ana's voice joined the mental cacophony, "He betrayed our family."

Alex bolted upright. Victor and Ana were in it together and that's because Lucas betrayed them both. What had happened with Victor's first wife?

Alex squeezed Lucas's hand again. "I know what you did, brother, but you didn't deserve this. I promise you, Lucas, I'll make them pay."

Chapter 20

The Hospital

Broken hearted and disillusioned, Alex said goodbye to what was left of his older brother. An inflatable doll, managed by tubes and pumps. He dragged out of the Intensive Care unit intending to return to Lucas's house and collect his motorcycle, then to Irene's for the kitten and his personal things. He hated that his brother was kept alive solely for Mata to be able to justify the misadministration of the medication. And administered by the director of a hospital, which was not Lucas's assigned IMSS. Everything was clear now, there was no possibility of recovery. The only thing left was for Director Victor Mata to pull the plug and deliver the news. And it would be Victor, with flowers, soft words, hugs—for Morticia—while he and his evil sister winked and gloated.

Alex descended to the ground floor, found Morticia. He tried to show a kind face so as not to worry her anymore, but he was so angry. *So angry.* His expression said everything. Morticia jumped out of her chair, tried to run past him. Alex blocked her. She started to cry. Oh, how he wanted to slam his fist into her face; to pound her into dust. Instead, he fixed her with his stare, a bug wriggling on a pin.

"Morticia, I warned you."

She turned her sad countenance toward him. He saw how gaunt she was. Her hair had a few streaks of gray. With the strain of the recent months lines carved around her eyes and mouth. It was obvious she knew what she'd done. And Morticia was paying—would pay for the rest of her life. Alex held out his hand to her. She stuffed a packet of papers into it.

"What's this?"

Her voice quavered. Speaking to the floor she said, "Uncle Victor sent me to an emotional support psychologist to help me. According to him, I'm emotionally delicate and this trauma on top of my operation might harm my health. Of course he's right. I had to sign some papers for treatment."

Then the decision to pull the plug had been made. Victor was preparing Morticia for the news. Half of his heart wanted to see her suffer. The other half ached for this woman who had been so betrayed by her own mother and uncle. He repacked his rage and grief into a deep fold within his heart and turned a calm exterior toward his niece. "I'll walk with you."

They walked in silence to the consultation room door, each suffering their personal hell.

"Morticia, call me when you're done; I'll take you somewhere to eat. You must be starving," he said, knowing she probably wouldn't call. As much as he hated her at this moment, he didn't want to leave her alone in the web of cover-up.

He knew what was coming, and Morticia was going to be devastated. Lucas had been her hero, just like

Enrique Deltoro Bandenboosh had been to him. He knew the loss. It was something you never forgot. And when Morticia found out the truth? He couldn't allow his imagination to go there.

Alex envisioned the ritual to disconnect Lucas. He pictured that final gasp. The satisfied smirk on Mata's face, the phony condolences, the hysterics of their shared niece. The moment was coming. He felt it settling onto his shoulders, the darkness closing around him. His limbs weighed heavy on the short walk to the parking lot.

He unlocked the motorcycle, mounted, and headed toward Lucas's in a thick fog. He would talk with his sister-in-law. He parked, locked the gate, and let himself into the entry hall. Ana sat at the dining table. When she saw him she started to rise.

"Not this time, Ana. We have to talk." He unzipped his leather jacket and removed the packet of papers he brought from the hospital, tossed them down. "You probably already know. The hospital is going to disconnect my brother from his life support today. Morticia is in counseling to help her survive this. You've ruined her life, Ana. Now you will complete your responsibilities to this family." He scraped a chair out from under the table and sat down heavily. Rifling the documents, he pulled out those requiring her signature and pushed them toward her.

Ana kept her lips pursed, face stony. Alex saw the red, swollen eyes and the muddy tracks of mascara tracing her cheeks. *What was she crying about? She'd completed her mission.* Her husband was going to be dead within the day.

169

"Here's what you are going to do. First, if you or the Mata family ever let your daughter know you were behind this, I'll personally send you to hell. Do you understand me, Ana?"

She lifted her chin defiantly, glaring at her brother-in-law, but she did not argue or try to defend herself. "Give me a pen."

After she signed, Alex said, "Where are the rest of Lucas's documents? The will, his instructions, and his wishes. He told me they are in a black briefcase—the case I saw him carry to your room some days ago."

"I don't know what you're talking about, Alex. I wish you'd take your things and leave."

"I will not, Ana. Not until I've received my brother's papers and you've taken care of the funeral arrangements in accordance with his wishes. You owe it to the husband who has given you everything you have."

"Oh, don't be so dramatic, Alex. Lucas will get well. After all, weeds and cockroaches never die."

"What a hypocrite you are. Cold." Was it his imagination, or was she wearing a malevolent grin? "Just do it. It's a matter of hours now."

"Me? A hypocrite? I didn't fuck my brother's wife. I didn't fuck my brother's second wife or my cousin's wife. I didn't turn him into a drunk. I didn't make him mis-manage our money or be a weak momma's boy, doing Irene's bidding over taking care of his own family. Oh, no, you fool, my husband did it all by himself, and I had enough."

"Well, Ana, in two days, Lucas will be dead and buried. Get the papers, call the funeral home."

Alex's last words as he slammed his way out of the

house were, "Do it, it's a matter of hours." He swung into Lucas's SUV and returned to the hospital to wait for his niece to call.

The call came. "Ten minutes," she said. Alex lounged against Lucas's SUV in front. Twenty minutes passed, then thirty. Wasn't this an awfully long therapy session? But what could he do besides wait? He wasn't sure he could trust Mata. The man acted like he loved his niece, but what if it was just that? An act? *No. I can't think like this.* He waited.

Alex's cell phone rang again. He activated it to hear Morticia crying.

"Bueno? Morticia, I'm here."

"Where, Uncle? I can't see you."

Her sobs made it hard for Alex to understand her. "Where am I? In front. Right on the street. I'll come in. Meet me in the main hall in front of the door."

He sprinted to the agreed meeting spot.

Morticia walked toward him zombie like, shuffling, unseeing. He was crestfallen. One look at the woman said she had not been spared any pain.

"Morticia! Over here," he called, waving as he approached her. She looked right through him, disoriented. In shock.

Alex hugged his niece without saying a word. How could he comfort her when she'd pulled the trigger? The pain was unbearable for both of them. He took her by the hand and led her to a nearby restaurant. Food would do them both some good. He doubted she had eaten since the morning. Nor had he.

Inside, he guided her to a table and seated her. Sitting made him feel a bit more comfortable; it probably helped her too. Morticia's absent stare gave way with the familiar sounds and smells of food. She looked at Alex and started to cry again. He let her cry, passing over a few napkins from the dispenser. She blew her nose and looked him directly in the eyes,

"Papi isn't getting better, Tío." She hiccupped and wiped her eyes. "Just like you said. How did you know, and Uncle Victor didn't?"

Alex reached across the table and took her hand. He couldn't answer. He wouldn't lie to her. It would kill her. Instead, he asked, "How did your session go?"

"Pure stupidity. They, there were two of them with me—I don't think either actually was a licensed psychologist. They said I had to be strong. For my mother's sake. I laughed at that. Where was Mami today? Not with my Papi."

Alex felt his heart crack open. For the family. For himself, but mostly for his brother alive because of machines. He deserved to lose his wife, but he didn't deserve to die. Alex stood and gathered his niece into his arms. She unleashed a torrent of tears.

The waiter hovering behind them had the sense to vanish.

Alex slowly pulled away from the embrace after a minute or so. He took Morticia's chin gently with both hands and looked into her eyes. "It hurts me to see you like this, beautiful. I think it would be better if we go home."

"Yes, please, Alex."

He guided her to the door, thanked the hostess, and dropped a fifty peso note onto the counter.

They drove directly to Morticia's house.

"Do you want to stay here or go to your parents' house."

"I want to be alone, Uncle. I don't want to see anyone."

Her raw pain cut him to the quick. How she must be suffering. "I'll ask Gabriel to sleep in with the boys."

Alex opened the passenger door, took Morticia's arm, and led her inside her house and to her room. Gabriel was with the boys watching T.V. Alex explained what had happened and asked he let her be alone. He said goodbye with a hollow feeling, not sure Gabriel was up to caring for Morticia, but he had to see his sister-in-law. Had Ana prepared the documents and made the arrangements? Lucas' transfer to the funeral home could be at any moment.

He rang the doorbell several times. He could use his key, but without Lucas, he knew he wasn't welcome, and he didn't feel right about it. He waited. Rang again. Ana didn't answer.

He stood outside the house for fifteen minutes, called Morticia—he needed to check on her anyway. But talking to her mother was a priority. If Ana wasn't here, that's where she would be.

The phone rang once. "Is that you, Tío? I feel so bad."

"I know you do dear, but do you know where your mother is?"

"No. I'll call her and get back to you."

Alex's head had begun to pound. He was so weary. All he wanted was a hot shower and to curl up with his little fuzzball, Daisi.

The phone rang. "My mom says she'll come down and open the door. She was in the bath."

Ana dawdled for five minutes, leaving him on the stoop. *To annoy me.* When she finally opened the door, he entered but they did not exchange a word. Alex noticed that her hair was dry, and her clothes were the same ones she wore hours earlier. She headed directly up the stairs.

He roughly grabbed her arm to stop her. "We'll make this short, Ana. I don't want any more to do with you than you want with me, but we need to take care of Lucas's wishes. Give me his documents and I'll get out of your hair." He gave her a little shake before he let her go.

She seethed, replying angrily, "No! I will know wh· when it's necessary." She fled to her room.

Alex lay down on the couch in the living room.

The night stretched toward morning. His phone rang—the hospital. Ana's door banged open and she and called down to Alex. He ran upstairs, knowing she'd just been informed.

Ana stepped into the hall with a mournful look.

"Your brother is dead."

Chapter 21

The Mourning

Thursday, April 30, 2020

A dark fog enveloped Alex. It filled the hallway, clouded his eyes, chilled his blood. His heart turned to stone. Lucas was dead; his brother was dead. The fog billowed, dissipated, leaving Alex staring at his sister-in-law who regarded him from her doorway. No hint of sadness. She delivered the news, but the loss of her husband? Not a flicker of remorse in her eyes. Ana closed her door—and that was it.

Alex's eyes moistened but he shed no tears. He knew this would happen. He had prepared for this moment. He crept back downstairs to collect his things. This house, its hate-filled vibes and infirmities. And Ana Deltoro née Mata—killer. *The she-devil.* She'd killed him. Worse, she'd intentionally caused her own daughter to murder her father.

From one moment to the next, everything changed. His family was gone. Alex was alone. He picked up his jacket from the floor where he dropped it. He found his bag in a corner, the laptop on the table where he last opened it. His shaving kit remained on the back of the half-bath toilet, a sweater in the corner. His minimal presence in this house left no trace. He would walk out the door and leave nothing of his occupation, especially the love he held for his brother. Regardless of what a disaster alcohol and greed had made of Lucas—they were still family.

He paced the living room and library off it, checking for anything he might have missed. There was the book he'd been reading. He replaced it on its shelf. They read books together as children. Lucas changed in adolescence, left Alex behind. Always abuses and problems, drugs and drink. But even so, Alex held a sincere love for Lucas—for his whole family. For Alex, there was nothing more important than his father and brothers. Like Morticia for Lucas, he thought.

But Lucas is dead. Alex had failed to prevent it.

The cool night air on the short ride refreshed him. Some of the weight he carried lightened as the distance from the Deltoro-Mata house increased. Idly he wondered if anyone had called his niece. He turned into Las Brisas then left into Calle la Islas. The *cerrada* was quiet. The roar of the motorcycle echoing off the stucco houses deafened him. The gate clanged like an alarm behind the bike. Even the rattle of the chain sounded ghoulish. But there was Daisi at the door waiting for him. She meowed and rubbed against his ankles purring. Alex scooped the little cat into his arms and let the tears flow.

He awoke when the first ray of sun sliced across his bed through the hastily closed curtain. He'd slept fitfully. Between the terrible events of the day before, and the dread of endless arrangements and posturing to come, sleep did not refresh him. A zombie, he moved through the shadowed house on automatic. He fed the cat, prepared scrambled eggs, which he barely touched. He bathed, dressing in jeans and a dark tee-shirt pulled from a bag of dirty clothes. They didn't stink too bad, but he didn't much care. He finished the carafe of coffee. Made another.

Finally, the caffeine kicked in and his fog brain cleared. It was going to be a long, tense, emotionally fraught day. He hoped he was wrong, and Ana had taken on the planning—*yeah, when pigs fly.* Alex opened the computer and called up a new Word doc. to make a checklist of all the tasks needing completion before Lucas would rest in peace.

1.Check on Morticia, give her the news
2.Get the folder of Lucas's wishes and arrangements
3.Talk to Ana/divide up the work

Then what? He didn't know and closed the laptop. It all hinged on Ana, but from what he saw last night, she wasn't going to participate. He packed the computer back into the bag, tucked his wallet into his pocket, which reminded him of his promise to Lucas— secure the wallet and cell phone. He stiffened, the hot prickles of tears stinging his eyes. *No!* Alex had too much to do to *feel.* He pushed his emotions into a lockbox in his heart and ran up to find and hide the wallet. It was right where Lucas said it would be. He moved it into a Ziploc bag and buried it into the bottom of the dish cabinet, Daisi looking on.

"You remind me, kitty girl. I might forget," he said, giving her head a scratch.

A glance at his watch told Alex he'd better get going. If he didn't arrive at Morticia's house soon, Ana might already have given her the news by phone. He preferred to do it in person. He knew her well and was sure that she would be hysterical. Alex gave the bike more gas. Three minutes later he was ringing the doorbell.

Morticia looked down from her second-floor window and locked eyes with Alex. "NO, TELL ME THAT MY DAD IS NOT DEAD!" she screamed.

"Let me in."

She thundered down the stairs and flipped the door lock.

She threw open the door, desperately grabbed Alex by the shoulders, shaking him, screaming, "What is happening, Uncle?"

Alex put his hands on Morticia's arms. "I'm in as much pain as you." He embraced her, crooning, "Your dad has gone ahead of us; he is in Heaven resting."

Morticia's, "NO!" deafened Alex. She sobbed, repeating, "Tell me it's not true."

He hugged her tighter. "Morticia, I wish it weren't so, but we have to join forces now more than ever to face this great blow." He paused to let her relax then said, "Come with me, let's go to your mother's house, I think she needs you now."

Ana lay in the recliner, gazing into space. The black case sat on the side table. Without looking at him, she extracted the folder and held it out. Alex took it from her hand and carried it to the dining room table.

All the documentation was there. He read for five minutes then contacted the funeral home by phone. It was the same placid, platitude-filled voice that took the details, much of which were already with the director. He assured Alex payment had been made.

The director gave him an estimated time for the family to arrive. The wake room and services would be ready at nine the next morning for guests to say goodbye to Lucas.

Because the facilities were far from the center of Veracruz, Alex decided to use their bus transportation to the municipality of Medellín where the facilities were located. The director suggested dividing into three trips for the comfort of the attendees.

With the arrangements for the funeral made, Alex took on the task of informing Lucas's family and friends of the bad news. Ana should be doing this, he thought. But Ana was unsuccessfully trying to calm Morticia, who wailed uncontrollably. Probably because Ana's words sounded insincere.

The first bus left at 8:15 a.m. Ana and her close relatives met at the house at seven-thirty. Among them, Victor Mata, who sidestepped every time Alex came near him; Ana's sister Gela and her daughter Leticia; Ana's cousin Mateo Zambada Mata, Morticia and her family, and friends of Lucas. In total about twenty people rode the bus. In the wake room, the crowd swelled to forty attendees.

Because COVID was at one of its worst moments, many people did not show up, but expressed their condolences by phone, calling Ana throughout the morning. Alex eavesdropped on several of the calls. Ana couldn't have been accused of graciousness, but she modulated her voice sufficiently that people who didn't know what had happened between Lucas and his wife weren't going to gossip.

The day dragged. The officiant performed a perfunctory service. The rosaries lacked luster. Ana sequestered herself in one of the bedrooms set aside for the family for most of the afternoon and night. Only the testimonials offered a bit of diversion from the senseless, sad affair. Lucas's work friends and colleagues turned out to be some fun-loving dudes. They recounted trips, parties, drinking, gambling. Some remembered others who had passed. Most from cancers of various sorts. They joked about the heavenly reunion Lucas was having.

Alex wasn't surprised so many had died from cancer. Most of Lucas's friends worked at the nuclear plant. Victor would have known this and used the knowledge to his advantage in the plot to kill Alex's brother. When he couldn't stand it any longer, he wandered out through the gate and turned down a narrow tree-lined lane to the river.

Warm sun sparkled off the calm water. Alex sat down on the bank and watched ducks poke about the reeds, breathing the perfumed air until he emptied of thoughts. The pain subsided. He closed his eyes and let the emptiness subsume him until he floated in nothingness. A loud quack and flapping of wings on water woke him up. It was time to return to the frigid room.

Eventually Lucas's body was removed to the crematorium, the last of the boisterous friends left, and the family and close friends settled down to mourn in the quiet of the cold, hothouse-flower-scented room. Alex sat with Morticia to await the urn holding Lucas's ashes. He felt like they were the only two who truly mourned. Certainly not Ana, or Victor Mata, holed up in that room. *Getting their stories straight?* At least they did not join Victor's wife, or the rest of that side of Ana's family having a grand time in the restaurant on Lucas's dime.

The director appeared two hours later with the silver urn and handed it to Morticia with the same gentle words he used weeks before when he handed across Irene's cremains. *You'd think they'd use a new script.*

Mata rounded up his family and everyone returned to the bus, the last of the day. When the transport arrived at what was once Lucas' home, Alex got out and waited for Ana to open the door and let her relatives pass inside. Trailing, he entered and beelined for the penthouse.

Lucas had said he hid his phone, "in the socks". Alex opened several drawers looking for socks. When he found the socks, the phone was not there. He open drawer after drawer searching. He couldn't find Lucas's cellphone anywhere.

Only Morticia had been present. Could she have taken her father's phone? Why? Lucas must have something important on that phone. Probably photos Morticia shouldn't see. How could he get it from her?

Alex picked up a beer he had no intention of drinking and wandered into the living room. The only sad face belonged to his niece. The rest laughed, joked, caught up. Food and plenty of drinks covered every surface. He sidled over to Morticia standing alone at the edge of the velvet curtains covering the front window. In a low voice he asked about the cell phone.

"Yes, I have it, but I'm not going to give it to you. It was my dad's and I'm going to give it to my mom. She asked me for it."

Alex adjusted the surprise and alarm from his face. She'd never turn it over if she thought it was important. Maybe her mother's interest had alerted her already. It confirmed what he guessed. Lucas wanted to hide something.

Alex gently said, "Niece, your dad specifically asked me to take care of it." He gave her what he hoped was his most compelling look of sadness and sincerity. "I don't want to let him down." His face dropped and he sniffed. "I failed him, Morticia."

Morticia hugged him. "We all failed him. I knew he drank too much. Don't worry, Uncle. You don't need to know; you cared for Papi."

He was too late; they had already investigated the information Lucas' phone hid. He stopped insisting. He'd aroused enough suspicion. *God, Lucas, what did they find?*

The next day the novena began. Alex had never understood the nine days of prayers and rosaries said for two hours each day to say goodbye. Alex arrived thirty minutes early. To avoid the Mata family, he ambled into the kitchen. Puff pastry sandwiches with mole inside, croissants with ham and yellow cheese, sweet bread and coffee for the guests. Better than his meager lunch at Irene's. He still hadn't had time to shop. He snatched a mole-filled puff pastry and a croissant, consuming them on the spot. People were arriving. He decided to move the food out to the dining room table.

Leticia, Ana's niece, saw him struggling with the door. She ran over and held it open, then carried out the rest of the trays with him.

"You're Alex, Lucas's brother. You probably don't remember me. I'm Leticia. Mom is Ana's sister."

"Of course I remember you, Leticia. I'm so sorry for your loss. I tried to offer condolences yesterday but somehow never crossed your path. Thanks for the help."

"Yeah, your bother was a fun guy. It's a shame. He was still so young."

Something in her eyes belied her words. Luckily Morticia arrived.

"Oh, Morticia, your mom asked for you. She's upstairs with mine. Come on, let's go up."

In moments, Ana's raspy voice filtered down the stairs. An argument had broken out. Alex took the stairs two at a time. Should he go in? The door stood open.

Ana shouted, "You had nothing to do with my husband? What do these little messages mean, Leticia. Listen, how nicely you talk." He leaned in, the sound was low. A recording of a woman's voice saying some very provocative things.

Ana continued, her voice rising, "How much did you get from that rich man you fucked? It was my husband Leticia—your uncle! But you couldn't have looked for another man, could you? You're a hopeless whore. Is this what your mother taught you?" She was crying now, and concluded her talk by shouting "Leave my house immediately."

Leticia fled through the door so quickly Alex couldn't hide. As he leapt out of her way, he saw inside the room. Victor and Ana's sister were there. Leticia continued her exit, almost running. Alex turned to go, glancing again into Ana's room, directly into Mata's baleful eyes.

Alex went down to greet the arrivals and get the novena started. He was not fanatical about religion, but he tried to fulfill his obligation as a Catholic. Morticia followed, first pulling him into the kitchen. "What do you think of how my father behaved, Uncle? I'm ashamed of him. Did you know about this? It hurts me how my mother feels."

Alex nearly shouted, answering the question, "What you did is unconscionable, you all violated my brother's privacy, which means a very serious lack of respect as well. Without justifying his faults, the one who seeks finds, Morticia, and that is what you and your mother did." He spun and stormed out.

Ana stopped him in the dining room, forcing him back to the kitchen. "What do you know about it, Alex? I'm tired of you. Leave my house." She shoved the phone into his hands. "Come back when you're ready to admit to what a waste of space my husband was."

Alex bit down on his tongue to hold back the retort he longed to shout over the rooftops, *You Ana. You and your brother and your daughter. You all murdered him!* He stepped past her to the living room but turned away, unable to concentrate on the ritual. He was shaking with rage. What great consequences and family damage would the information on Lucas' phone generate? He made his way to the door, then turned back. Mata's defiant, hateful gaze fixed on him.

Chapter 22

The Robbery

Friday, May 8, 2020

Alex brooded throughout the next week. At first he slept, exhausted physically, and drained emotionally from all that had transpired. His family was gone. His in-laws shunned him. Even Morticia, his ally though all the terrible and heartbreaking events since he left for Veracruz on March 29th, had abandoned him. He needed to be alone. He closed the windows, locked the doors, turned on the air-conditioning, and slept, the little cat by his side.

His dreams filled with dread. Masked doctors with hypodermic needles dripping red chasing him through hospital corridors. Cars speeding toward him without lights. Ana laughing, as she dragged him from his house. His fears seemed endless. When he awoke, he only had enough energy to feed Daisi before he had to sleep again.

On the third day after his eviction from the novena, Alex awoke rested, although his body felt beaten, aching for food and a gym. Not his emotions; they bled.

He fixed himself a large breakfast of potatoes cooked with onions, a jalapeño he found in the crisper, and half a longanisa sausage that didn't look moldy, topping the pile with three fried eggs. He poured himself a fresh cup of coffee and carried breakfast to the table to devour as his thoughts devoured him.

Ana. She was the nexus.

He pictured the scene outside the house after she'd shoved Lucas's phone into his hands. Instead of attending the novena, Ana followed him screaming nasty accusations and complaints against his brother. *What did she think I could have done about it?* Yet she blamed *him*.

"I gave you that phone, so you'd know what garbage your brother is. Just wait until you see. He's taken advantage of you too, Alex, so don't act so righteous."

He had replied, "I'm sorry, Ana. I'm sorry for everything. How would I have known he betrayed you? What should I have done?" *Except hidden the phone better.*

"You're an ignorant fool. He's betrayed you too! And don't think I'll come pick up the pieces for you. Get off my property."

He had looked past her toward the house. Her guests crowded the window, watching. Head high, he marched into the garage, put on his helmet, wheeled the motorcycle to the alleyway. Firing it up, he roared out of the callejon.

He washed down another tortilla-wrapped bite of egg with his now-cold coffee. *Poor Ana.* He felt sorry for her, but he carried critical information in the cell phone he thought he could use to better interact with Lucas's family in the future.

If he could unlock it.

Eating wore Alex out. He went back to bed, but this time he couldn't rest. Lucas's behavior appalled him. Ana was right. His brother was a self-centered, greedy pig. "Garbage" she'd called him. The contents of the phone was not his business, but he had to know. He sat up and plucked the device from his bedside drawer. For the next forty-five minutes he tried every possible password combination he could think of with no luck. He decided to get up and hire a cell phone workshop to hack the access code.

The cold shower improved his energy, and clean clothes lifted his spirits. He'd heard there was a plaza of tech repair shops in the port. He wheeled his motorcycle out of Irene's garage and traveled south to Veracruz's center, a fifteen-minute trip.

Circling through the congested streets, he found the computer plaza, a sprawling indoor market of about two hundred stalls dedicated to the repair and sale of cell phones and computers. Alex hurried to catch a technician willing to crack the code before closing at eight p.m. It was 7:35. After visiting three businesses that did not want to do this work, he was ready to call it quits. But he was here. *Might as well try one more.*

The owner of the fourth agreed to perform the job. Alex thought the phone would be opened immediately, but the man explained the process and the work ahead of him. He had to wait. The technician would call when the phone was open. At least the price was reasonable.

It had been several days since his last encounter with Ana and Victor Mata. He did not attend the novenas for Lucas. He felt sad, but he wanted to avoid a new confrontation with his sister-in-law. Anyway, he was still feeling lethargic and heavy. When he tried to sleep, he couldn't. His mind would not stop churning over the events since he arrived. He ached with guilt. Guilt for not realizing the depth of the problems, for not protecting Lucas—for not saving his life. Yet when he got up to do something, all he wanted was sleep.

If he could just set it aside—the "mistake" made by Dr. Víctor Mata. How was it possible the doctor did not know the contraindications of the drug? Then, ignoring Alex's warning of the side effects of the medication he prescribed, he still gave instructions to his niece to administer it. How could it be a mistake? The strangest part of the incident, however—Mata had driven to the house before it was reported that Lucas was reacting badly. In exactly twenty minutes. Morticia hadn't seemed to notice, consumed as she was by her own guilt and grief.

Alex wanted to justify his medical negligence due to lack of experience in this type of patient, since his specialty was gynecology and obstetrics. He couldn't. That last look Mata had given Alex when Ana ran him out? No, Victor Mata knew exactly what he was doing. And Ana had told him why.

On Thursday Alex contacted the technician cracking Lucas' cell phone. It wouldn't be ready for another day. Annoyed, Alex said, "We agreed it would be opened by today."

"It is more complicated than I thought. Your brother used two-step verification. That meant I've had to crack two codes."

"When shall I come?"

"Three tomorrow."

The next day, on the way to pick up the cell phone, he passed by Pancho López's house. Pancho was in the cerrada washing his car, and signaled Alex to stop. As usual Pancho wanted all the gossip on Lucas's death, but Alex said over the rumble of the motor, "Can't stop, güey. I have to pick up my phone from the repair."

"I hear you, man. I tried you a couple of times and wondered why I hadn't heard back. I thought you might like to go out for a beer. How long you going to be? Let's meet after you're done."

"Sure, where?"

"Same cantina."

Alex hadn't much liked the place. It was lower than a dive—a putero, hooker bar, but he said, "Okay, Poncho, see you at four-thirty."

Alex arrived at the electronics repair just before three. The technician showed him the cell phone was unlocked with all the information intact. He paid the bill. The small success made him feel stronger. He slipped the phone into his pants pocket, retrieved his motorcycle from the parking lot, and headed north to his appointment with Poncho, arriving thirty minutes early. It was a nice day, sunny and not too humid. He decided to wait for his friend outside. Poncho showed up early too. *Maybe things have started going my way.*

Inside, they found a table across from the bar and ordered the usual caguamas, toasting each other and the pleasant day. Like before, Poncho swilled his at almost three times the speed of Alex, who took it easy. By the time Alex was asking the slutty waitress for another, Poncho was finishing his third and excusing himself to go to the bathroom. He was gone over five minutes. Alex got up to see what was happening.

Poncho didn't appear to be in the bathroom. *Strange.* Alex used the urinal. Then Poncho's voice floated from behind the single locked stall door. His speech slurred, but the beer made him talk loud. Alex listened.

"Sí Anita, we're having a few chelas. I think we'll be here for about two hours. Go now. I'll keep him away from the house. Go!"

Alex finished urinating, tiptoeing out of the bathroom without washing his hands. He couldn't risk Poncho coming out and finding him listening. He'd been talking to Ana. Why would Ana be interested in Alex's whereabouts? He sat down at the table again and sipped his beer. Poncho returned in a couple more minutes.

"Everything okay, Poncho? I thought you fell in."

They laughed and Poncho went back to drinking and gossiping. He signaled the waitress then invited her to sit down with them, his crude leer too obvious.

"You're a sloppy drunk, Poncho. And a lousy tipper. Hit on me again and I'll have you run outta here," she said pleasantly, tipping her chin toward the entry where a burly man perched on a stool.

Alex flinched. Apart from the fact that he did not like the environment, he thought they might have problems. Lucky the girl was tough and didn't appear to suffer fools.

"Sorry for my friend. I think he's had a couple too many," Alex said.

She smiled at him. "Don't worry about it. Poncho is a drunk, but he's harmless. Want another?"

Alex smiled back. "Not yet." He tipped his head at Poncho. "Don't want to be where he is."

The girl giggled and wobbled back to the bar on her too-high heels, hips jouncing in the skin-tight, shiny black mini-dress uniform she wore. He'd seen dresses like this on the streetwalkers down on Calzada Tlalpan's rent-by-the-hour hotel district in Mexico City.

Poor Pancho was so crass, he couldn't even get a puta to pay attention to him. Alex shouted to get Poncho's attention. The dude was smashed. He kept a conversation, if it could be called that, going for a couple of minutes, then pulled the device from his pocket and announced, "I've got to take this. I'll be right back."

Poncho waved him off, head drooping, eyes glazed. "Ya com'n back?" he slurred.

"You know it, amigo." Alex doubted he'd be missed.

He had no intention of coming back. He wasn't comfortable in the cantina, and Poncho was getting stupid drunk. Was this what Lucas did? It didn't matter. He had to get back to Irene's and find out what she was up to. The one-sided conversation he overheard did not bode well. *What does Ana want now?*

Alex drove straight to Irene's, parking two doors down and out of sight of the house. He fingered the keys on his ring for the gate padlock before he realized it was open. He stopped. Should he go in? He plucked up his courage to enter unseen through the garage. From the garage he heard noises inside the house. There was no doubt, his house was being robbed.

He remembered his father's hunting rifles stored in his room. Could he get to the guns? It was dangerous but necessary. He entered slowly, silently, stopping to listen. Upstairs, women's voices? Familiar voices. Alex inched closer to the stairwell; he listened.

Morticia! Why is Morticia here? And she was talking to her mother. Alex's fear evaporated, replaced by anger. What the fuck were they doing in his house? He ran upstairs.

He caught Ana red-handed. "What the hell?" he asked, although it was obvious she was searching for something. The drawers hung open, some of his things had been dumped onto the floor.

Ana shrieked, jumping up from her knees where she searched under the bed. Her cheeks turned beet-red, and her jaw hung open.

Morticia flew in from Irene's room holding a packet. Alex knew what they were. Irene's financial information: invoices, deeds, bank statements. She dropped the packet. Ana lunged for it.

"You're stealing my mother's documents?" He couldn't believe it. Now he knew what happened to Irene's jewelry, his father's collection of fine, rare watches. "You disgust me."

Noise came from the other room. Sure enough, there was that good-for-nothing Gabriel rounding up electronic devices.

Alex went downstairs and called his lawyer in Mexico City. Ana, Morticia, and Gabriel stayed upstairs, presumably scrubbing the house of anything with value. He described the scene. The lawyer recommended that he go for the police and, if possible, they arrest them inside the property.

Ana realized Alex was on the phone. He heard her shout, "Let's go, there's no time for anything more."

He intercepted them on the stairs.

Morticia's boyfriend yelled at him, "Take off or we'll kill you!"

Alex ignored him and lunged for Ana. She'd stuck Lucas's wallet in her bra. The wallet he'd hidden. It contained all the credit and debit cards for Irene's and Lucas's banks.

"Give me the wallet, Ana."

"I dare you to take it, pendejo."

Morticia was not satisfied stealing the money and assets. She came down the stairs, handed the packet of documents to Gabriel, and grabbed the ashes of her grandmother, great-grandmother, and Alex's younger brother Hugo. Alex had put the urns on the table to take to the novenas to place with Lucas's ashes before Ana ran him off.

Ana sneered at Alex. "What are you going to do? This isn't even your house. You try anything and you'll be sorry."

Alex watched them hustle out with their prizes. He followed them, hoping to see a patrol and have them arrested, but his earlier luck had run out. They walked to the corner of the block and got into Lucas's SUV. Alex locked the gate and ran for his motorcycle. He followed them in the hope of seeing the police and getting them stopped with the goods. Again, no luck. They and their haul scuttled into Ana's house like the cockroaches they were.

Alex called his lawyer, Samia, again and gave her a blow-by-blow description of the events. She instructed him to go immediately to the prosecutor's office to file a complaint.

At the Fiscalia, they took Alex's statement and

informed him the trio would be arrested and jailed without possibility of bail. Alex felt those knives in his heart again. Ana and Gabriel? Lock 'em up right now. But Morticia? He had loved his niece; now she betrayed him. Could he send her to jail? What about her little boys? He paced, deliberating while the lawyer drummed his fingers on the dented metal desk.

The man finally cleared his throat, bringing Alex back to the office. "I'm sorry, Licensiado, I just can't put my niece behind bars. What else can I do?"

"Two options, go forward with this complaint, or file it as an informative act to use later if you need it."

Alex shook the lawyer's hand. "Thank you. I'll leave it as informational for now."

When he left the horrible government offices, Alex knew the score. All the events that had taken place since he'd arrived had been planned by Ana and Victor Mata—hadn't she as good as admitted it? But Alex had shown up and stayed, a wrench in the works, and Poncho López was brought in to deal with him. Worst of all, Morticia had been playing him all along—for the inheritance.

Alex might not be sending Ana to jail now, but he vowed not to let this rest. He would find justice for Lucas no matter what it took.

Chapter 23

The Lawsuit

Friday, May 16, 2020

An anvil of dread settled on Alex's shoulders as he maneuvered his motorcycle through the thick, disorderly traffic on Avenida Allende from shopping in el centro. He constantly looked over his shoulder, not for the usual crazy drivers, but for the malevolent specter dogging him like a shadow as he returned to Irene's house. He'd never experienced fear like this before. Is this what Lucas felt? Did he know his own wife was plotting his demise? He shot left on the green light around the Pemex station into his colonia, dodging potholes, a pesera, and several honking cars. It was always congested here between the bus stop, several takeout joints, the turns into the gas station, and the Chedraui shopping center.

Traffic eased as he dropped down the slight descent and bore left at the Y, again dodging the huge potholes filled with oily water from the last rain. His stomach growled. Alex realized he hadn't eaten since breakfast and considered the options close to the house.

Exhaling, his taut muscles softened a bit as he passed the car repair, the tire shop, the cell phone distributor, and several hole-in-the-wall green grocers. Familiar territory. People darted in and out of stores, hailed a looming bus, darted through the traffic crawling over the topes amid the honking and exhaust. He made the sign of the cross as he passed the barn-like church still hung with clear electric Christmas lights over its broad patio and fountain.

Later, locked into the house after inhaling a platter of carnitas, tortillas, refried beans, rice, and a liter of Tecate from a taqueria in the neighborhood, he wasted no more time brooding. With Daisi purring next to him, Alex meditated on his conundrum, saw the path open like a dawning over the placid morning Gulf. The course of action was clear—his brother had been murdered by his own family. He could not leave it to oblivion. He must make a written report and officially file it with the courts.

It was after midnight when he snapped the laptop closed. He had a five-page document ready, detailing everything from the voicemail from his mother, "She's trying to kill me", through the robbery of Irene's financial information. He'd added another page with his demands. If Ana and her brother Dr. Victor Mata were willing to murder Lucas for money and revenge, what would stop them from coming after him? His experience with attorneys had taught him to proactively protect himself first. You never knew when your mouthpiece was working against you. This Licensiado he found from an internet search, Fidel Godoy and he did not have a track record. The short call the day before hardly counted. All he knew were

Godoy's rates.

He'd seen how lawsuits could go. A wave of regret washed over him, souring his carnitas-filled stomach as he thought of his career back in Mexico City. His former career. Over the years, the laboratory had initiated several suits in which Alex had been a witness during his tenure. He knew once a suit was filed, the accused would be notified. A red flag for Ana and Mata. Alex had to make sure his name was kept out of it. If he were found out, he would need protection, and that meant a hearing with a judge. He couldn't file without these protections.

He yawned. Daisi woke up and stretched, closing a sharp claw into his thigh. "Ouch! Daisi!" he yelped and nudged her to the floor as he pushed away from the table. "Come on, let's go to bed. I have to see a lawyer tomorrow." Daisi meowed and followed him up the narrow stairs.

The next morning, Alex took his coffee to the table, found his note, and called the number listed for Godoy's office to make an appointment. The receptionist passed him to the attorney.

"Señor Deltoro, good morning. I hadn't expected to hear from you so soon. Have you decided what you want to do?"

"Yes, Licensiado. I've written up a statement and would like to sit down with you as soon as possible. When can you see me?"

"You're in luck. I just had a cancellation for this morning. Can you meet me at eleven o'clock in the Gran Café de la Parroquia? I have a lunch appointment in that part of town."

"Sure. I'll see you then. Thanks." Alex hung up,

hoping he'd recognize the man from his photo on the firm's website.

When Alex arrived, the man from the photo was tucking a bill into the pocket of a pretty, traditionally costumed dancer circulating through the tables for tips at the end of her performance. Her trio played in the background, a tune Alex recognized from the radio program his mother was never without as she attended her household chores.

He raised his hand in greeting and sat down opposite the attorney. "Good morning, Licensiado."

"Señor Deltoro," the man answered, signaling a waiter. "What'll you have?"

The waiter scurried over with a tiny round tray holding an order pad, a bar towel draped over his arm, poised to jot the order.

"Thanks," Alex said, "a black coffee, por favor."

The man nodded and hustled off through the swinging doors to the kitchen. Alex studied Godoy's face. He looked to be in his mid-fifties, a güero with pale skin, blondish, greying hair, and pale blue eyes. Argentinian, he surmised by the attorney's unfriendly accent, something between Castilian and condescending. Alex wasn't sure he liked the man.

"How can I help you, Deltoro?" Godoy asked.

"I'm not sure but call me Alex. Let me give you a summary of my problem."

The waiter delivered Alex's coffee. He took a sip and relayed the main points of his family inheritance, the robbery, and Lucas's death.

Godoy listened attentively, making an occasional note in a small book he pulled from his briefcase. The waiter circled by with a coffeepot and refilled Godoy's cup. The next band started up, snappy Caribbean rhythms driving a cheerful marimba. Fleetingly, Alex wondered why there weren't any marimba players anymore in nearby in Las Portales, a popular plaza with restaurants and hotels next to the cathedral. The balmy sea air, swaying palms, and happy music were what had made Veracruz and los jarochos, people of Veracruz, special.

"Alex, please explain again how your sister-in-law got into your house and what she took?"

"Ana had my brother's key. Or maybe her own copy, I don't know. I've changed the locks and fortified the points of entry over the walls. She took my mother's financial information and credit cards. She—they: my niece and her boyfriend were with Ana—tried to take the TV and did take my mother's and my younger brother's ashes. She has no right to those. They're *my* family." That familiar tide of sadness rose over him. "I don't know what I could have done to stop it."

"You've made a police report?"

"Yes, but I couldn't bring myself to have them arrested." Alex signaled the waiter for another fill-up.

"But the report is filed?" Godoy shot his icy eyes toward Alex. "And if you change your mind, it can be prosecuted?"

"Yes, but I'd rather try to recover the information, settle the inheritances, and move on."

"Of, course," the grating voice answered, "but should you change your mind, or it become necessary, it is best that the report is ready."

"So, what can we do?"

The happy marimba morphed into a haunting, mournful piece that matched Alex's mood. Talking about his dysfunctional family, hell, *thinking* about the family brought him down.

"Let me consider the problem and let's meet here in one week," the attorney said. "Meanwhile, please jot down everything you remember was taken. Have you notified the banks?"

"Yes, of course. I've included the losses in my statement." Alex slid the folder with his report across the table to the attorney. "Ana wasn't a signatory, only my older brother, her husband."

"Bueno. I'll have the office contact you. Let me get your coffee." Godoy slid Alex's statement into his briefcase, looked at his watch, and turned his attention to a file he pulled from the briefcase. The interview was over.

The meetings he'd attended over the past two weeks with Licensiado Godoy had been positive. He was getting used to his accent. But telling the story again and again reminded Alex of the dangers involved with gunning for Ana and Victor. Today he would bring it up, his list of non-negotiables. He folded the updated list into his jacket pocket in preparation for today's meeting with Godoy.

"Daisi, I've got to go," he said, setting a bowl of water next her crunchies. "I have to go all the way to Boca del Rio, Colonia Reforma. I think we're ready to file the lawsuit, girl." Daisi stood up, stretched, and yawned. "Oh, sorry Daiz, I didn't mean to disturb your nap," Alex said, laughing as he bent to give her head a scratch. She sniffed toward the bowls, turned up her nose at the food, and rubbed against Alex's ankles, purring. "Thanks, Daisi, I'm going to need all the luck

I can get."

The office wedged into a narrow, tree-lined side street overcrowded with residences and parked vehicles. Alex squeezed the motorcycle between two late model sedans and chained it locked. A chorus of birds tweeted from the foliage as he made his way back to the address. Tangles of service wires drooped and coiled at every pole and many of the electrical wires sagged into their connector boxes on the buildings.

Not at Godoy's office. The two-story building had been modernized with a smooth, steel-grey facade, white iron security trim covered large windows in front of closed black mini-blinds, and an over-sized steel door painted Gulf grey-blue, swung easily when the receptionist buzzed him in. He proceeded down a short hall paralleling the street to reception. The hall had been hung with framed modern art with sharp angles and rectangular planes of blues and greys with pops of hot color. Architectural.

Alex knocked on the glass door into the reception. Licensiado Godoy stepped into view and welcomed him with his Argentinian accent, unsettling Alex again.

But Godoy's words were kind. "Welcome, Deltoro. Please be seated. Help yourself to a drink," he said, gesturing to a bar setup crowning a mini refrigerator. "I'm with another client, but we'll be done soon."

"Thanks, Lic. Take your time." Alex sat down on a clean-lined grey sofa next to a black end table. The newspaper sat on the table, blaring its headline, *Zeta Leader Accused*...and a grisly black and white photo of several men splayed dead in the road. He picked it up, thumbing to the business section. One of these days he would need to deal with his lack of employment. He better catch up. If he didn't have his job in Mexico. . . *Activate the foundation?* But Ivan had made it clear he wasn't keen on the idea. No Ivan, no donated and discounted drugs.

The paper vacillated between sensationalism and Boca del Rio-specific news, mostly connected to tourism and condo sales. He dropped it back to the table and studied his surroundings. The office was carved from a house and had that new house smell, so the remodel had been recent. The place had been designed by one of those fancy interior decorators to look intellectually slick yet calming. Or so he supposed.

Finally, Godoy dismissed his client and instructed Alex to come into his inner office. This space had a different feel. Photos, framed degrees, a signed soccer ball and a vase of lovely flowers on the modern credenza. More personal, less angular.

"Please sit-down Alex. Welcome to the new digs. We're finally organized and operating."

"You just moved in?"

"No, my wife made me build her a house in one of those new developments, Marevera, down the Riviera Veracruzana. Remodeled our old house to be an office. We turned the upstairs into two more legal suites and have them rented out. My partner and I have the kitchen, and our assistant—"

The talk was interrupted by a woman Alex pegged, because of her Argentine accent and age, as Godoy's wife. He stood.

"Hello! " she greeted Alex. "Say, if this reprobate," she tipped her chin toward her husband, "doesn't do his job, let me know and I'll straighten him out." She laughed, a throaty guffaw.

Godoy answered with a wink. "Alex Deltoro, my wife and law partner, Magdalena."

Alex smiled and shook her outstretched hand. "It's good to make your acquaintance, Señora." He'd guessed she was an attorney and now understood the firm's name: Godoy y Godoy, Abogados.

Magdalena turned to her husband. "May I bring you gentlemen some coffee?"

He nodded and she left the private office with a swirl of her Frida Kahlo-style flounced skirt. Alex sat down wondering if Mrs. Godoy was telling him Godoy might play loose with his honesty, but decided it was just a joke. Minutes later a young man entered with the steaming cups of traditional *cafe de olla*. Godoy introduced his son, Eduardo, the firm's law intern.

"Dad, may I offer you and Señor Deltoro anything else?"

"Thanks Eddie, we're set. Tell your mother gracias. The coffee is muy rico."

Eduardo closed the glass door behind him and Godoy opened the conversation. "The investigations into the inheritances are going well; thank you for your detailed statement. We've substantiated your claims, and I agree, you have been cheated out of your share, but although things are looking positive for your claims, you know the law—it moves at the pace of a glacier. Just like everything else in Mexico." He laughed like this were a big joke.

Was this a stalling tactic? For more money? Alex bit his lip to refrain from making a snide comment. He knew too much about how things worked and shot the lawyer a wan smile. He said, "Sí, así es Mexico," and changed the subject to his brother. He summarized the whole terrible story, adding pertinent observations and opinions.

"Licensiado, from my brother's family physician to the emergency room doctors, to the internist, and Dr. Victor Mata, head of IMSS General Hospital 71, I think it was a conspiracy to kill my brother. He never had cancer. He was prescribed medicines that conflicted with each other, doing little good, and some, in fact causing him illness. I think his brother-in-law and his wife were trying to poison him. It's what finally happened."

Alex stopped talking. A heavy silence pressed down on the office. Licensiado Godoy tee-peed his hands and bowed his head in thought. When he looked up, he asked, "And you have proof of your accusations?"

"Of course. Well, I think so Licensiado."

Godoy replied, "Excellent, I'll need to review everything. If you have a strong case, then chances of winning it are upwards of 90%."

"Okay," Alex said, "and how much will this cost me?"

"Don't worry, the standard for this type of case is a portion of the award. I typically take twenty percent

Alex wrinkled his brow. "And what typically is the award in a lawsuit like this?"

Godoy replied, "It could be compensation between three million five hundred thousand pesos and five hundred thousand pesos."

The gleam in Godoy's eyes as he described the award alarmed him. How could Alex put a price on his brother's life? He knew perfectly well that this matter was dangerous, but he could not behave like a coward. Even if it hurt him to harm his niece Morticia, it was her mother and her uncle who committed this terrible crime. Loyalty to his family was his nature, and who closer than a brother? Yes, Alex wanted, no—needed—to avenge the murder of Lucas.

"Look, Lic, I want to lock Ana and her murderous brother up and throw away the key."

"Of course you want justice for your brother, but we can do both. I once had a law professor tell me, 'Don't litigate your cases to get even—litigate to make a profit.' Prison gets even. Bankrupting them...now there's punishment."

"If I'm going to file a suit against the doctors, I'll put myself in danger."

"Yes you will, Alex. You need to prepare for that."

"I have, Mr. Godoy." He removed the paper he'd drawn up from the jacket pocket, unfolded it, smoothed it out as he deliberated his actions, and finally looked at the lawyer, his jaw tight and eyes blazing. "Let's make a profit."

Godoy scanned the stipulations. "Okay, Deltoro, we can stipulate to keep your identity confidential until we stand in front of the judge. We can petition the Court to assign you security, although this will be difficult unless you can prove you are in danger. And I would add one more stipulation: we initiate for culpable homicide, and those that correspond against those indicated in the preamble and those who are responsible."

"What does that mean?"

"Let me explain."

Three days later, on June first, Fidel Godoy filed a formal complaint with the Attorney General's Office. It was received with the following stipulations:

1) That the corresponding investigation file be initiated for CULPABLE HOMICIDE, AND THOSE THAT CORRESPOND AGAINST THOSE INDICATED IN THE PREAMBLE AND THOSE WHO ARE ALSO RESPONSIBLE.

2) THE IDENTITY OF THE PLAINTIFF IS KEPT CONFIDENTIAL THROUGHOUT THIS PROCESS.

3) IMMEDIATE MEASURES TO PROTECT THE PLAINTIFF ARE SET IN PLACE WITH THE MAXIMUM LEGAL SCOPE, SINCE THERE IS A CONCRETE AND WELL-FOUNDED RISK OF [PLAINTIFF] SUFFERING PERSONAL INJURY OR DAMAGE.

4) A HEARING WITH A CONTROL JUDGE IS REQUESTED AS NECESSARY IN ORDER TO EXTEND THE MEASURES OF PROTECTION TO THE PLAINTIFF.

Chapter 24

The Hit-and-Run

Sunday, June 7, 2020

ADO's midnight bus from Mexico City swept into the city of Veracruz. The alarm on Alex's phone buzzed in his pocket, pulling him from a dream, something to do with gurneys and masked doctors. He wasn't sure exactly. Was it something to do with Lucas's death? He felt the moist, tropical air filling the bus as it slowed to a purr and traversed Avenida Diaz Mirón toward the station.

He pulled off his sweatshirt and stuffed it into his backpack behind the dirty clothes and his purchases. The vehicle slowed, rounded a corner, and eased into its slot in the row of sleek busses. The overhead lights came on at exactly five a.m. Passengers stirred, waking up from the overnight journey; Alex slipped the backpack over his shoulders and trundled down the aisle toward the door ahead of the few other travelers.

The driver opened the door, stepped down, and opened the luggage compartments. Alex didn't have anything to collect. If he could find a taxi, he'd be at

Irene's before five-thirty. Early enough he could grab a couple more hours of sleep before he got busy with his petition to return to work at Laboratorios Salud Integral.

It was still dark outside as he crossed the station lobby. At the exit door, he greeted the security guard with a cheerful, "Buenos dias." She looked adorable in her well-fitting uniform.

She dimpled and wished him a nice day as she held open the door. Maybe he'd come back and ask her to coffee, although she must be twenty-five years younger than him.

The wide sidewalk, usually crowded with people coming and going, was empty, as was the wide avenue. Not a taxi in sight. Alex crossed Avenida Tuero Molina and stopped on the corner of Diaz Mirón in front of the marimba, the painted crosswalk. The light remained red, the area quiet, and he felt lonely, anxious to get back to Daisi. Even so, Alex waited for the green light to cross the three-lane street.

Minutes ticked by before the light changed. Out of habit, Alex looked left. Empty. He looked across the berm to the northbound lanes. Empty. Hitching up the backpack, he stepped off the curb and aimed toward the wide, tree-lined median strip. As he reached the center lane, a car appeared traveling at an excessive speed—80 or 90 kilometers—with its headlights off. Before Alex could react, the vehicle blew through the red light. Alex bolted, jigging toward the median strip as fast as he could move, but the driver spun the wheel to follow him. Alex was too slow, there was no escape for his groggy mind and over-taxed body.

At the instant the white compact hit his leg, Alex

understood. *The lawsuit!* He shot up onto the hood and into the windshield. Time slowed. Everything stood out in crystal relief. The black, oily pavement, the patchy grass median, the slick bark and shimmering crowns of the trees as he floated above them. His mind remained alert, holding his body in a state of readiness, survival. "It's incredible," he wanted to say about how he was transformed, suspended, his mind seeing the accident in pure clarity. But wasn't he confused? How could Alex see the hood and the tops of the trees from under the car? His motorcycle backpack spoke out to him—*pull me over your neck. Use me. Protect your head.* He was suspended six meters above the trees and beginning to fall.

It would be the fall that would kill him. He yanked up the pack, with its built-in protection features, and curled into it like a gymnast, his hands pressing the pack into his neck and head. Falls from the motorcycle flashed through his mind, landing headfirst. Always headfirst. He pressed harder as the ground raced up to meet him.

The backpack absorbed most of the impact; the breath was knocked from his lungs. As he gasped for air, a searingly bright white light illuminated him from the topmost of a tree on the other side of the sidewalk toward the northbound lanes. He inhaled a rush of the light, which filled his lungs, quickly spreading throughout his body and bringing Alex back to life where danger surrounded him.

"Get up!" his brain shouted.

He needed to run into the median to prevent the car, which had slowed, from backing over him and finishing him off. He rolled from his back to lift himself up, but his left leg did not respond, the tibia and fibula were broken, poking through his skin. Alex fell to his back on the pavement. The white light dimmed.

"He's alive! He's alive!" echoed from the ADO station.

Alex turned his head. Across the way was a Ramada Inn, a woman rushing out the door, running toward him. "Don't move. Stay still. Your back, it could be dangerous."

"I can't get up. I'm not moving. Please stay, the car..." Alex couldn't utter the words, but he would be all right under her protection. He relaxed. Adrenalin seeped from his system. Alex felt the alertness fade and a kind of numbness set in.

"The car fled. A hit and run," she said. "I've called 9-1-1."

He couldn't feel the ground or his leg. It needed surgery, but what of his back, neck, and the rest of him? He began an assessment, first moving his spine, his neck, then arms and his right leg. Everything worked, mostly, except his left foot was upside down. A wave of nausea washed through him. He pushed it away. He had been lucky he hadn't sustained serious damage to more than his left leg. Nothing felt atrophied.

A kind voice asked, "Can I do anything for you? Are you cold?"

Alex shifted to see the ADO security guard's uniform. "No, I'm okay, thanks. I need an ambulance." He guessed he wasn't going to get a date with her now.

"We've called for the paramedics. They should arrive at any minute," the woman from the Ramada said. "The police, too."

But Alex did not receive medical assistance, although the Red Cross was just 300 meters away. He could see the ambulances parked from where he was lying in the left lane of southbound Av. Diaz Mirón.

The adrenalin had dissipated completely, and the pain was horrendous. He felt himself weakening as panic set in. Was he bleeding out? He raised his eyes up to the young woman's face. "What's going on? Why don't they pick me up? I need a hospital."

Overhead the sky was beginning to lighten, and Alex now heard birds twittering in the trees. Soon morning traffic would clog the avenue. "Where's the *pinche* ambulance? It's been over an hour," Alex shouted and tried to sit up.

The security guard knelt, putting her hand gently on Alex's shoulder, holding him down. "Take it easy. Don't despair, we'll get them here. It's typical Mexico. But the good news is, they caught the guy who hit you. He's here." She gestured over Alex's head.

He craned his neck to see but was forced to roll to one elbow. The Guardia Civil pickup blocked a white car, maybe one of those tiny Japanese or Chinese vehicles, against the corner curb. A man was pressed spread eagle against it as the officers fussed around. Why weren't they arresting him? Why return him to scene of the crime? The man was not handcuffed.

A few minutes later, the Cruz Roja ambulance arrived. A paramedic climbed from the cab and approached Alex. The paramedic nudged Alex's waist with the toe of his shoe with some force. "Have you seen who ran you over?" he asked.

What kind of question is that? "No. I can't exactly get up and look," Alex replied, "but he's right over

212

there with the Guardia Civil.

"Yeah, another old asshole like you." The man's voice dripped sarcasm.

The paramedic's attitude confused Alex. Something was wrong, but he really did not want to answer or fight with the man. He needed to get to the hospital. He looked up at the woman from the Inn. She was watching the exchange, her face frozen with contempt for the paramedic. A few meters away the police and the hit-and-run driver were arguing. He claimed Alex had crossed against the traffic light. The woman also listened. Her look of contempt stretched to Alex's attacker.

She angrily shouted, "It's not true! I saw you run the red light and swerve to hit him. You did it on purpose—you animal!"

A black sedan rolled up and parked next to the Guardia Civil pickup. Sunrise lightened the sky and cast shadows across the intersection. Alex could just make out *AXXA* stenciled on the passenger door. He heard the slam as the driver got out. *Insurance adjuster,* he thought. He recognized the name. So, the pendejo who had hit him was insured. But why wasn't he being attended to? The paramedic was watching the adjuster collecting his data and certifying the policy was in force. Alex groaned. He hurt. His entire body hurt. Why didn't they take him to the hospital?

Finally, Alex was given analgesics and intravenous fluid. He immediately felt relief as his pain subsided. The paramedic enlisted a Guardia Civil to help shift Alex onto a canvas stretcher and lift him onto the gurney, then rolled him into the ambulance. Alex felt the jostle of the emergency vehicle as the paramedic climbed behind the wheel. He turned the engine over, but the vehicle didn't move.

Alex could hear a conversation taking place, although he couldn't understand the words drowned out by the rumble of the engine. Then the engine shutdown and moments later the back doors opened and two Guardia clambered in.

One sat on a bench next to Alex. "We need your statement, Señor Deltoro."

Alex, body aching dully and head swimming from the drugs, slurred, "Can't it wait? I need a doctor."

The man responded sharply, "No, Señor, it cannot wait."

"I feel awful. I've been waiting for two hours. I demand to be treated," Alex responded with as much force as he could muster.

The officer insisted. "Your testimony is indispensable. We cannot put this off. Speak to us now or..." His voice trailed off.

Or what? It sounded like a threat. Alex narrated the facts of the incident, where he was coming from, how he'd waited for the light, how he'd changed directions and run when the speeding vehicle, operating without lights, came after him. As he finished, another man, the insurance adjuster it turned out, climbed into the ambulance and crouched at the end of the cot where Alex lay.

"Señor..." He looked down at his chart. "Deltoro, we are authorized to offer you first class medical services in exchange for letting the driver go." He explained the payout—*payoff* Alex thought— would act as termination of liability or responsibility of AXXA in the matter.

214

"The man purposely ran me over. I may never walk again. I'm not signing off until I know what my injuries are. I demand to be taken to the hospital. You cannot detain me any longer. I'm the victim here."

The adjuster heaved himself up and stomped out of the ambulance, followed by the officers. The doors closed, the engine coughed to life and Alex yelled, "Where are you taking me?"

"Regional Hospital."

Oh no! The horrors of what could happen flashed in front of him. Alex knew too much about these government hospitals—dirty, crowded, inferior care, lack of specialists and medications—*no, no, no!* They let people die from simple infections due to lack of antibiotics. It was impossible to trust surgeons, who he urgently needed if he wanted to save his leg. Besides, there always was a backlog. Coupled with the COVID pandemic, he'd wait for months. No, it was simply impossible to receive good care. *There's no time to lose.* "Take me to Star Medica," he insisted.

"You know they aren't going to pay you anything, you idiot," the paramedic said, gesturing out the window. Alex heard voices yelling to the adjuster, who returned to the ambulance saying, "If you tell me, you release liability, you'll get that care you want."

He remained silent. His care was first and foremost, but afterwards, he was going to make the bastard pay for what he'd done. The police should not have let him go. He'd run Alex down and fled the scene. That, of itself, was illegal. Add to it the intent and it was attempted murder. No, if he'd stopped to help, Alex might have released him from liability. Not now.

It felt like it took forever for the adjuster to complete his paperwork and give the go-ahead to the ambulance to take Alex to Star Medica, the premier hospital in the region. The adjuster passed the paperwork to the paramedic and shouted through the window, "You're a lucky bastard. The company is sending you to Star Medica."

Alex didn't understand the man's behavior, but the ambulance started up, pulling around the to head north on Diaz Mirón.

The twenty-five-minute trip was agony. The paramedic raced through potholes and over bumps without slowing. "Please, slow down! You're hurting me. Slow down!" Alex called out.

"Yeah? And the ride is so much smoother in Mexico City? No potholes or topes?"

Mexico City? How does the paramedic know I'm from Mexico? This was worrying, not because of the bad treatment the pendejo dished out from the beginning, but what worried him the most was that he knew where Alex was from. The subject had not been discussed. Now Alex was certain the hit-and-run was planned, and the only people who could have done this were Victor Mata and Ana Deltoro Mata. Maybe Doctor Fierro was in on it too.

The ambulance arrived at the emergency ramp of the Star Medica hospital, where an efficient team of professionals was already waiting for him. They transferred Alex to a wheeled gurney and whisked him inside. He heard the nurses complaining about the poor placement of the needles delivering serum and analgesics as they cut off his jeans. They replaced the needles with new and reconnected the medicines.

He was appalled at the condition of his clothes, filthy, greasy, and stained from the pavement and the car's bumper and hood. He'd forgotten until seeing the clothes that the friction on the ground raised him to a sitting position and dragged him for several meters. Alex thanked God that he was alive.

The hospital staff informed him that he had to contact a family member to be responsible for him. *It's my family who put me here.* He replied, "I don't have any family in Veracruz. I can sign any documents you need."

"No, Señor, your condition is extremely serious. It is urgent someone is aware and ready to act in case your condition worsens," she said.

"You mean, if I die."

She nodded but continued. "We can start with your full-body x-rays, so that it can be surgically intervened, but I repeat, a responsible person is mandatory while you are undergoing surgery."

Alex sighed. *Just get on with it.* "I have a friend in Mexico. Will he do?"

The doctor handed him a cell phone. Alex glanced at the wall clock above the intake desk. Eight o'clock. Julian Castillo would not like being awakened so early.

A groggy voice croaked, "Yeah?"

"Julian, I'm so sorry to call early but I need your help."

"That you, Alex? You sound weird."

"I'm in the hospital. I was hit by a car."

Awake, Julian shouted, "You what?" Alex pulled the phone away from his ear. "Where are you? What happened?"

"Slow down, slow down. It's just my paw."

More shouting and questions.

"Look, Julian, I need surgery. The hospital requires a contact." Alex summarized the situation for his friend. "Can I count on you?"

Julian's voice went serious. "I'm on my way, Alex." The line went dead.

"Where's my cell phone?" The doctor shrugged. "Then what's the number of this one?"

The doctor took the phone, and said, "You won't be needing it in x-ray."

Forty-five minutes later, after x-rays, blood tests, checks on his blood pressure and blood sugar, and Alex didn't know what else, he was wheeled into the operating room where he met his orthopedic surgeon. The doctor looked too young to be operating on him.

Alex asked, "How old are you? Are you even out of university?"

The doctor laughed. "I get that a lot. Don't worry, I have plenty of experience, I am a tibia specialist. Everything will be fine."

A nurse asked Alex his favorite music.

"That's easy, rock of the 60s," he said.

In a moment, the operation room filled with the groovin' sounds of the Rolling Stones. Someone injected him with a sedative and the doctor slipped the anesthetic mask over his nose and mouth. "Count to ten for me."

"One...two...three... four... fi—"

Alex was rolling on a gurney through brilliant white hallways. *Is this heaven?* The slight swaying made him drowsy. He closed his eyes. When he opened them again, he was in a recovery room, a familiar voice

218

floating out of his dreams, "How do you feel, Gato?"

Was that how God addressed people in heaven?

Two or three hours later, Alex fully rejoined consciousness. He surveyed the room. It felt comfortable, clean, and cool. He saw it was equipped with a TV. The white noise whir of the air conditioning soothed him.

Soon a pretty dark-haired nurse came in to check on him. She smiled. "You're awake. How do you feel, Señor Deltoro?"

Alex smiled back, but said, "I feel pretty bad, señorita. I just had surgery."

"The drugs are wearing off. Are you experiencing pain? I can give you something as soon as we get you to your room."

"My room? Where am I?"

"Recovery. Your friend has arrived and is waiting for you to get settled. Do you want me to send him in?" Alex nodded. "Okay, then, you can visit until the doctor comes to check on you. We'll move you after that."

"I'm thirsty." The nurse poured a tiny paper cup of tepid water and handed it to Alex. He eyed it suspiciously. "No Coke?"

The nurse laughed. "No Coke. Let me get Señor Castillo for you." She glided out on her rubber soles with a swish as the door closed behind her.

Moments later, Alex turned toward another swish. Julian strode in, red-faced and out of breath. A rush of emotion filled him. "Julian," he said, his voice hoarse, "thank you for coming." He held out his fist. Julian bumped it and grinned. "But you didn't need to run! They couldn't kill me—this time."

"That doesn't sound good, Alex. What happened?

You look pretty done in." He waved at the elaborate system of pulleys, cables, and tubes attached to Alex.

He looked around the room, eyes alighting on a chair next to a narrow bed, probably for visitors. It was presently empty. "Pull up a chair. I'll give you the rundown. First, when did you get here?"

The padded chair scraped across the floor as Julian positioned it so Alex could see him. "We were lucky, Gato, I caught the last commuter flight and arrived in Veracruz three hours after the call. You were just getting out of surgery. So, what happened? We haven't spoken for a month, man. I'm sorry about your mother."

"Yeah, thanks, bro. It was a blessing in a lot of ways. Besides having a lot of pain, had she known what my brother and sister-in-law were up to, she would have died from a broken heart."

"How is Lucas? I remember he was having some health issues. Drinking, right?"

"Yeah, but it wasn't just that. You think your family is dysfunctional? Wait until you hear about mine."

Julian leaned forward, all ears. "Now you have my attention, Gato. How can any family be worse than mine?"

"Lucas was murdered by his wife and her brother, the head of one of the local IMSS hospitals. Death by medication."

"No mames, Alex. Why? How?" he sputtered.

"Long story. You got time?"

"Nothing but time. You haven't heard my sad story. I've been laid off. I can stay as long as you need me."

"Because of that lying pendejo, Espinoza? What'd he do this time?"

"Sí, Espinoza, the thorn in my side; it's complicated. But you first."

"Pour me a water, would you?"

Julian filled another mini-cup and handed it over. "Pretty cheap on the water, aren't they? I thought this was the top hospital."

"Something to do with the surgery. I don't know. Irene died and almost immediately Lucas took sick. You know he was screwing Mami's caretaker? Dumb asshole. But that's not all he was up to. The pendejo couldn't keep it in his pants. He screwed Ana's brother's wife. Victor divorced her. He remarried and my drunk brother, screwed the new wife too. There's quite a list. Ana's cousin's wife. Ana's niece on her mother's side. Who knows how many more. The long and short of it: Ana and her brother Victor plotted revenge."

Alex chronicled the details up to filing the lawsuit against Victor Mata and his cronies. "I had to go to Mexico to see Samia about another related matter—did I mention I caught Ana, my niece Morticia, and her idiot boyfriend robbing Irene's—*my*—house of all the financial information, credit cards, and even the urns with Hugo's and mother's ashes? Yeah. Ana's been after my family's money all along. She admitted it to me. That was, what, a week and a half ago? It's all blending together. Maybe the drugs. This was the catalyst for filing a suit. It was originally a civil suit for malpractice, but one look at the facts and both my local attorney, and Samia, said it was murder. Godoy, the local guy, filed the suit with the Fiscalia Federal. A week later, you're here in the hospital with me listening to my horrifying tale of woe."

221

"So, it wasn't an accident?"

"Well, if speeding with no headlights and turning the wheel to be sure to hit me was by accident, then sure. What's more," Alex lowered his voice. Julian leaned closer, "the ambulance didn't come for two hours and when it did, the driver, who was the paramedic, knew too much about me. Someone is shelling out a shitload of money to get rid of me."

"You're dropping it and moving back to CDMX? What about your job?"

"What job. Ten years of hard work, innovation, and filling LSI's coffers didn't buy me any loyalty. I'm out. I need to pack up my house and sell it as soon as I can, but I doubt I'll be back on my feet very soon."

"You're staying here?!" Julian exclaimed.

"Until I put those bastards in prison."

Chapter 25

The Setback

June 2020

Two days later, Alex was taken home by ambulance. Julián went with him. Alex would need nursing care, and there was no way he could manage to climb the steep, uneven stairs leading to the bedrooms. He wondered, not for the first time, how Irene had gone up and down without falling.

Julian cleared a space in Irene's bedroom for Alex and settled into Alex's room. He had repaired the TV wires and reinstalled it on the wall in front of his mother's bed, a good thing too, since he was going to spend three months on his back staring at that wall.

Now Alex understood the request that a family member take care of him. Julian managed the kitchen and housework, as well as Alex's sponge baths and bedpan, while maintaining his cheerful demeanor. The friends fell into a rut.

Alex could barely sit up in bed. He felt isolated and alone, as well as angry. Julián recruited the next-door neighbor, Rosa Dorantes, to keep Alex company. Rosa brought over her granddaughter Carolina Jepes, a sophomore nursing student at a local college. The visitors helped boost Alex's mood, but it wasn't long before he got tired of lying down and having others do everything for him.

He began working to sit up, then stand, although the twenty-five centimeters of titanium rod and the seventeen screws that held his bones together made it difficult for him to move. But in a couple of weeks, he was able to limp to the bathroom and bathe himself.

Alex praised Julian's cooking and felt stronger each day, which he attributed to the amazing, mostly vegetarian meals he was served.

"An anti-inflammatory diet, Alex. You'll heal faster."

Maybe he was right. Alex's system improved. Within days, even the pain had subsided. By the end of the first week, he was on the phone with his lawyers, initiating a new lawsuit, this time against the driver of the car that had hit him.

Things seemed to be going pretty well until he started having tingling and numbness in his butt. He remembered his horrific landing on the pavement after flying through the air. The image of the frayed and dirty jeans made him shudder. A layer of skin had scraped off, but it should itch as it healed, *Shouldn't it?* "A healing scrape doesn't go numb and there shouldn't be tingling along your legs," he commented to Julian.

"I don't know. Call the hospital."

His doctor sounded alarmed when Alex detailed the symptoms. "Alex, an ambulance will be at your house in an hour."

"What? Why? Can't someone come here and take a

look?"

"No. The symptoms may indicate something more serious than poor circulation from lying on your back for days. I need you here."

The alarmist reaction of his treating doctor irritated Alex, but what could he do? Carolina would drive him, when she got home from school. If he took a taxi, it would be a lot less money than the hospital's ambulance. And money was becoming a problem. His savings account was seriously sinking; he had no idea how much longer he was going to live in this seedy house in hot, humid Veracruz.

Julián nixed the plan. "You're going in the ambulance, güey. I'm not risking more injury from a taxista."

He had a point.

An hour later, Julian and the ambulance driver lowered him down the impossible stairs on a stretcher and deposited Alex into the back of the vehicle.

"I'll see you soon, man," Julian said.

The door closed and Alex was whisked away.

At the hospital, the cute nurse Yajaira, who had taken care of him after the hit-and-run, stripped him naked and gently placed him in a gown. They chatted amicably for a moment, but Alex, sore from all the pushing and pulling, joggling and bumping, gritted his teeth, and closed his eyes. She said something about a CT scan. He felt his gurney move.

The scan lasted about forty-five minutes. His excruciating pain turned into the normal dull ache as he relaxed on the machine. Afterward, Yajaira and the technician gently moved Alex to a wheelchair. She pushed him back into the cubicle to dress him.

"Have you heard what the problem is, Yajaira?"

She tucked his legs back into his sweatpants. "No. They aren't going to tell me. Stand up so I can pull these pants over your hips."

Alex raised himself using the armrests of the wheelchair. "There." He adjusted the waistband.

"Arms up." Alex complied while she pulled a tee-shirt over his head. "I'll have to read your chart to find out," she said then wheeled him into the elevator.

"Where are we going?" Alex asked once the doors closed.

"Admissions. Your doctor will meet you there, explain everything, and you will have to pay."

"Admissions? Why? Oh, you'll have to read the chart..." They both laughed.

The silent elevator stopped with a sigh of air. The door slid open. Yajaira led him past the elegant reception and entrance to one of several stations in front of a cluster of offices in a long corridor. A well-coiffed older woman in a pastel blue suit greeted Yajaira in a soft voice.

"Thank you, nurse. I'll take the patient from here." She stepped behind the chair, grasped the handles, and bent toward Alex's ear to say, "I'm Mrs. Santiaga de Vega, your account manager. We are going to prepare everything for you." As if Alex were deaf.

The woman pushed him into the office and parked the chair in front of a tidy desk containing an Apple computer, a calculator, a pencil cup filled with pens sporting the Star Medica logo, and a file marked Deltoro, Alex. Their doctor joined them as Mrs. Santiaga de Vega sat down behind the computer. He contemplated the soothing seascape on the wall above her head.

"Doctor, what's going on? Do you have the results of the scan?"

The doctor sat in the visitor chair and scooched it around until he was facing Alex. "Yes, and I'm sorry to break it to you, but we need to perform surgery on your spine." Alex gasped. The doctor raised his hand. "The scan shows two fractured vertebrae. If we leave them untreated, we run the risk of paralysis."

"How long will it be until this happens? Another surgery before I've recovered from the last one doesn't feel good. Can I have a few moments to talk to someone?"

The administrator excused herself and glided out of her office.

"Certainly Of course. Do what you have to do," the doctor said.

Alex took his phone out of his pocket and looked for the number of Dr. Sergio Ulloa Lugo, director of Sheramex Laboratories, one of the best doctors specializing in orthopedics and traumatology nationwide. Alex was in luck. The doctor was available.

"Alex, my boy, how the hell are you?"

Alex explained his situation to him.

"Can you ask your doctor to send the scans?"

Alex raised his eyebrows at his doctor, who nodded.

In a matter of thirty minutes, Ulloa Lugo delivered his diagnosis. "Alex, that surgery is necessary."

As if by magic, Mrs. Santiaga de Vega reappeared and placed herself behind the desk. She gave Alex her reassuring smile as she reached out one hand and opened the file with the other. "Your credit card, Mr.

Deltoro, and we'll take care of everything."

Alex didn't want to delve into how dangerous the surgery could be. He stiffened as terror enveloped him. Mrs. Santiaga de Vega checked his card, then excused herself when Alex's new surgeon, Dr. Robredo, a spine specialist entered. They shook hands.

The surgeon didn't waste time getting right to the risks. "Mr. Deltoro, I won't tell you that there are no risks involved with this spine surgery. We're going to insert two titanium plates into your spine around the two compromised vertebra. The statistical success rate is eighty percent, excellent odds for a satisfactory recovery for a man of your age and health, don't you agree?"

Alex thought for a moment and dared to ask the big question. "Doctor, what consequences will there be after the operation?"

Robredo smiled. "Oh, there's nothing to worry about. Your only problem is that your insurance no longer covers these expenses. Mrs. Santiaga de Vega can guide you through the insurance gibberish if you wish."

Alex's butt was numb again and his head hurt. How much would the operation cost?

"Mrs. Santiaga de Vega tells me that it will be between four-hundred-fifty and five hundred thousand pesos."

Alex didn't need to think. He barely had enough on his card, but he could cover it. "Let's do it."

Like the bad fairy, Mrs. Santiaga de Vega materialized behind the desk and ran the card.

Still worried about his finances, but relieved that the charge went through, he asked, "Well, what now?"

She gave him her friendly smile again, but her tone said something else. "Your nurse will move you to room number 356, where you will stay tonight to prepare for tomorrow's tests and surgery. The kitchen will send you a small snack later, then you'll fast until after your surgery." The administrator pointed to the door.

Alex turned to see Yajaira enter. Fatigue took hold of him. He wasn't sure if he could stay awake until he reached his room, but Yajaira's sweet face somehow made the nightmare easier. She replied respectfully to the administrator while receiving instructions. She took hold of Alex's chair and walked them out the door. Alex realized how childish it was to fear his account manager, a woman who did her job of processing him efficiently if tersely. Not that he liked her any better, but his confidence rose under Yajaira's warm influence.

They took the elevator up to the third floor. Room 356 was tucked away in the northwest corner of the building with a blurry view of the distant green mountains through a large window. The room was cold despite its soft palate. The raised bed, sporting a gray wool blanket, reassured Alex that at least he wasn't going to freeze in the tropics from the facility's arctic air-conditioning. The bed protruded under a large painting of the coast on a partly cloudy day. *Not exactly cheerful*, but he found it soothing with a kelp green surf and foam bubbling at the tide line. The television occupied a third of the wall in front.

Yajaira helped Alex into bed and showed him how to use the various controls to get comfortable, run the TV, and call for help. They experimented with possible bed adjustments for Alex's maximum comfort according to Dr. Robredo's recommended poses to relieve pain in his spine and leg.

"Thank you, Yajaira. Can I call you that? I know how beds work. I've been here before." Alex's laughter sounded more like a pig's growl than a joy, even to him.

"I remember," she replied, "but it's my job to make sure *you* remember everything and stay as comfortable as possible." She put the TV remote in his hands. "Don't forget that I'm here to take care of you. Call me for anything, Mr. Deltoro..."

"Alex. Just Alex."

"Okay, Alex." She smiled. "Don't forget to call me. The button is here..." She pointed to a button placed on the bedside table next to a jug of water, a glass, an emesis basin, and some brochures about the hospital.

"Thank you, I'll call," he said. "Where's my phone?"

She answered, "In the closet. We don't want you disturbed by anything tonight." Yajaira pointed to a door near the entrance, partially obscured by a closet. "Call me. I'll help you get to the bathroom," she said, disappearing into the hall.

Left alone to rest, he turned on the TV and went through the menu until he found a Netflix movie he thought might be interesting. For a while he forgot about the serious problems that landed him in the hospital, but he soon obsessed again over new danger to his spine. What if he were paralyzed? *What if I can't go back to work? If I have to go to IMSS hospitals?* They would kill him, just as they did Lucas. *No!* He couldn't let that happen. But what could he do? Alex had never felt so powerless, so weak, so hopeless. Beyond trusting fate, the universe, God, whatever was manipulating life's slings and arrows, Alex was out of control.

The room went dark with the sunset. Alex tried to sleep, but he couldn't stop his racing mind. He knew something about the delicate nature of spinal surgery. Any failure could leave him crippled for life. And general anesthesia always carried a risk. *What if... What if...?* Finally, before dawn, Alex relaxed and slept.

The stretcher-bearers arrived too early. His snack remained untouched by the bedside. How could he eat when his stomach clenched with worry? The skilled assistants carried him from bed to stretcher and transferred him to the laboratory's clinical analysis area for the necessary tests and to collect his medical history.

Dr. Fabián Alcalá introduced himself as his anesthesiologist and explained what type of anesthesia he would use, with a brief explanation of the procedure.

"Do you understand, Mr. Deltoro?" Alex nodded. "Well then, assistants, please transfer our patient to the operating room."

There was no turning back, although Alex did not expect such speed. He tensed up. It was now or never, forever to remain silent if he didn't get off the stretcher and flee. On the other hand, he had no more time to worry—*obsess*—about the result. In minutes he was face-down on the cold metal plate with a huge lamp illuminating his backside. The anesthesiologist gave him the first injection. Again, Alex was asked what music he wanted to hear.

"Pink Floyd," he managed to mutter.

Pink Floyd's The Wall floated through the operating room, surrounding Alex. The sedative took hold, and he soared with the music, flying. A great peace descended upon him, enveloping him in intense and bright colors. The world seemed beautiful; his fear evaporated. Alex was half absent when Dr. Alcalá placed a mask over his nose and mouth and asked him to count from one to ten.

He reached three.

Alex woke up in the room assigned by the hospital, still under the influence of anesthesia. A soft voice resounded. "Alex. Alex! Wake up. Alex..."

He struggled to come alert, turning his head toward the door before realizing it was Julian who was calling him.

His friend got up from the visitors' sofa bed. "How do you feel, champion? It's done. The doctor says everything is fine, but you have the last word."

Alex was still dizzy. How was he? He didn't know. He raised and lowered his right hand, his left, his healthy leg, and finally his injured leg. *Working.* He shifted his rear to the edge of the hospital bed. A stabbing pain radiated from his spine. Alex groaned but continued to move to his feet.

Julián ran to stop him shouting: "No! NO! Don't move, buddy. Take it easy, take it easy Alex. Let me go get your doctor. Let him help you. Don't hurt yourself." He pressed the call button.

Within seconds, Yajaira entered the room and introduced herself.

"I'm Julián. Can you call the doctor? My friend wants to get up, but he's still anesthetized."

Yajaira replied, "Oh my God. I'll be right back. She rushed out of the room and immediately returned with the orthopedic doctor, who took control of the matter.

232

Almost shouting, he greeted Alex. "Good afternoon Mr. Deltoro, I'm Dr. Robredo. Everything went well, but now you have to rest. You must not move.

Alex stammered, "Can I walk?"

"Not right now. Everything went well," he repeated, "but until the effects of the sedation wear off, we require patience on your part. Later we can do some exercises to prepare you to use crutches." Robredo tilted his gaze toward the metal sticks leaning against the window frame. He turned to Julian. "For a few weeks, Mr. Deltoro won't get out of bed." He looked back at Alex. "But in time his life will be totally normal."

The fog of drugs in Alex's brain slowly dissipated. Was it the surgeon who was talking to him? "Will I be able to walk?" he asked as he struggled to sit up.

Robredo gently planted a hand on Alex's shoulder and pushed him down. "Alex, no nerves were affected by your accident. You'll be as good as new if you follow my instructions. But it's going to be a slow recovery and it's going to require a lot of therapy. You have to be patient and rest. I'll stop by later to see how you're doing."

Alex's relief at the doctor's words almost stopped the intense pain in both his leg and spine. But his inability to move at will frightened him. What if the doctor only *said* that he would recover? A dark despair enveloped him. "I need to go home," he growled.

"Soon, Alex. We'll be gone soon," Julian reassured him.

The hospital kept him under observation for two more days.

Julian arrived in time to help Alex into the ambulance. The transfer home was a piece of cake. That was, until they arrived at Irene's house and had to deal with the ridiculous stairs. Alex realized that, once he settled into his mother's room, he wouldn't go anywhere for weeks. In the hospital, it has been quite easy. Nurses and doctors took care of all his needs. Yajaira had given him exceptional care, tender, meticulous and good-humored. She had promised to visit him at home. Maybe she would.

At home it was a different story. His room was not prepared for the kind of care Star Medica gave him. Julián did the best he could, but he was just one person and not as cute as Yajaira. The worst thing was the daily sponge bath. Alex couldn't clean himself, and the sheets and mattress stayed wet all day. They had only spent a few days following the doctor's orders for Alex to lie on his back, but he felt like a pig. Worse than a pig: he and his room were starting to stink.

"Julián, what can I do? I hate myself like this."

"Could I put a sheet of plastic under you?"

"Wow, brilliant! Plastic. Go buy me an inflatable pool and we'll put it on the bed. Next, run a hose from the bathroom connected to the shower. That should work."

The next day the problem was solved. What a relief to wash his hair! He still needed help getting into his "bathtub", but the mandatory three months in bed would pass much more pleasantly feeling clean. For this, he was grateful. *God, time is moving slowly.* It would be a long while before he could use his crutches. Alex was usually active, and he felt like the universe had applied a brake. It was humbling. And depressing.

His mind was constantly agitated. The big question:
Will I ever be okay?

Julián, Rosa, and Carolina reminded him daily that
he was still alive. If it weren't for them, Alex would
have sunk into a dark slump. His friends taught him
to be grateful. But his gratitude wasn't enough to stop
him from envisioning the cabron who ran him down
languishing in jail for the rest of his life.

Chapter 26

The Battle

Tuesday, June 30, 2020

Alex's fury grew as he lay in his bed aching. Day after insufferable day. His hatred toward the culprit blossomed like one of those night bloomers giving off a noxious stink. He knew perfectly well it had not been an accident. The man had intentionally attempted to kill him. But why? His mind churned, turning inside out and upside down. He didn't have any enemies in Veracruz. Except his family. Would Ana try to kill him? Alex's mind fixated on the idea his accident was planned and the thought rose: *Do not wait any longer.*

He reached for his telephone and punched in Licensiado Godoy's number.

"Buenos tardes, Oficina de Godoy. Como puedo sirvirle?" crooned the receptionist.

Alex identified himself and his purpose. The woman put him on hold.

Several minutes later the attorney brayed in his grating accent, "Deltoro, how are you? I didn't expect to hear from you so soon. Did something new come to light?"

"Yes, Lic. I've just been released from the hospital
—"

"What? Why? Are you ill?"

"No sir. They tried to kill me." Alex relayed the whole terrible story to the attorney, who periodically asked him to repeat something. At the end of his statement, Alex said, "I want the bastard who hit me locked up."

Godoy remained silent for several beats before he said, "Of course you do, however, considering the hit and run occurred eight days after we filed the suit, I think you should consider including the doctors. I can file a complaint immediately rather than wait for our scheduled appointment, but please, I want you to repeat what happened."

Alex adjusted his position for as much comfort as he could find and began the story again. This time he added details he'd forgotten. Finally, he asked the important question, "When will you file the complaint?"

Godoy's sarcastic sounding laughter grated through the phone. "As soon as possible, Mr. Deltoro; it will not be more than a week."

Alex wasn't sure if the pins and needles he lay upon over the next days had to do with his injuries, or his anticipation of the complaints and Godoy's call, but he barked at Julian and snapped at Carolina when she visited. He was rude to Rosa. It wasn't the injuries turning him into a monster, Alex was dying of boredom and anxiety. Godoy's week stretched to two.

On the thirteenth day, the attorney called. "Mr.

Deltoro, I've filed the *anuncia estatal;* we now present the complaint to the Veracruz state prosecutor's office. It is required we ratify the filing of the complaint for injuries against Braulio, the driver.

"Today? IT'S DONE? That's great! Thank you, Lic." Alex's grin spread so wide his face hurt.

Godoy continued as though Alex had not spoken. "Your presence at the *Fiscalia* is essential. You must ratify the complaint with your signature before the authorities personally."

Alex stiffened. The grin contracted to a frown. How on earth could he do that? He couldn't even get to the bathroom five feet away.

"Licensiado, I can't get out of bed. It's impossible. I'm barely two weeks out of surgery and in a lot of pain. Bring the fiscal here."

Godoy barked a laugh, "As if it will matter to them. No, man, you need to make every effort. Your signed statement is indispensable. Be here in one hour. It won't take long, and you can get back to bed." He hung up.

Alex didn't need to think twice. The hate-filled voice in his head always muttering about the man who had ruined his life, shouted, *Go!*

"Julián! Julián," Alex yelled, scaring Daisi from her nap. She dug her claws into his good leg and bounded out the door.

Julián leaned out of his door. "No need to yell. I'm right here. That was Godoy? What did he want?"

"Can you bring me some clean clothes and help me get dressed? We have to appear at the D.A.'s office down on Blvd. Fidel Velasquez as soon as we can get there. Is Carolina next door?"

"You're loco, man. You can't go anywhere!"

"I have to. Hand me some clothes and call Carolina while I get dressed. Or a taxi."

Julián argued, "It's a huge risk, Alex. Get them to come here."

"Not going to happen. Just do it."

Julian could not hide his anger. His face burned red. Through a clenched jaw, he said, "Okay, you know what you want to do. I'm not wasting time arguing with you. You're a fool, Alex, and stubborn too. Nobody is going to change your mind. Certainly not me."

Without further discussion, Julián handed over clean jeans and a button-down shirt. A few minutes later, Alex was walking his body down the treacherous stairs with his hands, managing to lower himself without hurting his leg or his aching spine. He would not let go of his opportunity to initiate a second suit, one that clearly connected to the murderer of his brother.

While Alex lowered himself down the stairs, Julián ran next door to get Carolina. She backed the car parallel to the gate and opened the door while Julián mostly carried Alex into the backseat.

Carolina drove carefully, creeping through the potholes and over the topes. She ignored the idiots honking at her as she and Julián kept up a running conversation. Alex watched out the window half listening. As they turned right out of the colonia from Juan Vicente Melo to Dos Bahia, he noticed a blue car coming up too fast behind them in the side mirror. *Pendejo.*

He closed his eyes, gritting his teeth, heart pounding as they made the turn onto Dr. Joaquin

Perea Blanco and bounced over the giant speed bump. He kept his eyes closed, muscles tensed through the bumps and holes until he felt the car turning onto Dr. Rafael Cuervo in front of the Pemex and Chedraui.

"You okay back there, Alex?" Julian asked.

Alex looked forward catching the image of the blue car behind them in the side mirror. Still too close. "Yeah. I'm okay. Better now that we're on a maintained road."

"Only five or eight minutes more."

Thank God. He couldn't last much longer with the sudden braking every time a taxi cut them off, the swerves to get around slow drivers and traffic snarls, and the constant honking, causing him to tense up. Alex's arms ached from holding himself together, but there ahead, he saw the tall vertical fencing and guardhouse at the gates.

Godoy met them at the reception area. "Take a seat."

Alex gave him a dirty look. "Doctor's orders. I need to lie down."

The lawyer's eyebrows shot up, yet he aimed a sneaky smile at Alex. "Do it—it will help our case. I'll let the Licensiada know we are here." Godoy scuttled away.

Alex leaned on Julián and Carolina. The three sent daggers into Godoy's back.

"It's why he's risked your physical health—for sympathy. How much are you paying this guy?" Julián asked.

Godoy reappeared with a tall, fleshy woman in a severe charcoal-colored polyester suit with several stains on one shoulder. Her hair, a color of red not found in nature, was clipped back into a messy old-style twist, which did its best to escape the pins randomly stuck into it. She pushed a wheelchair.

"Mr. Deltoro, I am Licensiada Yolanda Zarate. I will be litigating your case." She held out her hand to shake, but Alex was gripping his friends. He nodded to the wheelchair.

"Yes, I see," she said. "Please help him into the chair and come with me." She hustled from the room into the short hall and turned right, Godoy matching her stride.

Carolina carefully placed Alex into the chair. Julián, pushing, raced to catchup. He rounded the corner as the lawyers turned into the next hall. "What's the rush?" Alex asked.

"I don't know where they went." Julián slowed down. One of the wheels wobbled.

Alex shrugged. He shouted, "Godoy!"

His attorney stepped out of a door on the left side of the hall about halfway to the end and gestured.

They entered moments later. Alex assessed the small office. Directly across from the door facing the back wall sat a metal desk piled high with paper stuffed folders and a couple of empty baby bottles. Those accounted for the stains. Baby puke. *Charming.*

Licensiada Zarate perched on her grey-padded metal chair, dwarfed by the mountain of paper. Godoy pulled up a chair by the similarly laden desk where a young man sat busily working at a laptop computer. The rest of the office was taken up with shelving, tables, the printer and law books scattered everywhere.

Alex did not have a good feeling about this

interview. The place was crummy—dirty and disorganized. Julián parked him in front of the lawyer, and he held out his hand. She took it leaving a smear of sweat across Alex's palm as they greeted each other. "Let's get to business, please Licensiada. I'm in terrible pain and I'm not supposed to be sitting upright."

"I'm very sorry, Mr. Deltoro. First, I need you to walk me through the accident in your own words." He flinched at her language. She took up a steno pad and pen, leveling her gaze on him.

Alex turned to Godoy, "What? You've got my statement. I'm here to ratify with my signature."

"I'm sorry, Mr. Deltoro, but this is our procedure. You must report the facts as you know them before we can take the next step."

Didn't they read the complaint? He couldn't stand and he couldn't sit. He half reclined as his pain escalated from a dull throbbing to excruciating knives stabbing him. He began the recitation, running through the details as quickly as he could. Sweat broke out on his forehead and he felt nauseous. The attorney stopped him repeatedly to reiterate details and ask for more information. Godoy piped up now and then with a detail or question. Alex felt like he was at the Inquisition, and he was the guilty party, not the victim.

"Everything I have just told you, Licensiada, is already declared and notarized in my statement with my attorney. May I go now?" he said fighting to keep the sarcasm out of his voice. He needed these people.

"I'm truly sorry, but we have more to do. We'll be done soon," she replied then turned to her computer and began typing.

Ten agonizing minutes later, she asked the young

man to hand her the copy. She read it over, signed and dated it, and handed it to Alex.

An official letter addressed to:

C. COORDINATOR OF THE DETECTIVE DIVISION OF THE MINISTERIAL POLICE CENTRAL ZONE VERACRUZ
Reference:
VER-ZN/D-XVII/UAT/2430/2022

The letter requested the video recording from the intersection and the official police report from the hit-and-run.

"I advise you to go see the investigating officers, Señor Deltoro. You'll have better luck with them if you go in person."

"Isn't that your job, Licensiada? I am not to be out of bed for another two and a half months—"

"I'll go, Deltoro. Don't worry." That Argentinian accent had Alex plenty worried. He had fallen into a theater of the absurd.

Licensiada Zarate handed him another document the young man had retrieved from the printer. A document requesting a classification and opinion from the State forensic expert on Alex's injuries to certify the legal basis of the suit. Finally, Alex was presented with three copies of an affidavit assuring everything he said was true, which he signed. The interview was over. Godoy called Julián back to take Alex to reception.

Alex and the lawyers shook hands again. Godoy and Alex coordinated their next meeting as they traversed the dingy halls of the Fiscalia Estatal.

"Should we go now?" Carolina asked.

"Go home, yes."

"No. I mean to see the forensic pathologist. I'm really interested in that."

"Carolina, I don't need to go. I need to send a report to him from my doctor at Star Medica. Anyway, he's probably in Xalapa. But you can take it to him if you really want," Alex said, attempting to smile at her through the rearview mirror.

"You have a report? Maybe I *will* take it to him. Who is he?"

Alex thought for a moment, gazing out the window. A blue compact car came up alongside them. The driver turned to look in at Alex with a sneer. "I don't know who he is. Could you slow down?"

Carolina took her foot off the gas; the blue car surged ahead. Alex caught YGU-8 before the car was swallowed in traffic.

At home, Alex shuffled through a pile of papers stacked on the table, slid one out, and asked Julián to get it copied and mailed, before crawling back up the treacherous stairs to his bed. He'd read it so many times, he could almost recite it by memory.

Within a week, Alex had a copy of the report signed by Dr. Francisco Delgado Druaillet, Forensic Medical Expert.

Based on the medical report [attached] from the Star Médica Hospital, June 21, 2020, signed by Dr. Robredo, with the diagnoses of: traumatic vertebral injury of T 12 (fractured vertebra specification) and T 11 injury, L 11, there is an x-ray plate in view where multifragmentation fractures of the tibia and left fibula is observed, which was surgically reduced.

Surgical wound 20 cm long—midline of dorsolumbar region, surgical wound 15 cm long. And another of 10 cm. in length on the anterior side of the left tibia region.

CONCLUSIONS:

1) Patient remains neurologically stable

2) Injuries are life-threatening

3) Injuries will take more than 15 days to heal subject to their evolution and sequelae

In the next few days, Alex called the lawyer to check on the Fiscal's request for the police report and video footage from the closed-circuit camera at the scene of the hit-and-run. The receptionist passed him to Godoy's wife.

"I'm sorry Mr. Deltoro, I have no information about this. My husband is away, but I'll ask him to call you. How are you doing?"

"I'm slowly healing, but I don't understand why my report has not been obtained. It's what he was paid for."

"I'm sure he's requested your police report and will be in touch as soon as he can. Buenos tardes, Señor Deltoro." The line went dead.

What happened to the charming woman who said to talk to her if things went wrong with her husband? He called Licensiada Zarate at the Fiscalia Estatal. No, the report and video had not arrived.

"You heard him. Licensiado Godoy said he would deliver the letter. How long does it take the police to send the report? Isn't it routine?"

"Yes, it is routine, and generally the report will be here in several days. However, you might want to consider your attorney has not acted properly on behalf of your case."

"What do you mean? We signed an agreement. Can you submit the letter?"

"As I said before, it's better if you go, but let's give it a few more days, Señor Deltoro."

Alex hung up. Over the next few days, he called Godoy's office repeatedly. Each time he got an answering service and left a message. What the hell was going on? It looked like his attorney had abandoned him, and according to Licensiada Zarate, the report had not arrived. Alex finally made a formal request of the Fiscalia to make an official request of the C. COORDINATOR OF THE DETECTIVE DIVISION OF THE MINISTERIAL POLICE CENTRAL ZONE VERACRUZ.

Nothing happened. Alex realized he'd been screwed.

Monday, August 10, 2020

La Fiscalia asked five times for the report and video. Alex suspected someone had been bribed to lose or destroy the evidence to stop his lawsuit from going forward. He had a copy of the file and, with nothing better to do, he read it over carefully, hoping the written record might shed some light on his problem. Sure enough, he discovered the prosecutor, the baby-puke stained Licensiada Zarate had made several

246

errors at the time of requesting the video. Three errors, in fact very important errors: 1. the date of the hit-and-run, 2, the time of the hit-and-run, and 3. even the year was wrong. *What was the matter with these people?* These errors would obviously hinder the investigation. He yelled for Julián, who had just returned from the gym.

"Hey man, get me up. I need to go to the prosecutor's office. They're screwing me over."

"No, Alex, you need to stay in bed. Call."

"Come 'ere, listen to this." Julián stuck his head through the doorway and Alex read the document with the errors.

"Chingao! Those weren't errors. Somebody bought off your lawyer."

Forty minutes later, Julián wheeled Alex into the state prosecutor's offices. Alex demanded the head of the department's office. Julián raced Irene's rickety wheelchair he'd found in the storage room into her office, surprising the department head and her secretary.

Alex waved the page under her nose. "Señora, look at this! Wrong date. Wrong year. Wrong time. This was Licensiada Zarate's work. I need someone who is not corruptible. She's been bought off."

The lead prosecutor blanched then colored. "Let's not make accusations, Señor. . . Deltoro is it? Let me issue you a new prosecutor." She held up a finger then dialed. "Carmela, I need you to take over a case. . . Yes, now."

Again, Alex had to repeat the story to the new public official, Carmela Soto.

"According to the investigation file, the person who had paid the insurance was different from the one who committed the hit-and-run, and they did not arrest the driver. The detectives didn't do their jobs. I want, in writing, the report of the officer who arrested and was present at the accident."

But the damage was done. When Alex returned a week later, he realized that the official document still had the wrong year. Alex had no doubts. The Fiscalia was intentionally hindering the investigation. How far would corruption in Mexico go? This was the state prosecutor!

Unfortunately, on September seventh, Alex underwent a second surgery on his tibia and fibula. The fracture remained; the bones would not heal. Julián insisted it was from getting out of bed too soon and too often to stress out at the Fiscalia. This time his surgeon exchanged the titanium plate for a larger and thicker one. To ensure healing, he made an incision in Alex's hip to extract a bone graft to be applied to the tibia.

How was he going to pay the credit card bill? Alex was nearly broke. Julián and Rosa generously fed him most of the time. Neither had two pesos to rub together. He could sell his mother's house, yet it wasn't worth more than a month's grocery bill. *Anyway, where would I live?* He pondered all this as he fell asleep in his hospital bed.

Yajaira gently awoke Alex in the morning with his tray of eggs, tortillas, papaya, and coffee.

"Good morning sleepyhead. The doctor will come see you sometime this morning. If all is fine, he's going to send you home. Julián is taking good care of you, I think."

"Good morning, Yajaira. What time is it?"

"Late. I let you rest. How are you feeling?"

"Tired. Beat up. I'm done with operations and lack of exercise. When can I get up?"

She laughed. "Oh, you pobrecito." She played a sad aria on her air violin. "Concentrate on healing, Alex. You'll be able to ask the doctor when he makes his rounds. You don't want to end up back here again."

"You're right there. I can't afford it. I haven't worked in almost six months. I don't know what I'll do."

"Do you have anything you could sell?" she asked while stuffing pillows behind his back so he could sit up to eat.

"I was thinking about that last night. My house isn't worth enough to bother selling. You've seen it."

"What about taking out a mortgage? Don't I remember you telling me you have a house in Mexico?"

"Wow! Good memory. I hadn't thought of a mortgage. You're brilliant!" *But how long before I can go back to work?*

"Glad to help, Alex. Eat up. The doctor should be by pretty soon. I'll come back later to see how you're doing."

Alex sank into a quagmire of hatred and depression. His suit foundered, Godoy never surfaced, and the Fiscalia did nothing. His attacker remained at large.

Wednesday, December 9, 2020

When Alex was able, he called Carolina to drive him to the Ministerial Police satellite office in Colonia Las Bajadas, out on the highway between Boca del Rio and Veracruz. He would obtain the police report the State Fiscalia failed to secure.

The small, run-down building was tucked into a pocket between the glassed-in ATM station of a bank, and a car lot stacked to the clouds with wrecks from accidents on Veracruz's highways. A gas plaza crowded with big rigs pulling shipping containers lay across the highway. The stench of exhaust, diesel, burning rubber, and dust made him sneeze. *Nice section of town.* The noise deafening for someone who had been confined for months.

Carolina let off Alex and his crutches, saying she needed to shop for fresh groceries for Rosa. "I'll pick you up in front in an hour," she said, and pulled back onto the northbound highway toward the next colonia where there was a big market.

Alex swung himself up the uneven steps and through the security gated door. He asked for the chief commander of the detective unit responsible for carrying out the initial investigation of his hit-and-run at the front desk, one Rolando Hernández Macho.

The burly Commander Hernández shook Alex's hand then invited him into his office. "How can I help you, Señor Deltoro?" he asked as he motioned to a threadbare chair hunkering before a beat-up metal desk missing one leg, perching on a stack of old manuals.

Alex explained his mission, including that the request had been repeated five times by the Fiscalia, and to date, there had been no investigation or response. He added, "The only progress was that the ADO bus station refused access to its files—obviously lying. Don't you, the authorities, have every right to the information?"

"I don't know about ADO's policies," he said, "but our department has never received requests from attorney Godoy. I remember the requests from the Fiscalia did not turn up any reports or video."

"Because the dates and time were wrong." Alex passed over his corrections and a copy of the document drafted by the prosecutor's office.

Hernández requested his assistant find the paperwork, which was readily available when given the correct date and time. "Typical incompetence," he muttered. "I'll have these sent over to the fiscal, Soto, you said?"

"Yes, Licensiada Soto, or that was the last one several months ago." Alex explained his operations and recovery, then and asked to be provided with a computer to write another additional document that he printed, signed, and handed over:

He requested: 1) A list of which agents from the hit-and-run to contact and provide a personal account of how the events unfolded, where, when, and how. 2) Information on the witnesses and how to locate them. 3) A copy of the document the prosecutor's office used to verify the case to the Ministerial Police, along with access to interview the alleged perpetrator. 4) Instructions to collaborate on the case to facilitate the ongoing investigation.

Alex printed two copies, signed and dated one, and

handed it over to Hernández.

Commander Hernández instructed him to wait for a call from an agent in January, since the December holidays were about to begin. He would provisionally assign him to Officers Daniel Gutiérrez and Manuel Barrera, but, he said, "They have not yet submitted their reports."

Alex's hope sank. *More waiting.* How he hated waiting. "Thank you, Commander. I'll be in touch in the new year. Feliz Navidad." He hobbled out of the office to wait for Carolina to pick him up. Finally, something was happening on his case.

Chapter 27

The Tail

Carolina arrived within ten minutes, leaving Alex enough time to survey the neighborhood. It looked rough, and he felt weak. He exhaled with relief when she pulled up and pushed the door open in front of the bashed-in Chevy he leaned against.

"How'd it go, Alex?"

He waved the copies of the reports. "I finally got these from the crime scene. Let's go."

"I need gas. Got any money?"

"No, but there's a bank over there." He pointed. "I'll get some cash. Park in front."

She pulled forward. Alex went through the maneuvers to get out and retrieve his crutches, found his ATM card, let himself into the locked station, and got into line for the machine. Four people waited. He turned to look out the window.

A blue Jetta slowly cruised by, probably looking for a parking spot, but he could see that the driver was checking out Carolina or appeared to be. Then he was looking into the man's eyes. He felt an uncomfortable sensation cross his back, but the car made a sudden U-turn across the four lanes and disappeared behind a pump in the station. Alex was imagining things. *Wasn't he?*

His lucky day. The line moved fast and in five minutes, he was back in the car and Carolina was ordering her sin magna gasoline. Alex could see the boot of the blue car between the rows of pumps. Something bugged him. He remembered a blue car following them, months ago when he went to the State D.A.'s office with the missing Godoy.

"I'm going to the bathroom. Be right back," he announced and clambered out.

He kept trucks and pumps between himself and the blue Jetta until he made out the license plate, YGU-877. YGU-8? That was the plate that he'd seen before. He crossed over the island around a pickup at the pump, behind the Jetta to the station and went inside to watch through the window. He had seen the driver's face before, but it had been some time. He watched, willing the man to turn around.

The man, dark-skinned, clean shaven, grinning plump lips, close-cropped dark hair under a black baseball cap, had finished pumping and paying. He turned the key and pulled out, passing close to the building. As he passed, he tipped his finger against the bill of his cap and pointed the finger salute directly at Alex. Alex could feel the squeeze of the trigger.

He didn't listen to Carolina's cheerful patter on the way home. Instead, he grunted monosyllables when she asked him something, and she finally punched on the radio and sang along to her pop songs. He kept his eyes peeled for the Jetta.

Rightly so. Carolina made the left into the colonia

and there he was, parked in front of the grocer's, picking through the carrots. Again, the grin. *He's waiting for me. Wants me to know he's after me.* Alex's bones chilled although it was a warm day. He hurried into the house, barely thanking the girl for her kindness.

Ready for a nap, he struggled up the steep stairs. This first day out had exhausted him as well as stressed him beyond his usual stoic tolerance. He was scared.

Julian's door stood open when Alex reached the landing, and he popped his head in to say hello. Julián's suitcase was open on the bed. His back was to the door, but there was no mistaking he was packing.

"You off?" Alex asked, his tone light.

Julián turned around, a stack of folded clothing in his arms. "How'd it go, güey? Come in, sit. Tell me you got the reports."

Alex lowered himself to the caned chair with a quiet grunt, then grinned. "I got them! With the correct dates and time there was no problem. It doesn't look like the Ministerial was bought off. Or we'll see."

"What about your demands? Will they give you the info and protection you want?"

"If they don't. . .pues we'll wait and see. That guy who hit me wouldn't be able to pay them off."

"Yeah, but I doubt Braulio, was running the show, Alex. Everything I know about this screams 'attempted homicide' and why would that guy want to kill you? No, it's someone, or a group of, say—doctors? Who has motive and means. I'm worried to leave you." He said, tucking another tee-shirt into his suitcase and closing it.

"You coming back after the holidays? I'm refinancing my house in Mexico. Getting a mortgage so we'll have some money until one of these lawsuits pays out."

"Alex, I feel terrible, but I have to get on with my life. I've got an offer. It's a good job, and you're doing so well since the last operation, you can manage. My mother called today and begged me to come. The family needs me. I'll miss our talks."

"Your wife?" Alex asked. He backed up to let Julián head down the stairs then followed.

"Dios, no. My kids. My parents. At least for Christmas. The job starts in January. I'll stay at my daughter's until I get a paycheck."

"You can stay at my house. It's empty."

Julian set his suitcase on the coffee table and collected up his book and glasses, tucking them in his backpack. "Thanks, my friend, but you know I can't pay for it."

Alex clumped to the door on his crutches. "A gift. For as long as you need it. I owe you, Julián." He stood the crutches up and hopped to his friend to give him a brotherly hug. "Thank you, amigo, I'd have died without you."

Julián chuckled. "Maybe not died, but I am glad to have helped. I want you to be smart, Alex. Don't go after these pendejos. Do your therapy, sell the house, come home."

A honk in the narrow street signaled the taxi. The men crossed the patio, Alex unlocked the gate, holding it open for his friend. They embraced again, clapping each other on their backs. Then Julián was gone.

Alex felt a chill wind. His crummy little world was disintegrating.

The following day, Rosa and Carolina appeared at the gate toting a package wrapped in colorful paper and a plate enfolded in a tortilla towel, mounded high with something that smelled heavenly. Alex let them in, inviting them to join him in a fresh cup of coffee.

Rosa settled herself on the settee while Carolina trotted after Alex to help with the coffee.

"What's under that towel, Carolina?"

She giggled. "You'll find out. I made them myself." She pulled three mugs from the cabinet, set them on the tray she'd taken from the top of the refrigerator, then poured a small pitcher of milk for Rosa. She carried the tray to the coffee table and sat down to unwrap her treat. In moments, Alex joined them, the press brimming with dark, rich coffee and poured each a cup.

"Guau, Carolina! You baked those? Hojarascas? He pointed to the now uncovered plate of freshly baked star-shaped cookies with silver and gold sprinkles.

The girl nodded, beaming. "Do you like them?"

"My favorite. How'd you know?"

"I didn't but they're my favorite, too, and good for Christmas."

"Thank you. I'm sorry I was not so nice yesterday."

"It's okay, Alex. Are you going to be all right here by yourself?"

"We—I-I'm sorry to see Julián go, but I've got Daisi. And you and Rosa." He smiled at his neighbors. "And a plate of delicious cookies." He winked. Carolina blushed.

"Alex, dear..." Rosa set her cup gingerly onto the tray, and leaned forward. "It's part of why we've come today. Do you have any plans for Navidad? We are leaving tomorrow for my family in Oaxaca. We go every year. Would you like to come with us?"

Daisi strolled in from wherever she'd been napping and wove between Rosa's legs. The old woman bent down to pet her; the cat turned up her one-hundred-watt purr.

"You've made a friend of my kitten, I see, but I don't know how I could go. Somebody has to stay home and feed her." He smiled. "Thank you for the invitation. I'd be honored to pass the holidays with you and your family, but Señora Rosa, I still have so much pain, especially in the car. I really need to stay home and do my exercises and rest." He reached over from his seat and squeezed her withered hand.

Carolina appeared oblivious to his subterfuge, but Alex thought Rosa could see right through him. It wasn't his pain; it was his shame. He was always taking from this kind grandmother. He couldn't bear to go and ruin her holidays—she wouldn't have many more.

"If you won't come, Alex, it's a good thing we brought your gift." Carolina handed over the package.

"For me?" Alex said, animating his voice. He grinned, took the package in his hands and gave it a shake. "Hmmm. Not a set of marbles."

Carolina giggled. "No, not marbles—or a jigsaw puzzle. Open it!"

Alex ripped the paper away to reveal a quality headset to plug into his phone. *How generous!*

"Guau...Just what I need while I exercise. Thank

you both so much. I'll miss you while you're away, ladies. But I'll keep the taxistas in business." He laughed and helped Rosa to her feet, gave her his arm and walked her to the gate, Carolina on the other side. At the gate, they hugged again and said their goodbyes.

Rosa's parting words echoed through Alex's brain. She patted him on the back. "Cheer up, hijo, you are a strong man, the strongest of the lot. Mark this old lady's words. You will recover from this, Alex."

"Feliz Navidad, ustedes," he called as they disappeared through their own gate.

Alex felt awash in sadness as loneliness crowded down on him. He missed his brothers, his mother, and most of all, his dad. He'd always been surrounded by family or friends at Christmas. Now he was totally alone—and still not recovered from what he referred to as *the accident.* But in his heart, he knew it had been no accident.

Alex locked up and hauled himself up the stairs, balancing the plate of cookies in one hand and propelling himself with the crutches in the other. He lay down, clicked on the television, and flipped through the channels. Announcements, laugh tracks, Christmas carols. He wasn't feeling the holiday spirit, but he settled on a Christmas rom com on Netflix. He half-watched and half-dozed until the next movie started with a loud soundtrack that jerked him from his fugue state.

He ached. The bed was too hard and his thoughts too low. This was when Alex wished he liked to drink or take drugs. He could knock himself out and sleep until January. He didn't have anything else to do.

Except, he didn't do those kinds of things anymore. He was a responsible, law-abiding member of society who took his duties seriously and strove to be a reliable, caring human being—and look how that turned out.

The TV cast its bluish glow across the room for the remainder of the night while Alex brooded, and a gnawing fear germinated in his gut. The blue car. The attempted murder. The robbery. But mostly, his abandonment. How could he protect himself?

Chapter 28

The Threat

Sunday, December 20, 2020

Alex only ventured out of the house when he needed food. Maneuvering the cobbled streets of his neighborhood on the uncomfortable crutches was risky. He could fall or be knocked over, but taking the motorcycle was riskier. He remained vigilant watching for the blue car. Most of the time, he rattled around his mother's house, now his house, between the T.V., the kitchen, his laptop, and the living room chair with the good light where he read the few books he found on the shelves.

Late in the afternoon, he was reading, his leg pillowed onto the coffee table, when the sound of a motorcycle echoed up the street. It stopped outside his wall putting, but no one shouted out their wares for sale. *It must be visiting across the street.* He turned back to the book.

Moments later, the dining room window exploded with a sharp bang, sending shards clattering across the tile floor. Something hit the table. Alex's heart stopped. Had someone come to rob the place? He grabbed a crutch, ready to swing. "Who's there?" he shouted as he lurched from the chair, moving as fast as he could toward the table. No one at the window; no one climbing the gate. The motorcycle roared between the stanchions closing off the street and whined into the distance, leaving Alex in silence.

He shivered. His hand shook as he reached for the light switch, fear rising up his gullet. What had come through his window? The table contained the accumulated clutter of papers from the D.A.'s office and his lawyer, his computer, but something had hit. He pulled out the chairs. A river rock wrapped in paper and bound with twine rested in the second chair. He plucked it up and untied the twine. A list scrawled on the paper in black marker read:

Drop the lawsuit
Go back to Mexico
Or join your brother

Alex's blood boiled. A direct threat. *This was proof! But of what? Did the hit-and-run driver, throw this through his window? Or the doctor?* He dialed Godoy, but on the second ring he disconnected. Godoy had never gotten back to him. He'd gladly taken Alex's retainer, but never followed through on what he contracted to do. Either incompetent, or they'd bribed him to stall and produce incorrect or misleading information. *Dios, he hadn't even gotten the date right. No.* Godoy wasn't going to help. What should he do?

In the past, when things got too complicated, Alex walked. But first he needed to take photographs of the damage and the note. He hobbled upstairs, rummaged through the wardrobe for his running shoes and put them on, then searched the dresser top for his phone. Swiping it open, he saw he had a text message from an unknown number beginning with the Veracruz exchange. Probably the new attorney from the D.A.'s office. *Took her long enough.* He opened it.

"Consider yourself warned. Next time it won't be a window," an unfamiliar, gruff voice said. Alex couldn't place the accent, but it wasn't jarocho. Or chilango.

For once the crutches weren't burdensome. With two threats, Alex wished he carried a gun rather than two metal sticks, but at least a crutch wielded like a Japanese bo-staff would be some protection. *But against whom?*

Outside, the day shown bright, warm and crystal clear. Neighbor's Christmas decorations glittered on fences and walls; the strains of Christmas carols wafted from gated entries as he limped the slight slope toward the little neighborhood market. A boy he did not recognize was kicking a soccer ball several doors down.

"Buenos tardes, joven. Have you been out here long?"

"Feliz Navidad. For a while. Why?"

"Did you see a motorcycle come up?"

"Yeah. It stopped in front of Irene's house." He pointed to Alex's house.

"Did you see what he looked like or what he did?"

"Yeah. He tried the gate, but it was locked. I thought it was Irene's son, you know the chilango."

"What did he do?"

"He climbed up on the gate and threw something

through the window. I heard the crash."

"Then what happened?

"I don't know. Grandma called me. When I came back out, the motorcycle was gone. Why would Irene's son break her window?"

"It wasn't her son, I'm her chilango son. My mother died earlier this year."

"Oh, sorry man, I didn't mean anything."

"It's okay. I'm Alex." He held out his hand to shake. "Did you ever see a blue Jetta here?

"No." The boy looked up at him. "What happened to you?"

"Hit by a car. You Lupita's grandson?"

"Yeah. Rafi. I'm ten. The blue Jetta hit you?"

"No. Another car. You're good with that ball. You going pro?"

"When I'm big enough. But that's not for a long time." He frowned at his ball.

"Maybe you would like to earn some pesos while you're here."

The frown morphed into a grin, and the boy nodded. "How? Wash your motorcycle? I'm leaving after New Year's to go back to school."

"Pues, that too. Twenty pesos sound about right? But no, I need someone who's outside in the alley, maybe practicing his footwork, to keep an eye on who goes to my house. If you see anyone, will you check them out? Try to describe them? Don't approach anyone, just watch. Ring the bell if you have news, okay?"

He handed the kid twenty pesos. "Twenty now, twenty next week, and twenty before you leave. The bike is extra."

The boy hopped a glee filled dance and stuffed the note into his short's pocket. His grandmother called him. Grabbing up the tattered soccer ball, he shouted, "Adios, Alex," and bounded into the house.

Alex hobbled onward. The blue Jetta bothered him. It was the only option, well, except the mysterious motorcycle-riding, rock-throwing, man. He was certain he'd see the Jetta in the neighborhood again. He was also certain it was connected to the rock thrower.

Alex bought bread, meat, and vegetables, skipping the beer he would have consumed if he hadn't given the retainer to Rafi. Filling his backpack, he hefted it over his shoulders and started home. He didn't see the Jetta.

The short walk exhausted him. But it served its purpose. He knew what he had to do, and concluded that calling Samia, his attorney in Mexico City, was the only choice. He could trust her. The lawyer answered on the third ring.

"Good afternoon, Señora Samia. It's Alex Deltoro."

"What a pleasure to hear from you, Mr. Deltoro. How can I help you?

"Are you busy? I have quite a story to relate. I need your advice."

"I'm free this afternoon. Go ahead."

Alex related all the salient facts, including the earlier threat. He added his opinions on who was behind the attempted murder.

She responded with, "Mr. Deltoro, this is dangerous. My initial opinion is you should abandon your suits and leave well enough alone. But it's your choice. I can only give you some minimal support from Mexico City, I'm sorry. I can recommend a trusted colleague who lives in the Port of Veracruz and practices criminal law."

Alex paused for a few seconds. He weighed the danger, but something compelled him to continue. He wouldn't cower and run back to Mexico with his tail between his legs like some street cur. *No!* He had to avenge his brother and get justice for himself. Family obligation had turned to self-motivation, he realized—they'd tried to kill him! He sucked in a deep breath, letting it flow out slowly. "I understand what you are telling me, and I know the risks. I'd like to talk to your contact."

"Give me a few minutes, Mr. Deltoro. Let me review my notes and find his information."

An hour later, Licensiada Samia called back. "His name is Ramiro Altamirano, his telephone No is 2295 563777. Confirm you agree that he speaks on my behalf."

Alex contacted Licensiado Ramiro Altamirano who listened carefully to Alex's story.

"Mr. Deltoro, did you get the license plate of the Jetta?"

"Yes." He spelled out the letters and numerals slowly.

Altamirano repeated back the plate number. "Tomorrow I will contact you. I'll research the owner of the car through the public vehicle registry and CarFax MX. I trust we will move the matter forward."

Licensiado Altamirano wasted no time. The next day, he contacted Alex. "I have news for you Mr. Deltoro. The Jetta belongs to a former Policia Ministerial named Enrique Silva, and he is currently a private investigator. He was terminated for corruption some years ago. Rumor says he's extremely dangerous. Please forgive my over-stepping, but you must be careful, Mr. Deltoro. These people are garbage; they have no morals or scruples—they'll do anything for a few cents. I repeat, you have to be careful. Now I've become involved. We need to tread lightly."

Alex fell speechless for a few seconds, then straightened from his slump. "Lic. Thank you for this valuable information. But why would I be investigated, unless the hit-and-run was planned? The pendejo who hit me had no reason to want me dead, which convinces me this has to do with my suit against the doctors who inadvertently, or more likely purposely, killed my brother."

Altamirano concurred.

"I have to end this matter once and for all. I want justice for my brother, and a lot of money for my pain and suffering," Alex said, adding in a snarl "And loss of income. Can we meet this week, get my cases turned over to you?"

"I'm sorry, but I'm booked for the next several days, then it's the holidays. We'll have to leave things until the beginning of January. But so will they."

Alex slumped; the fire of his resolve tamped to smoldering coals. He had to wait. Waiting was not his thing—he was a man of action. But Christmas was only a few days away, and the New Year would have to bring him satisfaction. He couldn't continue to live like this, beaten down at every turn. With Julián, Rosa, and Carolina gone, all he had was Daisi—a small, purring comfort, but not enough. Even his weekly therapy was on hold until after the New Year. As well as the near weekly visits to the Fiscalia.

The more he obsessed over the progression of events, the more certain he was that a powerful, wealthy opponent orchestrated the setbacks and delays. Altamirano would be his second privately hired attorney, Godoy having taken his retainer and disappeared suspiciously. The wife had lied to him. At the D.A.'s office, he was on his third state assistant D.A. Each had been replaced after he caught the stupid mistakes they made in his file. *Really?* The wrong date for the hit-and-run? *The wrong year?*

It kept happening. The D.A, would pull the case when Alex found the errors, saying it was for revision, then assign him a new attorney. How much money had the doctors funneled into the state retirement fund or the holiday party—or directly into the pockets of the attorneys? There simply couldn't be so many incompetent lawyers working at the State of Veracruz D. A.'s offices. Add the cost of the attempted murder and the P.I.—why the hell didn't the doctors just pay *him* off and be done with it?

Chapter 29

The Holidays

Finally, Christmas day arrived. For Alex, locked in his mother's crummy house, the day passed slowly. Alternating between restless sleep and watching stupid holiday movies on Netflix, he stayed in bed with no appetite to prepare anything for dinner. The best he could do was pet Daisi as she ate her crunchies.

He couldn't stop himself from thinking of past family dinners full of smiles and hugs; the clinking of glasses and shouts of "salud!"; the exchanging of gifts —watching the eyes of the kids light up with joy at a new doll or train or soccer ball. The thought that this would not happen again stabbed his heart. It trembled with sadness. His father was long gone. His mother and younger brother gone, lost to cancer. And Lucas. Poor sick murdered Lucas. Alex curled into himself, clutching his middle, wracked with dry sobs.

He spent the better part of Christmas week alternating between sleep and checking for the blue Jetta, or any vehicle in the neighborhood, which didn't belong. Hard to do during the holidays, when family came from all over to visit his neighbors.

A couple of days after Christmas, he conferred with his ten-year-old halcon lookout. "So, what have you seen Rafi? Anyone interested in my house?"

"No, Señor Alex. I know who all the cars belong to. I haven't seen anyone sitting in a car or any motorcycles except Amado's, but he's in Guanajuato and it's been locked up in the carport since before Christmas."

"Good work, man," Alex said. "Here's twenty more. Keep your eyes open. Check in right away if you see anything. And thank your abuela for the delicious tamales. They really made my Navidad." He ruffled Rafi's hair as the boy stuffed the money into his pocket.

"She's making sopapillas today. I'll bring some later. Bye!" Rafi scampered down the narrow street. Alex re-locked the gate.

It was a lovely warm day with not a cloud in the sky. He was feeling stir-crazy. Maybe he should call for an Uber and walk along the Malecon. Or plant himself at Cervecería Heroica on the Plaza de las Armas with a beer and listen to the bands, which would surely be performing all afternoon and evening. Maybe he could catch a mass at the cathedral anchoring one end of the park while he was there. He'd missed the Christmas Eve mass.

Going out into public could be dangerous. The Malecon wouldn't be crowded enough, but the plaza might be. Especially if he were sitting against the restaurant's wall. Dios, he had to get out of this ghost-filled house and live a little. He could buy groceries at Chedraui on the way home. There was nothing in the refrigerator beyond some limp lettuce and moldy beans from a week ago.

Daisi rubbed against his ankles as he stood at the kitchen counter assessing the staples for what he might need. His list was growing. He'd need quite a bit of food to tide him over to the new year. Maybe it would be better to take a taxi from the plaza to the Soriana closer to el Centro—the one with the ATM machines, and Uber home from there. He could be recognized too easily in Chedraui.

He stowed the list in his pack with enough cash to cover his beer and comida, then hobbled into the shower, hoping he had something clean to put on.

In the shower, Alex mentally assessed his financial condition. He could eat, but his cell bill and the electricity were due around the fifth. Not to mention Altamirano's retainer.

If it wasn't one thing to worry about, it was another. He hadn't been this broke in three decades, he realized as the cool water splashed over his head. Not since right after his father died and grieving, he insanely abandoned his job to spend months running around the country with a girl from California in her VW camper.

It had been the balm to heal his broken heart. He'd poured his soul out to her as he drove. Reina didn't speak much Spanish. But she loved him and supported him until he healed. It hadn't ended well— how could it have? She was on a tourist visa; she wasn't staying. But she had done her job, taking away his pain and restoring his confidence. He needed a new Reina.

But look at how far he'd come. Pinche Lucas. Lucas had knocked him down. *Will I ever get back on my feet?* Once the lawsuits finalized, and he could get out of this wretched city, could Alex beg his way back into his job?

He thought about Reina again—what was her real name?—as he toweled off. He wondered what she was up to. Maybe he'd Google her, see if she could be found. He had her name somewhere.

On the thirtieth Plaza de las Armas teemed with holiday merry makers. The restaurants overflowed with diners; it was the hour of comida after all, and more people poured out of the cathedral at the end of a service. Hawkers, mostly indigenous children, wove between the outdoor tables displaying their wares, and stopping whenever anyone looked interested in cheap sunglasses, woven belts, or one of the myriad useless objects and tourist trinkets these poor kids were selling. Were they forced labor for Los Zetas?

He grabbed a chair at a small table backed up against the cevecería, lowered the crutches to the tiles behind the chair and sat down. He waved away the little boy selling Chicklets.

A short man dressed in black pants, a white shirt with a grey-blue towel wrapped around his hips like an apron, carrying a black plastic tray scurried over. "What can I get you?" the waiter shouted over the blaring salsa rhythms of the band set up in front of the tables. The singer had a nice voice.

He replied, "Bring me a tarro sized Corteza de Bronce, please, and what's to eat?"

The man slapped a menu in front of him. "I'll give you a minute." He hustled inside to the bar to fetch Alex's order.

He returned in moments with a jar of dark beer topped with a froth of dense cola-colored foam.

"Anything to eat?"

Alex shouted over the music. "Thanks, yes the hamburger Mamastronica with everything, medium rare."

The waiter bent toward Alex's ear. "Very good. Salsa? Guacamole?"

"Guac!"

The waiter shot a thumbs-up and moved on to the next table. The place was getting crowded. Alex wondered if he should move inside. The music was great, but he'd be able to hear it loud and clear from the elegant dark wood appointed taproom. No one outside would be able to see him.

A crowd of twenty-somethings swarmed through the neat rows of outdoor tables, funneling under the portico past Alex into the taproom. A wedding party maybe, or a pre-New Year's Eve celebration. They'd fill all the tables, if they weren't running back and forth between clusters of friends, ruining his supper and peace. He'd stay put.

Fifteen minutes and half the beer later, his burger arrived. Alex's stomach growled; he hadn't eaten a decent meal since Julián left. He dug in, turning his attention to the giant, juicy, fully loaded burger. His first bite told him this was worth the inflated price. He ate half of his meal like tomorrow would never come, finally coming up for breath when he felt a rush of heat up his neck as an out-of-place movement caught his eye.

A man's gaze concentrated on him. Dark hair, tanned, black muscle tee showing off his beefy arms, cutting across the several restaurants' outdoor dining areas like a cat—too fast for a man his size. His eyes bored into Alex, telegraphing mal intent. Alex whipped out his wallet, deposited some bills onto the table. In a smooth motion he slid the crutches from behind his chair and propelled himself into the pulsating throng inside the restaurant, beelining toward the bathrooms. He raced through the hall, the kitchen, and out the delivery door into the callejon running behind the row of restaurants.

The kitchen workers shouted as he swung himself down the narrow alley toward Calle Independencia. He needed to hide, but where? Behind a dumpster? In a dumpster? Too obvious. A door banged open, almost hitting him as a chef appeared hefting a bag of garbage. Alex darted inside while the man's back was turned and awkwardly crutched his way to the bathroom—the women's bathroom—and locked himself into a stall.

A cluster of women came in. The other stalls filled. He could hear chatter at the sinks. There must be a line, he thought, as doors opened and closed. He couldn't hear any music. Probably a break.

Suddenly the outer door banged to some shrieks. The women in line started shouting, "A man!" "Get out!" "Women's!"

A scuffle sounded and a man's voice said he was sorry to the rhythm of slaps and shoves. Would his assailant take his reception as a sign Alex wasn't there? Or better yet, would he leave the restaurant entirely?

Alex waited for another fifteen minutes while women came in and out before he heard the band, a new band by the sound of it, strike up. The flow of traffic dwindled. He crept out of the stall and made his way to the door, heart pounding. Now would be the reckoning. He pushed the door open slowly, studied the empty hallway, stepped out, checking both ends.

Like the Cervecería, the restaurant was filled with revelers. Several large parties milled around trains of tables coupled together. He studied the crowd. No Ray Mysterio in a muscle tee.

He maneuvered his way to the front door, poked out his head to take in the diners and drinkers on the plaza. With five restaurants filled to capacity along the park, it was nearly impossible to assess the danger. Then there were the trees and shrubs in the park, which could easily hide a watcher. At least the many people prevented the guy from taking a shot at him, or so Alex hoped. He decided to make a run for it, calling for a taxi to meet him on the other side of the cathedral.

In eight minutes, Alex was safely out of the Zocalo and standing on the curb in front of Soriana. He often bought groceries here as it was practically in the Fiscalia parking lot. He hobbled into the store, made his way to the far-left end, got cash from the ATM machine, grabbed a cart somebody left at the entrance to the bathrooms, and headed toward produce. He ticked off his purchases and finally added a treat of pan dulces. The half-eaten burger wasn't quite enough to tide him over to breakfast.

The line to pay snaked out into the wide cross-store aisle. Alex pulled up to the end and used the wait to call for an Uber. It would arrive in fifteen minutes, but the line moved fast—mostly folks picking up pan dulces or something for supper. At the register, he grabbed two giant bottles of Coke from the end-cap refrigerator and started through, paying cash.

Balancing his crutches and several bags of food, he limped toward the exit where he could watch the parking lot. No blue Jettas stood out, but anyone following him could easily be driving another car. Despite the congestion of shoppers coming and going, Alex would be readily recognizable out on the curb. How many middle-aged men with curly light brown hair would be on crutches? Better to stay next to the security guard inside.

"Hey man, how's it going?" he asked the blue uniformed attendant.

"Looks like you need a hand."

"I'm resting for a few, waiting for my Uber, but thanks."

The guard looked about thirty-five, fit, and bored under his black buzz-cut hair. "What happened to you?"

Alex wasn't one to discuss the details of his problems with strangers, instead he quipped, "The car won."

"You got hit? Where?" The man's voice sounded incredulous.

"Crosswalk on Avenue Salvador Diaz Mirón." His phone buzzed. "My ride is here. Catch you next time." Alex began his balancing act.

The guard said, "Here, let me get those bags." He picked up three and asked if the silver Tsuru at the curb was his.

Alex nodded, the guard headed out the door, with Alex hustling to keep up behind him.

The man handed over the groceries. "Here you go. I

hope you got some compensation. Good luck," he said,

Alex bent to shove the crutches and food into the backseat. He straightened up to get into the front seat. A car backfired. The guard grabbed his muscled arm. A woman screamed.

The security guard shouted, "Shooter! Get down. Get down!"

Alex dropped into the front seat with the driver, who was already half lying across the seats. He watched through the side mirror as the guard wrestled his gun from its holster, a red rivulet running down his arm. He'd been grazed. But he used the car as cover, crouch-walked to the rear bumper to survey the parking lot.

Over the shouts and screams of frightened shoppers, Alex heard a motor rev. He sat up to see a black car speed to Avenue Rafael Cuervos. Its tires squealed as it shot right into the stream of traffic and disappeared.

"They're gone. Let's go," he shouted at the Uber driver. "Take the back exit, we'll enter Las Brisas a different way. I'll direct you."

The driver grinned. He was missing his front teeth. Hopefully he wasn't a meth head. That would be the last thing Alex needed.

The driver threw the car in gear then peeled out of the Soriana lot onto Playa Palma Sola. Once away from the supermarket, the driver said, "They thootin' at you? Wha'd you do? Am I goin' to have some big problemth now?"

Alex wasn't going to discuss his situation with a potential drug addict, although the young man didn't look like a drug abuser, other than the teeth. He countered with, "What happened to your teeth?"

"Yeah, ith why I'm driving' for Uber. To pay a dentitht. My day job conthruction. I got hit when a load of lumber thlid off the truck. What's your excuth?" He laughed.

Alex directed him to the right onto Playa las Brujas. "It's a long story. I did my familial duty and took out a malpractice suit against the doctor who killed my brother. But it turned out to be intentional. A guy came after me. Turn right. This'll bring us into my neighborhood." He fished in his pocket for some of the cash. Here's some extra for your trouble, man. If you turn here, you can drop me at the end of my street. I'll walk. It's just one house in."

"They know where you live?"

"I don't know who *they* are. I'll have to take my chances. Slow down."

Alex craned his neck to see down his narrow cerrada. Daylight was fading, and it was hard to see, but there were no cars parked at his end that didn't belong to neighbors. If he kept to the wall, he could probably make it through his gate. Especially if he left the crutches on the street. He picked up the bags and began a slow limp pressed up against the wall of his neighbor's house.

Chapter 30

The Shooter

New Year's Eve 2020

New Year's Eve was its usual raucous event on Calle las Islas. Colorful papel picado cris-crossed the cerrada, fluttering in the gentle evening breeze. Christmas lights decorated gates and walls. Neighbors moved outside to entertain families and friends, the smells of cooking meats, steaming tamales, and tortillas floated on the air with sounds of salsa tropical, banda, ranchero and the traditional mariachi music blaring out of doors and windows throughout the fraccionamiento, neighborhood.

Even rap tangled into the cacophony, punctuated by hoots and hollers of laughter, greetings, horns, and to Alex's chagrin, cuetes, firecrackers. Every pop had him ducking to the floor. How was he to distinguish between the kids blowing off rafts of cuetes, and an assassin shooting into his house? At least his little halcon was out there watching for anyone who didn't belong or who carried a gun. Alex made sure of that when Rafi showed up at the gate with a plate of his grandmother's piping hot tamales and a pitcher of her delectable ponche.

All he could do now was keep a low profile with his terrified kitty and wait for the quiet of New Year's Day, then get back to work on his lawsuits and refinance. There was a lot he could do from the house. His groceries would last almost to Day of the Three Kings. His chauffer, Carolina, would come home the next day.

He hadn't realized how much he would miss that intrepid young woman, and especially her grandmother, Rosa. She'd become his rock, his oracle—his therapist. But it was better they were away. He feared his problems would land on them. They might be shot or held hostage or—his mind ran crazily through scenario after ugly scenario—and he'd be at fault.

But on Monday, it would be Licensiado Altamirano listening to him, giving him advice. This man was more likely able to protect himself, or so Alex hoped. Guilt nagged that Godoy's involvement in the suit was the cause of his disappearance. Pues, if he had actually disappeared. Maybe the pendejo was just cheating him out of his money. He prayed, however, that Rosa and Carolina would return home after he and the lawyer had terminated the threats. Protection was what he needed.

As darkness fell and Alex finished the savory tamales, saving the sweet ones for midnight, he checked that everything was locked up before turning off the lights. He limped up to the guest room and pulled the black-out curtains shut. Since the incident with the rock, he'd moved from his mother's room to the other bedroom. It was smaller, lacked a bathroom, and he had to buy a wardrobe for his clothes, but the bed was infinitely more comfortable. Not to mention, the window overlooked one roof and the blank wall of another house's second story, not the street. *Just a precaution*, he told himself.

Both houses fronted Cabo Catoche, the street to the west of his. Unless a shooter came through one of those properties, he was relatively safe. His window gave him easy access to the neighbor's roof if he needed to make a quick exit. Wouldn't whomever lived there be surprised to see him hobbling down their stairs? If he could hobble after leaping a meter from his window ledge to their roof. Anyway, he'd checked it out on his way from the local grocery—the roof was only accessible through the house.

The noise from the neighborhood was slightly muted by the houses, but the popping of the firecrackers bounced off the walls, making the night sound like a warzone. Crackcrackcrackcrack! Daisi, cowering on a tee-shirt crammed between the bed and the wardrobe, flinched with every blast. Alex scooped her up and cuddled her against his chest as he settled himself into the pillows to scroll the internet. The rum from the ponche had given him a subtle buzz, and he relaxed with the purring of the cat. With only the glow of the cell phone the two were soon asleep.

Alex jerked awake as something exploded. A dozen tiny knives stabbed at his chest. Daisi streaked off the bed as the sound of revelry in the street below intensified.

"What the hell?" Alex shouted. He looked at his chest. Droplets of blood oozed up from at least ten punctures. Daisi had gotten him good.

He lumbered off the bed, wondering if the explosion was a palomas, a giant firecracker, blowing out windows...or something in his dream. *It must be midnight.* Unlocking the deck door, he limped out onto the roof patio to see what was going on.

Another crack! Something whizzed into the stucco above his head. He turned—his mother's bedroom window was gone. Only jagged shards remained behind the iron grillwork. The fiesta raged, too loud for revelers to hear, but Alex knew—someone was shooting at him!

He ducked and half-crawled back into the house, bolting himself into his bedroom. He dug one of the hunting rifles from under the bed. No one would be coming to protect him.

New Year's Day dawned overcast and cold. After his shower, Alex applied antibiotic cream to the cat claw punctures. Just what he needed to add to his precarious existence—cat scratch fever. Daisi had returned from her hiding place in the wee hours and cuddled in with him, but he'd slept poorly anyway. Both his leg and back ached. His head ached. He felt drained of every ounce of energy except for the throbbing.

Happy New Year, pendejo. While he stood in front of the blown-out window, Alex chided himself for ever coming to Veracruz. Glass was everywhere. He turned in a circle. Holes fanned the back wall above the window. At least that window was still intact. He stepped out onto the landing, closing the door behind him. Tomorrow he'd call a glazier. Today he'd have to call the police, except, *what would they do?*

He turned the stove on under the frying pan and heated up some tortillas to go with his huevos mexicanos while he beat the eggs. Alex pondered his predicament. They knew where he lived and were coming after him. Of course they knew where he lived. It was probably Ana's idea to attack the house. *That bitch.* A bolt of electricity shot up his spine. His sister-in-law had sunk to the classification of his ex. Greedy, vengeful, harridans. But what had Avelina needed to avenge?

Avelina. He hadn't given her a thought for several months, but now, he could see her type. Ana's type. Ana led his stupid brother down the primrose path—straight to alcoholism and cheating his family. He wondered again what Reina was doing. Was she married? Kids? They might have been his. A familiar current of shame washed through him.

He ripped a tortilla nearly to shreds and used a piece to fork a portion of eggs and salsa into his mouth, almost choking on the hot mass. He coughed and shoved the half-filled plate onto the coffee table, too angry to eat. He'd done it all to himself. Now look at him. Crippled, weak, ruined, and sticking to some sense of familial duty he no longer believed in—if he were to admit it. Maybe he should cut his losses, drop the lawsuits and go on—

Banging on the gate interrupted his pity party. A high-pitched voice called out "Señor Alex! Señor Alex." Another bang. "Are you home, Señor?"

Rafi. It was only eight o'clock. *What's he doing here so early?* Alex unlocked the door and looked out. Yep.

The kid, bouncing up and down like he had ants in his pants. He called back, "Hi, Rafi. Happy New Year. Hold on."

Alex shuffled through a bowl on the credenza behind the table and grabbed the padlock key.

The moment he stepped onto the stoop Rafi started babbling. He spoke rapidly. Alex could only understand a few words, but one stuck out, "gun".

He dragged his aching leg faster across the small patio, fumbled with the padlock, and managed to let the excited boy in. "Hola, Rafi. Slow down, you're about to explode.'

"I saw him. I saw him!" Rafi's smile widened.

Alex propelled the kid toward the door. "Who?"

"The man with the gun. It wasn't a regular gun, it was a cuerno de chivo. A Kalashnikov. He had it in a bag. I followed him through the people and hid in the yard across the cerrada. He waited until midnight. When all the cuetes went off he shot at your house. I heard the glass break. Then he ran away through the posts. A car started up and drove off fast."

"Had you seen him before?"

"No. Yeah. Maybe? He looked sort of like a man I saw sitting in a car across from the gym when I went for more fruit for the ponche."

"Would you recognize him if you saw him again?"

"I don't know. It was kinda dark. I mostly saw the gun."

"But he came in from Ursula Galvan? You're sure? Yet he left through the stanchions?"

The boy nodded. His tone defensive, he said, "Seguro. I did exactly what you said, Señor Alex. I followed him. He talked to a couple of people, grabbed a beer, and acted like he was invited. I heard him say something about Señora Rosa."

Alex's heart flopped. *The shooter knows Rosa?* "Okay. What did he say, Rafi?"

"I dunno. Something about how it was too bad Señora Rosa was missing the fiesta. It was loud, but I remember he said he wanted to give her a present."

The story of the shooter's movements didn't add up. He was going to give her his gun? Something in the paper bag with the gun? "Rafi what aren't you telling me? Sit down. Time for the meeting I've paid for."

"I, uh, I told you it." Rafi said, his voice sounding stoney. He watched the floor as though something interesting was going on. A cockroach race, perhaps.

Alex sat, adjusted his tone. "But he didn't stop and leave something for Rosa, did he?"

"No, it was just an excuse." Rafi perched on the chair.

"Did he go to her gate?"

The boy swiveled around to look toward Rosa's. "No. He crossed to the empty house and hid behind the wall. I couldn't see him anymore, but the bag was there after he broke your window."

Alex's eyebrows shot up. "He walked out of the cerrada openly carrying a Kalashnikov? *There's a set of balls for you.* So why did he leave that way, not back through the crowd?"

Rafi watched the cockroach race more intently. His shoulders barely lifted into a modest shrug.

"Rafi. . . what aren't you saying?"

"I think he left that way because he saw me."

"He saw you and didn't try to conceal the gun? What makes you think so?"

"I was just walking. I had some cuetes to set off. I saw him holding the gun after shooting the window."

"You mean, he saw that you followed him." The kid shuffled his feet. "Show me where he was standing."

Rafi led Alex to the gate and pointed to a shallow niche where the neighbor's wall ended, and the empty house began. Yes, Rafi's story was starting to make sense. "Can you describe him at all?"

"Not as tall as my dad but big. Like he worked out at the gym."

"Skin? Hair?"

Rafi looked up at him. "Black."

"Like an indio or an Africano?"

"No, like a Mexican."

Alex smiled, said, "Come on back in, kid. I've got a bonus for you." He put his hand on the boy's shoulder, gave it a pat. "You did a great job, although you put yourself in danger. Next time, don't let the person you're following see you. Did he see where you live?"

"No."

"Thank God for that."

They returned to the living room. Alex fished around in his catch-all bowl and came up with three twenty-peso notes. He handed them to Rafi, who lit up.

"Señor Alex, do you know who the man is?"

"I haven't been formally introduced. Who you described came after me a few days ago. Listen, that's sixty pesos. Twenty for this week, twenty to wash the motorcycle, and twenty extra for your good work. But promise me if this man comes to our neighborhood again, you'll stay far away from him."

"I promise."

His little face took on a cherubic glow Alex didn't

believe for a moment. He hardened his voice. "I'm serious, Rafi."

Again, Rafi hung his head. "Okay," he mumbled.

"Great. You still have those cuetes?"

The boy jumped up and pulled a string of firecrackers from his pocket.

"Okay, shall we set them off after washing the bike?"

"Can we, Señor Alex?"

"You betcha kid! Way more fun than boarding up the window, right?"

Chapter 31

![decorative border with skulls]

The Assessor

Monday, January 4, 2021

Rafi and Alex scrubbed up the motorcycle to gleaming, splashing in the soapy bucket and squirting each other with the hose. For a short time, Alex relaxed in the sunshine and enjoyed himself. Rafi was a cute kid, smart, perceptive, and good humored, the kind of boy Alex would have wanted if he'd had children. However, Rafi's report disturbed him.

Once his grandmother called the boy home to eat, Alex had time to consider the implications that the shooter knew, or knew of, Rosa. Was the man aware Rafi was watching him? Was his comment about Rosa a threat? That the shooter knew Rosa's name couldn't be coincidental—could it? He didn't believe in coincidence, or not this one. Alex brooded. If anything happened to Rosa or Carolina, it would be his fault. He needed to protect them. *Gracias a Dios they're away.*

Late into the night, Alex still brooded. An unknown assailant had shot a high-powered rifle at his house. Was he trying to scare him or kill him? He'd threatened his kind neighbor and sweet Carolina, too. Fear gripped him. If that man could enter his neighborhood openly in front of all the neighbors, then shoot up his house once, he could do it again. And Rafi —he'd seen Rafi.

As dawn crept between the slats of his blinds Alex finally dozed off. He'd considered the threats from every angle as he tossed, turned, shifted, paced, curled, and cried. The hit-and-run, the rock, the surveillance, the attack on his house, and the murder of Lucas tied together. He weighed his options. Abort his mission to avenge his brother—it's what they asked for—and limp back to Mexico, a loser, jobless, and broke? He pictured the derision he'd encounter, the delight of Avelina seeing him broken, the pity in co-workers' eyes. *No!* The rush of anger exploded through his body and into his gut, freezing in a diamond-hard lump of resolve. No. Alex Deltoro was no weak coward. He owed it to himself.

The weekend passed without a visit from Rafi, an incident, a threat, or sleep. Monday dragged Alex's eyes open from a nightmare. He was running. Running, masked, white-clad surgeons chasing after him, scalpels gleaming under blinding floodlight. One brandished the intubation tube. He couldn't let them catch him. He needed to protect his family, Rosa, his mother. He ran, searching. Their motors revving, they were coming. . ..

Alex lay still, contemplating the meaning of his bizarre dream. Daisi nestled, sleeping in a ball pressed into his chest, purring, her little motor intensifying and diminishing with her breath.

Victor Mata was behind everything. And probably Ana. Maybe why she was so keen on getting the Deltoro family money—to assassinate Alex. He was the last Deltoro standing. And he could barely stand without crutches.

He had enough of thinking. It was time to take charge. At nine o'clock, he would call the Licensiado Altamirano, get an appointment and ask him for protection for his and Rosa's houses—*if the police haven't been bought off, that is.*

"Good morning, Altamirano and Associates. How may I direct your call?" purred a woman's voice.

"Alex Deltoro for Licensiado Altamirano."

"He's in court but let me connect you to his cell phone. Please hold." A scratchy instrumental version of an old standard, Besame Mucho, cut in.

Yeah, I hope I'm not kissing more money goodbye on this.

"Deltoro, Happy New Year. Are we ready to fight?" Altamirano's cultured voice sounded over the line.

"To you, too. Yes, Lic. I'm ready. Do you have time to see me today?"

"I'm about to go into court, let me see how long this will be. Hold on." The song had changed, but it was as scratchy as the last.

"Yes, I'm free for an hour this evening at six. I'll transfer you to Señora Ivonne. She'll take your information and have everything ready for our meeting."

"Thanks, see you th—"

The music started up again. In several minutes another woman, a smoker by the gravelly sound of her voice, came onto the line. "Ivonne speaking. How may I help you?"

Alex introduced himself and gave her a synopsis of his situation. The Licensiado already knew about the P.I. following him, but he detailed the events of New Years with the implied threats.

"It goes deeper than threats." He counted up the three incompetent assistant DAs he'd used, plus the disappearance of Godoy.

"I see. I'll brief the licensiado when he comes in. Please bring a copy of your statement along with the documentation you have, and the latest file from the Fiscalia. Lic. Altamirano will be ready to see you at six." She gave him the address downtown, in one of the lovely old buildings built during the Porfirio administration.

Alex did not see the blue Jetta, or the black car, but he knew full well whoever was watching him could have changed vehicles. He was ninety-percent positive someone was back there, binoculars on his Uber, but he arrived punctually at Zamara Park, a graceful white stucco building with an arched colonnade running the length of the side fronting Avenida Independencia close to the fire station. He had the driver leave him mid-way along the colonnade near an entrance into what looked like a garden.

He assumed Altamirano's office could be accessed off this central garden, but as he wandered past Porfirio era iron benches and an elegant gazebo situated in the middle of the lush tropical park shaded by towering palms, he realized there was no number 206. His GPS had directed him to the well-known Veracruzano Gran Cafe del Portal restaurant under another set of arches. He was going to be late.

He dialed the office again and the smooth voice explained, "It's on the second floor, Señor Deltoro. Look for the door in front of the tram."

Alex scooted as quickly as he could from the garden locating the door to the interior. The outside of the building had been kept up, but the inside needed maintenance. The wooden stairs, grooved from decades of foot traffic, creaked; the carpeting was threadbare, and the walls looked dingy under inadequate artificial lighting. But at number 206, as he pushed open the door, he found the atmosphere elegant and well cared for. He stepped up to a polished counter with two attractive, well-groomed attendants. The receptionist with the smooth voice pointed toward a hall. "Mr. Deltoro, the Licensiado is waiting for you. Second door." She smiled warmly.

Alex headed in the direction she pointed, after saying, "Thank, you." The executive office was partitioned by an entry with file cabinets, files stacked every which way. Polished bookcases were crammed with law books journals, and more files. They created a passage leading into the airy, bright office where Altamirano sat at a broad mahogany desk, also laden with files, one of which lay open in front of him.

He looked up. "Deltoro. Glad you could make it. Have a seat." He gestured to the two comfortable looking upholstered chairs facing him across the expanse of desk.

"Thanks for seeing me on such short notice, Lic." He leaned over the desk and shook the attorney's still-outstretched hand, then gave him the thick file he'd carried in. "Here's everything you asked for, minus what I haven't been able to get my hands on. That's part of my problem." He sat down. "I think the DA's office has been bought off."

Altamirano shut the folder in front of him. "Can you give me some time to look over your case? Perhaps you'd like to go down to the café for a coffee while I get up to speed? I'll join you when I'm done. We can talk about our plan while we eat. I didn't expect such a thick file." His chuckle sounded low, rich.

"You don't want to hear what I have to say?"

"Of course, but first I want to look over the State's case. It's this we will be fighting, no?"

"Yes, you're correct. I'll wait in El Portal."

An hour and a half, two Cokes, and a slice of almond cake later, Altamirano joined Alex at his small table, slapping down the rubber banded file and giving Alex a knowing nod.

"You've had four assistant DAs on this case and not one has managed to get the correct date, although it is clearly noted on your ambulance receipt and the medical admittance sheet. These alone give you a solid case. I'm ready to listen to your story." He raised his hand and beckoned the waiter. "I'm famished. Nothing since a late breakfast. Care to join me? We'll put it on my tab."

"No thank you, Lic." Alex's stomach had been growling for the last hour, but he needed everything he had to hire Altamirano. One soda had been his limit. He'd had two.

The waiter appeared, "Your usual, Lic?"

"No Tony, I'd prefer enchiladas suisas, a Fanta, and coffee—black. It's going to be a late one tonight.

"And for you, Señor?" the waiter asked Alex, pencil ready to jot his order.

"Just a coffee, por favor." His empty gut twisted dreading the strong acidic invasion.

Small cups of delicious coffee arrived immediately. The men sipped and chatted pleasantly through the ten minutes it took for Altamirano's order to arrive. Alex made a mental note that the food was fresh and fully prepared to order. He hadn't eaten here before. Not counting the slice of cake.

Altamirano dug into his enchiladas while Alex related his story. "The lawsuit initiated under federal jurisdiction for denial of medical care to my older brother." He recounted Dr. Fierro's criminal behavior and collusion with the IMSS floor coordinator. The attorney's eyebrow went up for that.

Alex pulled the document of the acceptance to the FGR and explained the situation. "After the investigation folder FED/VER/0000405/2021 was integrated, I went to the prosecutor's office to read it. The 3rd Prosecutor, Blanca Estela Cuauhtémoc, gave me the folder, but seemed reluctant and nervous. When I started to read it, she snatched it from my hands, saying I could see it later, and made me leave. I only managed to read that my sister-in-law and niece had been interrogated and lied when they claimed they did not know Dr. Fierro. He was the family doctor who attended to everyone! Even I went to consult with him with my niece Morticia about the medicines my brother took. Fierro gave us prescriptions for medicine that was not suitable for my brother, an alcoholic, and that should not be taken together, risking Lucas's health and finally his life."

"I assume there's more. I saw the prescriptions. And the notes on contraindications and cautions."

"Yes, Lic, there's plenty. The next day I showed up demanding to see the file. I was told I no longer had access to the investigation file, only the direct victims had access; in this case, Ana Mata, the wife of my brother and sister of the murderer, and my brother's daughter, Victor Mata's niece." Alex paused for a sip of his now‑cold coffee and winced.

Altamirano signaled for a refill. "Didn't I see you'd contracted with Fidel Godoy? What did he have to say?"

"I retained Godoy to initiate the first suit in April, but he never did anything. Then he stopped taking my calls. I reached Mr. Godoy by telephone once before I left the Federal DA's office. He advised me he would request the investigation folder. The next day, he gave me the written request to present. I immediately went to enter it into the investigation folder, and I again made an appearance at the FGR. I was taken to the 3rd prosecutor, and this time she handed me a document stating I was denied the status of victim, and I did not have access to the information—exactly what she had told me verbally. I had my cell phone and searched to find out what articles of law the prosecutor used to deny me access. It turned out that they referred to femicides and things totally off topic."

"I assume you went to the prosecutor."

"Of course. Her response? 'Go talk to your lawyer.'" Alex described his trip to Colonia Reforma and Godoy's surprise. "I said to Godoy, 'I don't believe it's possible to commit a crime so easily—this cannot be!' Godoy took on a malevolent expression and responded with 'It is,

Alex. I could tell you shocking stories, but if I did, I would be breaking attorney-client privilege. I advise you to sell the house and leave things as they are.' Godoy was bribed."

"Fidel Godoy was more than bribed, Alex," the attorney said. "He has disappeared and is presumed dead. I'm going to advise you to first get help from the CEAV. In light of what I've read, and what you've told me, I believe you are the victim, not your sister-in-law. That group can establish your legitimacy and help you get your case going."

"Will you be working with me?"

"Yes. As your assessor, defense attorney." He made the check-please signal and Tony scrambled over with a chit, which Altamirano signed. He waved away the pesos Alex offered for the coffee. "Let's go back to the office, settle our terms, and get the retainer in place. I think you have a strong case. I don't believe your brother was accidentally killed. With all the shenanigans going on behind the scenes, I'm convinced the man was murdered. I'm starting to understand Godoy's disappearance."

"You think the doctors had him killed?"

The two men trundled up the creaky stairs.

"I don't know. I have a niggling feeling he's not with us anymore. I know a few things about him. He got himself involved with the Zetas. That's probably what did him in."

Alex balked. "You're telling me he was working for the narcos?"

Altamirano shrugged, opened the door, and held it for Alex. "I assure you I am not now, nor have I ever represented a narco. Come on, sit down. It's getting late."

Alex sat. "Look, there's something I need you to do. We know I'm being watched and threatened." He related the incident on New Year's Eve. "I'm scared. For myself and for my neighbors. I want round-the-clock protection from the Feds."

Altamirano pulled up a contract onto his screen and asked Alex for his personal information. In a few minutes, he reread what he'd typed, making several corrections and printing the contract, handing a copy to Alex. "Check this over and make sure everything is correct. You'll see I have added the request for police protection. Take your time and I'll answer any questions you have."

Alex read through the contract. He was becoming an expert on these things; he didn't see anything out of the ordinary except his demand for protection. What he did notice was the price. Altamirano wanted both an hourly rate and a huge percentage of the awards.

"Is this percentage negotiable?"

"I can't go too low, Señor Deltoro. I'll be paying bribes to the police to keep all of us safe. If you can't do it, I can recommend another attorney who will charge you less."

"What's your lowest ask?"

Altamirano laughed. "I like you Deltoro. Forty percent."

"Thirty."

"Thirty-five—it's the best I can do."

Alex crossed off the original figure, entered 35%, initialed it and reached across the desk to shake on their deal. Alex dug into his pocket and handed over 10,000 pesos. "Let's get started."

Chapter 32

The Homecoming

Wednesday, January 6, 2021

The Uber let Alex off outside the physical therapy office ten minutes early. His therapist, a young man who called himself Doctor Bones, wanted to see him for a review of his progress before the session began.

Alex had religiously performed his daily exercises over the holidays and was able to limp around the house without his crutches. No way Alex Deltoro would end up crippled. He might not have quite the same youthful vigor and flexibility as a year ago, but he'd be dammed if he let Victor Mata and his pendejo ex-judicial police take him down. He snorted. *Flexibility?* With titanium rods and plates screwed into his bones? It was going to be difficult passing airport security. But then again, it would be a hell of a lot harder to break him now. *I'm the bionic man.*

Doctor Bones greeted him from behind the counter. "Happy New Year, Alex. Where's your chauffer today? Sit down, sit down. Look at you walking without crutches. You've been doing your workouts."

"Happy New Year to you, too, Doctor B. Of course I have. What did you want to see me about?" He handed over his payment. Bones put it into the till. "I'm surprised you're open today."

While Bones wrote out a receipt, he said, "We'll celebrate the three kings with cake after your session." He laughed. "But seriously, you're almost done with your therapy, four more sessions. I want to assess your progress today with a series of tests to find out where your weaknesses are, then we'll concentrate there, just as long as you keep up your daily regimen."

"I appreciate what you've done for me, doc. I never thought I'd walk again. I'm obviously able to hobble around and determined to walk normally, even run, again. How will you assess me?"

"Take it easy, Alex. You gotta walk before you run. If you are diligent, you'll meet your goal. You probably have another year. But let's worry about that later. Come on back."

Alex followed his therapist to the workout room, removed his shoes and performed some stretching exercises. After fifteen weeks of therapy, he could touch his toes for the first time. They moved into standing leg lifts, balancing exercises, and modified squats. When Alex was warmed up, they went to the mat. Together worked through a routine of yoga poses: cat and cow for his back, planks for his core strength, and to strengthen his legs, downward dog for his hamstrings and back flexibility. More leg strengthening and balance with the warrior pose. They moved slowly in tandem, breathing deeply.

Bones observed Alex's progress, sometimes pausing his routine to guide his stance. Alex relaxed. His worries floated away as he watched his progress in the mirror affixed to the wall; he could see his energy and strength stabilize.

Eventually a tiny bell chimed. Doctor Bones said, "Good work. Now for the test. I want you to walk to the end of the room and back."

Alex complied. His limp had diminished slightly.

"Now do as many toe lifts as you can on your damaged leg."

Alex stopped at twenty. When he first started, he couldn't do one.

"How much weight can you lift? Where will you lift from?"

Several barbells in several weights lay on the mat. Alex went to the first, 10 kg, squatted and stood pumping the weight to his chest, then over his head without strain. He moved to the next, 20 kg. He was able to pick it up, but the months lying down had left him too weak to fully stand up without pain.

"Good job, Alex. You're healing much faster than most with the severity of your injuries. I believe you *will* run again. Let's go have a slice of Three Kings Cake. My girlfriend made it. Bones led Alex into the little employee room, cut two slices onto paper plates, and poured each glass of fresh squeezed orange juice. Alex drained half of his glass in one swallow then cut into his cake. Something plastic poked his tongue. He spit it into a napkin. A tiny plastic baby doll. Bone slapped his thigh, laughing. "Alex, you're hosting the party, man! And I know you'll be ready."

On the way out, Doctor Bones said, "Hold on. I have something for you," and ducked behind the counter, returning with a lightweight metal cane, exactly the right height for Alex. "Dump those crutches man. Happy graduation."

In the morning, Alex ran through his exercises then got on the phone to his realtor in Mexico City. Daisi sat on the couch watching him, tail swishing.

"Señora Zentella, can you help me take out a mortgage on my house? I need a loan against the value."

They discussed the situation; the realtor agreed to act as his intermediary with the lender. Alex knew she trusted him. They had worked together several times, and she knew the value of his house.

"Señor Deltoro, I'll make arrangements today. We'll email the papers for signature. Once you've signed and notarized, express them back and I'll transfer the cash to the account you designate."

"Thank you so much, Mrs. Zentella. I'll watch for your email."

The money couldn't come soon enough. He was down to the wire. He wished he could just sell the dump he was living in and move on. Hadn't he endured enough in the name of familial duty? And what had that duty bought him? He'd always been the outsider, the *okay—unconfirmed*—bastard son.

Alex—the Cinderella whose job it was to clean up everyone's messes. Like right now. He finished scouring the patio tiles and started cleaning the living room. Rosa and Carolina would be home today. Surely they'd stop in for a visit.

After cleaning, Alex lay down for a nap. Bones had told him to take it easy. He still had time to get to the store for some fresh sweet breads and soda after a rest.

But his body ached and his mind swirled. Had Altamirano started in his file? Would the Feds give him protection? Round and round he went, finally getting up and, using his new cane, limped the block to the store.

"Perfect timing, Señor, the panes just arrived," the owner said, displaying a tray filled with delectable looking donuts, cakes, pastries, and cookies. Her smile and the aroma of fresh baked treats invited him to pick up the tongs and circular metal tray.

He grinned. "Mmm. They're what I came for. I need some drinks too." He inspected the tray now prominently displayed by the register. Carolina was fond of custard filled pastries, cuernos. Rosa preferred flaky arejas and the guava-filled pastries. He loved a warm concha and the sticky panque. He selected two of each, adding a couple of vanilla cookies and a croissant for his coffee in the morning.

While he dithered at the cold case, the dueña rang up the pastries. Coke was a no-brainer. He selected two liters, but what did Rosa like? Probably tea. He added a liter of milk in case she wanted it. Carolina, he knew, was a Sidral Mundet apple soda addict. He added two bottles to his basket.

Once rung up, he carefully balanced the purchases into a brightly-colored woven tote, something left behind by his mother, and thanked the owner—he really should learn her name, he shopped with her often enough. He picked his way down the crooked steps to the sidewalk and limped across the shady street, heading up the slight rise toward his corner.

A movement caught his eye. Someone was watching him from inside a black sedan parked across from his street. Watching way too intently to be waiting for traffic to pass and pull out. He stopped behind a tree growing up through the uneven paving to catch his breath—walking was still an effort, especially carrying a bag of groceries—and checked out the car and the driver as much as the tinted glass allowed.

Rock music pounded out of the gym. A glint of light flashed off the watcher's aviator sunglasses. A black shadow stretched across his chin. Alex felt a current of malevolence emanating from the vehicle.

The man grinned and pointed what looked like a handgun at him. Alex pulled back behind the tree, shouting, "Gun! Gun! Help!"

Javier, his buddy and owner of the gym, with half-dozen body builders, poured through the door carrying dumbbells. Alex pointed and they charged into the street fanning to surround the vehicle. The Nissan Versa roared to life then shot from the curb, disappearing over the hill. But not before Alex got a photo of the plate.

The gym rats scuttled back across the street and into the gym. Several stopped with Javier to find out what was happening.

"Hey, Alex, what was that? How are you, man? We haven't seen you for months. I thought you'd gone back to Mexico." He looked Alex up and down. "What the hell happened to you? Come on in. Have a beer."

Alex checked his watch. He had time; the women wouldn't be home for at least an hour, and Altamirano would be at comida. "Javier, you aren't going to believe a word of my tale."

Forty-five minutes later, Javier had organized a team of his regulars keeping an eye on the neighborhood. They'd call Alex if anyone dawdled too long, record license plates, and run them off. A couple of the hulking weightlifters looked like thugs themselves, but everyone welcomed Alex. He remembered what it was like to be part of a group enjoying a beer and banter. He promised to start working out as soon as the doctors gave him the okay.

Carolina's car still ticked as it cooled outside her grandmother's house. Alex stopped and rang the bell. Rosa appeared in the courtyard, her eyes lighting up to see Alex.

"Welcome home, Señora Rosa! I've missed you two. I'm on my way back from the store with fresh baked panes. Will you and Carolina stop in once you've settled? I want to hear all about your trip."

"How lovely, Alex. We'd be pleased to join you. Will thirty minutes be too late?"

"No, just perfect, Señora. Shall I put on some water for tea?"

"Yes, dear. I'm happy to see you without those crutches, Alex."

But you won't be happy to hear you're in danger. "Thanks, I'm getting along much better. See you soon."

In the house, Alex busied himself with arranging the pastries on a platter and heating the water. Daisi meowed excitedly. *She must know they're home.* But his excitement was of another sort. Anxiety. How would he tell his neighbors about what had happened? He finished laying out the glasses and cups with the snacks when the bell rang.

He poked his head out the door expecting to see his neighbors, but Rafi was waving between the gate's bars.

"Hi Rafi, I thought you'd gone home."

"No, school starts on Monday for me. I'm leaving on Sunday. Señora Rosa is home!"

"Come on in, Rosa and Carolina are on their way over to tell me all about their trip. We have pan dulces."

"Conchas? I love conchas. And those huge yellow cookies."

"Vanilla. Me too. I bought two."

Hovering over the plate, Rafi asked, "Can I have one of—" The bell interrupted Rafi's request. He bounced out the door and came back with Rosa in tow, Carolina left behind to lock the gate.

She came in and settled onto the couch with the squirming boy, whom she tickled. Rosa poured her tea while Alex filled glasses with soda. Everyone selected their favorite pan dulce.

Rosa asked, "How was your Christmas, Rafi. Did you have fun?"

The boy regaled them with enthusiastic lists of presents, feasts, and what fun he had on New Year's Eve. When he started to talk about being a lookout, Alex shushed him.

"Not now, Raf, let's hear about Rosa and Carolina's holiday."

"But then I get to tell Rosa."

"Tell me what, dear?"

"The man who wanted to give you a gift."

Her brow creased. "What man? When?"

"I'm sorry, Señora. I'm to blame. I planned to tell you about what happened after hearing about your trip."

"Can I tell? I want to tell," Rafi blundered on. "I

305

saw the man shoot out Alex's bedroom window with a big rifle. And he told the Señor across from my abuela he had a gift for you, but he said you were away, and he didn't leave it." He paused to catch his breath.

Carolina asked, "Alex, was it that guy who followed us?"

"I didn't see him, only my young halcon here did." Alex explained the goings-on since they left, including the incident earlier. "The man looked to be in his forties, five o'clock shadow, aviator glasses, short black hair, but I couldn't get a good look through the tinted windows—"

"Yeah, he was really tall, well taller than Grandma's neighbor, and kinda thin, but with muscles —I could tell. And he had a black jacket. That was him. His voice sounded sorta foreign."

"Foreign how, Rafi?" Carolina asked.

"You know, like from Mexico, or el Norte."

"He sounded like me?" Alex asked.

"Well, kinda. Not like here."

"But what did he say, dear?" Rosa interjected.

"Something like, 'I planned to leave a gift for Señora Dorantes.' But he only carried the rifle in the paper bag."

"Grandma, do you know who he is?" Carolina asked.

Alex answered for her, "I don't think he's someone any of us know. And I think the gift was a ploy to find out if the señora was there. Thank God you were away."

Rafi watched the interactions between the adults with interest as he crammed a concha and both cookies into his mouth. He was reaching for one of the cuernos when a voice in the street bellowed his name. He shot out of the house yelling, "Estoy aqui, Abuela."

Alex followed and let him out the gate. Abuela said it was time for dinner. Rafi replied, "But I'm not hungry."

"Tell Rosa I'll drop in on her tomorrow." Abuela dragged Rafi down the lane to his dinner.

Soon Carolina and Rosa returned home, Daisi trotting with them, tail up and meowing her happiness at seeing them. They'd set up a signal system in case this man returned. To Alex's relief, Carolina agreed to drive him to his appointment at the CEAV in the morning.

Chapter 33

The CEAV

Monday, January 11, 2021

Alex's appointment with the CEAV, the Executive Commission for the Attention of Victims, was for ten a.m. Traffic on Cuervo was light. The journey across the city of Veracruz took less time than anticipated, even though Carolina drove carefully, keeping to the speed limits. He'd be early. Alex wasn't one for waiting. He liked action, getting things done—hell, he'd been sitting around for months now. He needed to move forward with his lawsuits before Mata and his cronies killed him, not wait around another legal office.

"Carolina, turn left up here. We're only few blocks off the Malecon. Let's cruise the beach. We have time."

She turned. The morning was glorious, sunlit below a clear, blue sky, even the Gulf of Mexico shone a glistening blue-grey rather than its usual dull green. A line of tankers queued beyond the island, floating cities of silver, blue, and rust. Alex opened his window and let the cool salted air rush in. He breathed deeply, relaxing. His tension and anxiety let go. He would enter the Federal office calm to present his case.

On the beach, birds flocked on the wave-slick sand, sentinels taking in the sun. No people were out sunbathing or swimming. It was the hour of nature, before the vendors, hawkers, tourists, and beachcombers arrived with their umbrellas and music and trash. How he'd missed the beach these many months.

"Slow down, this is a tricky intersection, Carolina. At the light, make a right. At the next light turn left and make the next left you can. That's the building," he said, pointing to an old three-story beachfront home in need of paint.

Carolina followed his directions, pulling into an empty parking spot on the side street with five minutes to spare. She steadied Alex as he limped up the stairs to the front door, relying on his cane to make the steep climb.

Inside the cramped foyer, a security guard at a reception counter said, "Good morning. How may I help you?" He was perfectly stationed to prevent anyone entering a hall into the interior or fleeing up the stairs to the next floor. Only two short flights of stairs were accessible, leading to the restroom on one side and the waiting room on the ground floor.

"Good morning. I'm Alex Deltoro here for a meeting with Señora Angelica Borzo."

The man scanned the appointment book. "Please take a seat in the waiting area. She will be with you shortly." He waved to the short flight down to his right.

The waiting area was an L-shaped room, bright with sunlight from the many windows. At one time, with its view of the Gulf, it would have been a pleasant room to relax in. Now, buildings across the wide boulevard blocked the view. The short end of the L contained two beat-up tables shoved together, cheap folding chairs surrounding them, presumably for conferences. Beyond, a Coke machine purred. The rest of the room held worn seating for waiting clients.

The wall above the chairs, and on either side of the stairs, held dozens of posters: Wanted posters with photos, vital statistics, crimes, etc. And more upsetting, posters of the missing. Alex and Carolina perused these, aghast at the numbers of young men likely kidnapped by the cartels. Probably dead. And the women—girls really—snatched. Tearful pleas by families wanting to know what happened to their children, wives, husbands, accompanied many of the posters, telling Alex it was families, not government, posting. He took a deep dislike to this depressing place.

Carolina, tears in her eyes, pointed to posters of small children missing. Some had been gone for years. The last wall, closest to the windows, contained posters for the most recently disappeared. One face looked familiar. Alex leaned in, fished his glasses from his shirt pocket. Fidel Godoy! "Carolina, look. It's Godoy, my lawyer. It says 'presumed killed by Los Zetas'. That's what Altamirano thinks."

The guard leaned into the stairwell. "Señor Deltoro, Señora Borzo will see you now. Please go up the stairs. Her office is the third door on the right."

"Don't you have an elevator?" asked Carolina.

The guard gave her a sour look.

She continued, "No, it's for him," jutting her jaw at Alex.

The guard grunted something and shook his head. Alex started up the stairs, pain shooting up the titanium rod in his leg. Carolina returned to the waiting room. She'd brought her schoolbooks and planned to study.

At the top of the stairs, a brassy red-headed woman, nearly as wide as she was tall, waited for him by her open door.

"Señora Angelica Borzo?" he called out.

"Sí, good morning, Señor Deltoro. Please come in." She waddled into the brightly lit office, her dimpled rear jiggling in her tight shocking-pink pants and plopped onto an oversized rolling chair at the far desk to fan herself with the only file visible.

Alex followed. He bet himself *she* arrived on the second floor in an elevator. Her area looked tidy while the second desk, located in front of the windows, was piled high and cluttered like most of the government offices he had visited. The youngish man with dark closely-cropped hair, dressed in a white collared shirt and a loosened black tie, uniform of the bureaucrat, nodded and returned to his laptop perched on a stack of files. There were no bookshelves or books, but the printer stand was stuffed with files, bound reports, papers, office equipment, and supplies. The atmosphere felt close. He wondered why the slatted coverings over the windows, which must overlook the Gulf, were closed.

"Please take a seat," Mrs. Borzo said. "How may I help you?"

Alex moved some books from the chair closest to her desk and sat. *She doesn't know why I've come.* Alex recited a summary of his suit filed against Doctor

311

Mata.

No longer fanning herself, the Licensiada opened the file then passed it to him. "Look over the documents we have received from Fiscal Paola Zamudio. Your attorney, Lic. Altamirano has asked we re-evaluate your victim status, which I see has been revoked. I will need these documents from you: your deceased brother's birth certificate, birth certificates for yourself, your parents and your other siblings. I also need the death certificates of these same family members. I cannot certify you as the victim without these proofs. Señor Deltoro, once I receive the documents, I can begin your validation and will see you here again once I have finished." She closed the file and drummed her pudgy fingers on its cover.

Alex assumed the meeting had ended. He stood, reaching out to shake the brown sausages, when a piercing scream echoed through the hall. The attorney's jaw dropped. Then shouting, a crash, more screams and finally the sound of a door slamming. *What the hell?*

"Carolina!" Alex shouted and started for the door.

Hampered by his injury, it took several minutes to descend the wide staircase to the first floor, calling for Carolina with each step. At the reception, he found the security guard groaning and getting to his feet, and Carolina cowering behind the counter, tears streaming down her face. Shards from the door's sidelight window scattered cross the entry.

He helped Carolina up, gathering her shaking form to him, and held her until she calmed.

The guard was on his cell phone calling the police.

"Carolina, what happened?"

"Let's get out of here, Alex. I want to go home."

"Where are your books?'

"Down there." She pointed to the empty waiting room.

"I'll get them. Wait here."

"No, I'm coming with you. Don't leave me."

"Come on then. Help me on the stairs."

Back in the car, Alex asked, "Are you okay to drive?"

"Yes, if that man doesn't follow me." She turned over the ignition and eased out of the parking space, checking her mirrors. "I don't see him on this block."

Alex frowned. "What man, Carolina? Someone followed us? Why didn't you say something? Was it the man from before?"

"It wasn't the same car. This was a black Nissan Versa. The man was thin and muscular, short black hair, a stubbly chin, wearing a black cloth jacket. His skin tone looked yellowish. Not white. He was old."

"Old like me?"

"No, like forty maybe." Carolina rounded the corner then waited at the red light for her left arrow.

"Cruise the Malecon. We'll be safer there in the traffic. I'll keep watch for the car. I know it. It's the car from yesterday." He mentally reviewed the license plate number. He'd call Altamirano today for the name of the driver.

The light changed; Carolina turned left into the curb lane. The story rushed out. "The man came in and sat down near the stairs. I thought he was someone waiting for his appointment. I didn't pay any attention because I was taking notes from my book. I-I was at the end of the table with my back to him. The next thing I knew he'd grabbed me by the arm and put his other arm around my neck. His hand covered my mouth. Then he dragged me toward the door. I kicked him and wrenched free at the stairs. I screamed. The guard ran in from somewhere shouting. The man pulled harder on my arm trying to get me out the door. The guard pulled, too. I screamed. The man let go. The guard and me fell; he slammed the door so hard the window shattered."

"Did the man say anything?"

"Only that my abuela would get me back when you drop everything. But I could see in his eyes he wanted to hurt me."

Alex gazed at the water. The line of container ships had shortened. Clouds were forming and the water chopped with a breeze blowing up. This was exactly what he feared. Victor Mata—he was certain it was Mata behind all of it—would stop at nothing.

"I'm sorry, Carolina." The words rang hollow.

At home, over the phone, Alex pleaded for Altamirano to get security for them. The Feds owed it to him, *didn't they?* Now innocents were involved.

Luckily, the Deltoro family birth certificates survived Ana Mata's greedy thieving and remained locked in a safe Alex had purchased to guard what remained from future attack. All he needed was death certificates, easily obtainable through Veracruz's Civil Registry.

Instead of calling Carolina, Alex Ubered to the offices located in el Centro on Benito Juárez in another of the lovely old government buildings forming a U around a manicured park, complete with statuary and white iron benches. The clerk assured Alex the documents would arrive at his house the next day. *I'll believe it when I see it,* was all he could think, but sure enough, the following day a messenger rang the gate bell, handing over the packet of death certificates. Carolina appeared. She asked what he was doing.

"I'm calling for an Uber to go see Mrs. Borzo. I've got all the certification she asked for."

"I'll drive you. I'm bored. But I'm coming up with you. I heard the best way to stop being afraid is to face your fear, so I'll go there and face what happened."

"Carolina, no. I don't want to piss your grandmother off."

"It's okay, she's playing cards with some neighbor ladies."

"So, it's okay to do what she doesn't want you to do as long as she doesn't know?" He shook his head as if to say, *kids!*

She laughed. "Get in the car, Alex."

From the vehicle, he let Licensiada Borzo know he was on his way. They trooped up the stairs and knocked on the office door.

The young man let them in.

"Mr. Deltoro, good afternoon," the advocate said as Alex handed over the documents. "Give me a few minutes to review these, and I'll make a determination."

One set of louvered slats stood open. Alex confirmed the office had a magnificent view of the sea. He elbowed Carolina, tipping his head toward the window. She walked over to look out, jumped back, and returned to Alex to whisper, "I see him out there. He's watching the building."

"Señor Deltoro, everything is in order. Please sign this document to confirm you accept my representation before the authorities as your legal advisor. I am going to request you be returned to the status of victim. Next week I will have news for you." She hefted herself to her feet, saying, "Thank you," as she walked them to the door.

At the reception landing, Alex asked for a back door, explaining the threat. The guard agreed that calling the police was futile then escorted them out through the garden. Carolina made a U-turn in the street. Alex directed them back to Calle las Islas without passing the tail.

Nine days flew by. He did not hear from Mrs. Borzo. Alex's confidence in the CEAV dwindled. Finally, a call came demanding he come to sign more documents, then making him wait for over thirty minutes before he, once again, had to conquer the stairs.

"I have bad news. They have denied your petition. But I have another trick up my sleeve, Mr. Deltoro."

He looked at her flabby arms squeezed into a black stretch top and wondered where that trick might be hiding, but quickly scanned the several pages she held out, before signing. "What's your trick?"

"I've talked to my superior who will insist."

Oh good. Alex was not confident about this trick. Yet, four days later he was contacted by Licensiada Borzo. "I have good news. Come to my office please."

Carolina was in school. Alex took an Uber to the now-familiar CEAV. He noted the broken sidelight had been repaired as he huffed through the door after the steep stairs.

"Hi, Lucho. You know where I'm going."

"Hello, Señor Deltoro. She's there. Go on up."

The advocate dispensed with the niceties, handing Alex a document and telling him to read it carefully and sign. When he looked up and nodded, the Licensiada described how her boss proved the articles of law used to deny the victim status did not apply in the case. He had demanded justice be served. Alex was again granted the sought-after status as victim in the eyes of the federal government. All he needed now was to make it home without being the real victim—again.

Chapter 34

The FGR

Wednesday, January 27, 2021

Wednesday would be Alex's last physical therapy session. He woke up feeling sad. He enjoyed the sessions with Doctor Bones. They had helped him maintain his sanity for how many months now? Almost eight.

He made a coffee, showered, dressed in his usual shorts and tank tee-shirt, wondering if Bones would miss him. They got along fine. Maybe he should stop on the way and pick up some beers or tequila. *Does Bones like tequila?* Maybe some kind of gift? *Nah*, tequila would do it.

He laced up his gym shoes, went down to the kitchen to make something light to eat, and topped up Daisi's bowl. *Pinche cat.* She'd gone home with Rosa on the seventh and never returned. He missed his little fuzzball, although now she was a skinny, near grown cat. Or she had been. The couple of glimpses he'd had of her, she was really filling out. *Probably eating well at Rosa's and coming in at night to eat here.* Some critter was.

Alex shuddered. In the space of ten months, he'd lost his mother, his brother, his job, his health, his cat, and now he was losing his physical therapist. At least the mortgage came through; he had plenty of money—ironically, money he would need to pay the mortgage until he could work again. The damn lawyers were bleeding him dry.

The Uber let him off in front. He found Bones behind the counter speaking with a client. He sat down, the Casa Dragones Tequila Blanco in a box with a silly holiday bow on top. But it was a surprisingly refined tequila, considering his pedestrian neighborhood store.

The woman finally stopped talking and limped toward the door, saying, "Buenos tardes," as she passed.

Alex hopped up to open the door for her. "Buenos tardes, Señora."

Bones sang out, "Such a gentleman, Deltoro. You ready for graduation day?!"

Alex picked up the tequila and carried it over to his therapist. "I can't wait to get away, Bones." He winked, plunked the box onto the counter, and added, "This will help you through your grief."

The men laughed. "Go on in. Let's see how you're doing. I'll get a couple of glasses."

Two hours and several shots later, Alex was on his way to the Fiscalia General of the Republic, the FGR, to read through his file. Would his titanium *enhancements* set off the security alarms?

On arrival, he was told to wait, his attorney would come get him.

Idly, he considered the differences between the federal and state D.A.'s offices, Where the state was unsecured, dirty, cramped, inefficient, and teeming with people, many of whom were outright criminals, the fed's offices had a manned guard entrance, nice, manicured gardens, pristine maintenance, and tight security to get in to see anyone.

His lawyer did not come for him; instead a polyester-clad clerk escorted him to the lawyer's office and handed him a file, saying that, "For the 'improvement of the investigation', the prosecutor has made some changes." Alex took 'improvement of the investigation' to mean 'straighten out the dishonest behavior of the preceding prosecutor, fiscal #3, Paola Zamudio.' He'd added that Ana and Alex's niece were waiting to make statements, so he could not take the file away. A copy would be ready for him the next day. *But Ana and Morticia have already made statements. False statements.* Alex's hackles rose. Something was off.

He took the file and was shown to an empty storage room smelling of dust and mildew, filled with boxes of files surrounding a table and a lamp, where he could read. The statements from Ana and Morticia were missing. In the last three days, the D.A.'s office had interrogated many of the doctors who treated Lucas in hospital, including the emergency doctors, internists, pulmonologists and more.

Alex remembered the kind doctor who had consoled him. Now he understood her strange reaction. A total of twelve doctors were questioned and named as defendants, but curiously, Dr. Mata, the man responsible for the death of his brother, had testified as a witness.

Chingao! This wasn't right! Alex realized the doctors who treated Lucas were covering up for their boss—director of the hospital—Dr. Victor Mata. His blood boiled.

Continuing to read the thick file, grateful for the speed-reading course he'd taken years before, Alex detected contradictions in what was declared by each of the doctors under investigation. Some of the declarations were made before it was possible to know the facts, or by practitioners who would not have access to the information. It was clear why Ana had insisted on the cremation immediately, over his request for an autopsy.

Four of the emergency physicians, who had the first contact with Lucas, stated: "When the patient arrived in critical condition with severe respiratory failure from sepsis, they intubated him immediately. **Margin note: acting directly against Lucas's instructions notarized in his hospital records.**

Alex realized they failed to mention the cough with greenish expectoration he suffered three days before, the dyspnea at moderate level two days before, and a temperature of 38°C, all information given to the admitting doctor by Alex himself. He ticked off the statement and added his thoughts to the margin.

He couldn't believe the lies—or the incompetence. He'd taken care of Lucas. He knew the truth. *Who would believe a family would let an infection run long enough to cause respiratory failure?* Especially if the patient's wife was sister to the head of an IMSS hospital! *Three doctors in one department so naïve?*

Anyway, the only person who actually could enter

the symptoms into the hospital records was Mata. He'd brought Lucas in, and he had signed as the responsible family member alongside Morticia. He hadn't told the intake doctor diddlysquat. The intake log had nothing more than Lucas's name, the date, the time and that he couldn't breathe. Remorse and pain stabbed Alex's heart as he recalled that day when Morticia administered the fatal drug to her father. He read on.

The internist gave contradictory declarations, claiming, based on her conversation with Alex, Lucas died of septic shock, although all the laboratory tests clearly showed no infections. He made another note in the margin: **blaming me?** She went on to state Lucas had a tumor in his digestive tract—where?—and had been insulin-independent for six years. **Margin note: Lucas never took insulin. No medical proof of cancer.**

When Alex got to the part where the internist declared she'd never met Lucas, yet she was the one who had certified "her" death, he laughed. *Probably her one bit of truth.* If she'd seen Lucas, how had she missed the moustache? Alex counted error after error, noting: **date of admission, date of death, number of days in the hospital, failure to report the fatal injection prescribed.**

But the lie that galled Alex the most? The doctor used Mata's party-line. She signed the death certificate that Lucas died of cancer in direct contradiction to the medical file.

The last joke came in the form of the statement by one Edison Doblado, a resident at IMSS #57 who rambled on about his interview with the brother of the patient—**Note: I was never interviewed**—and repeated word-for-word the lies already stated by Mata's cronies. *Another coverup for the murder.* But how would he prove it?

Alex turned back and forth between the hospital statements. The discrepancies glared at him. They were trying to hold him responsible. How could the internist have this data if she acted immediately? The medical data corresponded with the emergency doctors' statements signed with the day and time—**note: minutes after Lucas's admission to the hospital. *Impossible.*** Right after the doctor's "interrogation" of Alex. The one that never happened.

No way was he coming back "tomorrow" for the addition of Ana's and Morticia's statements. He was staying right here until he had copies in his file.

He called Altamirano. "Lic, I need you to come right now."

"I'm on my way."

Alex finished skimming the file, checking for the corrections he had requested. The fiscal, Blanca Estela Cuauhtémoc, was either inept, possibly downright stupid, or paid off. Her work on the file had "lost" the statements by his sister-in-law and niece, admitted Lucas to the wrong IMSS, and put date of death in 1919. He paced the small room for the next forty-five minutes until Altamirano finally arrived. The lawyer convinced Alex to return to the waiting room, and the assistant to leave the file in Alex's hands.

The licensiado led Alex to the far corner of reception, out of the main view of anyone entering from the front, or the offices access. Alex sat facing the hallway Ana would have to cross, one eye out for her and the other on the file. In low voices, Alex explained the new lies and blame being aimed at him. "I can't wait to see what Ana Mata has to say. You already have the inheritance case, so you know what she thinks of me. I'll wager she's made some damning claims. My niece will have said the same things in the same words. Can you find out what happened to the missing declarations by the two? Their first statements are missing from this file."

"You have copies."

"When you read this crap, you'll agree, it won't matter. Mata and company are trying to frame me. That's in case their threats don't succeed in making me back off. Or they haven't taken me out by time of the trial. Lic, please get me some protection. And can't you get a date with the judge sooner rather than later?"

"Mr. Deltoro, we need some corroboration or some proof. I have to read the new file. And we must wrestle this case away from the state. It is not a murder, it's a conspiracy by a federal agency."

Alex sighed. *It's not malpractice, it's murder. It's not murder, it's conspiracy.* What would it be tomorrow?

Finally, Ana and Morticia appeared. If Ana's smug expression didn't tell the story, Morticia's nervous hold on her bag and constant sideways glances did. They'd lied through their teeth. Suddenly Morticia stopped and covered her face, exclaiming, "Tío!" Tears rolled down her cheeks before she hung her head.

But Ana's head snapped around to glare at him. Her look could cause blizzard conditions in hell. She marched toward Alex, dragging her daughter by the wrist, shouting, "What are you doing here? Haven't you caused enough trouble? You killed my husband. You sent your family to the poorhouse!"

Altamirano stood up, strode toward Ana, his bulk and height diminishing her assault. She stepped back, lowering her voice, but the epithets still rained.

"Madam, if you wish to communicate with Mr. Deltoro, please have your attorney contact me." He handed her a business card. In a soft voice Alex could barely hear, he said, "Be careful with what you say and declare. Lies in your declaration are perjury. We *will* prosecute. You and your daughter have a nice day now."

Morticia broke free, running for the door as Ana stopped mid-expletive to stare at Alex, eyes heavy with hate. She turned and stomped from the Fiscalia, her footfalls echoing from the stucco walls.

Altamirano approached the receptionist, apologized for the disruption, and asked how much longer before the fiscal would bring the statement to add to Alex's copy of the file. To Alex, it looked like he was flirting with the young woman. Of course, he probably was in and out of the FGR often. He realized it was the only reason Alex was getting this special treatment. Samia had done him a good turn, suggesting the lawyer.

"Another fifteen minutes. Alfonso Cardona is preparing the signatures now. The D.A. is with your fiscal. Frederid is a pal of mine; we play golf together. I'll introduce you if he comes out. We've already discussed your case. He's interested. It would be a big win for him."

Or a big payoff.

The phone at reception rang. The woman answered, looked their way, said something, and hung up. She skirted the counter and approached, smiling. "Licensiado Altamirano, the assistant is on his way."

The sound of a door closing ushered in the same clerk in his pilled poly pants and scuffed black oxfords, carrying a file tied closed by twine, which he handed to the attorney.

"Thanks, Max. Give your best to your mother, will you?"

"Yes sir, Señor. She'll be glad to hear from you." He nodded to Alex and almost ran back through the door marked PRIVADO.

"Listen, I have twenty minutes before I'm seeing someone here. Let's read those." He untied the string, held out one of the pages to Alex. They sat down again to read, exchanging sheets as they finished.

Again, mother and daughter had produced coordinating declarations; however, the original statements had changed. In the new version, neither had ever gone to consult with Doctor Fierro. Alex made a mental note that no mention was made of the prescriptions or the injection. They both claimed Lucas died of cancer, and Victor Mata had gone to the house in previous days to deliver the bad news that Lucas was dying from cancer. Alex was disgusted. They lied, and they declared using the exact same words.

"Lic, they were prepared. Probably by Ana's brother or his attorney. Except for Mata coming to the house, it's pure lies."

"Deltoro, this is what we have to prove."

Chapter 35

The Strategies

Alex leaned back into the leather bucket seat to stare out the window as Altamirano slowed for the next tope. The rundown neighborhood, Colonia Tarimoya, depressed Alex more than he already was.

"Lic, I'm out of ideas. They've bought off every prosecutor and advocate—possibly even the Policia Ministerial, although I finally got the accident report at the beginning of the month. I need to add it to the file."

The lawyer didn't reply. Alex studied the neighborhood. Buildings looked uncared for, half the cross streets were dirt, and in every dip, small ponds of oily rainwater collected. Businesses limited to street tacos, tiny food stores, and bars. "Don't drive through that, Lic. It's too deep for this Porche."

The lawyer swerved to the very edge of the pond and slowed. "Stop worrying, Deltoro. There's still time on the murder case, which, by the way, I do not want prosecuted by the state. Or combined with the hit-and-run." He braked to avoid a ragged man jerking across the street in front of the car as they pulled back onto dry asphalt. *Tweaker,* Alex thought.

"Why not combine them? Victor Mata paid the guy to run me down. How he knew where to find me at five a.m. that day, I don't know."

"Tapped your phone, maybe."

"I only have a cellphone."

"Listening device in the house?"

"Sounds a little high-tech for Mata. But what do I know?" He grabbed the OhJesus strap as Altamirano sped around the corner out of the shitty neighborhood.

"Who was in your house?"

"My sister-in-law with my niece and her no-good boyfriend, Gabriel López. They robbed the place of all my mother's financial information. Credit cards, bank statements, anything they thought had value. Ana even took my mother's and younger brother's ashes. I caught them in the act."

"Why aren't they in jail?"

"I couldn't bring myself to have them arrested. I filed a complaint with the police. They said I could revisit it if I felt they needed to be prosecuted."

"I don't understand. Why would they take your mother's things? Where is your mother?"

"Passed. Stomach cancer. My younger brother too. Long story. Ana is after my family's inheritance. She and my brother got plenty of it, but she wants the rest. It's part of why she and her murdering brother killed Lucas."

"What about the status of your inheritance?" He slowed. A line of cars idled behind the flashing lights at the railroad crossing. La Bestia—as the twice daily train from the southern border up to the northern border and back was called—was on its way. "Relax, we'll be sitting here for twenty minutes."

Alex straightened up to watch the Beast slowly chug by. Some days the northbound trip carried sad, famished·looking immigrants flocked on the car roofs, fleeing from the violence and poverty of Central America. Sometimes he recognized Venezuelans as their country sank deeper into what Alex deemed communism. Today the train ran south and was empty. "Yeah. I'm glad it's not hot. The inheritance? I don't really know. Lucas was the trustee. I don't think Ana can access any of the accounts. I was hit before I could reconstruct everything and talk to the banks. She told me she deserves it all for what Lucas did to her."

"Why don't you open that file and read Mata's declaration to me."

Alex twisted to reach the file placed on the floor. The car was a beauty, but not a car for a tall man with a bum leg he could barely bend. He dragged the thick file into his lap, flipping through the pages until he came to Victor Mata's sworn declaration.

"Lic, it says here his declaration is as a witness. That's pure bullshit. He says, 'I never attended to the patient Lucas Deltoro. I did follow up on the ultrasound performed on the patient on April 6th at the request of Dr. Aurora Rodrigues, and I consulted with the patient's brother, one Alex Deltoro, regarding booking an MRI for Lucas Deltoro. The result of that MRI showed lesions in the patient's stomach.' Lic, the records of the MRI are not included in this file," he said, as he scribbled a note in the margin. Continuing, "'and for this reason I referred the patient to an IMSS gastroenterology specialist to determine if the lesions were of malignant cancerous origin. The medical record states that due to the inflammation present because of an infection in the patient's throat, the gastroenterologist could not perform an endoscopy, therefore the cancer was only theoretically certified'"

Altamirano interrupted. "Deltoro, this statement negates cancer as the cause of death. This is in your favor. What else did he say?" The train blasted its whistle at another crossing a mile or so down the tracks. The clacking of the wheels tapped out a sad rhythm as endless tanker cars riding high in their carriages, rolled by, graffiti advertising Paco from Nicaragua's or Chepe from Guatemala's sad commentaries on life.

Alex thought these were the lucky ones, the polleros. They had money for spray paint. The chickens? By Veracruz they'd been robbed of everything, beaten, raped, and sometimes killed. He looked back at Mata's statement. "One of the things I read in here said Lucas was intubated, which was true. Yet he could not be scoped out by the gastroenterologist because of inflammation in his throat. The intubation tube is much bigger than the endoscopy equipment. Can we use it?"

"Yes. I'm already thinking of a doctor I know in Mexico City we can bring in as an expert witness to testify—one of the president's team."

"Mata is smart. How is it he's made so many errors?" A dinging sounded at the crossing. Light flashed as the gates opened and traffic began to move. "No, don't answer. I've been trying to figure the whole thing out since last spring. I mean, why did he go to all the trouble to deceive Lucas and the family that Lucas suffered from advanced malignant cancer with metastasis to all organs? Was it to torture Lucas? Punish him? Ana was in on it. I swear that Mata family is evil. The cousin, Mateo Zambada Mata was in on it too, although I don't have anything on him. I don't think Ana much liked Lucas. You know, Lucas stole Mother's portion of my younger brother's estate left to her."

"Not to be indelicate, but why did you stay in Veracruz to care for Lucas?"

"Turn here. You don't think I ask myself that on an hourly basis? Yeah. All I can say is duty. And some misplaced love for my big brother leftover from long, long ago. Right again." He pointed at the turn.

The Porche grumbled into low gear and descended the slight hill toward Calle las Islas. And there it was, the black Versa parked several cars down the slope on the left "Lic! Pull over! Now."

Altamirano veered to the curb and cut the engine. "This your house?

"No!" Alex almost shouted. "It's the guy following me. I think he's the one who shot out my window and tried to kidnap my neighbor's granddaughter."

"Whoa, hold on Deltoro, it's a black Nissan just like the thousands of black Nissans in this city."

"No man, the placa—black on white. I memorized it. YF-J-800-A. That's him. I was going to call you."

Altamirano turned the key, revved the engine, spun a U from the curb, and shot out of the neighborhood.

"What are you doing?" Alex shouted over the engine roar.

"We're going for a drink. I know a place nearby. Then I'm calling a buddy who will take care of this. We'll get to the bottom of these threats by morning."

Holy mother of God! Was he going to have the man tortured? Not that he didn't deserve it. "Okay," Alex said, dragging out the word. Then he said, "You don't mean the putero over on Ursula Galvan."

The attorney leveled an incredulous look on him. "A whore bar? What kind of places do you drink in?"

Alex broke into laughter. "I really don't drink much, but the decoy to get me out of the house when Ana robbed it took me there. Dios! I needed three showers after that."

They backtracked, turning up past the IMSS Tarimoya and ended in front of a thatched roof restaurant/bar nestled into a pleasant tree-lined neighborhood Alex didn't really know. It looked more prosperous than *his* shabby digs. Altamirano pulled to the curb right in front. The sign read Palapa de Jaiba —Mariscos. Altamirano got out of the car, leaned in, said, "Bring that file, man. We'll get some work done while we wait for El Puño."

Oh, great. The Fist.

The hostess, who turned out the be the owner, welcomed Altamirano with a hug and pecks to his cheeks. "Ramiro! Bienvenu, bienvenu. It's been a while since we've seen you. Laurant was asking about you just yesterday. Come, I have your table ready." She spoke in French.

Altamirano replied, in accented French. "Is the bouillabaisse fresh today? I have a taste for your signature dish. And a bottle of whatever will pair best. Bring two bowls. My client needs a few bites of heaven today." He introduced Alex to Señora Amélie Roux.

Señora Roux smiled and gestured to a round bistro-style table in the garden next to a bubbling pond filled with lily pads. A couple lunched at a similar table on the other side of the garden next to a white stucco wall grown over with a heavily pruned vine making an interesting pattern in the bright winter sunlight.

Seated, Alex surprised them both when he replied, "Merci, Licensiado. C'est gentil de ta part." He smiled at the petite Amélie. "Ma grand mère était française. Her bouillabaisse was my favorite. Growing up, we always spoke French with her."

"I like your client, Ramiro. Let me get you your wine. May I offer you a bowl of olives? We have fresh shrimp today. A little platter to go with your bread. Señor, would you prefer butter or olive oil with your bread?'

"Please, call me Alex. You too Lic. Is the oil from Provence?"

"Oui."

"C'est parfait."

Mrs. Roux proved an efficient host and an excellent cook. She explained she made typical French luncheon dishes, while her husband came later to prepare the dinner menu. Laurant was a Michelin starred chef.

"How have I never heard of your restaurant before?'

"It's a long story. Perhaps your lawyer will tell you one day." She scurried off to get the starters. Alex raised his eyebrows at the attorney.

"Later. We need to cover some ground."

The men discussed the problems with the federal file. Alex agreed to make a list of the errors. He was discussing the omissions when his telephone rang. He held it up, and said, "The state prosecutor's office. I better take it." He punched on the speaker.

"Alex Deltoro."

"Señor Deltoro, I'm calling on behalf of Fiscal Zamudio. She has arranged your hearing with the control judge on February 4th at eleven a.m. I will send an official notice with the date, time, and location to your address on record. Is this still your address?"

"Yes, Calle las Islas. But I'm sorry, I haven't reviewed the file. Would you please ask the fiscal to postpone? She knows we're not ready."

"I'm sorry, Señor, it's not in my hands. You have to talk with the prosecutor. I only do the notification. Good afternoon." She hung up.

Alex thought she really did sound sorry and wondered how many of these distressing calls she had to make each day. He looked at Altamirano, speechless.

"We'll pay the fiscal a visit first thing in the morning. Meanwhile let's order another bottle of that Pommard pinot noir. Now tell me the problems." He signaled the owner, pointed at the bottle.

"You know some of it. We need the declarations of the two witnesses and the video from the ADO entry. I have the police report now, so we have to certify it and enter it into the file. That's easy enough, but without the declarations, we won't win. We must postpone. Can you exert your influence? So far, the state hasn't listened to me. I've had three prosecutors. Lic, they're paying them off somehow."

"So, you've said. I agree. It will be near impossible to put the file in order by the fourth. Meet me at the D.A.'s office at nine."

Señora Roux brought a new bottle and two plates containing warm tarte tatin with a little dollop of cream atop each.

Alex licked his lips. "I haven't had a tarte tatin

since Grandmother died." He took a bite and sighed. It was delicious. He turned back to the lawyer. "This is not the first time I've been summoned. Twice the judge postponed at the request of the defense attorney under the pretext they would talk to me to set up a negotiation. I told you we met in the conciliation office. Braulio's lawyer asked for an evaluation of expenses for my hospitalizations and recovery to make a compensation proposal, but we were stalled as they claimed they were waiting on the hospital to calculate missing expenses, or some nonsense. I had receipts for everything I paid. To make it short, no proposal was made. Instead, I got the doctors' version of plata o plomo, except, the plata has never come to me. They tried to kill me. Now they're trying to run me out of town after I've been ruined physically and financially."

"Forget it. . . Alex, if there was will on their part they would have already settled. Braulio doesn't have money, so whoever paid for his services is dragging their feet to tire you out and evade their responsibility. I take it the driver has never revealed his employer."

"No, of course not. You know how these things are handled. I wouldn't be surprised if the doctors got to the judge. He said at the last meeting, my presence was not obligatory. He could carry on without me; only the accused is required to attend. Did he think I was new? The prosecutor whispered that I shouldn't worry; they'd find a way to stop any hearing."

"Yes, exactly as I will. We'll call you in sick. Have another glass of wine."

Alex had drunk three glasses and was feeling light-headed. He finished his tarte and ordered a coffee. Just as it arrived, Altamirano's phone rang.

The call was brief. The lawyer turned to Alex. "It's done. You won't see the black Nissan or it's driver again." He paused. Alex pictured the driver shot. Killed. Altamirano smiled, tapping his forehead. "Which reminds me—I have a piece of good news. Frederid has organized twenty-four-hour protection for you until after the trial."

Chapter 36

The Ally

January 28 through February 2, 2021

The doorbell echoed throughout the house at seven a.m. Disoriented, he reached for his phone, knocking it to the floor. The bell rang again, and he realized someone was at the gate. He padded to the balcony to peek over. A uniformed policeman raised his hand, calling out, "You Alex Deltoro?"

"What's this about?" He wasn't about to give this stranger any information before he knew why he pressed his bell so early.

"Pérez. Your day-shift protection."

"Who sent you?"

"FGR arranged it. I'm with the Policia Ministerial."

"Okay, I'll be down in a minute. Let me get some clothes on."

Alex pulled on a pair of shorts he found crumpled on the floor by the chair, and a Pink Floyd tee-shirt someone gave him, then slipped into his flipflops and grabbed the cane. At the gate, he checked the man's credentials then let him in. "You want coffee, Pérez?

Take a seat. How is this going to work?"

"Yes to coffee. With milk if you have it." He sat on the couch facing the kitchen. "Me, González, and Hernádez pulled this special assignment. One of us will be with you every eight hours until your court date. When you are home, we'll be watching the old lady next door also."

Alex ground the beans and prepared the French press. "What about the granddaughter? She was attacked in the lobby of a federal agency."

"CEAV. We know. The man is in custody—*so Altamirano's El Puño didn't kill the stalker*—not expecting further problems, and the girl will be protected when she's with you. Best we can do. We don't have enough manpower to put two on a shift."

"I get it," Alex said, as he put a mug of steaming coffee and the carton of milk in front of Pérez. He'd bring it up with his lawyer at the meeting. "But they know her car. She's been driving me around for months now. The next guy could snatch her at school or the supermarket. Christ, she's only nineteen."

Pérez shrugged. "These are our orders. When you're home, we watch your house and the neighbor's. When you go out, we go with you." He put down his cup. "Let's look at the house. I need to see what I'm up against."

Alex gave the man a reluctant tour. He didn't trust the federal police on principal. Showing the guy the house could be an invitation to robbing it—or worse, showing a killer where he could get in.

"Look, you've seen it. I have to get ready for a meeting. You have a car?"

"Yeah. I'll drive. You buy the gas."

"Fine. Help yourself to more coffee." What was he going to do? Pérez had seen the layout and the contents. Not much to steal, but he guessed he'd be carrying his laptop wherever he went from now on.

Pérez drove him into the compound dropping him in front of the walkway leading into the lobby. This time, Alex dressed for the Fiscalia. Slacks, pressed button-down shirt, loafers, and his computer bag slung over his shoulder containing both the laptop and the file. He'd been at it half the night, but he had every error, typo, and lie documented.

Altamirano greeted him at the entrance, wearing a lightweight suit that gave him the air of a gringo from Houston or Atlanta, or somewhere like that. What did he know about the American South?

They shook hands.

The attorney said, "We have an appointment with Fiscal Zamudio in fifteen minutes. You ready?"

"As ready as I can be. How will we get this woman to make the corrections, get the missing evidence, and change the appointment?"

"Guilt-trip her. Or threaten her." He grinned. "Or maybe I'll drown her in my charm."

"I feel like I'm participating in a con."

"That's exactly what it is. Who was that guy who drove you here?"

"Pérez. He's the day shift protection. Thanks for getting that arranged."

"Don't thank me. Frederid took care of it. I owe him a big one. But if he takes this suit and wins, he'll owe me again."

Alex felt a little queasy. Cronyism wasn't the

democratic way, but it certainly was the way of Veracruz.

A buzzer sounded; the voice of the receptionist called for Licensiado Altamirano and Señor Deltoro. They approached the desk.

"You can go back. The fiscal is ready for you."

Altamirano did the talking. Beyond the platitudes and "making nice", the Licensiado was as hard as steel. Fiscal Paola Zamudio didn't stand a chance. It was beautiful to watch the dance as Altamirano almost had her admitting she'd taken a bribe. He probably was worth the fifty percent he originally asked. But most of this payout, if he won the suit, went toward what the hit-an-run had actually cost him.

"I sympathize, Licensiada. I know you're overworked and just haven't had time to go after the ADO for the video or find and take statements from the witnesses. But how can we stand in front of the judge without the facts? You understand; without this key evidence, the judge is unlikely to lean in our favor. Do you want to see my client, already injured, be reduced to penury through no fault of his own? Of course you don't. It's why you went into law enforcement. It's why I did too!"

Zamudio hung her head. "I can change the hearing date, and I promise, I'll go get the evidence. I need a letter from you saying Señor Deltoro is sick. That will act as reason to postpone. But that judge will reschedule for the next week. Can you be ready on February 11th?"

"Why, Licensiada, that's up to you." He handed over an official looking letter requesting postponement.

"We're counting on you. My client will go over the file and show you the errors, inaccuracies, and omissions. I'm surprised at the sloppy work coming out of this office. Let's make it right. Don't you agree, Licensiada?"

Zamudio's face turned rosy as a childish expression of guilt took her over. Alex shook his head with silent disbelief. *How could the State hire such incompetent lawyers? No wonder they were corruptible.* This was his third—each worse than the last.

Altamirano still chastised the woman. "I assume you received the accident report from the ministerial police?" She shook her head. He handed her the copy Alex had received. "Then you will chase it down, locate and interview these witnesses, as well as exert your legal power to obtain the ADO video. Correct?"

Again, Zamudio barely nodded not taking her eyes off her ridiculous spike heels.

"Excellent. You'll get the file completed accurately for our return on February second to review it. By the end of next week, you will have the video and the statements of witnesses. Am I clear?"

Alex sat down by the desk and opened the file, eyebrows raised. He expected her to sit and cooperate.

Altamirano turned to leave, but spun back, narrowing his eyes and tightening his voice. "You won't let us down, will you, Licensiada?"

Alex took a lesson from his attorney, using some of his techniques to manipulate the licensiada as he went over the problems. She wasn't as docile with him, obviously resenting a mere victim telling her how to run her prosecution case.

She tried to defend her predecessors' work, but Alex

341

wasn't having it. "Licensiada, those fiscales were removed from the case for incompetence. Two of them are suspected of accepting bribes." He didn't know this, but her face said it all. "Zarate and Soto still working here?"

He smirked at her reaction. She'd heard the gossip. Of course, a place like this would teem with gossip, and maybe Zamudio had been approached too. She sure responded like she was guilty of something.

Alex smiled kindly and softened his tone. "I know you want to keep your job, maybe rise up through the ranks, be the Attorney General for Veracruz one day. Let's cooperate and win this case. It's your first big one, isn't it?"

"Yes, Señor Deltoro. I'm new here."

"Okay, then don't be defensive, listen and learn."

They spent the next several hours going over every item on Alex's list. He helped her with the official letter to ADO demanding a copy of the video for the hours of five a.m. through eight a.m. on the morning of June 7th. Finally, he walked her through the departments to locate the report from the Policia Ministerial, leaving a trail of disgruntled assistant prosecutors and support staff in their wake, but eventually finding it "lost" in a stack of inter-office correspondences in the Fiscal de Distrito's office.

On the way back to Zamudio's office, her tappy heels echoing off the tile floor, Alex said, "Great! Now you have the names of the witnesses. Get them in here for their statements." He paused to think, "No. Better yet, maybe go to them and take the statements. We'll coordinate with Altamirano. He'll know how to handle this."

Zamudio sighed. She obviously wasn't happy about her day. Probably because she'd been instructed by the boss himself. Altamirano was going to have a field day with this. *That is, if we can get proof.* He was on the phone to his attorney the moment he walked into his house.

Over the weekend Alex, Carolina, and Rosa established a routine with the three guards. The men seemed pleasant enough, married with kids, and enough sympathy for the grandmother and granddaughter that they arranged to drive Carolina to classes and pick her up when she was ready to come home.

Rosa remained vigilant at home, keeping an eye on the neighborhood through her group of card playing friends. No one had seen a strange man or car. Alex didn't quite believe the doctors would drop it, but for several days, he was able to breathe easier and sleep well.

As promised, Altamirano and Alex visited the State D.A. prosecutor's office. Fiscal Zamudio's spackled·on makeup didn't conceal the dark circles under her red, droopy eyes, and she didn't look happy to see them.

Altamirano started in with his obsequious compliments to be rewarded by a slight smile and the fat file thrust into his hands. He passed it to Alex.

"Licensiado, Señor Deltoro, please take a seat. I have done as you asked. Every correction has been made. The police report is included, and I have our people collecting the video from ADO now."

"Well done, Licensiada! We'll go over the corrections while we wait for the video. Then we'll watch it together," Altamirano said, his voice jovial. "How about the court date?"

"Yes, I received a call from the judge's assistant. The 11th at three p.m. will work for him. But he said this was the last change."

"Wait a minute. I've never changed the date before. It was Braulio's lawyer delaying," Alex defended.

Altamirano waved his hand dismissively. "It's not important. We have our date. Let's dig into that file. Alex, why don't you borrow the assistant's desk."

The man looked at the Licensiada, who nodded. "Take care of the copying—" she tipped her head toward an overflowing metal basket by the door— "and take the rest of the afternoon off. I'll vouch for you."

Alex wondered where he'd been last Thursday. He sat down and opened the file, pulling up his copy of the errors on his laptop. The slog through the hit-and-run file had begun. Altamirano left to work with another client and fiscal, saying he would return to check on progress when he was done. Alex knew he had an appointment with the Veracruz district attorney. His attorney held something over the man—probably why things seemed to be moving smoothly.

Periodically, he stopped and asked a question or pointed out something she had missed, which she was able to correct and replace the page in the moment. That was lucky. The review took a full three hours, but finally! It was done.

"Thank you, Licensiada Zamudio. We're almost finished. Has the video been delivered?"

"Let me check." She turned away and punched several numbers then spoke softly into the desk phone. In a moment she dropped the receiver back to its cradle and turned to look across the room at Alex. "Yes. My boss and your lawyer have reviewed it. They ask that we join them. Come."

She wore another pair of ridiculously high shoes jeweled with fake sapphires, although her skirt was a dowdy brown down to her calves. *Whatever floats your boat.*

He followed her to the left and up a flight of stairs to a suite he hadn't known existed. This area was carpeted and relatively tasteful for a government office. They stopped at the assistant's desk.

Zamudio showed her badge. "Señor Deltoro regarding Deltoro vs. Braulio to see the boss."

"Go right in, Paola," the secretary said, brushing the air like waving away a mosquito.

Interesting dynamics within this organization, Alex thought as he stepped into the Attorney General's office.

Altamirano greeted them, praised the excellent cooperation of the licensiada, and helped her into a chair. Alex leaned across the desk, introduced himself, shaking the man's hand. He pulled up a chair from the far side of the bright, spacious office.

The conversation flowed primarily between Altamirano and the Attorney General, mostly a lot of back-slapping and we-done-its. Obviously, the men had come to an agreement. Alex hoped it wouldn't include a payoff to the civil servant. He'd quiz his lawyer later.

Eventually, Humberto Picharra said, "I've agreed to view the ADO video with you." He turned his giant computer screen toward the seated audience and hit play. At first there was nothing. Alex's stomach churned.

The empty sidewalk and the intersection. A truck, then a car passed, the car turning left at the intersection. Then nothing until Alex walked into the frame, his motorcycle backpack slung over his shoulder. He strode to the corner, crossed Tuero Molina and stopped in front of the painted crosswalk until the light on Tuero Molina turned green and it was safe to cross.

Alex's heart rate sped up; his body tensed. He didn't want to watch.

The camera caught him looking both ways. No vehicles were in sight. When Alex reached the middle of the lanes, an older white Tsuru appeared without lights, running at a high speed on Diaz Mirón. It ran the red light.

Alex was shaking now, fearful he'd vomit right onto the Attorney General's highly polished desk.

He sprinted out of the vehicle's path, but the car swerved toward him. Alex was caught sailing over the car which drove from the frame, the license plate in view. The video showed *Alex hitting the ground and the ADO night security running toward the accident. In another moment, a second woman entered the frame at the accident.*

Both women were clearly visible on the recording, and identifiable as the D.A, zoomed in. Alex remembered the angels who soothed him. Not angels, real women. He had said good morning to the ADO guard as he left the building. He couldn't watch any more of the video.

"Sorry, I can't take any more of this." He stood up and took a step toward the door. His injured leg buckled, and he nearly fell. Licensiada Zamudio jumped up and caught him, helping him from the room. "Lic, you'll watch the whole thing?" he called over his shoulder.

"I have a copy, Deltoro. Call your driver and go home. I'll phone you later."

His fiscal helped him limp to the waiting room. He sat down. She leaned close to his ear to say, "I didn't believe your story, but what I just saw was a brutal attack happening exactly as you claim. I will make sure you win your suit, Señor—even if it costs my job."

So, she had been bribed.

Chapter 37

The Judge

Thursday, February 11, 2021, 10:00 a.m.

Fiscal Zamudio was as good as her word. She tracked down the witnesses, took their statements, and carried the investigation further—to the first responders. Interviewing the police individually, she corroborated the captain in charge, how he let the driver go after he was caught. She took statements saying that the ambulance, stationed only meters from the accident took an hour and a half to arrive, but her search for the attendant/driver was a bust. Cruz Rojo did not employ a driver with the name given to the police. Everything was in the file, fully and properly documented and authenticated on the Sunday before the appearance. Zamudio's work was perfection.

After the Fiscalia de Estado and the video, Alex and Altamirano sequestered themselves several times. The attorney admitted his suspicion about the D.A. taking bribes, and he happened to know Picharro attended the same club as Victor Mata. Word had it they were friends.

"Alex, are you aware he claims the case against Mata is a straight murder, and therefore needs to be prosecuted by the State as per the law? I think Mata originally paid him off to dismiss the murder case. My conjecture is that when Mata paid that disgraced judicial to kill you, Picharro protected his buddy, Mata, by separating the suits and doing everything he could to prevent the case from going forward. Whatever the truth, we go to court soon, and we're going to win. We should discuss the award, Alex. I've got your accounting of costs, but what do you want for loss of income and pain and anguish?"

"Lic, I have the documents from my former employer making me the department head and the raise that came with it. I was on a vacation leave, planning to return to work the next week and start when that pendejo ran me down. Multiply eight thousand dollars a month by the eight months since I was run down, and I've lost sixty-four thousand dollars. Plus, the bonus of sixty thousand pesos I would have received at the end of the year."

Altamirano was totting up the figures as Alex gave them. "So, in addition to the sixty-eight thousand, you think we should ask for," the calculator clattered, and he said, "what's your hospitalization and recovery? And your health and peace of mind. What's that worth?"

Alex contemplated a reproduction of Picasso's Don Quixote drawing. Finally, he said, "How much do you think I'll get? "

"Generally, about two thirds of asking. I'd ask for several million pesos."

Eventually they agreed on an asking price. The lawyer said, "I'll submit this. Let's plan to meet before the hearing to go over how the court will run. I'll prepare you. Say Wednesday at four o'clock?"

Alex nodded, they stood and shook hands. "Thank you, Lic."

At home, things settled into a routine. Pérez showed up for coffee and breakfast at eight. He made his rounds, chatted with Rosa on the stoop, sometimes playing cards with her. Depending on Carolina's class schedule, he drove her after making sure Rosa was safe with friends or locked into the house with Alex. He enjoyed lunching with Rosa. It was an opportunity to visit Daisi. The little cat rubbed along his legs and sat in his lap purring. Maybe she'd come home when all of this was over. He missed her.

At four, González brought Carolina home, often after they stopped off somewhere to pick up dinner for everyone. Sometimes he drove both Carolina and Alex to the Chedraui to shop, trailing behind them watching every shopper like he or she was a stone-cold killer. The man was pleasant enough, but more of a loner, preferring to keep to himself cleaning his gun or whittling. *Who whittles these days?* One way or the other, González was no conversationalist.

At midnight, Hernández came on. He scared all three of them. The man was a spook and rarely interacted with anyone. He patrolled the two houses and the neighborhood all night. His only social skill was the terse "gracias" when Alex handed him a cup of coffee.

By the morning of the eleventh, Alex had settled into a sense of security, almost boredom, but the looming hearing wiped out his complacency. He guzzled his coffee, slopping it on the patio table with his shaky hands. His wild thoughts morphed into fog; he barely registered Hernández's presence. He jittered back and forth through the house until the security guard demanded, "Take a breath, güey."

Carolina had taken his "funeral" suit to the cleaners; his shoes were shined to a high gleam. Once dressed, his too-long curls gelled back, he collected his file, laptop, and his courage. At eight-thirty, he said, "Let's go," to Pérez, who had replaced Hernández, and was drinking coffee on the patio.

Pérez walked the cup to the sink. "Calm down, boss. You got this. Vamos."

"Everything cool next door? No one following us?"

"Quit worrying. I dropped the kid at school while you showered. Granny is baking today. I'll be back in an hour. Your lic said he'd bring you home later."

"Okay, then, I guess that's all." While Alex closed the passenger door and hooked the seatbelt, Pérez slapped a bubble light onto the hood then started the engine. "You know where we're going?"

Pérez, annoyed, said, "Take a nap or meditate, man. Of course, I know where the Judicial City of Veracruz is—Colonia Ortíz Rubio." He laughed. "You have any idea how many times I've testified?"

Alex tuned out, grunting or laughing during the few pauses in Pérez's ongoing monologue.

Twenty-five harrowing minutes later, Pérez was making jokes with the security at the entrance to the courthouse. The man laughed and waved him through. He dropped Alex at the wide plaza stretching in front of the wedge-shaped building.

Alex searched every face for Altamirano. The Licensiado was nowhere to be seen. But Alex was early. He picked his way along the esplanade passing banks of solar panels and the towering flagpole, the symbol of Mexico undulating in a slight breeze, to cane his way up the wide stone staircase to the glass entrance mirroring a line of palms with the Gulf of Mexico stretching into the blue, cloud studded sky. Would he see justice today? He began to sweat.

The day proved unseasonably warm. Approaching the entrance, he jabbed the attorney's number into the phone, but the call dropped. Probably service was jammed, or too much metal in the modern, two-story building. He passed through the security check and metal detectors, showing his summons. The attendant waved him toward the cafeteria.

Inside, it was cooler. Already the building hopped with activity. Many wore masks. Lawyers and clients, press with their camera crews, scared-looking wives, grandmothers corralling children, police, and bureaucrats. Alex recognized several faces including the Fiscal del Distrito de Estado deep in conversation with two suited men. He glanced at Alex, causing Alex to shiver. Was that criminal here to screw him over? He limped into the cafeteria and bought a tall Coca-Cola with ice. Still no Altamirano. Still early.

The Coke and a round of deep breathing cooled Alex. He tried his phone again and this time the call went through.

"Alex, I'm right here. Look up."

The lawyer waved from the cafeteria doorway. Alex stood up and raised his arm in an 'I'm here' salute. The lic nodded, pointed toward the coffee, and joined him in two minutes with two steaming cups.

Alex's watch read nine-thirty.

Altamirano looked cool in his Southern gentleman's linen suit, vest, black tie. That perfect Atticus Finch standing up for right and justice. Why didn't Alex feel confident? No, he felt like Tom Robinson—the system prejudiced against him from the start. *Or bought off.*

"Deltoro, I know that look. Don't worry. You've got this. You'll win."

"Don't worry, be happy? Why don't I feel positive then, Lic?"

"Listen, this is what's going to happen." For the next fifteen minutes, Altamirano detailed the procedure. When he finished, Alex had a vivid picture of the hearing. But the rock in the pit of his stomach still weighed him down.

"Come on. This way to courtroom 4." The attorney pushed back from the table—his chair scraping on the linoleum—and led the charge.

Room 4 reminded Alex of every courtroom he'd entered. He wasn't new to the judicial system. He'd acted as an expert witness on occasion in the capital when the suit involved something to do with Laboratorios Salud Integral.

The door opened onto the back of the room with a wide aisle bisecting horizontal rows of seating, to the dark wood podium and judicial bench, flanked with a flag and topped by three microphones. A stand-up microphone stood in front of the podium between two polished desks with three microphones each.

Altamirano led Alex to the left desk, pulled out the middle chair and told him to sit down. The assessor took the left seat. Shortly, Fiscal Zamudio entered the room dressed in a tailored suit and her signature heels, this time in smooth black leather matching her briefcase. She smiled. "Good morning, Señor Deltoro. You ready?" She opened her case, pulled out the file and her notes, then proceeded to study them. Alex saw the slight tremor in her hands as she turned the pages.

In a moment, Braulio was escorted into the courtroom by two people—a pale woman Alex thought could pass as a man. A very short man. Maybe she was a man—flat-chested, man's haircut, a man's mode of dressing in jeans and a pressed, short-sleeved white shirt. He pegged her to be about forty. She kept pushing her large square-framed glasses up her straight nose. The prescription made her eyes look like a bug's, popping out of her head.

He didn't know the other man, but the briefcase shouted attorney. He was another character, older, maybe seventy-five, his hairless pate shined above the tufts of white hair bristling at the nape of his neck. Like Altamirano, the lawyer was impeccably dressed in a suit that rode perfectly on his extremely thin frame, the silk coffee-bean-brown shirt gleaming under the banks of tube lighting, as they traversed the room to their desk to the right of the podium.

Before Braulio stepped around the desk to sit, he gave Alex an angry stare as if saying 'you were supposed to die'. Alex stared right back. It was his first good look at the man who had tried to kill him. He was short, like his lawyer, but stocky. Maybe they were related, except he had a brown, weathered face making him appear older than his sixty-eight years—just a poor slob in his ordinary, well-worn jeans, a thin, wrinkled striped polyester shirt, and cheap black tennis shoes. Probably a ploy to garner sympathy. Alex knew Braulio, an ex-policía judicial, or Federal Policia Ministerial, as the agency was now called, was a cunning bastard, fired from the meanest, lowest, most criminal department in Mexican law enforcement. Alex smirked.

More people filtered into the courtroom. The judge's assistant took her place at the little desk off the right corner of the podium against the wall. Alex noticed the video screen mounted above her head. He looked around and counted the video cameras covering the entire room. No one was going to get away with any bad behavior.

The assistant announced, "Please rise."

The participants and the few spectators stood up as the judge crossed from his chambers door and assumed his seat at the desk. The room sat.

"Good morning, I'm Judge Eugelio Romero. Senorita Geine, will you please read the charges and lead us through the results of the investigation."

The señora gave the details of the hit-and-run with the judge stopping her periodically to ask questions. Now and then he directed a question toward Alex or his would-be assassin, Braulio. In these instances, the lawyers spoke. Altamirano was smooth, eloquent, and dignified, the fox. He slipped in the suggestion Braulio had been hired. Braulio acted like the ass he was, shouting, denying, trying to hold to his statement that Alex had stepped in front of him crossing against the light. His lawyer tried to shut him up, but finally the judge threatened to hold him in contempt and have him removed to jail.

The assistant played the video.

At this point, the second attorney started in. It turned out he was from the insurance company. His story amounted to the company trying to weasel out of paying anything. The judge told him to sit down.

Finally, after all the evidence was presented, the judge proclaimed it was sufficient to continue with the criminal proceedings against Braulio. "I hesitate to rule now. I want to study the case file further before settling on compensation for Señor Deltoro and punishment for Señor Braulio. Licensiada, you will be responsible for bringing the accused in every eight days. If he does not appear to sign, he will be arrested and go to prison, and I will rule in favor of Señor Deltoro. My final ruling shall be made thirty days from today in this court." He banged his gavel. "Court dismissed."

At an early lunch at Bokoba, another seafood restaurant under a thatched roof, this time on the Malecon, they discussed the hearing.

"Alex, this isn't quite over, you know. You have a meeting with Zamudio at four o'clock—she did well today, didn't she," he said. It wasn't a question. He continued, "the fiscal will pose a list of questions to you in order to beef up your statement. Because the judge wants to close this case as quickly as possible, you'll need to answer, in writing of course, right away. I don't know exactly what they are looking for, but I fear it's something the Fiscalia del Distrito del Estado can use to tie the hit-and-run to the murder of your brother."

The conversation continued as they entered Altamirano's office. The attorney had planted himself behind the desk with a glass of whisky. Alex had declined; the beer at lunch had been sufficient for him. He still took some pain killers.

Alex sat. "This is bad? As far as I'm concerned, it is exactly what happened. I want to see this guy go down for taking a bribe and intent to murder along with Mata."

"But not through the state, Alex, not the case against Mata. If the state links the two, which it is trying to do, it will take the case and instead of being a case against government corruption, the IMSS hospitals and the group of IMSS doctors involved, it will only prosecute Mata. You might win, but with all the help he had, he will walk free and the corruption within our government will continue. Business as usual. I doubt you'd win though. Picharra will run the time out with incorrect date, false leads, everything he did on today's case to delay, mislead, and obscure. His thinking, I'm sure, was to send you and your case to court with such flimsy evidence it would be thrown out.

"To top it off, if your case stays with the state Fiscalia, I don't have a chance to take down that shady bastard. You want that, don't you? You must. You may be the last honest citizen in this forsaken country."

"Yes, Lic, I want all the pendejos who killed my brother, covered up for them, and tried to prevent me from getting justice, to pay. Money for me. Prison for them. So, what am I supposed to do?"

"Talk to your fiscal. Take the questions home. Call me if you need help. You won't lie, but you'll spin the answers to keep the cases separated and the murder with the feds."

"Lic, I'm out of patience with the game playing, the kickbacks—it's all about money, isn't it? I might be just as bad. I want money. A lot. Victor Mata and the entire progression of greedy fucks stole my livelihood—my life. I need to get back to Mexico City and start over."

"And so you shall, my man. Now," he said, checking his Rolex, "let me drop you at the Fiscalia."

Fiscal Zamudio waited for Alex in reception at four. *That's a first.* She greeted him professionally, inviting him back to her office.

"Congratulations, you won today," she whispered, once they entered the familiar hallway.

"You were pretty impressive, yourself, Licensiada. I'm glad you decided to come over to my side." He looked down at her. Her cheeks pinked. *Pleasure or shame?*

They entered her office. She closed the door, not something she had done before. "What's this about, señora?" Then the stench hit him. Marijuana! Along the back wall instead of the copier, bricks upon bricks of mota stacked halfway up to the ceiling. *What's going on here?* He sneezed.

"Sorry. Evidence. Have seat. I've been instructed to expand your statement. The judge has ruled favorably for you to win the suit, and win big, but there are some holes in your declarations we need to fill."

"Holes? Like what, Lic? I've written everything as it happened. You know that. You've seen the video."

"Listen, I didn't suggest this, the Fiscalia del Distrito has asked these questions. I'm just a messenger."

"Pues, what kind of questions? Why are you acting

secretive?"

"Here." She thrust a typed paper into his hand. It listed ten questions. "Take them home. Answer them tonight and bring me back your typed statement tomorrow. It's a matter of urgency. We have to convince the judge while he is favorable toward your case."

"You aren't making sense, Licensiada."

"Just do it and meet me back here at the same time. Congratulations again." She opened the door and ushered Alex out, closing the door behind him with a click.

That night Alex sat at his laptop and concentrated on the questions. What's so significant? he wondered. Every question but one had been answered in his original statement. Fiscal Zamudio had included: Was it raining on the morning of the hit-and-run? That was an interesting question. He began typing.

At the time I arrived at the bus station, it was not raining, nor had it started at the time of the hit-an-run. I lay on the street for about forty minutes before it began to rain. The private security agent, an employee of the ADO, was still with me. She produced an umbrella and covered me for approximately an hour until the police arrived with Braulio, the person who ran me over, then fled the scene. In a couple of minutes after they brought Braulio back, the Red Cross arrived and she closed the umbrella, wishing me good luck and left. It wasn't raining any more. If I had had a hemorrhage, most likely I would have bled to death over the hour and forty minutes.

He worked on each question, thinking back to the attempted murder. None seemed out of line or unusual. Anyone could answer—they'd all seen the video. He did not call his attorney. Instead, he fell into bed exhausted.

Chapter 38

The Attacks

Friday, February 12, 2021

His first thought upon awaking concerned those stupid ten questions. The judge wanted to verify Alex had been telling the truth? When the stupid *juez* watched the video he'd have a little more trust, but *ni modo*, he'd answered as required and would ask Pérez to drop him at the Fiscalia at four. González could pick him up.

He pulled on his shorts and grabbed the cane. It was early; he could make coffee after he finished his routine. Alex had missed his exercises the day before. Hernández was probably next door anyway. He and Rosa had formed some sort of bond, to the irritation of Carolina who said the ministerial police officer was "creepy".

Alex tended to agree with her. But so far, things had gone well with them. He had their protection until March eleventh—unless he and his neighbors continued to be threatened and Altamirano pursued his buddy Frederid, the Federal D. A. in Veracruz.

Since the hearing, a great weight lifted off his shoulders. The juez would award him a bunch of money, and hopefully, *fingers crossed,* put Braulio away. He had priors and a dishonorable discharge from government employment. Alex's gut, a great judge of outcomes, insisted he would score for his team. Speaking of teams, he should put up a basketball net and toss hoops with the dude across the lane. Good exercise for his leg.

The bell rang, Hernández appeared from the back of the house somewhere. He was like a cat, silently slipping around from hidey-hole to hidey-hole. He let Pérez in and slinked out the gate.

"Good morning, Alex." Pérez's cheerful greeting filled the room with sunshine. "It's a beautiful day!"

"Good morning. You ready for coffee?"

"Sure. What's on the agenda? I'm driving Carolina to school at ten and picking her up at three-thirty. You got anything?"

Alex handed his bodyguard a mug. Black.

"Can you leave me at the Fiscalia at four? Also, do you know how to contact González? I need him to pick me up, also at four, so no point coming here first."

"Sure, I'll text him. Maybe you better come with me to pick up the kid. You know how traffic can be at that time of day."

"Ja ja, you mean at all times of day—except at five a.m. when the killers are out."

"Yeah, man—what happened?"

Alex gave a synopsis of the hearing and subsequent meetings.

Pérez' eyes lit up and he shouted, "High five, bro'."

Alex slapped his palm then refilled their coffee

mugs. They talked amiably until Carolina shouted at the gate.

"Ay, gotta go. See you in an hour. If you have nothing to do, would you go next door and keep Rosa company?"

"Sure. She's baking." For once, Alex had nothing to do. Altamirano would handle things; he was working on the murder suit.

He shrugged into a clean tee-shirt, slipped his cell into his pocket, and locked the house.

As always, he looked both ways before exiting the gate. No one lurked at his end of the cerrada. He quickly relocked the gate and planted the cane to hop over the curb to Rosa's gate.

She smiled with delight. "Alex, you're just in time. I've baked panque and have fresh strawberries Carolina brought home from that fancy market in Boca Del Rio. Come in. Come in!"

He passed into her courtyard as the old woman banged her gate shut. "Rosa, lock it. Pérez is off driving Carolina. It's not over yet."

"Yes, of course dear. But you must tell me everything. Carolina said you went to court yesterday?"

They walked arm-in-arm into the house. Alex followed Rosa to the kitchen where she fixed two plates of cake with berries, placing them on a tray that held a coffee pot and two mugs. "I asked Pérez to invite you over. Let's go up to the balcony, dear. It's pleasant in the morning. We can keep an eye on things."

Alex picked up the tray. They climbed the perfectly built staircase to the landing accessing the balcony. Rosa's sported a charming bistro table with an embroidered cloth covering it. He put the tray down to help the older woman into her chair. She poured and they chatted while enjoying the still-warm cake.

Alex shared his news about the hearing. Rosa described her Oaxacan Christmas with the rich black mole, and the new baby. He was the high point of her trip. "Three months old and already a comedian like his father, my grandnephew. He'll be a handful when he can actually talk!"

They sat in shrinking shade as the sun rose higher in the sky. Alex was just considering suggesting they go inside when noises came from down at his gate. The sounds of the cerrada rose, seeming to come right from the balcony. Glancing at his watch, he confirmed it was too soon for Pérez to be back. He held up his hand, putting a finger to his lips. Rosa stopped talking, cocking her head to hear. He rose silently and edged to the wall separating their two houses to peer around it.

A stranger stood at the gate pulling the chain through the staves, forming a loop big enough to slip a bolt cutter through. The chain was too heavy for the tool, which disappeared into a market bag at his feet.

The man was a non-descript, but well-muscled twenty- to thirty-year-old moreno, with the stature and bone structure of a Oaxacan. Alex saw a wispy smudge over his lip. Maybe younger than twenty. He dressed like any man on the street. Jeans and a tee-shirt. No bulges under the shirt; he wore sandals so no place to stash a gun or knife.

The man grabbed the bag and moved away, passing through the stanchions closing the street and disappearing. Alex sat back down and told Rosa what he saw.

"Call the police."

"I'll call my lawyer if he comes back."

In moments, the man was back without his bag, but with a rope coiled over one shoulder. *Did he think he was going mountain climbing?*

Alex pinged Pérez.

—Where are you? Pendejo trying to break into my house Watching from R's
—Passing store
—Come thru cerrada
—👍

Alex watched the stocky cowboy prepare his lasso. Ready, the man scanned the houses and street for anyone watching. *Not very smart.* He never looked up to catch Alex spying around the connecting wall. He wasn't sure what the vaquero thought he'd lasso. The idiot circled his loop faster and faster, then let it fly. It made a perfect landing around the urn of dead flowers on his balcony railing. Impressive. The man, kid really, yanked on his lariat. The pot flew off, crashing onto the entry patio. The cowboy ducked, scrambling out of view behind the electrical box on the street.

In moments, when the crash hadn't caused anyone to investigate, he recovered his rope, then edged to the border of the property looping it around a poke of rebar jetting up from the front wall. He started to walk up. Amused, Alex thought any other human could have scrambled over with nothing more than his arms.

The intruder leaped into Alex's patio almost soundlessly, creeping toward the door. Pérez appeared at the cross street. Alex rushed down, keeping out of view. From either edge of the front wall, they watched the man try to break in. Through a series of hand signals, they formed a plan. Alex would enter through his gate as soon as Pérez was over the wall and had him down. He would use the idiot's rope to restrain him. Pérez hoisted himself over, leapt toward the man, barreled into him, knocking him over. Alex opened the lock; threw himself through brandishing his cane. Perez flew up from the tiles. The Oaxacan pounded to the wall. Jumped. Missed! Pérez on his tail. The boy, a vicious bear cub, turned—something in his hand.

"Knife!" bellowed Alex, jumping aside as the kid rushed past him and out the gate, lightning fast like a rat to its nest. Pérez couldn't catch him, but Alex was able to shoot photos of his face.

They stood panting as the whine of a motorcycle faded away.

"I don't know what that was about. Robbery? An attempt to catch me off guard and kill me? I'm pretty sure the threats are over, Pérez. It's either kill me or leave me alone."

"I agree. It's weird. I don't believe it was a random attack. We ought to call the police."

"They won't do anything. I'm sending you photos of him. Don't you have a data base you can search?"

"Yeah, okay. I'll be right back. Check on Rosa."

Pérez returned with Rosa and a platter of quesadillas, rice, beans, fruit, panque, and her sewing. Alex produced two Tecate's and a cup of tea. After an early lunch, Pérez would have his department identify the interloper; Rosa would remain at Alex's. Alex would call his lawyer.

The phone rang. Mrs. Borzo.

Once his victim status renewed, he'd followed the advocate's directions, reviewed the federal file, clarified the facts, delivered the corrected file to the CEAV offices. What did they want now? He let it go to voicemail.

Altamirano was in court. When he listened to Licensiada Angelica Borzo's message, she requested he appear—again. Something about managing the facts and discarding the straw.

He loved how these people talked, never making sense. *Why can't they speak plainly?* Metaphors just didn't cut it in court. He dialed.

Borzo answered, "Señor Deltoro. Thank you for getting back to me."

"What's up, Licensiada? You received the file I left several days ago?"

"Of course, I have reviewed it. I don't find any compelling reason for the Federal Government to prosecute your file and am sending it to the State as a common murder trial."

Alex erupted. "You're what?" He couldn't believe what he heard.

"It is not a federal case."

"You assured me ten days ago you were calling for a medical opinion to certify the management of my brother's medical treatment. No medical arbitration commission would accept the treatment Lucas received as proper care." Alex talked fast; his anger and frustration built. "Did you include the information about the MRI? What about the prescription of the NUBAIN20? It was all there. We've gone over this. Call them back, or better yet, make an appointment for me with this board. I'll present my case."

"I can't do that, Señor Deltoro, but I will review the file and make any addition that may have been left out. I can forward the information tomorrow."

"You were to send the file a week ago."

Her voce dropped; she used that stern tone of a schoolteacher out of patience. "Señor Deltoro, these things take time."

"You mean you never delivered my information. How can I have been denied if you failed in your job? I expect you to deliver that file to the Medical Arbitration Commission today, or I will be forced to contact Xalapa. Call me as soon as the file is submitted. Good day, Mrs. Borzo." Alex hung up and dropped his head in his hands. *Why is this so hard?*

Pérez's expression mirrored how Alex felt. "You having bad luck, too?

"The office isn't getting any matches for this guy. With nothing to go on, my hands are tied. We need to remain vigilant. I've sent the photo and report to Gonzalez and Hernández. I'm going to make a perimeter check." He put on his protective vest and let himself out the gate.

"Alex dear, I don't know exactly what's wrong, but I think you should call your assessor. May I make you a nice cup of tea?"

Alex smiled and nodded, dialed Altamirano—again.

"Lic, we've got a problem with the CEAV." Alex repeated his conversation. The lawyer remained silent for a few moments. "You on the line, Lic?"

"Thinking. I don't like the conclusions forming. Alex, I think your advocate at the victim's commission has been bought. Are you free tomorrow between nine-thirty and twelve?"

"Of course. What will we do?'

"I'm going to have a little conversation with Frederid later. Then you and I will pay a surprise visit on Licensiada Borzo tomorrow."

"Oye, Lic, I haven't let you know yet, but a kid tried to break in here today. He was fast with a knife. Pérez is looking into him, but so far, no success."

"I'd hoped Mr. Puño would put a lid on the threats. Stay alert, Alex. We're in the home stretch."

The connection disconnected.

The surrounding houses cast long shadows into the patio as the sun inched toward the mountains. "What time is it?"

Pérez, still in his vest, leaned through the door, and replied, "Time to get going. Señora, I don't think it's wise to leave you alone. Do you mind sewing in the car?"

"No. I'll just freshen up a bit and get my purse."

"Let me escort you. Alex, lock up and meet us at the car in five minutes."

Alex kept watch for motorcyclists following, or drivers appearing too interested in them. As usual, Pérez stuck the bubble to the roof of the car and turned on the lights. Unless the kid was plain stupid, he wasn't going to mess with the police. Nobody would; traffic raced to get out of their way.

Pérez knew where to pick up the girl, and according to Alex's watch, they arrived exactly on time, but Carolina was not in sight. Students milled around awaiting rides, talking with friends and laughing. Alex scanned the faces. No Carolina.

Suddenly Pérez jumped out of the car and ran toward a scuffle on the sidewalk eight car lengths ahead of them. A girl screamed. Voices called for help. The mass of students parted as Pérez ran through— Alex saw the Oaxacan shoving a girl into an SUV. Carolina!

He took off, yelling, "Lock the doors, Rosa!"

By the time he arrived, students and professors clustered obscuring the view. "Carolina!" he bellowed and pushed his way breaking through the onlookers to find the young woman sobbing in the arms of a woman, the boy in handcuffs on the ground, and the SUV gone. A siren wailed.

When Carolina saw Alex, she pulled away and ran to him, tears streaming down her cheeks. He encircled her in his arms.

"It was so awful, Alex. That boy grabbed me. He tried to push me into an SUV. Why me?"

"Did he say anything?"

"Only to be quiet."

Her shaking had begun to subside; she was getting angry. Alex could tell by the shift of tension turning her body rigid. "Your gran is in the car. Come on let's go sit with her. Let me tell Pérez."

"Yo, Pérez, I'm taking Carolina to the car. What do you need to do?"

The guard tossed Alex his keys. "Go take care of your delivery. I called my department, some guys are coming for this pendejo, but it might take a while. I'll come by for the car later."

"Thanks man. Carolina, you feel up to driving?"

"Okay." She broke away then gave Pérez a hug.

Rosa was relieved to see her granddaughter.

Carolina got them to the Fiscalia on time. Alex handed over the responses to Zamudio's ten questions and they returned home.

González posted himself on Rosa's balcony where he could keep an eye on things.

Chapter 39

The Fight

February 23, 2021

Tension ran high. Two attacks in one day were two too many. Alex tossed and turned; restive sleep interrupted with nightmares punctuated by long minutes of brooding wakefulness. Pérez came, got his coffee, and went outside. Carolina texted that she and Rosa would stay locked their house.

Alex showered and put on his slacks. He pressed a shirt then called an Uber to meet Altamirano at nine-thirty at a coffee place near the CEAV. The Uber pulled up in front of the torta restaurant as he rounded the corner. His leg hurt from running the day before, and he was happy to sit. The thirty-minute ride gave him time to parse the problem he faced with the Victims Commission. Altamirano was right. The doctors had bribed Borzo. *What else could it be?* His lawyer cited several behaviors on Borzo's part that corroborated their suspicions.

Inside, the guard signed them in. Altamirano led them up the stairs to Borzo's office, Alex grimacing with pain. The Licensiada was on the phone when they barged in. She slammed the receiver into the cradle, a guilty look on her downturned face. It didn't last long.

She began to shout. "What are you doing here? How dare you enter my office without an appointment! I'm calling security." Altamirano was already on his phone. "Who are you calling?" The woman was loud.

"Licensiada, I'm calling Fernando up in Xalapa. Unless you have anything to declare regarding the Deltoro case." He held out the cell phone, finger poised to dial.

Her voice calmed, sweetened. "Licensiado Altamirano, everything is fine with the Deltoro case. Is there something I can help you with?"

"Yes, there is. Some key pieces of evidence for the case file were missing when it was delivered to you, and I want to doublecheck all is now in order. The Medical Arbitration Commission can't make an informed decision without these pieces of information. Mr. Deltoro assures me he has made a complete statement regarding the death of his brother, including information about the drug NUBIAN20, and the conspiracy to withhold medical treatment at the IMSS 6. Mr. Deltoro said he delivered this crucial information to you, and we wish to verify it has been entered into the case file."

Borzo blanched. She'd been caught in a lie, and she knew it. "I-uh, I must have forgotten this. I'll add it to the file today and send a copy to the commission right away."

Altamirano's smooth voice purred, "Isn't that what you said before? Is there some reason you have been derelict in your duty? Perhaps someone has interfered with our business?"

Fear rolled up in her eyes. "The addendum slipped my mind. We're short-staffed right now." Her left eyelid fluttered—a lie.

"Then you will make corrections today."

"It would be best if Señor Deltoro resubmitted the information with an affidavit explaining it is to replace lost documents."

"If that expedites the matter, we will attend to it immediately. Thank you, Licensiada Borzo. Good day." He got up and headed to the door. Borzo shot Alex a hateful look. He smirked, turned, and limped out.

They drove to a nearby stationery store. Alex ran in, copied his information, wrote out a short letter explaining the addition, copied that and returned it to Borzo within the hour. Again, she was on the phone. Before he went into the office, he listened. She was talking to someone about him. ". . . suspect I've been compromised. That attorney is going to call Xalapa. I'm not going to lose my job over this, Doctor. . . Okay, okay. Yes, I'll complete this one more thing." She hung up.

Alex opened the door.

Several days later, he received the email saying the Medical Arbitration Commission had ruled against the federal prosecution of the Suit. The attached document detailed the decision. They had failed to take into consideration the addendum Borzo was to submit, nor did they consider the contradictions in the doctors' statements. The file was sent to the state prosecutor.

Alex was livid, and ashamed for his country. The ones with money could buy impunity. He couldn't let those murdering doctors win.

He clearly remembered the words of the prosecutor who gave him the copies of the original filing, "Señor Deltoro, your brother was murdered." It seemed like a millennium had passed since he'd initiated the suit. That first prosecutor offered him two options: reach an agreement to settle or continue with the investigation. The next prosecutor pointed out the previous prosecutor's modifications to his declaration—the scene of the events, dates and times—all wrong.

"I shouldn't tell you this, but there is no other reason for these errors than to hinder the investigation so the ministerial detectives would drop it in the dead file."

It came as no surprise the Federal government was trying to disassociate itself from its responsibility by sending the matter to the State. According to his attorney's meeting with Fiscal Frederid, the Commission's ruling claimed the murder of Lucas had occurred outside the IMSS facilities, arguing the medication causing respiratory arrest was prescribed and obtained outside the IMSS complex. Simple—it was a straightforward murder. *But how is it possible the FGR does not take into consideration that the medication was prescribed by the director of the IMSS Hospital 51?*

Someone up the chain had sold his honesty. A hundred thousand dollars? A quarter million? What was the price of professional ethics? Alex burned. No, he would not give up.

He and Altamirano agreed fighting through the CEAV was the best avenue. Working with the Victims group was free to Alex, a plus. Altamirano did not come cheap and every meeting, notary, change—you name it —with the Fiscalia cost him.

Besides, within CEAV were both federal and state advisors. He could take Borzo to task for not providing the essential information to the Medical Arbitration. Then demand a new advocate. Alex's metaphorical master's degree in the shady environment of lawyers confirmed the old saw: it's easier to find a perfect banana than an honest lawyer.

Eleven days later, Alex entered the familiar agency to meet his new CEAV advocate. At the reception, the guard asked him to join the licensiado at the conference table in the waiting room. As he and Altamirano stepped into the room, two men stood to greet them. They introduced themselves as Armando Padilla, the advocate, and Fernando Locona, the attorney heading the Veracruz branch of the CEAV down from Xalapa to oversee the proceedings.

After the official rigmarole of signing documents authorizing Padilla as his legal advisor, Fernando Locona apologized for the poor work of Licensiada Borzos, and explained she had been let go. Padilla would now look after his interests. "Mr. Deltoro, please bring us up to speed on your case so we may understand what happened, and how it has been handled."

Alex sucked in a breath and slowly exhaled his rising blood pressure to normal. He was going to waste more time repeating eight months of this nightmare. He summarized. Locona spent another half hour saying everything except what CEAV would do for him. The advocate, Armando, said nothing.

Finally, Altamirano said what needed to be said, "With all due respect, Licensiado, we are all aware of the corruption throughout our government and legal system. I've listened to everything you've said, but I have failed to understand exactly what your agency will do to assure justice for my client, our client, Alex Deltoro and his family."

The advocate tried to hide a grin. Alex smirked behind a cough. *You tell 'em, Lic!"*

His boss turned a shiny color of copper. "I'll leave you in the capable hands of Licensiado Padilla." He excused himself saying he had an important meeting back in Xalapa.

Padilla took over. He was young, fair-skinned and clean cut. "Let's go to the prosecutor's office and get the ball rolling."

"Shouldn't we discuss your intentions and agree on a plan of attack first?" asked Alex. Altamirano nodded in agreement.

"That's the second part of the plan. We need to know exactly what the fiscal—"

"No, Licensiado, we need a plan. Our goal is to bend the FGR to our will, not the other way around," Altamirano interrupted.

Alex added, "Look the feds—with this commission's help—sent my case to the state. Let's not waste more time fighting over it, I want the prosecutor to know we will not stand for this abuse. I want a plan."

The advocate looked annoyed. "Okay, Mr. Deltoro, but please be brief."

Alex expressed his point of view. He pulled his prepared arguments from the folder he carried. "This investigation has totally stopped since the file was sent to the state. Mata needs to be investigated fully. My statement clearly documents that he prescribed the medicine while on duty, and the IMSS reception guard handed that prescription to me. The investigation does not coincide with the problem. The prosecutor's investigation has not taken into account the malpractice of the doctors who attended the emergency. Furthermore, Licensiada Borzo failed to submit the proofs I provided to the arbitration board. Neither the CEAV or the FGR actually investigated to verify claims the emergency doctors interviewed me, or took into consideration that the symptoms mentioned in the medical record did not exist. The biggest omission? The manufacturer's contraindication of the drug itself. Alcoholics, the label says in capital letters, should not take it because of the risk of respiratory arrest—in twenty minutes, exactly as it happened to my brother."

Altamirano covered Alex's wrist with his hand. "Calm down, Alex. We have corrected all of this in the file with your full statement. Lic Padilla here can read that. Let's talk about the main legal problem with your suit."

"You mean the actual complaint? Yeah, about that." He pulled another set of papers from his folder and pushed his signed copy of the original filing across the table. "I filed against IMSS Hospital for malpractice. Look! This says the complaint is against a Family Medicine office located at another address, which denied services and abandoned treatment. This shit is pure lies! Almost every finding misinterprets the facts or makes up its own." Alex's voice rose. He felt his blood pressure aiming for the roof, and hot pinpricks stabbing his eyes.

He glared at the advocate who began to speak. "I agree, Señor. We have a serious manipulation of this case file. Since your pages," he looked at Alex's printed notes, raising his reddish-colored eyebrows, "detail the errors and omissions, let me take twenty minutes and read them."

Alex nodded, slid the papers to Padilla, then got up and bought a Coke from the machine on the back wall. His lawyer steepled his hands and closed his eyes.

When the advocate finished reading, he folded his hands over the notes and cleared his throat. Alex stopped pacing; Altamirano opened his eyes.

"First of all, we agree the file must be returned to the federal level, yes?"

"Yes," they chimed.

"Then let me state my opinions. I believe that the intention of the government is to release responsibility of the FGR and have the case handled as medical negligence on the part of Dr. Mata—a civil matter which would ultimately wind up with a payout by Mata's professional insurance. Since the common jurisdiction is outside the powers to be able to judge the IMSS, a federal institution, this strategy would release everyone else involved, including the hospital and the deceased's family doctor. It would give the aggressor, Doctor Mata, an option to pay a fine for a misdemeanor, allowing him to continue practicing.

"This man is part of your family. Only you, Señor Deltoro, know the extent of the punishment due to him. To proceed, we need to know what you want to do."

"I haven't been clear enough, Licensiado? Throw all of the doctors in prison. Lose the key. And make them pay me millions. Jail my sister-in-law too, while you're at it."

"Yes, I hear you. But here are the realistic options. We can separate the crimes into three scenarios:

One, return the lawsuit as lack of patient care by the family doctor.

Two, open another lawsuit against the hospital for the crimes of cover-up and professional malpractice committed by the workers to obfuscate a deliberate murder by Dr. Mata. This would not be murder, as there is no report that the patient arrived dead."

"Hold on," Alex interjected. "They kept him alive with artificial respirators and a pacemaker—just to carry out Mata's malevolent plan of deceiving my family into thinking Lucas died by natural causes. The big lie—cancer—"

Altamirano interjected, "Of course you are angry and bereaved, but put it aside, and let's determine our strategy."

Chastised, Alex said, "Yes, Lic."

Padilla continued, "If the government insists there was a medication prescribed outside the government institution, handle that separately as a second complaint against Dr. Mata by the common jurisdiction.

"With a fourth approach, handle it as it has been happening, all in a single file with further investigation and taking into account the omissions and inconsistencies." He added, "We have all the necessary elements, more than enough to do it, Mr. Deltoro. What will it be?"

Altamirano stepped in. "Let's go with wrestling the current case back from the state before initiating one of the other options. The Fiscal over there has higher political aspirations. If FGR prosecutes, he stands to have a big win, and Alex stands to see real justice done."

"Okay, let's go to the prosecutor's office or they'll all be gone for lunch."

Licensiada Margarita Fernández, Eighth Prosecutor in the Integral Unit of Law Enforcement of District XVII, met them in the hall as she stepped out for lunch. A woman of medium height with a bitter face. Even from a distance, Alex read extensive experience. She didn't look happy, but she graciously said, "Please come in and we'll see what we can do. I thought you weren't coming."

"Sorry, Fiscal Fernández, we appreciate your time," Padilla said before making introductions.

Alex assessed this new fiscal as she pulled a file from her cabinet and sat at her desk. Would she be the only honest prosecutor in Veracruz? Approximately sixty-five years old, salon-dyed auburn hair; a good quality, if severe, suit, and something rare in tropical Veracruz— stockings that made her legs look good in the red high-heeled shoes she wore. She topped her professional look with gold-framed bifocals.

"Please sit. Let's make this quick, my lunch is calling me." She smiled. "This is about the federal investigation folder Number FED/VER/0000405/2021 that was sent to the State?"

"Yes. May I enter my credentials?" Padilla handed over his legal agreement with Alex.

"Thank you." She tucked the accreditation into the file. "I'm listening."

"My client wishes to return the file to be prosecuted by the FGR."

The fiscal grumbled a bit before getting to the question. "On what grounds, Licensiado?"

Padilla clearly explained, adding that the victim's medical file was never integrated, despite the fact that the prosecutor's office requested it on several occasions.

Mrs. Fernández interrupted Padilla's speech with a curt voice. "We are going to take it one step at a time. First we are going to ask for the return of the file for review. On our next visit, once we have obtained the medical record, we will continue our conversation. Send me your official request in writing and be ready to meet." She stretched out her hand to say goodbye, which to Alex rather felt as though she were blowing them off.

"Thank you Fiscal Fernández. When might we expect a callback?"

"Within ten days, Mr. Altamirano."

Back at the CEAV, Padilla wrote up the document to recall the case and obtain the medical record. The three signed it, made copies, and Alex called for an Uber. The document was in Fiscal Fernández' hands as soon as she returned from her comida.

Chapter 40

The Turnaround

March 2021

Seven days later, Alex was summoned to the prosecutor's office in the morning to review a copy of the medical file. Fernández ushered him to a conference room and told him to read and annotate. Shocked, the document was completely made up.

His note read:

No documents from family doctor, Dr. Fierro

No documents from the doctor who requested the last ultrasound

No medical report of the ultrasound study

No MRI study

No record of consultation with the gastroenterologist and his results

No record of the medication prescribed by Dr. Mata

False statements—erroneous dates—lies

Alex noted the numbers of times false information was repeated with a clear lack of continuity. And he noted the total lack of expertise in the use of the computer. No secretary would make formatting errors.

And the grammatical and punctuation errors!

Alex requested the fiscal demand key documents in order to support and prove what Alex denounced. Hell, he had copies of receipts proving some of the lies.

Fiscal Fernández huffed, but Alex sensed she had taken a keen interest in the case. Perhaps Frederid had gotten on *her* case. Perhaps she was truly honest. The one thing he was sure of, Mata had tried to sway things. Something she'd let slip about a phone call. *Yeah, I've heard that call,* he thought, remembering the last advocate. He waited for the shoe to drop.

But it didn't. Another week passed. Alex and Padilla were summoned to Fiscal Fernández's office.

"Sit down, gentlemen. I have excellent news." Keeping them in suspense, the fiscal sent her assistant to bring tea for everyone. While the girl was out of the office, she said, "The state has relinquished the file. We have all the evidence documents, which support Señor Deltoro's claims. The judge is in agreement and has calendared a date."

The assistant returned with a tray containing a China teapot and four matching cups and saucers with a small pate of almond cookies, which she set on the desk for the attorney to pour. Alex accepted his cup, and a cookie passed by the girl. *Get to the punchline!*

Padilla added a drop of milk to his tea, then said, "The date?" He grinned at Alex.

"Yes, Mr. Padilla. We'll get to the date. Melisa, will you fetch some lemon slices?"

Again, the girl trotted out of the office. "Licensiado, Mr. Deltoro, in light of the threats and attacks on you and your neighbors, only us three, Fiscal Frederid, and the judge, may know this date. Call it a secret, but for your own protection, it must be so. The defendants will not receive this information until shortly before Semana Santa."

"But the date?" Alex asked. He felt like a kid anticipating Christmas gifts.

"April fifth."

"And the victim's chances of winning?"

"Mr. Padilla, the Fiscal wouldn't have wrested this case back from the State if there were any chance of losing." Her tone was imperious. *Well deserved.* She was the top winning prosecutor in the Veracruz department.

"Excuse me Fiscal, but I have a question. On the eleventh, I will hear the judgement on my hit-and-run case, and my protection will be terminated. May I request I have protection through the trial?"

"Who is protecting you?"

"Policia Ministerial. Three officers. My dayshift drove me here."

"That sounds rather luxurious. Why do you need protection?"

Alex summarized the various attacks, threats, and attempted kidnapping.

"I see. And this was not included in your complaint?"

"I was run down eight days after I filed. The State handled it."

"Let me talk to the Fiscal about it. Perhaps your assessor can intervene."

Alex knew better with this one not to press his point. "Thank you, Fiscal Fernández."

At home, Alex, Pérez, who was becoming a trusted

friend, Rosa and Carolina rejoiced. Pérez produced a bottle of halfway decent tequila, and even Rosa was convinced to give up her cup of tea for a small glass. She'd been cooking; a pot of chicken poblano warmed on the back of her stove.

González arrived to relieve Pérez.

"Señor Pérez, can you stay for comida? I'll just cook some rice and bring everything over. Carolina, come make a salad," Rosa said.

Carolina obeyed reluctantly, Alex noticed, giving the bottle a long, sad look. She dawdled, chatting with the security.

The men enjoyed a few more shots with plans for the end of the assignment. Only four more nights through the eleventh. González was happy to go back to his day shift and his family. Pérez was sorry to leave his cushy assignment.

Soon Rosa and Carolina appeared with the dinner. After eating, Alex put on some music. He convinced Rosa to take a spin across the floor with him. Carolina invited Pérez; the dancers swirled, laughing until González rushed out of the door, pistol in his hand, scaring the poor water bill collector, and reminding everyone of the danger surrounding them.

For three days, things remained quiet at the house. Alex felt at loose ends. He was accustomed to working on the suits. Now all he had to do was nothing. Pérez was edgy, so was González, and no one had a clue what was going on with Hernández. Rosa locked up tight; Carolina, usually garrulous, had nothing to say. The judge was about to make his ruling.

Alex anticipated the Fiscal's decision regarding

continued protection. He went to bed early, leaving González on duty, and fell asleep quickly. In his dreams he was chased by a faceless threat, or he hid from a monster he never saw, or he was attacked by a hooded human shooting. Bang! Bang! Then footsteps running up tiled stairs and—he woke with a start.

Someone was in his house, coming up his stairs. He flew out of bed and eased through the window to the ledge.

God save me!

He pushed off with his damaged leg and flew across the gap to the neighbor's roof, miraculously landing on his good leg and rolling on his side. The window crashed open, glass and bullets flying. Alex clawed his way to standing and ran to shelter in the stairwell. The assailant roared with frustration, but did not follow.

Alex crept down the stairs pounding on the neighbor's door. A woman answered. "Who are you? I'm calling the police."

"Yes, please. I'm your neighbor in Calle las Islas. I've been attacked. Call the police. Call my lawyer." He shouted the number.

Trapped. Alex couldn't go home—the woman wasn't about to let him in. He'd never be able to jump onto the window ledge now that it was covered with glass shards. He fumed and anguished for fifteen minutes until the door opened a crack, then all the way. It was Rosa. He'd never been so happy to see anyone in his life. The woman let him in demanding to know what was going on. Rosa relayed the story until Altamirano arrived and took them home. The assassin got away.

Alex did not have the gate key. Carolina appeared, anxious, but relieved to see Rosa unharmed. She climbed the wall. She'd barely started across the patio when she screamed.

"Carolina, what is it? Are you okay?"

"It's González. He's been shot!"

"Get the key."

In moments, Alex was tending the security guard. The lawyer got on the phone to the police. Carolina called for an ambulance."

The rest of the night was a shit-show, but Alex and Altamirano were in courtroom 4 at nine a.m.

So were quite a few others.

Thursday, March 11, 2021

The judge entered. Everyone rose. Everyone sat. Altamirano approached the bench and called for a meeting in chambers, which lasted twenty minutes. Braulio was summoned. Ten minutes later, he returned to the courtroom stony-faced. Alex was called in.

"Señor Deltoro, I've heard all about the attack on you last night. I understand you and your neighbors have been harassed on several occasions. I have spoken with Mr. Braulio about testifying for a reduced sentence regarding who is behind these attacks. With your assent, I will rule with that caveat. Be assured, Señor, he will see jail time. I will also increase your award. Is this satisfactory?"

Alex nodded. *Braulio is going to denounce Mata!*

The ruling was almost anticlimactic, but not entirely. Braulio, after receiving ten years with parole in six for good behavior, was arrested and led away in cuffs, but not before turning to give Alex a hate-filled sneer. Alex was awarded three million seven hundred thousand pesos—a hundred eighty-five thousand dollars—to be paid by Braulio and the auto insurance company within the week.

Altamirano and Alex strode out of the courthouse, down the imposing stairs, and onto the esplanade, before simultaneously turning toward each other and whooping.

"We did it, Lic! We did it! Do you think they'll pay?"

"We'll know in a week. You're the fighter, Alex. Most would have given up long before now. Let's get out of the open—go see if we've won the next skirmish, yeah?"

Fiscal Fernández waited for them at the reception area. She appeared happy to see them.

"Good afternoon, Señora. You've heard the news then," Altamirano said.

"Congratulations, Señor Deltoro. I'm happy for you. Come on, let's go back to the office."

She guided them through security and chatted amiably as they walked along the well-tended lawn and foundation plantings to her office. Once inside, with the door shut, a broad smile took over her face. "I have good news and better news. Which do you want first?"

Alex said, "Give me the good news."

"The Fiscal has arranged for you to keep your protection through April fifth. They're in place and doing a good job, I understand."

"Thank you, Fiscal Fernández. I really appreciate you going to bat for me. We'll probably be getting a new man though."

"Why is that?"

Altamirano answered. "The evening man was shot on shift last night when an assassin broke in. Alex managed to escape over the rooftops to a neighbor's house. The threat isn't over, but we have good news from today's ruling. Braulio has agreed to turn State's witness for a reduced sentence. Once he fingers Mata, and/or his group, we'll have the final proof of murder, attempted murder, and conspiracy. What's your better news?" He grinned, eyes twinkling.

"Licensiado Altamirano, you're a rogue. You've stolen my thunder. I was going to tell you about Braulio. No matter, let's have a toast then I've got to run." She pulled a small tray with an excellent bottle of silver tequila and three blue-rimmed tequila glasses, caballitos, ready to be filled, from the credenza and poured, handing each a glass. Holding up her own she declared, "To winning!"

They echoed, "To winning!" and threw back the smooth, smoky liquid.

Alex, his lawyer, the CEAV advocate, and the prosecutor worked tirelessly for the rest of the month. Besides attending and sometimes testifying at several hearings, Alex continued to help build the case. Braulio did indeed name the person who hired him. But it wasn't Victor Mata. Dumfounded, he gaped at his attorney.

"Ana Deltoro Mata was arrested this morning. You may as well act on your complaint against her for robbing your house. But hold off until tomorrow. I'm betting she's going to turn on her brother. Mark my words."

"I wish I could have seen her hauled away. No one deserves it more. Can she be implicated in Lucas's murder?"

"Your prosecutor is working on it."

They smiled at each other with evil glee.

Alex analyzed every word in the final case file. As the doctors' house of cards flipped and flopped, more and more evidence was entered to support Alex's claims. Once Mata was accused, others changed their tunes and their declarations. The real medical file mysteriously appeared at the FGR reception. Everything pointed to an intentional murder of an IMSS patient by IMSS employees.

Altamirano and Frederid were right. The case was big. All Alex wanted now was for Mata to accuse Ana and Morticia—the whole family would go to prison.

But Alex felt empty. Revenge wasn't so fulfilling.

Also, he was not out of danger. He'd been shot at twice riding with Pérez to one or another of his legal appointments. Carolina had to miss classes when someone followed her on campus. Luckily her teacher was aware, and called security to grab the man before he could flee. The last week before Semana Santa, Alex was confined to the house except for legal appointments. Rosa and Carolina escaped with relatives to another city for Easter Week.

One of Alex's outings was to the hearing on the charges of contracting with Braulio to run Alex down. Ana did not appear. On the way to the car, he asked Altamirano what was going to happen.

The attorney said, "The judge will take it into

consideration in the punishment. One thing for sure, you will be paid a benefit." He opened the backdoor of his brand-new Mercedes and put the file he carried on the seat, then extracted his briefcase. "Alex, get home safely and have a pleasant afternoon. I've got to rush back on another matter. Pérez is waiting at the gate for you. Be careful."

Things happened fast. On the eve of Holy Week, Alex was notified for the hearing on April fifth as promised. The three judges had completed their rulings. The case was to be decided.

Altamirano warned him, "Get ready for the verdict, Alex. We're in the final stretch."

Chapter 41

The Verdict

April 5, 2021

The days crept by. Alex's only reprieve was the company of Pérez and a brief visit from Daisi when she was hungry. His nerves stretched taut. Sleep eluded him. What would happen? Would he win the suit? Not even Altamirano was around to quell his fears.

Finally, Monday, Pérez escorted him to the courthouse cafeteria per the licensiado's instructions. They were early.

Altamirano met them at the door. "Alex, you look tired. Let's get coffee. I have some news."

"I could use a cup. I haven't been able to sleep." The lawyer, he noted, appeared as fresh and well-dressed as ever. *Easy for him.* "When do we go in?"

"I'll be called. They'll be late. But that gives us time to relax and catch up. Black?"

"Yes. Thanks."

Altamirano returned with two tall cups of steaming coffee. He set one in front of Alex and sat down. He tested the coffee. "Ay, hot!" He set his cup on the table, cast a serious look on Alex. "You understand what this hearing is, don't you?"

"The judge will rule. I get money and vindication, or I'm fucked."

"In a manner of speaking, yes. The judges have already ruled on the law. This is a formality. The issues with the IMSS system have already been determined and penalties meted out. We were correct about your sister-in-law. She turned on Dr. Mata, as did the hospital doctors, including Fierro. Although there were separate charges brought against Fierro and the floor supervisor."

"So, Fierro isn't being charged in this hearing?"

"No, I didn't mean that. He was charged with malpractice and dismissed. The floor supervisor as well. Fierro is also charged with accessory to murder."

"All the other doctors? Mata's cousin?"

Altamirano laughed a deep guffaw as he banged his cup onto the table. "Down to a man, they turned on Mata. Zambada lost his license. He's gone. Some of the others have been fined and suspended for varying periods of time. The hospitals couldn't afford to lose personnel during this pandemic. Staff is short as it is. But this is why you'll see them as witnesses." He glanced at his gold Rolex Cosmograph Daytona. "We better get over to the courtroom."

Alex swilled the dregs of his cup and pushed up from the table. "New watch?"

"A little gift to myself for winning."

The courtroom was similar to the last one, but this one had had a stately mahogany desk with a cedar chair upholstered in wine-colored leather dominating the dais. To the left of the judges' bench, a table filled. Alex realized it was for the defendants and their attorneys as he recognized a couple of the defense lawyers. To the right sat the two fiscales, and an auxiliary legal advisor. Altamirano pulled out a chair for Alex. They sat down. Behind them, witnesses filed in, as well as relatives of the accused, or so Lic whispered. Alex recognized several of the doctors. The galleries filled up with spectators. Two uniformed police officers guarded the main door.

"Check out all the meat going onto the grill," Altamirano muttered.

Exactly at eleven the judge's assistant bustled through the door behind the bench and tapped the microphone. "Good morning. This fifth day of April 2021 at eleven o'clock we hear the verdict of Investigation File number FED/VER/0000405/2021 for the crime of homicide against Dr. Víctor Mata Arriola and Dr. Arturo Fierro. Please turn off your cell phones and other devices. Photography is not allowed in the courtroom."

The door opened again, and the judge stepped into the courtroom.

"Please rise for his honor Judge Benancio Silva Benítez," the assistant said. She seated herself at a small desk behind the dais.

The judge took his seat. "Be seated. Pursuant to articles 53, 59, and 104 section 2 of the Code of Criminal Procedure I shall read the defendants' rights."

Alex couldn't keep his foot still. Taptaptaptap. Did these murderers really have rights? He tuned out.

"...I call the defense and the prosecution to the floor." The judge sat back down.

The defense spoke first claiming malpractice not homicide. The prosecution rebutted with facts from the case file. The courtroom atmosphere heated up.

Judge Silva intervened. "Thank you, Licensiados. Witnesses, please approach the bench."

The witnesses filed to the dais; their attendance confirmed per legal process. The judge instructed them to conduct the trial according to the law. Next, the crowd of doctors and various other witnesses were led out to await their turns at the witness stand. Alex yawned.

Silva launched into a discussion of a series of articles of the penal code, which applied to the accused. Alex had trouble keeping his eyes open. Only his nervous tapping kept him from falling asleep. He forced himself to pay attention in time to catch the judge turn the process over to the prosecution.

Altamirano stood up, and began speaking, his voice calm, reasonable, sincere. "Your honor, gentlemen, ladies. With this file," he paused to hold up the case file, "I present conclusive evidence of the deliberate, planned, homicide of Mr. Lucas Deltoro by his brother-in-law, Doctor Victor Antonio Mata, and accomplice Doctor m Fierro Martinez, in retribution for Dr. Mata's wives cheating on him with Lucas Deltoro. It's an old story, as old as mankind itself. Statements by the interrogated doctors demonstrate intentional lack of attention on the part of Dr. Fierro, the patient's family doctor, with the support of the IMSS floor coordinator, who illegally denied service available to the victim, all this to support his friend and medical colleague Dr.

Víctor Mata, who wanted revenge."

He stopped speaking and gazed over the audience shaking his head. Alex heard a couple of gasps from the gallery.

Altamirano continued. "The indiscretions of Dr. Víctor Mata's wives did not give the doctor the right to murder. It's a sin. And murder is against the law.

"But how was this murder enacted? First Mata instructed his friend, the deceased's family physician, Dr. Fierro, to misdiagnose stomach cancer, then prescribe conflicting medications and medications contraindicated for the decease. Secondly Fierro was to deny treatment, tests, and procedures. Finally, when Lucas Deltoro was sufficiently poisoned, Dr. Mata prescribed NUBAIN, specifically contraindicated for use by alcoholics, which sent the victim into respiratory arrest. At the hospital, Dr. Mata intentionally orchestrated the attempted cover-up by his fellow hospital members to try to hide the malpractice that led to the patient's death." He waved the file again. "The proof is in the file." He sat down.

The courtroom was deathly silent.

The defense offered a few weak arguments and requested the presence of the witnesses. They were called one-by-one to the courtroom to testify. Mostly the doctors pointed fingers at Mata, claiming threats or ignorance as to what was going on. Alex had heard enough. He wanted to leave. None of this would bring his brother back. It was just plain boring.

Until witness Ana Deltoro Mata was brought in.

He straightened up. Ana barred her teeth at him.

One of the defense lawyers stood to question Ana. "You are the widow of the victim, Lucas Deltoro?"

"Yes."

"What was your role in the murder of your husband?"

"I guessed what my brother was planning. I saw it in how my husband's health deteriorated. I tried to stop Victor."

"Why didn't you go to the police?"

"I was ashamed."

Alex snickered. Ana's expression looked as defiant and angry as she usually did. Whispers and rustling came from the audience. No one believed her. The judge shuffled his papers.

The last to be called was Morticia. She wasn't being accused of murder, was she? He shot a glance at Altamirano who gave a tiny shake of his head. Alex smiled at her, but she didn't meet his eyes.

Another of the defense attorneys questioned her. "Miss Deltoro, your uncle has been accused of murdering your father. You have been caring for him during his illness. Do you believe the accusations? Might the death be accidental?"

"I refuse to testify. I don't want to know anything about this. You're accusing my family!" She started to cry and ran out of the courtroom.

Altamirano held Alex back as he started out of his seat. "Later, Alex," he whispered.

The judge droned on about testimonies and evidence. The people present shifted in their seats, restless. Alex drummed his fingers on his tapping leg. *Why don't they get to the verdicts?*

Eventually the judge noticed the restless courtroom. "Well, I think we've fully complied with the law. Shall we get to the main event now?" A patter of chuckles sounded from the gallery. People had come for the salacious details and the severe punishments. Alex wished he believed in capital punishment, which had been outlawed years ago.

"Then let us get on with it." Silva detailed the related verdicts first.

The majority of the doctors were penalized with a hefty fine payable to the Federal government, with a percentage of the total award to Alex. He noticed that despite being losers, these doctors acted as if the court had ruled in their favor. *What? Are they lunatics?*

Alex intently observed the proceedings. The judge sentenced Dr. Fierro to ten years in prison. He was led away restrained in handcuffs, head hanging.

"And you, Mr. Victor Mata, this court has found you guilty of the premeditated murder your brother-in-law, Lucas Deltoro. You will serve twenty-five years in prison without option of parole, pay restitution in the amount of thirty million pesos to the stated victim, Alex Deltoro, and pay a penalty to the federal government of ten million pesos."

Neither man would practice medicine again.

Mata swung his head toward Alex, hatred darting from his eyes. He was dragged away shouting, "I've been set up! I'm innocent. It was Ana Deltoro." The crowd roared.

The judge called for order; the courtroom quieted down. "We have one more verdict. Bailiff, please bring Mrs. Deltoro to the stand."

Ana was half dragged in, screaming obscenities and denials. "It was Victor. It was Victor! I'm innocent. I'm the victim."

"Mrs. Deltoro, you are convicted of obstruction of justice and being an accessory after the fact in the murder of your husband. You will pay the court one million pesos and spend seven years in prison."

The greatest impact to Alex was Ana's sentence. He closed his ears to the vile things she shouted as she was hauled away.

At last, both he and Lucas were avenged. Ana had been behind it all, the heartbreak, the terror, the pain. His former sister-in-law would spend seven years in prison without parole. A new investigation folder had been channeled to the State D.A.'s office to investigate and return the Deltoro family assets to Alex, including Irene's bank accounts, investments and properties. She'd get another sentence for the robbery.

Morticia had been left out of both parts of the suit. Later, Altamirano explained the judge had fined her a substantial sum to be paid to the State.

Court was adjourned. He was vindicated. The results were satisfying, but the cost had been high. Possibly too high. Alex turned toward his empty future.

He began by inviting his team for lunch. It was the least he could do for what he believed was the only group of honest lawyers and ministerial police in Mexico.

Altamirano asked, "And now Alex, will you stop working or will you plow a new field to plant? What have you planned?"

Without hesitation Alex informed the group the first thing he would do was sell his houses and move to a city with good year-round weather, maybe

Cuernavaca or Guanajuato. "After this, I want a quiet life. Get a dog. Write a book. Study law?" Everyone laughed. Alex continued, "Maybe reconnect with an old love."

"Oh? Who's the lucky one?" the attorney asked.

"Today, because of all of you," he circled his arms to encompass the table, "*I'm* the lucky one."

Case Closed

CAST OF CHARACTERS

Family
Alex "Gato" Deltoro—Brother, Director of Sales at LSI
Lucas "Loco" Deltoro Ramos—Brother
Hugo Deltoro Ramos—Brother
Irene Ramos Deltoro—Mother
Enrique Deltoro Bandenboosh—Father
Ana Luisa Deltoro Mata—Wife of Lucas
Morticia Deltoro Mata—Daughter of Lucas
Dr. Victor Antonio Mata—Brother of Ana

Laboratorios Salud Integral (LSI)
Ivan Castellanos Palacios—Director General
Margarita Ledesma—Director of Development
Levi Abramov—Director of Marketing
Samuel Zugasti—Director of Operations
Avelina Fogel—Former employee and Alex's ex, now with
Bonilla

Doctors
Doctora (Dra.) Milagros Bondad—Section Chief, IMSS #58
Dr. Lionel Fierro Martinez—Deltoro family doctor, IMSS #57
Dra. Aurora Rodriguez—Ordered the ultrasound
Dr. Juan Carlos Figueroa—Gastroenterologist, IMSS Tarimoya
Dr. Robredo—Surgeon, Star Medica
Dr. Fabián Alcalá—Anesthesiologist, Star Medica
Yajaira—Nurse, Star Medica
Señora Santiaga de Vega—Account manager, Star Medica
Dr. Jose Gordillo—Veracruz M.E.

Attorneys
Licensiado (Lic) Fidel Godoy—Attorney who disappeared
Yolanda Zarate—Fiscal delEstado #1 (State D.A,)
Carmela Soto—Fiscal del Estado #2
Paola Zamudio—Fiscal del Estado #3
Fiscal Humberto Picharra—Veracruz State D. A.
Blanca Estela Cuauhtémoc—FGR #1, canceled Alex's victim
status
Alfonso Cardona—FGR #2
Margarita Fernández—FGR #3
Melisa—Assistant to Margarita Fernández

Fiscal Frederid Osnaya Domínguez—Head of the FGR for Veraceuz
Licensiado Rafael Altamirano—Alex's victim defense attorney
Licensiada Samia—Alex'sattorney in CDMX
Assesor Angelica Borzo—CEAV #2
Assesor Armado Padilla—CEAV #3
Lencho—CEAV security guard Licensiado Fernando Locona—Head of the CEAV Veracruz

Police
Chief Commander Rolando Hernández Macho—PFM Veracruz
Daniel Gutierrez—Officer at the scene of the accident
Manuel Barrera—Officer at the scene of the accident
Pérez—Alex's security dayshift
Gonzáles—Alex's security evening shift
Hernández—Alex's security nightshift

Supporting Characters
Gabriel López—Morticia's boyfriend
Aimee—Irene's caretaker
Poncho López—friend of the family
Rosa Dorantes—Alex's next-door neighbor
Eduardo Braulio Falfan—Driver of the white Tsuru
Julián Castillo—Alex's friend from CDMX who takes care of him
Carolina Jepes—Rosa's granddaughter
Rafi—Alex's ten-year-old neighborhood watcher
Javier—Owner of the corner gym
Señora Amélie Roux—Owner of the fish restaurant
Señora Patricia Zentella—Alex's Mexico City realtor
Enrique Silva—Driver of the blue Jetta
El Puño—Altamirano's fixer

Acronyms
Federal General de la República (FGR)
Comisión Ejecutiva de Atención de Victimas (CEAV)
Institutu Mexicano del Seguro Social (IMSS)
Policia Federal Ministerial (PFM)

GLOSSARY
Spanish—English

Abuela—grandmother
Artesania—crafts
asi es Mexico—"this is Mexico" used in resignation
Atole—a rice drink served with tamales
Autopisto or pisto—toll road
Aver—let's see; I say!; show me
Ay—Oh; a nonsense exclamation
Barrachos—drunks
Bueno?—how a telephone is answered
Buenos días—good morning
Buenos tardes—good afternoon
Cabron/a—bastard; asshole; ass
Caguamas—very large beers
Cajeta—goat milk caramel
Callejon—alley
Calmate—calm down
Cariño—dear
Cervecería—brewery
Chelas—beers
Chiles en nogadas—stuffed chilies in walnut sauce.
Chingo—lots; many; much; way cool; really good
Concha—a pastry
Crepas—crepes
Cuernos—a filled pastry
Cuetes—firecrackers
Doctor/a—doctor
Dueña/o—owner
El centro—city center
Flan de coco—coconut custard
Guau—wow
Güero—fair skinned; blond
Güey—dude; fool
Halcon—lookout
Hermano/ hermanito—brother; little brother
Hijole—OMG!
Hijo/a—son/ daughter
Ja ja—ha ha
Jaiba—crab
Torta de jamón—ham sandwich
Jarochos—people from Veracruz
Jefa de pabellon—floor manager

Joven—young
Juez—judge
Licensiado/a—title of a lawyer
Los gangleos—lymph nodes
Madre de dios—Mother of God
Mariscos—seafood
Morena/o—refers to dark skin
Mota—marijuana
Ni modo—no matter; never mind
No mames—I don't believe it; look
No te preocupes—don't worry
Novena—the nine masses held after a funeral
Ojalá—God willing, from Arabic
Pan dulces—pastries
Panque—a sweetcorn cake
Pendejo—asshole
Pesera—a type of small municipal bus
Pinche—fucking, used as an adjective
Placa—license plate; shield; badge
Plata o plomo—silver or lead, referring to Narco threats
Pobrecito—poor you
Polleros—the people who lead immigrants across borders
Poncela—give it to him
Ponche—traditional Christmas punch, often spiked
Por favor—please
Privada—a gated community; dead-end street
Pues—then, well, oh. A place holder
Puta—hooker
Putero—hooker bar
Que amable—how nice
Rico—delicious; rich
Salchicha—sausage
Salud—health
Seguro—I'm sure; safe
Semana Santa—Easter week
Sin magna—lead free
Sopapillas—a fried snack
Taxistas—taxi drivers
Te amo—I love you
Topes—speed bumps
Torta de jamón y queso—ham and cheese sandwich
Tu mamá—your mother
Ustedes—you people

Author's Note

North American culture approaches life very differently than Mexican culture. For this reason, I think it's important to jot some notes for the English reader to better understand Mortal Revenge. Some of the story may seem exaggerated or unbelievable, but I assure you, the depiction of the Mexican health and legal systems are ripped right from reality. In fact, this book is based on a true story.

Mexicans place great importance on the family, to such an extent that even people who can't stand their parents or siblings, are unconditionally loyal, honoring the obligation to stand with family with total fidelity. Family comes first. It's ingrained within us as children, and we in turn pass this to our children. Asi es Mexico.

Corruption and impunity are so common, they have become a way of life. People expect it. The mismanagement of the government leaves no other option. For example, police as a rule, make so little they use their badges as authorization to legally shakedown citizens to pay the rent of their patrol cars, or pay the *mordita* (little bite) due their supervisors—on up the chain of command. The same type of behavior occurs in all government offices such as prosecutors' offices, courts, federal police, etc. Authorities are bought. The winner of the legal case is the person who bribes the authorities to obtain victory even if they are the criminals.

Another common example is the obtaining of social benefits. To get a housing loan, Mexicans must pay what is commonly called a *mochada*, which is nothing more than bribing bureaucrats to prioritize our requests, regardless of who has priority. An important point is that the corruption influences the lack of important social services such as education and health.

Before the MORENA government, theft by public officials stole money from programs, but there were still services. Now, the centralization, or federalization, of programs has made it easier to defraud the public. Our health system has deteriorated so much, our hospitals don't have enough funding for essentials such as bandages and medicines. There is no money for building and equipment maintenance, meaning that there is no equipment such as respirators or ultrasounds. This current government, instead of improving essential health services, has cut it by 50%, eliminating the Seguro Popular (Popular Insurance System), serving people not entitled to Social Security (IMSS) or ISSSTE (state or government workers' insurance) because they were informal workers—essentially the impoverished.

The government steals without limitations, but the Mexican mentality is, "what can I do?" In part this attitude is pure Mexican, and the other part is lack of education. Mexico is currently 30% in poverty while 10% of the population holds 80% of the wealth. Instead of improving national education, it is now dedicated to the dumbing down of the population, to the eventual ruin of my beautiful Mexico. Hola Cuba.

To add to our collective identity, we have an epidemic of obesity. Our ancestral diet consists of tomatoes, corn and beans, not inherently fattening. Then why is the vast majority of the population obese? The objective is to satisfy hunger. Foods fried in lard and wrapped in tortillas taste good and are cheap. People have not been educated about nutrition. I'm not criticizing them; the vast majority of the population has no idea what I'm talking about. There is no dearth of fresh fruits and vegetables in the markets, but the food traditions have been handed down through the centuries, and "asi es Mexico."

While not specifically political, I wanted to tell my story to show the world what happens when people don't fight for their rights. Unlike in Mortal Revenge, as of this writing, my lawsuits have not settled. I am angry and tired, but I'm still fighting. My attorneys have been bought off, my evidence disappeared, and my story is no different from any other victim's story. We all know it, and yet Mexicans still do not wake up. This may be the biggest difference between our English-speaking cousins and us. You fight. Mexicans say, "Asi es Mexico."

Fernando León Torrens

Your Next Read
Kickback

A Dafne Olabarrieta Mexico Mystery
Book 1

Excerpt From Chapter Two

The light on her landline blinked again. She punched the code, and the message started. Static or some sort of crackling. As she reached to drop the receiver into its cradle a familiar voice sounded.

"Help. Please, Daf, please help me."

She put the receiver to her ear and started the message over. Static. Maybe sobbing? The sound so low she could barely hear the voice.

"They've kidnapped my girl. Aisling. They've taken her. My baby!"

She was listening to bloody Alba Falconi. Dafne hadn't heard that voice in years. Not since Alba admitted she'd been in a relationship with Oliver. *Her* Oliver. *Her* fiancé. And they were getting married.

Dafne's gut clenched and her head pounded. Hang up the phone. That's all she needed to do, then she could forget again. It had been a small consolation that Oliver acted his usual cheating self and did something stupid to Alba. Dafne had heard through the grapevine she was back in Mexico several years later. How long ago had that been? Dios! Ten years or more.

The message was still running. "Help. Please, Daf, please help me." Then clear sobbing and a choked-out telephone number.

Should she call? A kidnapped child! But Alba had betrayed their friendship; let her call the police. No. That was petty. She checked the time stamp: 8:20 this morning. A lot could have changed since then. The room dimmed as Dafne's heart sank under a wave of black self-loathing. She couldn't punish a child for her mother's disloyalty. She'd sidelined as a hostage negotiator since university. At least she could find out what happened. She played back the message again. This time scrawling the number on her pad.

"Alba? It's me, Dafne."

"You got my message. I-I wasn't sure you would be working there. I thought you weren't going to call." Breathless she added, "Dafne, I need you to get Aisling back!"

She pronounced her daughter's name ASH-leen. "Oliver's daughter? When was she kidnapped? Could he have taken—"

"Disculpame, por favor, Dafne. Please! Find my child," Alba said through her rising sobs. "It's not Oliver. He has no interest in Aisling."

The terror and pleading in Alba's voice frightened Dafne. This was real, but she wasn't ready to forgive. "You betrayed our friendship, Alba. Call the police."

"They told me not to involve the police or I'd never see my daughter again."

"Who are they? What did they ask you to do?"

"I don't know who they are. I only have a number. Dafne, help me! She's only a little girl..."

Something was off. "Alba, what do they want you to do?"

Her sobbing intensified. She gulped. "They'll sell her to the cartel."

"Give me the number."

Her sobs subsided. Alba hiccupped and spoke in a near whisper. "1722-597-0930."

"I'll find out who it belongs to and call you back. But I need you to tell me what's really going on, Alba. There's a special FGR unit, the Policía Especial Anti-secuestros. They know how to help you."

"No!" she wailed. "Please, meet me somewhere." Dafne's voice softened.

"I'm at work, Alba. I can't get free before four-thirty —"

"Pues, meet me at Coffee and Deli on Gobernador Rafael Rebollar in San Miguel Chapultepec at five."

Readers Choice 5-Star Review

"Manwaring skillfully blends intense action with emotional stakes, ensuring readers are as invested in Dafne's internal struggles as they are in the plot. I loved the high-stakes story, the intensity of the action, and the character development that accompanied the plot. There was never a dull moment. I finished this book in one sitting and enjoyed it immensely. I highly recommend it."

About Ana Manwaring

Ana Manwaring is the award-winning author of the JadeAnne Stone Mexico Adventures, three volumes of poetry as well as many essays, short stories and flash memoirs. Her recent release, Kickback, received a Gold Book Award and has been short-listed for the 2025 Chanticleer International Clue Award.

Ana teaches creative writing in California's wine country. Founder of JAM Manuscript Consulting, she coaches writers, assists in developing projects, and copyedits. She also produces the North Bay Poetics, a free monthly poetry event. Https://northbaypoetics.net

She's visited Mexico's garbage dumps, explored a mortuary, sampled tequila in a 150-year-old cantina, lived on houseboats, consulted brujos, camped in Mayan ruins, swum with dolphins, and out-run gun totin' maniacs on lonely Mexican highways —the inspiration for The JadeAnne Stone Mexico Adventures. Read about her transformative experiences living in Mexico in her award-winning memoir, Saints and Skeletons.

With a B.A. in English and Education and an M.A. in Linguistics, Ana is finally able to answer her mother's question, "What are you planning to do with that expensive education?" Be a paperback writer.

***

If you had as much fun reading Mortal Revenge as I did researching and writing it, please consider going to your favorite online bookseller and leaving a review. Reviews help other readers find our books and help us continue to write for your enjoyment. As the adage goes, a book is not finished until a reader reads it. Thank you.

To find out about new books and upcoming events, please take a moment to sign up for my mailing list at www.anamanwaring.com. To connect with me on social media, find all my information at www.linktr.ee/anamanwaring